LOVERS &

NEIGHBORS

Also by SB Gamble
The Last Party

LOVERS &

NEIGHBORS

SB GAMBLE

The Good Fight
Publishing

FIRST EDITION
10 9 8 7 6 5 4 3 2 1

Names: SB Gamble, 1984-
Title: Lovers & Neighbors
First Edition: Chicago, Illinois 2017.
www.sbgamble.com

This is a work of fiction. Names, characters, places, and incidents are a product of the author's imagination. Locales and public names are sometimes used for atmospheric purposes. Any resemblance to actual people, living or dead, or to businesses, companies, events, institutions, or locales is completely coincidental.

The Good Fight Publishing
ISBN: 978-0-9973869-2-9
(Paperback)

Cover photo by Tiffany Bryant, PzAxe, and Peeterv
Cover design by Marlon Joshua Namoro
Author photo by Naiyah Scaife

For Sheena

1

ank Parks's mouth tasted like vomit. Nausea shifted the floor under him as he lurched over the toilet. His eyes blinked slowly in the grainy light of a colorless Chicago day that slanted through the window and onto the tiles. The cold from the tile seeped through his knees and traveled through his body. He was racked with a chill, and a dullness throbbed in his back. His body was one knotted slab of pain. He reached for his face, but his arms were lead. He was crouched over the toilet bowl. He steadied himself with a breath and stretched out his hand for his phone sitting on the countertop next to him. The consequences of alcohol have dislodged him from time to time. He had no idea how long he'd been here, emptying his stomach. Instead of grasping his phone, his hand tipped the device over. The sound of plastic hitting tile shot tendrils of sharp pain deep into his skull. He cried out and rolled off the toilet and onto his back. He tugged a blanket he'd brought in earlier over his body.

Surely, he was dying. Last night's beer and whiskey shots were out to kill him.

Hank heard footfalls come toward the bathroom in the small apartment. The steps in the small living room stopped outside the bathroom, and there was a deep exhalation, a sigh layered with a biting exasperation. He pretended he hadn't heard it. He screwed his eyes tight and feigned sleep. There was a creak as feet shifted on the floorboard. The heat of a gaze crawled along his skin. He slowed his breath, keeping it even and deep.

For a moment, he indulged in this desire to die. He considered whether this would be better than watching a decade of life become categorized, organized, and then placed in those shit-color brown packing boxes overtaking the apartment. Cups and glasses were wrapped in old newspaper. Clothes were wound in tight, angry rolls and shoved into ratty old suitcases. Even the scrawl on the boxes was damning in constricted black letters. The words KITCHEN DISHES—FRAGILE seemed to reach out from beneath layers of packing tape and seethe at him.

Death from a hangover was better than a scorned woman turning him into a villain.

Feet scuffled, and the heat from the gaze relented. There were more footfalls and the scraping of boxes being assembled. Packing tape was pulled from the roll, and the shrill screech it produced was akin to gunshots to Hank's skull. Kitchen cupboards detonated in the silence as their doors opened, and then slammed shut. He gritted his teeth, and tears rose in his eyes.

Andrea, please, he wanted to cry.

This was being done on purpose. She was making him pay. Andrea's vengeance had been small, needling him throughout the course of the week. However justified, she had declared war on him, a war in which he now lay pressed alongside the toilet, completely outgunned. Her once-loving stares made room for narrow-eyed glares that stalked him from room to room.

The slow drip of her malice started with the withdrawal of meals. The kitchen would blossom in the rich smell of baked chicken or the sizzling of a steak—oh, how he loved a good bloody steak—and then a plate garnished and a table set for one. She would sip her dark merlot and cut her steak, glaring at him in perverse glee as if she could hear the pained howl of his stomach. She would delicately cut from the steak, holding the small square of meat before her so he could see it before she ate it. He would almost choke on his own spit.

Andrea was an unemployed sous chef. When she had been working, she was employed at, in Hank's simple opinion, a pretentious overpriced Italian restaurant in downtown Chicago called Cibo e Amor. It was a beautiful space with a wide-open view of the street. A place that took months on end for a pedestrian like himself to get reservations, even with Andrea working there.

Hank tugged the blanket over his head to hide from the banging from another set of cupboards deeper within the kitchen. Maybe he could smother himself with the musty blanket. He realized that Andrea would probably revel in celebration. He saw her on her phone, dialing her friends and planning the celebratory drinks at one of the bars in Wicker Park.

A cold breeze rattled the window. It was a long, harsh winter with an ungodly cold that penetrated the core and stayed there. Hank was always shivering, and he could never get warm enough. The cold would rip at him as he climbed the stairs of 'L' train platforms. He and sour-faced commuters would huddle underneath heating lamps posted along the train stops. He was certain the lamps were decorative and served no purpose at all, just another indignity the Chicago Transit Authority subjected the populace to. The cold was so pervasive that all memories of another time, of seamless, cloudless blue skies and warm weather, were plucked from him, lost along the gusts of wind like one of the many pieces of debris caught midflight, only to be consumed in dirty black snow. Those unavoidable humps of snow crowded every curb and gathered en masse along the corners of parking lots and the shadowed paths in alleys. They weren't even fit for Hank to walk on them. The ice had ravaged the streets more than normal. Cracks in the pavement split into potholes like a meteor storm had hit the city. Everything was so frigid and so mercilessly ugly.

Hank adjusted the blanket Andrea had left him because it was too ugly to pack. The blanket, colored a weathered gray from too many washes, was barely long enough to cover his body. He drew into himself and screwed his eyes shut.

When Hank awoke, the apartment was dense in darkness and silence. He lay there for a moment as if he were floating in a pool. He blinked slowly while he adjusted to the dim glow of the streetlight from outside. The air had a stillness to it, and he held his breath to wait for a sound inside the apartment. All he heard were the muffled intonations from the couple that lived above him and Andrea.

He hated that couple. He was an unwilling witness to their lives. Days in the apartment were punctuated by their conversations and their footsteps. The melodies of sickeningly cheery pop music and rolling laugh tracks from sitcoms invaded the thin, poorly insulated floors. And when Hank started to hate his apartment, he reminded himself how lucky he was to find such a reasonably priced apartment in Ukrainian Village. He reminded himself how close he lived to the Western train stop and how quick his commute was to work. He told himself this, almost chanted it in a religious fervor.

It almost worked, too. He decided to close his eyes and sleep when a slow, rhythmic squeak of bedsprings was heard overhead. Then, like a rising tide, the intervals between the squeaks shortened, followed by the percussion of a bedpost against the wall, and then the scratching of the bedframe's legs against that sound-conductive floor. The moans started, the unbridled cries of a woman, and by the end of it, Hank was fully awake.

When he and Andrea had sex, they never lasted that long into the night. And they certainly weren't that loud. Maybe that was the problem. Hank couldn't remember the last time. Months passed, and even when they were both drunk, they never touched one another. Hank would look up at his ceiling and wonder how long two people could fuck.

He cursed loudly, knowing his upstairs neighbors couldn't hear his obscenities over their own. The noise went on for nearly an hour, and Hank was torn between his bourgeoning erection dripping in his boxers and the unrelenting need to sleep. He thought about the occasions he bumped into the woman from upstairs, passing her in the narrow hallways of the apartment building or at the rusty mailboxes in front of the doors. When he saw his upstairs neighbor, he couldn't look her in the eye. He feared his erection would reappear.

Lately, whatever poison had emerged between Hank and Andrea had somehow infected them. Those trysts became less frequent and gave way to arguments. No longer were soft moans heard, but instead, fervent intonations. Once, a clash ignited so loudly the light fixture flickered. And in those perilous moments, it seemed like everywhere Hank looked, love was burning around him. And although his life below these people was separated by plaster, wood, and brick, he couldn't help but wonder if his conflicts caused the couple above him to fight. If the booming rows he engaged in with Andrea had somehow signaled the couple above him somehow beckoned conflict into all of their lives. This notion was always a short-lived thought, yet it was prescient, coming back to him now even as he lay on the bathroom floor.

When the noise finally stopped, he realized he was alone in his apartment. Relief unwound his muscles. He left the bathroom, turned on the light, and ignored the boxes that Andrea had stacked in the corner. The apartment was half empty, and Andrea had slowly removed objects from the walls and closets. He walked through the apartment, surveying the space. Last night's liquor no longer plagued him, but as he entered his room and pulled opened the empty drawers, he felt the first tingles of a different type of sickness.

He turned to the closet and the sounds of his footsteps reverberated in the emptiness. There was a mass forming in his stomach. He couldn't believe how much room Andrea had taken up in the apartment. She had filled tables and shelves with kitschy knickknacks found from thrift stores and covered the wall in cheap art from local artists. She crowded bookshelves with so many books the wood bowed in the middle from the strain. Andrea was always burning an assortment of candles, trying her damnedest to combat the smells of old wood floors and dusty plaster. Almost every counter, table, and surface had held the limp melted candle stumps. The apartment had been covered in her texture, and now it was flat.

Hank made his way back to extract his phone from the bathroom. He made a quick phone call. There was a steady ring tone in his ear, and for moment, panic struck him. He thought no one was available.

"What's up, man?" a voice answered.

"I gotta get out tonight, Noah."

"It's cold as shit out," Noah said. "I'm at the office and headed back home. You could come upstairs to my place."

"I'll buy you drinks," Hank said, and then wondered if he'd tipped his hand too soon.

There was a brief pause as his friend worked this out, and he contemplated enduring the cold wind and the frozen mounds of snow. But true to form, Noah was never in a position to pass up free liquor. Honestly, who was?

Noah groaned. "Fine, I'll meet you at the usual spct."

This was a given, a routine carved out over the years, although the always reluctant Noah could rarely say no to Hank.

Soon, Hank was dressed as warmly as he could possibly be and renewed with purpose. Thick long johns were underneath his jeans. Wool socks itched at his ankles. His only scarf, a gift from Andrea, no less, was wrapped around his neck, stuffed into his coat, and partly pulled over his mouth. He was armed, trudging through a black glacial night. As a numbing breeze sliced into him, he briefly contemplated retreating into the apartment. But there was no liquor at home—he had finished it last night. And he couldn't anticipate when, or if, Andrea would be back tonight. He couldn't face her without the assistance of alcohol.

He grunted against the wind and stuffed his hands in his pockets. He bore down and rushed along with careful footsteps. He was wary of the ice until he heard a rumble over the hush of the night. He scuffled, slipped, and slid his way up to the train platform. He took the stairs two at time, knowing each step brought him further from the cold. Hank dove into the train as the doors chimed before they shut.

He was relieved as he was carried through the steely night high on train tracks. He stood peering out through the windows, watching white rooftops and plumes of smoke blurring into the night. Around him were people wound tightly in various layers, all knotted and braced against the cold. Everyone's faces were marred with frowns, united in this collective misery as cold found a way past their layers and beneath their coats.

When Hank's muscles were finally thawed, his legs freed from the tingling, and his fingers no longer limp and numb, he arrived at his stop in Wicker Park. He drew in a sigh and followed the small trickle of people onto the street. A mix of black snow and hard pebbles of salt crushed under his feet. Hank felt as though he was the only one outside in this city. Around him were nearly vacant streets. The bars and clubs glowed around him on the strip and tainted the dirty snow in neon luminescence.

He pushed through the door of his destination, a dim lounge bar name Stratosphere. As if for its namesake, the walls were black as a night sky, and dark lights from above cast everything in an unearthly blue. He met the doorman, who grimaced at him for bringing in the sharp winter air. He flashed him his ID and scanned the room for his friend. He saw no familiar faces among the crowd. He rushed through the people, found a stool at the bar, and waited.

He squirmed, a bit at odds with himself, and peered at a beautiful woman behind the bar. He ordered a beer and turned in his stool to face the crowd. He wondered if they, too, were as desperate to escape some problem like he was. The only thing that could force one out into that type of cold was some sort of desperation. Or was he too alone and projecting onto them? He sighed again and let mutters of conversations and the pulse of bass coming from a hidden sound system roll over him.

"You look lonely."

A woman stared back at him in an unwavering coolness. Her skin was pale in the pool of blue light from the black lights, and short, bluntly cut hair the color of the night sky hung around her face. Her beauty was startling, almost surreal. A black leather motorcycle jacket was draped around her small frame, and its collar was popped up, making Hank think of a shark fin breaking through an ocean's surface. His stomach shifted as if her gaze had put him in danger. He squinted at the woman to obscure her . . . or maybe in the hope of finding a recognizable fallibility. After a moment, he found nothing, and heat flushed his face when she continued to stare at him.

"You must not get out much," she said, turning away from him to an empty martini glass in front of her.

Hank snorted in feigned indignation against her icy glare. He returned to his drink, staring down but very much aware of the gravity she now occupied in his peripheral vision. The bartender came by, and the woman pointed at her glass.

"Can I have another?" she asked, then said, "Put it on him."

Hank all but gasped, and the bartender turned to him in question. Hank grimaced and reluctantly nodded in consent. The bartender took the woman's martini glass and walked further down the bar.

"So, you insult me and I buy you drink?"

The woman smirked at him. A fluttering stirred his stomach so immediately he was afraid he might have been sick.

"When's the last time you've bought an attractive woman a drink?"

"So because you're an attractive woman, you get to insult me and I owe you a drink?"

"Should we go into the privileges you have as a—I'm assuming straight—man? Because we'll be here all night."

"I am straight."

"Well, I'm glad for you."

"I mean, not that I have a problem with gay people. I mean, they're great. I love them. Well, I mean, not love them. I mean, they're cool."

The bartender appeared with another martini, only to leave them again. She brought the drink up to her lips and sipped from it with deliberate relish.

"My favorite kind of vodka," she said as she placed the drink back on the bar.

"What type is that?"

"The free kind," she said, and chuckled at Hank's deepening grimace.

The woman finished her drink and stepped from the stool. She gestured to Hank to follow her. His head was submerged in a thick liquid, and as she made a path through the crowd, it was as if her hips flowed. Soon, he was zipping up his coat and keeping in pace with her out to the salt-graveled sidewalk.

He shivered as he watched her draw a cigarette to her lips. She smiled at Hank and handed him a lighter. Obediently, he flicked it open and placed the flame to the cigarette's tip. She drew in smoke and exhaled it slowly, and a cloud of smoke and breath ballooned around her head, luminous in the streetlight.

Hank felt his chest compress, and somehow, she saw this and grinned with that unfaltering beauty. He was utterly outgunned, and she knew she had him. The woman offered him her cigarette. The filter was stained red from her lips. When Hank placed it in his mouth, it was damp, and it thrilled him like nothing had in the longest he could remember.

2

Emily Jones steadied herself as she slipped on heels in the hallway between the bathroom and the living room. Inside the bathroom, Derek Bagley turned the faucet, and a deep, pained groan shuddered the tap and traveled through the walls. She peered into the bathroom, and his reflection trembled back at her as the gasping pipes choked with water. Derek instinctively stepped back as if the pipe would burst through the wall. Soon, the tap sputtered and spat out yellow water. She frowned as the piss-colored water ran for a moment before turning clear. He washed his hands and flushed the toilet.

Derek stepped out of the bathroom, his face pinched in a frown.

"Jones, are you sure you want to go out tonight?"

Out of necessity, she took to being called her last name years ago after a public school education where she shared the name Emily with too many perky girls.

"Yeah," she said while spot-checking her mascara.

"It's just tomorrow is the big launch," he said, and stood for a moment, examining Jones. "I don't want you wearing yourself out."

She tried to listen to him, but the groan of the water pipes was still reverberating in her skull. They were another item to add to the growing list of complaints she had about the apartment. She knew that all her calls to the landlord would, of course, go unheard. For the last four months before the cold had arrived, she'd been harassing him about the jammed window outside her bedroom that led to the rusty iron fire escape. During the summer, she crawled out through the window and roosted on the windowsill. She would gaze through a thicket of trees and rooftops into the drone of the city that expanded everywhere she could see. It was a place of perspective, her place of respite, and one day, for an inexplicable reason, the window was fused closed. She spent an hour bashing at the window frame, but it didn't move. Derek reluctantly toiled at the window to no effect. So the fire escape, the only feature she would actually admit to liking in the apartment, was closed off forever. After that, she grew caustic toward the building and the landlord.

She tossed back her hair and pouted in the mirror, and Derek smirked back at her.

"Girls' night with Isabelle," she said, fighting to keep her focus on the mirror and turning her effort to her long auburn hair, curled and sprayed into submission. "I won't be out late."

"Do you have to go out at all?" Derek asked as he walked deeper into the hall, wedging himself behind her.

Jones felt the heavy heat of his hand on her outer thigh. She ignored him and held her breath. Her body tensed like a rope being snapped taut. Derek licked his lips, and his hand crept from her outer thigh to her inner thigh. The arch of his thumb slid up into the crotch of her jeans. He nudged her body into his, and his breath was hot on the top her head. The loose curls she had spent so much time on, her arms still a bit worn from holding up the curling iron, were flattened against his chest. Her mouth pinched into a thin red line.

"Derek, I'm going to be late," she said as his hands fell to her side.

Derek keeled forward to kiss her neck. His lips were wet and slick against her neck, and Jones resisted the urge to wipe away the spit left on her skin.

"Isabelle lives downstairs," Derek continued. "She can wait."

"She ordered a cab already," Jones said in tight, sharp words.

Derek moved back as if her tone had injured him. His eyes widened as if he was suddenly aware of Jones's mood. He crept back over the warped tile into the shadows of the hallway.

"You realize tomorrow is a big night for me," he said, his voice bristling.

Jones sighed and turned to him. "I'm aware. Believe me."

"The launch is going to be huge, and I need you by my side," Derek said, his face extended into a severe pout.

"Derek, I'll be there," Jones said. "It's tomorrow night, not now."

"You won't drink too much?"

"Yes, I promise."

Derek crossed his arms and leaned against the bathroom doorframe. His glare hardened, and he opened his mouth to say something, but he quickly closed it.

"Derek," Jones said, "work has been really intense these few weeks. And I understand the launch party for the app is tomorrow. I just need to get away from all of it."

He shook his head, and his heavy footsteps boomed down the hall, likely causing unnecessary injury to the splintering wood panels under them. "You don't understand the sacrifices I've made."

Jones flipped her hair over her shoulders and moaned at her now deflated curls. She moved through the tiny old apartment to the living room. There, Derek was sitting on the secondhand leather couch, with its cracked skin that pinched anyone brave enough to sit on it. In his lap was the open screen of his laptop computer. He stared at the screen, and light fluttered over his face.

Jones pulled on her thick overcoat. She watched him for a moment, the grief in his face tugging in the depths of her stomach. She briefly considered calling Isabelle and rescheduling.

Derek had thrown everything he had into launching his app. He drained his trust fund, spent an inheritance from his late grandfather, quit his full-time job, and picked up shifts as a barista for a flexible schedule. The pressure was splintering between them—his constant development meetings, the liquidating of all his assets, and pouring everything into this app. In the beginning, the prospect of it had thrilled them both, and she curled up next to him, one ear pressed to the chest, hearing the thrum of his heartbeat, and the other ear filled with his lofty dream that he would become the next Mark Zuckerberg.

And although she coasted along the current of his dreams, she wouldn't depend on his success. She questioned his steps, and a small bell went off in her head. His aspirations drew a small splinter between them that was slowly deepening into a gulf.

As she buttoned her coat, she wondered if she should have confessed the news that she'd been holding since Friday. Jones had been so blindly thrilled that she'd told her friend Isabelle before she even had a moment to converse with Derek. The tugging in her stomach was almost painful now, and she began to string together words, arranging them into a sweet bouquet, pulling off all the thorns, washing away the venom, to give them to Derek.

A drawn-out squeal escaped from the computer. A series of guttural cries quickly followed. Derek slipped his hand into his sweatpants.

Jones flinched, stammering for words. "Are you watching porn?"

Derek shot a cold, affirming sneer.

"Enjoy yourself," she said, winding a scarf around her neck, then rushing toward the door. She threw the door closed, and the slam was too sharp for her ears. She took the creaking stairs down one level. The hallway smelled of musky wet carpet, trampled and stained by a mixture of salt, mud, and melted snow. She reached out for the banister, its ornate woodwork nicked and worn from neglect and age. Huge white paint chips flaked off as she passed, exposing a mucus-color green underneath.

She knocked on Isabelle's door and it flung open and a woman paced out with her phone to her ear. A beautiful round afro extended around her head like a plume of raven smoke, and her mahogany face was taut with a frown. She locked eyes with Isabelle and smiled quickly, then returned to her frown and her phone call.

"Is the artist going to have the piece ready or not?" Isabelle said into the phone. She then rolled her eyes and pressed the phone to her chest, and said to Jones, "I'm sorry, babe, come on, the cab is outside."

Isabelle led the way down the groaning stairs into the small lobby. Cold air flooded them, pouring in from a broken glass panel in the door. Isabelle continued her terse phone call as they moved past mounds of black snow heaped along the sides of the walkway to the cab in the street. Jones opened the door and crossed the gray slush of undetermined depth into the cab. Isabelle, unaware, stepped off the curb on the street, and with a loud slopping noise, her foot was swallowed past her ankle into the frozen slush.

She yelped out and tumbled into the cab.

The cab driver peered into the back seat over the partition.

"Sorry," Isabelle offered, turning to shake the slush from her boots. "Take us to Stratosphere on Milwaukee."

Jones watched their apartment in an icy glow underneath the streetlight like a shameless exhibitionist exposing and flapping its parts at her. The building's brick skin was covered by bare black vines stretching along like a network of veins. Thick frozen ropes of icicles piled upon each other, jutting down from rain gutters at the various corners of the roof and giving the ugly structure a sharp set of teeth. The building was a surly old senior with a ceaseless series of creaks and grumbles. Once, in the throes of balancing a heavy bag of groceries up the treacherous flight of stairs, she overheard a neighbor saying that the building once had asbestos somewhere in the basement. And she was certain the paint chips that littered the halls were lead-based. Then there was last summer, when in the swell of heat and humidity, the nauseating vapors of gas leaked from the apartment two floors above her for what seemed like a month. It was as if this building, a survivor of World Wars, corrupted and bankrupted by city politics and the morphing topography of Chicago, was trying to bring its residents down in its death, crumbling brick by crumbling brick. The building would maim with its broke pipes or trip a resident with its loose steps.

The surrounding houses and buildings had undergone transformations—resurfaced brick, new paint, redone porches. Full teardowns would reveal linear architecture in a matter of months. A rise of suburban kids came into the nearby expensive housing to displace the long-lived locals like pioneers or pilgrims with shotguns to the heads of the indigenous natives. But instead of shotguns, they were armed with rent hikes, and failed businesses found new tenants and new life as boutiques and slow-drip coffee shops.

Fortunately for Jones, the rent still remained cheap in her building, which was why it stood out on the block like a festering wart. The building's ugly face growled at the otherwise beautiful snowcapped arrangement of the street. Jones even caught looks of disgust and confusion as she entered the building. On the rare occasion when she was brazen enough to invite a friend to her home, she would watch them nod at the surrounding area, and then watch the inevitable slack-jawed terror as she led them to her door. Often, she would feel like the Grim Reaper taking his ward to the mouth of death. She was able to pocket hundreds of dollars each month on rent—a much-needed discount with respect to Derek's entrepreneurial endeavors. Nevertheless, this embarrassment was growing to be too much, and she couldn't help but feel relieved every time she left the building.

Isabelle concluded her phone call with a series of curses and turned to Jones, looking back at their building.

"Don't stare at it directly," Isabelle said with a smirk, and Jones chuckled.

"Work?"

"Yeah, the artist who co-owns the gallery is being a prima donna."

"The white guy with dreadlocks?"

"Yeah," Isabelle said, fluffing her afro for effect.

Jones rolled her eyes at her friend.

"But enough about that," Isabelle said, shaking herself in the seat in an effort to be free to take on the night. "Did you tell Derek?"

"No."

"Why? This is a good thing."

"How do tell your boyfriend you got a promotion and you'll be making three times as much as he is now?"

Isabelle raised an eyebrow. "Just like you told me, except without the money part."

"He's going to want to know how much I'm making," Jones said. "He'll probably try to get me to become an investor again."

"Don't tell him how much," Isabelle said. "You guys aren't married."

The cab traveled east through the city into Wicker Park and alongside Stratosphere. When the cab came to halt, Isabelle glanced at Jones expectantly.

"What?"

"You have new promotion making three times the money Derek makes, and subsequently, more than me," she said, her smirk playful on her face again. "I'm not paying for this cab."

Jones grinned at her and paid the fare. She noticed Isabelle's timid step onto the curb, careful not to end up in slush this time. They rushed into the bar, finding a booth far from the door and the occasional burst of chill air as someone stepped in or left. A tattooed waiter came by, and soon, the women were drinking from champagne flutes.

"Look, I know this is going to be tough on Derek," Isabelle said, "but I'm going to celebrate your promotion. I shall now refer to you as The Director."

Jones flushed with heat. "Stop it."

"You are the director of Chicago Modern Art Magazine," Isabelle said, and raised her glass. "And you didn't suck anyone's dick to get there."

Jones smiled flatly. "I'm happy."

Isabelle's face screwed into skepticism. "Yeah, you're not convincing. I'm going to need you to get it together, okay? Because you'd better believe I'm coming to you for artists for my gallery. Do you know how hard it is to push art in this economy?"

Jones upturned the flute into her mouth.

"Damn, what is it?" Isabelle asked. "Did you suck someone's—"

"No," Jones said. "I can't tell Derek right now because we're not in a great place. When I left, he was watching porn."

"He's a guy."

"We're not good having sex."

"What? Derek looks like a really good lay."

"We tried tonight, but I just haven't been in the mood," Jones said, looking around for the waiter to refill her glass.

Isabelle snorted. "Do you know it's been so long for me that I'm considering buying battery stocks?"

Jones laughed, almost able to escape the tugging that crawled its way back into her stomach.

"No, what's really wrong?" Isabelle asked, as if she could sense the tremor of dread through the invisible threads of their friendship.

"It's Derek," she said. "I thought that at some point he'd get it together."

"What do you mean?"

"He's a part-time barista," she said, "and he's been developing this app for three years."

"Jones . . . sweetie . . ."

"Seriously," Jones said. "I can't be the man and the woman in this relationship."

Isabelle sucked her teeth. "What does that even mean? It's not the fifties. Times change, and things aren't how they used to be. No one has money, and barely anyone has a job. And those who do are taking jobs they're overqualified for."

"Oh, that's bullshit, Isabelle, and you know it. I got a damn promotion and you seem to be fine."

"You haven't seen my checking account, and look at the apartments we live in. I sleep with a full respiratory mask on to keep from dying from the carbon monoxide I know is in that building."

"I know Derek," Jones said. "He's going to make me feel bad for being successful. He always does."

"Well, don't let him. This is your night, and tomorrow is his."

Jones nodded and scanned the narrowing spaces in the crowd. Within the few minutes that they'd sat at the booth, the crowd seemed to surge, dragging in snow from boots and searching the corners and stools to set down their coats. Jones even saw a group of girls get scoffed at by the bartender for flopping their coats over the speakers. All the faces in that crowd held a cold, raw, red-faced determination, hands reaching out for liquor.

In the multitude of those faces, now pale in the immersion of dark lights, Jones only saw Derek's pout spring up like a buoy in her mind. And the thought of him brought a wrenching into her gut

3

Noah had left work early, and after circling the block, he slid roughly into the parking spot. His wheels made a sickening smack against the curb. He choked down his heart as the car idled. The sky above him breathed melancholy snowfall heavily onto his car across from the frighteningly sterile brick building. The snow dropping from the shifting gray above developed into a series of brown puddles along the street. He tried to focus on the building as if he had never seen it before, as if this wasn't his fifth attempt to enter it. He drifted from the building to his phone in his pocket, and then settled on a potted yellow tulip he held in his lap. He didn't think for a while, entangled in growing reluctance. Then, he finally shook his head, breathing in deeply and allowing his muscles to tense. His breath began to fog over the window, shrouding the outside world.

He glanced at his phone and noticed a missed call from his mother followed by the blinking icon of voicemail. He played the voicemail on speaker mode to break the heavy silence that began to crowd him.

"Noah, dear, I know this is hard for you," his mother said.

Her voice, by design, was harsh, and although she quit smoking nearly a decade ago, the damage left a rumbling timbre. But this time, her words contained a dark depth. And as soon as Noah heard it, he was arrested in the car, not knowing what to do with his hands, moving them from the bright tulip in his lap to the steering wheel and back again.

"Your father is getting worse, Noah. I know you are busy with the business. I understand but, dear, you need to come see him before it's too late. You need to come see him before there's nothing left. I love you. Call me, please, when you get this."

It was as if Noah had shrunk half his size, and when he tried to look up at the building across the street, it was completely obscured by the fog his breath had left on the windows. A familiar guilt lapped over him, and he often seemed to be grabbing at pieces of himself, trying to keep them from crumbling.

The car was growing cold, and he thought about calling his mother, but with his phone in his hand, as if sensing he was in need, Hank had called and pleaded with him to join him. Noah held on to a thin irritation at Hank's call. But honestly, he was relieved. He shifted the car quickly into gear and was sliding into a U-turn back to his office in Wicker Park, abandoning the yellow tulip on the passenger seat next to him.

There was no graceful or cool way to move through the snow as Noah progressed down the sidewalk. Most businesses had the sense to make some attempt at shoveling for the pedestrians. But the few vacant storefronts, which stood out like blacked out teeth in a smile, had no one to clear the walkways of the ice and snow. As Noah passed one of these, his combat boots struggled to make traction, and for a full fearful minute, he flapped his arms and his feet blurred underneath him as he fought to stay upright. His feet now planted on the ground, he outstretched his hands like a tightrope performer until he was safely on shoveled ground. He cursed Hank to himself as he turned the corner to see Stratosphere up ahead. There was a small group huddled near the door waiting to get inside, and Noah felt another stab of annoyance.

Hank was the brother Noah wasn't sure he wanted. Their lives over the years had become inexplicably tangled together. At first, they lay together like the neat rows of braids, but as time went on, they were tangled and choked off cords. They co-owned a computer servicing business, and over the plastic, metal, and glass entrails of fax machines, computers, and smartphones, they worked together. They rented space a few blocks from the Damen stop in Wicker Park atop a Thai restaurant that added the heavy scent of peanut sauce to the smell of burned wire and electrically charged air.

One could have considered this healthy, but forty-plus hours was only the beginning. A few years ago, Noah had been on the losing end of his quest for an apartment when a vacancy in Hank's building became available. The building itself was a horrid eyesore that left Noah wondering if he should call the Health Department or notify some bureaucracy. Hank advised against it, and in a lowered tone, he shared a grave secret with his friend—he said that was how the rent was kept low. And now, two years later and with enough excess cash to take cabs to the far reaches of Chicago, Noah has lived one floor above his friend.

Forever together, the commentary on each other's life ran like a record on repeat. They ebbed and flowed, fighting, working, laughing, and trying to keep afloat.

Noah would have been happy to retreat to his apartment. It was, after all, his weekend to man the shop, but he could see Hank spinning in misery in his breakup with Andrea. It played out like a car accident in slow motion, and just when Noah thought it couldn't grow any grislier, it did.

So instead of binging on Netflix and frightening himself with the scratching in the wall that meant the return of the cockroaches and rats, he was now out trying to keep from busting his ass on the pavement.

As he approached Stratosphere, he saw Hank was a member of the group outside. He watched as Hank and a woman, who somehow blended the hard edge of a dominatrix and the lustful longing of an adolescent's wet dream, passed a cigarette back and forth. Hank stared at the woman, slack-jawed with a pigeon-toed dopiness.

Noah slowed his steps. Certain congratulations were in order, and he didn't want to interrupt Hank's success. Hank had been in a relationship with Andrea for the entirety of their twenties, whereas Noah had slept with more women than he could count.

A grin, like that of a proud parent, pulled across his face, exposing his chipped front tooth in his otherwise handsome face. And like a flash of light, the woman clocked his expression, and her face darkened. She leaned toward Hank and said something. Hank responded in a series of quick gestures and shrugs. The woman chuckled and moved down the street and away from Hank.

When Noah came to greet him, his friend was slumped like a deflated balloon.

"Hey," Noah said. "What was that?"

"You ruined my game."

Noah tilted his head. "How?"

"She asked me if I wanted to get out of here," Hank said.

"And?"

"I freaked out."

Noah cackled, holding his stomach, forgetting about the cold.

"I know," Hank said as they stepped through the doors of Stratosphere, checking in with the bouncer and elbowing their way up to the bar.

Noah had returned to this bar like a creature stepping back into his natural habitat. Sounds of clinking glass and the rising crest of conversation all displaced his mother's voice and the guilt. Here, he could hold on to who he was, not the antiseptic hall of the St. Rose Community Living Nursing Home, watching his father sinking into the abyss of dementia. Noah, now relieved, smiled and nodded to the bartender for his drink.

"So, what's going on with Andrea?" Noah asked with a beer finally in hand.

"All her shit is packed up."

"That's good."

"It's fucking strange."

Noah sipped from his beer and shook his head. "Look, you need to be single. You need to bang a lot of women and get Andrea out of your mind."

Hank blinked at him incredulously.

"You're twenty-nine, man," Noah said, "and you've been locked down by the girl you lost your virginity to. I'm not saying you're pathetic . . . just a bit sad."

"What does that even mean?"

Noah glanced around the bar and squinted from face to face of women moving like constellations in the dim bar. He moved in close to whisper over the rise of low tempo music. "Dude, you can officially have any of these chicks here. In fact, watch me work."

Noah spotted a woman who lived next door to him in his building. She was sitting next a beautiful black woman who had a halo of hair around her head. He stared at her long and hard until she felt the pressure of his eyes. The friend of his neighbor returned his stare and Noah smiled.

"What are you doing?" Hank asked.

"Going in for the kill," Noah said, and cleared his throat. "You see, my young pussy-deprived pupil, her friend s our neighbor, thereby being connected to me and far enough to screw."

"The hot black chick?"

"Yes."

"She seems familiar. And do you really want to be hated by our neighbor when you bang her friend and never call her back?"

Noah whipped back to Hank, holding his cheek in mock offense.

"You see, my friend," Noah began, "this is how the game is played."

"And how you end up the creepy old single guy at the bar, shaking a bottle of Viagra."

Noah scowled at his friend and nodded to a passing waiter balancing a tray with empty shot glasses.

"Hey, give those girls a refill on me," Noah said, puffing out his chest in bravado.

"Are you sure? They ordered a fifty-dollar champagne bottle," the waiter said flatly.

Noah winced like he'd been stabbed. "Who does that?"

"It's okay," Hank said, patting his friend on the shoulder. "Sometimes, you can't get them all."

Noah shrugged off his hand and held up his head and nodded to the waiter. "Get them another refill on me, please."

The waiter and Hank exchanged looks. Soon, the waiter came to the women with Noah's offer and pointed back at him. The women followed the waiter's gaze, and Noah flashed his chipped smile. His neighbor narrowed her eyes while her friend with the afro waved back.

"Got her hooked," Noah said.

"Yeah, it only cost you fifty dollars plus tip and the dignity you should have."

Noah laughed and shook his head at his friend. "Shame, dear pupil, is for weak people, and where I may not have your version of dignity, as least I can't count the chicks I fucked with one finger."

Hank extended his middle finger. "You mean this finger?"

Noah ignored him and headed toward the booth the two women sat in. Hank followed him closely.

"I'm going to need you to run interference."

Hank expelled a deep sigh.

"Keep her friend busy. I don't think she likes me even though I bought her the next drink."

"Really? Do you think she can smell chauvinism?"

Noah halted, and Hank ran into him, nearly spilling his drink. He turned around, a bit indignant.

"Sorry."

"Look, man," Noah said, "Andrea will be out soon enough. I promise you it's not going to always feel this way. Your breaking up is a good thing."

Noah tried to smile at his friend, but Hank glared back at him like someone who had been lost for a very long time. There was a spasm in his stomach as he realized he'd left the tulip for his father in his passenger seat and wondered if it would survive the night in the cold.

4

Isabelle Boldwyn believed that the older people became, the more assured they were of their place within the world, or at least it seemed this way. She was envious of the people around her, navigating the city in the condensed subway trains, congested streets, and tight spaces of alleyways and sidewalks. The people around her rose from their beds with a certainty that, if she had ever had it, was now gone. Not always, but with a growing occurrence, a sort of slow drip, she would awaken in the blackness of night watching the square glow of the streetlight from her window on the ceiling until all the shadows retreated into dawn. There in that still, mournful quiet, in those isolating moments, she was certain she was the only person in the world. She was standing on the edge of a cliff, staring down into the mouth of a promised doom.

The common sense that she had stood so firmly upon, the very cornerstone of her life, had become malleable in that ceaseless exhaustion.

She hadn't figured out what had been the root of her misery—insomnia or anxiety. They seemed to cycle each other, a dog chasing its tail. This rotating wheel fell on her like an undeserving curse. And it was only a matter of time before either one completely usurped her. Fear left her breathless and damp with sweat under her sheet, fear of almost everything, one dark thought leaping to another.

Thoughts led her to the deepest harshness her mind constructed, from the absurd to the plausible. It was only a matter of time before something awful stalked her down and took her under. Maybe it would be never-ending unemployment, a terminal illness . . . cancer? She did have a weird bump just out of reach on her back. Or it could be gun violence. Someone was always getting shot in Chicago . . . someone was probably getting shot right now. Or could she become the next victim of the increasingly frequent racial attacks in this country?

Isabelle almost prided herself in her uncanny ability to picture the most colorful and varied forms of her demise. It was a twisted game she played with herself, a bitter solace in those nights.

She had been lucky that this had only happened to her once this week. She had two nights of light sleep, fitful, as if pushing a rock up a steep incline. When she awoke the next morning, her limbs were heavy. This feeling was foreign and startling. At first, she didn't know how to process it. Even though the sleep had only amounted to a few hours here and there, it provided her with some relief.

She hadn't felt this good in so long. How she could trust it?

She could convince herself that she was one of the lucky people and that this airy benevolence, this strange rested cheerfulness, passed itself to Jones's promotion. And although she kept herself well insulated in a gallows humor, this rare lightness left her feeling charitable.

Although this feeling made it easy to celebrate, that same lightness made it nearly impossible to gather enough sympathy for Jones and her boyfriend. Isabelle didn't want to pity her friend. She wanted to feel good with her as long as she could. Before the insomnia remembered where it placed her. Before she would be back to staring at the ceiling in a silence only broken by the grumble of her old refrigerator. How could she feel bad for the woman before her who had a man who would love her? Yes, he was in the wrong tax bracket—and likely to stay there with his app company, ill-planned and likely to fail—but surely, Jones had to watch the news or, at the very least, catch headlines every now and then. Yes, the economy was speeding to a banana republic, and they were lucky they had jobs.

At least Jones wouldn't be a spinster with chin hair and a hoard of cats waiting to consume her corpse if she died— a fear that reoccurred frequently in Isabelle's stretches of sleeplessness.

Isabelle was aware she should have been suspicious of all of this—her happiness, should she call it happiness. It felt flimsy for such a word. She should have produced some sympathy for her friend or at least, for her own sake, returned to the open arms of her familiar misery, but there she sat in the booth with Jones, bookended by two men who claimed to live in their building. One was black and the other white, pulling on Isabelle's sense of irony as they appeared to be the male counterparts to Jones and herself.

The white man was named Noah, and he kept on smiling at her with the chipped-tooth smile that played like a snare drum—ba-dum-tish—at the end of his jokes. Isabelle found herself laughing and forgetting how many glasses of champagne she had drunk. The dim blue light, and possibly that last shot of tequila, softened the bends and angles of Noah's face.

The four of them struggled for room in the booth, forced to be so close. Their limbs were nearly heaped upon each other. Something about it felt self-congratulatory—the easy combination of their collective beauty. It was easy to believe that peace had always existed.

Noah's arm, with no place to occupy it, was stretched behind Isabelle, and as the night progressed, as their compressed closeness grew familiar, his arm slipped around her shoulders. His body was solid and made up of compact ropy muscles, like she knew men to be, but warm like she had forgotten they could be. Tension left her shoulders, and she reclined into him. Empty shot glasses, champagne flutes, beer bottles, and elbows fought for room on the small table they gathered around. Their voices sounded over the drone of conversations and the steady pulse of music. Isabelle had to lean in to hear Noah speak, pushing herself further into his space and deeper into his warmth. She smiled, looking at him but not quite hearing what he said over the babble.

She knew this turn of good fortune was deceptive. Deep down, past the dim bar, the sharp bite of his cologne, and the rise of his voice straining over the music, her desire to be touched couldn't be trusted.

But she wanted it anyway. She had broken through the surface of her agony, splashing up where there was air, breathing the reprieve in deeply. It was only a matter of time before the insomnia would pull her under, and shouldn't she enjoy the surface world while she could? She should breathe, and feel, and drink in all this light. The end would come soon, and it would unfold itself in its various forms tonight or tomorrow night or some other night.

The sudden heat of Jones's gaze pulled at Isabelle. It tugged her out of the lightness and out of Noah's words and their flowing meter. Concern was locked on Jones's face.

For a moment, Isabelle wondered if her resolution was obvious to the table. Was she shamelessly throwing herself at this man, whom she just now recalled seeing in passing through the hallway?

Jones gestured to her friend, and they excused themselves momentarily. Jones hooked her arm in Isabelle's and elbowed through the crowd toward the bathrooms.

"Are you okay?" Jones asked.

"I'm fine."

"Are you sure you want to sleep with a guy in the building?"

"I won't sleep with him."

Isabelle couldn't quite commit to the lie. Jones's eyes narrowed in disbelief.

"I don't think you should sleep with him."

"Give me one good reason why," Isabelle said.

There was a lurch inside Isabelle. A threat against her lightness. She glared at her friend, who had so much, trying to deny her something so small. Isabelle sucked in a breath and began to turn away. Jones said something, and she, like her words, receded into the blackness and bodies of the bar. Isabelle trudged back to the booth that was now snatched up by another group. Her shoulders sagged in defeat when Noah's voice called for her.

"Hey," he said, pushing through the crowd up to her. "Looks like we lost our spot."

"Where'd your friend go?"

"He left."

"I guess it's just us."

The populace of the bar surged around them. People churned against each other in the darkness with their voices rising, their warmth pushing Isabelle and Noah together. They were once again forced into intimacy with one another. Noah had been full of wit and bravado among their friends in the booth, but now he stared at her softly in the blue light. He opened his mouth to speak but no words came out, and instead, he settled with his chipped-toothed smile. He was mute from intoxication and he tried to speak once more. His mouth hung ajar, but no words issued, no rhythmic voice, no charm.

His eyes widened, almost panicked as if he had lost something, as if he had dropped his voice somewhere in the bar. Isabelle smiled at him reassuringly and Noah's open mouth settled back into that smile. After that, everything was broken into fragments. The constraints of thought became unhinged, beaten down by a warm collective drunkenness shared between the two.

Somehow, they made it out of the crowd, out of the dark bar and into the dry cold. Isabelle leaned up against the bar, and Noah stood in front of her, still smiling. Outside on the street a few yards away, other refugees from the bar gathered in clumps, shivering fingers pinching and holding cigarettes. Noah and Isabelle were so close, still clinging, as if by instinct, to that intimacy they'd found in the bar. Isabelle inhaled Noah's breath that was rising around her in a soft cloud against the cold.

Again, he tried to speak and failed. His eyes fell to Isabelle's lips and stayed there for a moment. Isabelle clutched the fibers of his thick winter coat and drew him closer. His body pressed her against the frigid brick, and his breath turned heavy against her cheek.

Isabelle turned her face slowly and their lips met. A soft brushing, a gentle parting, and then deep probing leading to avid tasting. Isabelle could feel the strength of his ropy arms winding around her. She didn't know how long they were holding each other and kissing. Time slipped from her. Everything slipped from her. All that remained was her shivering, his kissing, and the warmth he continued to give off, as if he was the source of all warmth.

A whip of frigid air brought her back to the street. She pulled back and gathered herself. Noah did the same. Isabelle then stepped over the snow-encrusted curb onto the edge of the street. She waved down one of the cabs convening at the bar entrance. Inside the cab on the way home, she was back in Noah's arms. They stayed like that until they were in front of the ugly face of their building. Noah had given up trying to speak altogether as they scaled the creaking stairs of the hallway and entered Isabelle's apartment.

She led him through her apartment, sure-footed in the darkness. He trailed behind her, his fingertips reaching to fill the small of her back. Inside her bedroom, they reached for each other's skin, past layers and layers of clothes. Noah seized Isabelle as they backpedaled onto the bed.

Once again, Isabelle was inhaling his breath between kisses. The drunkenness that had betrayed him before was gone as he lay on top of her, using every part of himself to explore her. His wide hands searched the surface of her skin in the darkness, squeezing her breasts and tickling her nipples. His touch slid along her throat, along her pulse.

Isabelle held her breath, and her heart marched in her chest. She turned to her nightstand and rifled through the drawer, extracting a condom. Noah continued to kiss her, then he gripped her thighs and opened her legs. Isabelle reached down, groping in the darkness, past his panting chest, and her fingers brushed the stiff, wet tip of his ccck. She traveled down its girth and seized it in her hand as tightly as she could.

Noah gasped and shuddered on top of her.

She held him there and handed him the condom. In the dim light rolling over them from the streetlamp outside, she saw the question in his face. She nodded to him and released his cock as he hoisted himself up to roll the condom on. He lowered his weight back on her, and again, Isabelle's hand was around his cock. She led him to her entrance and teased him with her warmth.

Noah quaked, and his arm that held him up nearly buckled. She playfully dragged his tip along her, squeezing him to prevent him from fully entering her. He began to whimper, soft and pleading. She felt his cock swell in the condom. She held his gaze, and headlights from cars moving along the street outside flooded his face. Shadows spun around the room and around their bodies. It was then that Isabelle realized how hot his body was, how the heat flowed down from him, and Isabelle questioned whether she would ever be cold again.

"Please," he said in a strained whisper.

His voice, finally found, made its way into the darkness with such a softness that it startled Isabelle.

She released him, and he slipped into her.

5

The nudge from the springs in the couch were painful enough to awake Hank. He tried to shift his weight on the couch to no avail. The jab moved from his ribs to his back. He rolled once more, binding his upper body in the thin afghan. He cried out, kicking at the couch. He knew it wasn't the true tormentor.

No, Andrea lay comfortable and warm in the bed in the other room.

With a heavy sigh, he sat up, staring in the black apartment. He thought going out tonight would have taken his mind off things. For a moment, it had worked, and his thoughts lingered on the woman he had met at the bar. He still had the haunting pleasure of sharing a cigarette with her outside. He licked his lips to hold on to the sensation a bit longer. He thought of how she deliberately moved when she walked. He took in each of her steps, and his breath fluttered when she moved away from him, her arms swinging in time with the gentle stride of her legs, and the tight roundness of her ass was jabbing him sharper than the broken spring under him. He hadn't felt that way in so long. What had she awoken in him?

He didn't even know her name.

And there, his mind turbid with alcohol, he was afraid he could forget her. He steadied his thoughts and fortified her image. He lay back down and wondered if Noah was somewhere down the hall from him with Isabelle. He was certain Noah had gotten lucky while Hank only had a mirage of a woman to cling to.

He collapsed back onto the couch, and the springs punched his back.

He growled at the packing boxes still stacked on the side of the room. Darkness fell over them, shifting them into watchful figures in the shadows. Hank walloped the couch, and its springs cried as they popped him back.

"Fuck this!"

Hank was off the couch, and his unsteady feet led him in the path of one of the packing boxes. Affronted, he shoved the box out of his way. It smashed to the floor, and something within shattered on impact. He marched into the bedroom and ripped back the covers on Andrea's still body. He dove on the bed and pulled the covers over himself.

He sighed, stretching out on the mattress, enjoying it like the company of an old friend. The knots within his neck and the long length of his back uncurled.

Andrea stirred next to him and rolled to face him. Her expression quickly grew from confusion to rage, and she began to yell. She drew back and kicked at him.

"Get out! Get the hell out!"

Hank sat up in bed. Righteous indignation shot through him, and the pain in his muscles doubled.

"No, dammit! I'm done sleeping on that couch!" he said, grabbing his injured neck.

"I swear to God—"

"What? What are you going to do?"

Andrea sat up and turned on the nightstand light. Her hair was a network of tight braids covered in a silk scarf and her face was florid with anger. Her small fist gathered tightly at her side.

"You did this to yourself," she said.

"Oh, not this shit again. I was being honest when I said I wasn't happy anymore. How are we supposed to work if no one is happy? Stop punishing me for that."

"I don't want to do this. It's late and you're drunk—again."

"Well, I have to numb the pain somehow."

Andrea climbed out of the bed to sneer at him. "Get out!"

Hank lay back on the bed and placed his hands under his head to pantomime his comfort. He let out a loud, overly expressive sigh. "Nope, and you might as well leave—you're the one out of bed."

"Are you kidding me?"

She stared at him, drawing her mouth tight. He could see the labor of contemplation was slowed down from exhaustion. She began to pace the border of the bed.

Hank patted the area where she had been lying, enjoying the torture he inflicted. Alcohol had made him brave—perhaps too brave. He'd known Andrea for ten years, and the only reason he had the upper hand was because he'd struck while she had been asleep. He would pay for this, and the thought was a hard weight in his stomach. As she stalked the bed, he was filled with the urge to backtrack and yield the bed to her.

Andrea came to a halt at the foot of the bed. She must've seen him wavering. She placed her hand on her hip and stared at him. Had she figured out her counterattack that quickly?

Hank gulped and tried to smile. "Baby, I'm sorry."

"I'm not your 'baby.'"

"It's just that the couch is causing me back problems."

"Well, then you sleep in here," she said.

Her voice was ice, and there was strain in her face. Lines deepened around her mouth.

"I'm just a little drunk. I shouldn't have come in here like this."

Andrea drew back like she wanted to spit, and she moved away from the bed and toward the door.

"When we broke up, I couldn't see it," she said.

"Couldn't see what?"

"What you meant when you said, 'I wasn't happy anymore.' I see it now."

She walked out of the room and closed the door behind her. The old metal hinges squealed and the door slammed. Hank clicked off the light and lay there trying to work out why her words stung him. He rolled around in the bed, flipping the pillow over, trying to find comfort in his bed.

The ache in his muscles dug deeper into his back, moving in a jolt along his spine.

The sheets were saturated with the flowery smell of Andrea's shampoo. This forced him up, and he tore them from the mattress. He yanked the pillows from their cases and lay back down on the bare mattress. He scooped the comforter from the floor and drew it over his head. He screwed his eyes closed and rotated his shoulder, waiting for sleep to come.

His fatigue brought him to the precipice of unconsciousness. There, alone in the darkness, he traveled back to the woman he met at the bar and her lips curling around the length of their shared cigarette. His cock aroused as he pulled it from his gym shorts and stroked himself in sync with the way he'd seen her move.

i

The bottom had fallen out beneath Marcie Ellinger.

To most people, her best days would have been their worst. Her best day, she stood before men with her flesh exposed, the thump of her heart muted by the howl of music and dollar bills crumpled at her feet. This was something she had accepted long ago with a smile. While her best day would offend the propriety of most people, she reveled in her life. Shame was for weak people. She thrived in the netherworld that was pressed so closely up against the everyday mundane that she could hardly tell the difference. She knew what other people didn't—she'd peeked behind the veil. They all existed within the same system, the same cycle, feeding off one another. The upstanding, respectable man who wore a tailored suit behind the desk, making his cunning decisions, would be the same man she danced for. Night would fall upon the city, the veil would be drawn, and this man who believed he was hidden would creep into black narrow alleys to come see her. This man, so powerful in the day, a king among the highest people, would kneel before the sweep of her naked hips and the supple slopes of her breasts.

Elsewhere, outside the dense city, along stretches of green yards and the quaint suburban developments that they belonged to, a woman so upstanding, so well-to-do in her cardigan sets, wielded an unmistakable influence. She was the ideal, the upstanding American mother, in service to her family, the school, and her neighborhood. But a closer, more critical examination of this affluent woman exposed those fine cracks from the pressure spreading on her surface. And when the safety of night rolled over her suburb, she would venture into the city and visit Marcie's boyfriend.

Marcie's boyfriend, a fellow denizen of her netherworld, had a jagged scar parting the hair in his beard.

He looked at the well-to-do woman with his face designed for violence and navigating the dark cold nights. She, in exchange for his professional discretion and supply of Percocet, would pay him handsomely. Albeit, this woman's excursions into the city were not an easy feat, but it was better than the narrow-eyed, wary look of suspicion from her doctor. Any length to ease the needling pain of the cracks from the weight of perfection.

One night, after the kids had been put to sleep and her dear husband had been away on business, she sat before the fireplace in her recliner. She was relaxed at last, pills washed down with a glass of Malbec. She was so relaxed, plummeting down the darkest, warmest depths, that when the first break of morning light washed upon her, she didn't stir. That morning, her daughter and son, respectively twelve and eight, came down the stairs to find the upstanding well-to-do woman's face blue in death and her lap stained purple from an overturned wine glass.

The outrage and shock detonated an explosion, and early in a morning an exact week from this woman's death, another explosion broke through Marcie's door. Panic seemed to blind her as several armed men rushed her apartment. Even now, nearly a month in the wake of that, she couldn't recall much of what she'd seen. Only the sounds of boots, the cries of her boyfriend, and her child weeping in the next room haunted her.

No morning felt safe.

It wasn't existing in the netherworld that plagued her or a desire for the mundane. No, it was a lack of control in any of them. Now, she wondered if somewhere else existed between those two places. If there was somewhere else, she could escape the collect calls coming in daily from the county prison from her boyfriend. She had answered the first time he'd called, and the defeat in his voice left her sick and fearful. He wanted her there. He pleaded on the other end for her support. But she came up empty, and her voice was hollow when she spoke to him. He must've known and only called because there was no one else.

The man in the tailored suit was now loosening his tie and bringing a cigarette up to his mouth. No one was supposed to smoke in the VIP room, but with each cigarette he lit, the more generous he became. Marcie let him slide another twenty-dollar bill into the front of her G-string. His steely eyes were wet stones in the dim light of the room. There was a ruthlessness to them, a keen knowing, and this was why he was her favorite. That hard glance was a shared trait between them, and they recognized it within one another the way one predator acknowledged another of their species. This was why she disregarded the rules with him.

The music pulsed overhead in the speakers in the small room partitioned off from the rest of the club by a thick velvet curtain the color of blood. Marcie moved slowly to the cadence of the song, hitting every other beat as she reached for the strap of her bra.

He reached for her hand, causing her to stop. His eyes flickered, and she let his hand linger before shrugging it off. She smiled and pointed to the old cameras in the ceiling.

"Security is watching," she said. "There's only so much you can get away with."

His eyes probed her, and he smiled. "That's a lie."

She thought for a moment to continue her story but decided against it.

"You know what I want," he said.

"You don't even know me."

"Another lie."

She looped her thumb behind her bra strap and pulled it down, exposing her breast to him. She stretched forward, inches from his face. The intensity in his face didn't flutter, even when Marcie pressed her breast into his face.

He leaned back and took a drag off his cigarette.

"How long are you going to play this game?" he asked.

"How long do you want me to?"

He blew out smoke and an exasperated sigh. "Come away with me."

She had been dancing for him for a year and a half now. A year and half of watching the blush of arousal in his face bloom into something else, something complicated, something that pulled at her. Marcie cultivated it because she leveraged money from him. But he would do more than watch her dance. He would talk to her. He would chronicle the daily happenings of that mundane world he ruled. He would speak with the anguish of a predator who didn't kill and of the lulling death of domesticity.

It hurt her so to see him so pained, so sometimes, she slipped him pills. And sometimes, she let him touch himself while she danced for him. She did it to see the sharp edge in his eyes, to see his veins pop out like cords in his neck, and to celebrate his power. A power equal to her own, but unlike him, she didn't yield it to anyone.

"Come away with me. Let's leave it all."

The cry in those powerful eyes shook her. Those deep pools reminded her that life was trying to take her under. He just wanted a reason, just needed her to give him permission to take back what he'd lost so long ago in that office job, investment options, and a condo somewhere downtown. He started asking this a few months ago, trying to advance past her defenses and become a resident of her darkness.

In the dim light, his tan skin was the color of night. All the things that made him dangerous were illuminated, the tightness in his mouth and the wide bulk of his chest. Marcie let the temptation roll around inside her to the rhythm of her hips. The image of him navigating her realm came with ease to her, and the taste of it was sweet.

She turned around and sat on his lap, rocking slowly against his mass. She arched her torso and brought her head back. His lips tickled her ear. Emotion parted within her, and she was settled in knowing that she never wanted to see her boyfriend. His weakness, his ability to be taken from her home, had to be purged. He would eventually come to this understanding. He would inevitability stop calling and realize that he was merely a placeholder for her. He was like so many before him and after him.

The world did grow more severe, but Marcie was a predator.

She was alone with a sickly child who siphoned money from her with inhalers. A child who, at five years old, still refused to use the bathroom, and the scent of urine clung to him like an offending phantom. A young boy who only cried to communicate and never spoke more than a few words at a time. Her boy was never sweet, never kind, merely a tumor pulling her down into the heavy sands of guilt.

He was the living, breathing reminder of the one time she'd let herself yield to circumstances. The one haunting moment she hadn't listened to the predator inside her.

Before the baby came and stretched her body, she had been great.

When she entered her apartment after work, her child would unfold before her like a scene from a movie she didn't want to watch. The shrill of her little boy's voice would ram through the scraps of peace she had. The smell of his urine would ensnare her as he stepped up to her, clinging at her legs. His hands and face were impossibly gray. Even though Marcie didn't keep the cleanest apartment, she couldn't have imagined where he'd collected the dirt.

On the couch would be a friend who'd fallen on hard times nodding in and out of sleep, and if her friend were conscious, he would have a blunt burning between his forefinger and thumb. In a funk of weed and piss, Marcie would come in and fight for room on the couch. Her friend lamented about his failed DJ career while her filthy child wailed like an animal and her boyfriend called collect from prison.

So much weakness around her.

"I have a gift for you," the man in the tailored suit said while she bobbed on his lap.

He reached into the pocket of his suit coat and revealed a small glass snuff bullet filled with coke. He dangled the tube in front of her face. Marcie's breath knotted in her chest. She jumped up and shot her head through the curtain and surveyed the bar through the flashing strobe lights. The fat, lethargic security guard watched a woman slide along the pole. She returned to him, certain they were undisturbed.

"I can't do this."

He coaxed the rubber top off the glass tube and handed it to her. Marcie placed her bra back on and knelt, inhaling the coke up her nostril. She felt a burn shoot through her head and a flux of heat. She glanced up at the man in the suit.

A smile extended along his face. His smile was dazzling. His smile was dangerous.

Marcie collected herself on his lap and listened to the seduction of his proposition.

"Where would we go?" she asked.

He began to speak about a winter home in Miami, but Marcie didn't care where it was as long as she was far from the weakness that smelled like piss.

6

There was a gentle slope into consciousness. When Noah opened his eyes, the room was filled with brilliance as light resonated off a world covered in white. He turned to the woman next to him, and her deep brown skin was radiant. She stirred in the falling and rising of her breath.

He stared at her for a long while, traveling along the rich curves and bends of her lithe form. His leg lay next to hers in the coiled sheets. The smooth tightness of her flesh aroused him again.

There was a slow grind against his temples and an uneasiness in his stomach. These consequences from last night's liquor weren't severe. Noah succumbed to them, but just for a moment. This wasn't the first time he'd woken at a strange woman's apartment. Although unlike before, he couldn't find the urge to retreat, to creep out as if he'd never been there. That was so unnerving he could almost look past the agony of his hangover.

The white light from the cold morning was thrown upon him. He glanced around her bedroom, which, because they lived in the same building, had the same layout as his. Yet somehow, everything was different, and not just the watermarks making paths along the ceiling. Her room was draped in rich blues and purples, and the walls held paintings and shelves brimming with odd kitschy knickknacks and jewelry. Everything around him sang with textures and life. The familiarity of the layout made it hard to leave.

He felt settled, as if he'd come to the end of a long journey to wind up here in this bed.

She rustled, then turned on her side away from him. Her leg slipped away from Noah. He remained still, now tracing her spine and the perfection in the angles of her shoulder blades. Eagerness to touch her bristled within him, and his arm journeyed out as if it weren't just knotted bedclothes that separated them, but miles. He pulled his body closer to her. He breathed in the scents of her sweat, her sex, her perfume, and last night's liquor like they would sustain him. He gathered her in his arms. Their bodies were fused together again, and she awoke with a sigh.

She spun to face him, and a tired smile pulled along her face. She covered her mouth with her hand.

"Morning breath," she said underneath her palm.

Noah hesitated but allowed himself to follow his desire. He gently pushed her hand away from her face and kissed her. She laughed and pulled away.

"I have mouthwash for both of us," she said.

Noah's face heated. "Sorry."

"It's fine," she said.

She gathered the sheet from the bed and, with a hard yank, freed it from the mattress. She draped the sheet around her body and stepped through the door into the bathroom.

"Come on," she said, and Noah quickly pulled on his boxers and followed her to the bathroom.

There, she handed him the lid to the mouthwash filled with blue liquid. She held out the bottle and raised it up as if it were a drink. Noah did the same with the lid, and then downed the mouthwash, swished, and spat it in the sink.

"I'm surprised you're here," she said as she turned the sink's faucet. Within the walls, old pipes shuddered, shaking the mirror, and finally, the water washed down their mouthwash.

"Why is that?"

She walked through the hallway, and Noah followed her back into the bedroom. She sat on her bed, glancing at Noah, and her face tightened in suspicion. Noah wanted to join her on the bed, maybe try to kiss her, maybe try to relive last night in the now blazing cold winter light.

He took a tentative step toward the bed.

"It's just that you do this a lot," she said, and the accusation stopped him where he stood.

"Do what a lot?"

"Fuck women a lot," she said, and tightened the sheet around her body.

"No," Noah said. "Come on, it's not like that."

"Well, you live above me," she said with a smirk. "And I'm pretty sure you do."

"Shit," Noah said, and his head dropped.

"It's not your fault this building is made of matchboxes," she said. "And honestly, it's okay. I was drunk, and I wanted company."

Noah began to speak, but words became thick and gummy in his throat. He coughed, trying to force them loose. He glanced at her, and she pursed her lips at him skeptically.

"Do you have a speaking impediment?" she asked. "It's not a dig—just curious."

Noah grew flushed and swallowed in a vain attempt to keep his mouth from drying. He longed for his workstation with his tools, looking through a magnifying glass at the guts of a computer. There, along the open parts of silicon, copper, and zinc, the pathways of things conformed to order. An order that could be resumed if disrupted, unlike like flow of this conversation with this woman.

"I look for you sometimes in the hallway," he said. "I haven't told anyone this, not even my best friend, but I look for you sometimes. I hope I bump into you. When I saw you at the bar, I had to say something."

Her eyebrows raised high onto her forehead and her lips parted. The sheet around her body loosened, exposing the contours of her cleavage.

"Rochelle, I really want to get to know you."

She held her head back and drew in a breath. Her face screwed into a grimace so caustic Noah reeled a few steps backward. The connection that had existed moments before was severed so quickly it almost seemed audible, like a plate shattering on concrete.

"Rochelle? Who's that?"

"What do mean?"

"That's not my name," she said. "It's Isabelle, remember?"

"No, I meant that," Noah said, holding out his hands in protest.

Isabelle bent down and collected his clothes. She shoved them into his chest with enough strength to nearly knock him off his feet. She marched through the apartment toward the door, and Noah rushed behind her.

"I'm sorry," Noah said. "I really meant Isabelle."

"Sure, you did," Isabelle said. "And for a moment, I almost believed you."

"But I'm serious."

"Look, this was just a quick fuck," Isabelle said. "I understand that. I don't need you to pretend it was something more because you think that's what I want to hear."

She opened the door and pointed out into the chilly hall. Noah struggled to pull his shirt over his head, dropping his pants and shoes. Isabelle quickly scooped them up and tossed them out into the hall.

"I don't like being lied to," she said.

Noah sighed, defeated, and accompanied his scattered belongings in the hall.

"Oh, and women don't like to be stalked," she said, and slammed the door mere inches from Noah's face.

7

Rattled nerves popped like small explosions in Jones's stomach. Her mouth was coated in a bitter metallic taste. How could her body turn against her? She straightened her back against her chair and glanced out at the two men in her office—an office that she still hadn't decorated yet.

Was the ground pitching back and forth underneath her? And moreover, whose idea was it to call a meeting on her first day?

The finance director, a stout guy in his early thirties, peered over the black Wayfarer glasses dominating his small face. The dread in his face was a palpable flood and Jones could drown in it. She swallowed again, stretching her diaphragm.

Just hours ago, she had been elated. She had woken before her alarm when off. Jones had allowed herself the unspeakable in the morning lull, something that she rarely let herself do—she relaxed, an indulgence to believe in the rightness of the universe. There in bed, next to Derek, she reveled in her serendipitous fortune and believed in her diligent work and her unfaltering intelligence. A warm flame of satisfaction sustained her in the cold apartment as she stood in front of her closet, deciding how to dress the successful woman she had become.

Her stride was deliberate, and she stood tall in the line for her latte that morning. She trotted through the swells of gray, flat faces hurrying along colorless concrete and steel buildings, lustrous against the pale chill of winter. Nothing had been able to muddle her impudence on this day, on her way into her office, ample in possibility . . . until the despondent face of the finance director, along with the senior accountant, scurried in. Their heads were downturned, and they carried reports in thick manila envelopes into her office like pallbearers towing the dead.

"I spoke to our distributors. If we don't find another source of revenue," the finance director said, "we'll all be looking for another job by the end of the quarter."

His words were nomads roaming toward Jones down a long hall, arriving to her out of order. Jones nodded to him in feigned comprehension. He continued to talk, and Jones's eyes rested on her hands interlaced on her desk. Her muscles stiffened as he listed the profit and loss margins. Muscles wrenched along her shoulders and neck as if they were under blows.

This day had so much promise to it.

But maybe this was the penalty for her hubris.

She turned from her hands and past the ominous words, looking through the glass walls of her office to the floor space of the magazine. There, the staff of art directors, editors, and assistants stirred with vigor. Morning light the color of ash came through the skylights onto the open space, populated with Ikea furnishings and cubicles that snaked in the shape of an elongated "S" along the carpet. It was a modest staff of thirty-eight people made of dogmatic art history majors and chimerical liberal art majors. The staff, with their tattoos, leather, piercings, and ripped denim, strained the borders of acceptable business casual attire. One of the art directors strolled along the office like a harbinger of coolness in a pink bob. The burden of herding those smug transcendentalists and the irrevocably hip to the point of cynicism and all their cavalier efforts into profits promised to crush her.

The finance director and accountant left a mournful nebula in the office when they left. Jones's resolve began to erode when the phone rang.

"This is Jones."

"Are you going to be able to get off work early?"

Derek's voice on the other end was edging close to shrill. She could picture him alone in the apartment, succumbing to the current of his mania. She swilled in more air as the nerves in her stomach doubled over.

His launch was tonight, and she had left so quickly this morning she hadn't been available for the requisite words of support, the benevolent strokes to his greedy ego.

"Is everything okay?"

"God, no," he began, and as he spoke, it seemed as though the walls of her office inched in closer to her, expelling the oxygen she required to breathe.

Jones attempted to be a person of deliberate actions. She withheld her promotion from Derek for the sake of her ownership. The decisions and the money she owned would be hers alone. Jones had kissed, fucked, and breathed next to Derek long enough to follow the pathway of his thoughts and words before they condensed in his head. He would pry at every decision she made. He was a nefarious bastard who propped up statements in the form of questions to allow a slow incubation of doubt. And if he did offer a compliment, it was bloated with so much conjecture that Jones wondered if she had been insulted.

No, this promotion, however ill-fated, whatever havoc she brought to the magazine, whatever decisions she made in the hyper-modern pastiche office space, was hers alone. Her conviction didn't waver. This morning, even peeking behind the veil at profits and losses so dismal she understood the swift retreat of her predecessor, she hardened herself against those pangs of guilt. Maybe today, when he came walking through the door smelling like the acrid burn of Kenyan coffee beans, she wouldn't feel guilt at all. And even if she did, it was better than having him poke at her, having him bolster himself up as an expert to dispense his questions and advice, all the while seething at her.

The man Jones shared a drafty old apartment with grieved over his internet start-up. And he added his groans to that of the floorboards, his sobs to the cracks which traveled along the plaster walls, his sighs to the shutters of thin glass in the peeling window frames. A year ago, over dark draft beer, rising clouds of marijuana smoke, and an unjust, yet impregnable arrogance, Derek and his friends had devised a plan to digitize interior design. Derek had the capital, and a childhood friend had skills in marketing, while another had skills in design. During nights spent over the same potion, they finalized details.

Tonight was another one of their lavish parties in the name of the business, and nothing in Jones wanted to attend. She devised some sort of false sickness that could keep her home, but she doubted her ability to commit to the act. She had enough secrets chafing between them. With the weight of the magazine perched on her shoulders, she arrived at her apartment at the end of the day without much fight.

Derek met her at the door wearing nothing but a button-down shirt and boxers. His anxiety seized him, and he began talking to her in half sentences. In his state, he over-gelled his hair, and the buttons of his shirt were misaligned. Jones fought against her desire to resist him. She took a steady breath and retreated to the bedroom where a skimpy red dress lay disembodied on the bed.

She narrowed her eyes at it as Derek rushed up behind her.

"You don't expect me to wear that?" she said.

Derek scowled. "You look amazing in that."

"It's twenty degrees outside."

"I want to impress the investors," he said, going to the closet and stepping into gray suit pants.

"So you want me to be your ring girl?"

Derek swept his hand through his shellacked hair and frowned at the excess product left on his palm. He glanced at her helplessly. Jones bit her bottom lip and nodded, to which Derek rushed over to her, hugging her and unintentionally smearing gel on the back of her coat.

Jones quickly showered, wedged herself into the dress, and pinned her hair away from her face. Under normal circumstances, she relished any opportunity to elevate herself beyond casual denim, but tonight, she couldn't find any of her usual joy. When the Uber finally arrived at their apartment, she had committed to her quiet misery and preserved it silently as they journeyed east into the city, against the flow of ardent commuters.

The Uber driver was a spirited man who was most likely from a far suburb and followed the fare into the city. His hesitation resulted in several punitive honks. When they arrived downtown, he missed the destination and Derek gleefully sharpened all his nerves into ire at the poor man. Despite the driver's promise to turn around, Derek insisted he stop the car two blocks away from their destination.

Jones glanced down at her black heels and the slick, icy sidewalk and began to object, only to have her voice lost in the battle between the men. She sighed deeply and stepped out of the car, certain she would fare better in the cold than in the car. Derek climbed out, cursing at the man, and slammed the door for punctuation.

He adjusted the collar of his shirt and raked his hand through his slick scalp. His grimace pulsed a deep red, and Jones wondered briefly if she would be next.

She decided to test this. "The man didn't deserve that."

Derek didn't register her words at all. He instead looked through her at their destination. Silently, he linked hands with her and led her down the street. The Chicago River rippled like mercury in the bronze illumination of streetlights, parallel to them, and around them, buildings of phosphorescent concrete and glass reached up into the inky night. The streets palpated in traffic, and sirens echoed off the high walls of skyscrapers.

They arrived at a bar at the bottom of one of those buildings as snow began to fall. The walls of the bar were constructed of tempered glass, overlooking the river and the city night, and cast the city in a soft lens, like the ancient headshots of old Hollywood. Above them, dim light was refracted through glass installations, diffusing the room in such a beautiful incandescence that Jones trusted nothing her eyes saw. The entire bar of mahogany and stainless steel furnishings all read false.

The hostess led them through the back where downtempo music pulsed, and when they arrived at the gathering of equally dressed and primped people, Jones knew nothing was real. The small group applauded his arrival and raised drinks. His coconspirators swooped him away from Jones and began their campaigning. This party was naturally Derek's idea and was supposed to be evidence to the several investors that he was established, that he was bankable and worthy of their time and money. He had even been brazen enough to fly the few who were willing from Silicon Valley to Chicago.

On each table, an armada of iPads was posted, displaying his app and encouraging the guests to try out live demonstrations. An unseen projector transmitted the company logo on the wall. From what Jones had managed to deduce, the party planning had gone off without incident. Only a few investors had declined Derek's invitation, and the people swirling around her were delighted in the liquor, but what bristled her was that no one seemed to be interested in the iPads or the app itself. Not once did she see a single person pick up an iPad.

This event was Derek's Hail Mary—his final card to play before he had exhausted all of his capital. She knew if no one offered his company a check, this would be the end.

Jones suspended her apprehension when a fellow partygoer, loosened up from the free-flowing booze, questioned Derek's idea behind strained smiles and whispered to her.

"This is an amazing party. Is Derek responsible for all the marketing?" a woman asked her.

The woman was dressed smartly in a blazer, and Jones almost instantly regretted letting Derek convince her to wear this red dress. Jones could only nod at her, desperate to mask her own doubt. The woman walked away and met up with a group of men, who all darted glances of skepticism.

Jones quickly pushed through a few people to reach Derek, who was surrounded by people. He spoke earnestly to the small group. She attempted to catch his gaze to warn him, but he avoided her eyes. She waited, tapping her left heel into the marble tile beneath her. Finally, at a lull in the conversation, she pounced on him. A flicker of annoyance passed over his face. She ushered him aside into the beam of the projector, where he stared back at her with his company logo emblazoned on his face.

"Do you have any investors yet?"

He bit down hard. "I don't have time for this."

"We need to get them on the iPads," she said, her voice clipped by panic.

"I got this," he said, his face flushing pink.

"If we can get them to try it out, I'm sure you can get at least one."

"Jones," he said in a low hiss.

"I can help you. We can develop an ad for the magazine—"

His forehead and cheeks blushed into a deep crimson. "All I need for you to do is smile and look pretty. Understand?"

He hooked his finger in his collar and whipped away from her, flipping his scowl into a smile back to the crowd. The air was knocked completely out of Jones, and she staggered away, trying to retain normalcy. She made her way to the bathroom, which was as dim and metallic as the rest of bar, and into a stall. She reached behind her and unzipped the tight dress and exhaled deeply. She opened her clutch with her shaky hands, extracted a Xanax, and placed it on her tongue. She leaned against the stall until her natural breathing had returned.

She returned to the bar and ordered a vodka and lime. Jones took a quick swig, taking down the alcohol and the pill. She perched against the bar with her gaze through the windows to the rippling density of the river outside the glass.

She was witnessing Derek's end in real time.

8

The front door to the apartment was propped open by a bereft red brick. As Hank approached, he saw footprints through the snow toward a weatherworn moving truck. He went slack, and the icy biting breeze channeling through the hall led him up the stairs and into his apartment. He opened the unlocked door when two men, as beaten looking as the moving truck, carried boxes past him, against the breeze and along their path to the vehicle.

Hank stepped into his apartment, and all the boxes that had inhabited the walls and the corners of the room were gone. His steps over the creaking boards echoed. The apartment was now half full, as if Andrea had been omitted, a cavernous emptiness that stretched into the rooms and closets and cupboards. Hank felt himself choking, knowing he alone wasn't up for the task of filling this space. How was he supposed to tread through this foreign solitude?

Andrea emerged from the bedroom, and as they stood there hooked in the strange spell of the emptiness, her face dulled with contempt for him. The tightness in her mouth and heaviness in her eyes spoke to him. Those eyes, which he had looked into for over a decade, now told him that he had brought this ruin upon them and to their home.

Andrea adjusted the strap on a gym bag stuffed with her clothes.

"Do you need help with that?" Hank said, and the echo returned his words to him.

Andrea let out a bitter chuckle. She pushed past him toward the door.

"I'm sorry," he said, as if it could return the furniture into the apartment and repair their brokenness and seal the fissures that had deepened between them.

Andrea stopped, and from behind, he saw her hand tighten on the strap and her muscles bunch from the weight. She dropped the bag as Hank swept it up. Now next to her, maybe for the last time, a cold panic licked across his chest. Her face, her body and voice, had been all he'd known. Her presence was like a chronicle of his own do-nothing life. Andrea, as she was at that moment, had been by his side throughout the ghastly landscape of his adolescence. Both of them had been two awkward figures clutching to one another. She had been his first everything, and all of that life was laden there within her face, so much of who Hank had been, who he wanted to be, who he had promised her he would be.

There was a time when he believed they would always stay together, but that sentiment was misplaced and packed away like an aging keepsake, a victim to time and decay.

Andrea's shoulder brushed up against his as he compensated for the weight of the bag. The contact of their bodies was fraught in desperation, caught in its finality. She seemed as if she would have always been there for him to touch.

Now where he stood to touch her for the last time, he recalled their first touch on a hot, restless summer night in Ohio. Heat cooked the black tar, filling the spaces in pavement till it oozed and took the imprint of his running shoes. Hank had waited on the side of his house, leaning back on the searing metal of his garage door. He lay back there, testing his endurance until the pain was too much. He couldn't have been older than thirteen and had been preoccupied by the developing strength of his body.

No one was home that night. His father and mother had to attend some work party. Hank's father, wound up from anxiety, had spun around the house. Hank's mother, flushed from the heat, stuck last night's meatloaf in the microwave for his dinner. Even through their various states of emotion as the first generation to both have college degrees, they couldn't hide the pride beaming from them. His parents both emerged through herculean effort from that perilous housing project in Detroit, removed now but still able to recall, as children, the smoke pillars and broken glass of the Detroit riots and the later carnage between crack and the war on drugs on black bodies. Now, they had arrived at their own American dream, becoming what they promised themselves they wanted to be.

Attempts to pass what they had endured on to Hank had failed miserably, and as his young desires fell into suburban angst that neither of his parents could speak to—an affront to their joint struggle and Blackness itself—Hank was left to develop in the narrow, safe confinement of suburbs with his grandparents, still residents within the crumbling metropolis of Detroit, telling anecdotal stories of what had been around the holidays.

His parents had left over an hour ago, and by now, dinner had grown lukewarm and had gathered that objectionable look that only leftovers had. Hank's nerves wouldn't allow him to eat, and he saw Andrea moving through the shadows of trees along the sidewalk.

She walked through the grass and smiled at him, and he reached out his sweaty hand and took hers. She said hello and engaged in other small talk, but Hank couldn't hear over the sound of his heart flooding his ears. Andrea was there in all her blossoming femininity, the beginning hints of her breasts rising upon her chest and the slope of her hips. She was the daughter of the only other black family in the neighborhood, with parents with a similar story except they came up from the south. They were an inevitability, drawn to one another. Adam and Eve in the garden, standing in the shadow of the Tree of Knowledge.

They had entered the quiet refuge of his house and took to the basement, where the humidity wasn't as thick. And in the basement, they tiptoed through an artless conversation as if traversing over the open mouth of a bear trap. He had been shaking then, and he wiped his swampy palms on his jeans. Now when he remembered the kiss, it had been the clean smell of sweat on her skin that tipped him over. He kissed her quickly, a mere soft peck, a touching of lips. But that hapless fumbling of youth in a suburban basement led to exploring in the backseats of old cars and brought him to an entire tactile life through exploring her spaces, her tears, her mouth until he knew them like his own.

Her hand had interlaced with his, both of them plump faced and acne inflicted, traveling the ceaseless expanse of strip malls, mega stores, and the steaming troughs of buffet restaurants in the dullness of Ohio. They deluded themselves in the heedless arrogance of youth that after college they would escape the unwavering propriety of fat Midwesterners to the city. Somehow, they would reach some sort of Darwinist state of evolution that neither of their parents had reached from the bustle of the city.

Hank had been so open to the world, so ready to get away from the familiarity, only to find that he had never truly left the rut of his old life behind, that in fact, it was there in her, lying next to him, growing older and twenty pounds heavier. And the visceral comfort from their fucking turned sterile and mechanical. He began to see the dumpy figure of her pedestrian mother prevail in Andrea when she stepped out naked from the shower. Had she been a seed of this suburban dullness all along?

And the higher state of being, this purported better life in the city, was the beginning of her culinary career and conversations of more opportunities for her in San Diego. Hank couldn't imagine a worse defection than moving to the west coast of the country, and it wouldn't be possible with his business here in Chicago.

Andrea now led the way through the apartment and into the hallway. Hank lugged the bag down the stairs, hobbling under the surprising load.

"I expected to be gone by the time you got home from work," Andrea said as they trudged through the new snow.

The men in the moving truck were packing away the last of the boxes. Behind the truck, Andrea's friend was sitting in the driver's seat in a small sedan. Through the glass, her friend puckered into a harsh grimace at Hank. He opened the back door of the car and placed the bag on seat. The sneer of her friend followed him.

Hank turned back to Andrea. "I'm glad I had a chance to say goodbye."

Her face wrinkled and her eyes shimmered with tears. Her breath was unsteady as it came out in small white puffs.

"You told me you weren't happy, and now I won't be standing in your way," she said.

9

Exhaustion had lost its formality long ago with Isabelle and came to bother her like an old friend. All day, she was moving through its heavy fog. She climbed out of the subway and onto the cold street of downtown Chicago. There, cold air whipped through the gulf between buildings, railing against raw-faced pedestrians and forcing urgency in everyone's steps. Ahead of her was her destination, Harrington College, a small private art college that rivaled Columbia College. She brought her hand against her face to block out the snow and gaped at her alma mater (that she was still indebted to, receiving a monthly reminder from Sallie Mae). The tall old building stood brazen in its Beaux-Arts architecture against the sleek glass, modernistic faces of its neighbors.

Memories of her past self pressed up to the present, and Isabelle found herself reaching back through the years, wishing she could warn herself. Her small gallery wouldn't have been operating at all if not for several favors that Isabelle had cashed and a grant sponsor from the state that gave work and internships to college students. But those funds were drying up soon. If she couldn't come up with a solution soon, her gallery would have to close.

Isabelle found an alley next to Harrington College, where a few students were smoking, regarding her with a wary look reserved for adults. She didn't know if she should feel insulted that they regarded her as an outsider to a tribe that she had once belonged to or be relieved to be free from it. She turned her face up toward the cold. Snow traveled and swirled on planes of wind toward her tired body, beaten by sleeplessness and failed by sleeping pills. The coldness felt soothing, as if her whole body had been raw nerves.

She had a meeting with the head of the art department in the hope of obtaining a grant. She was prepared to fight like hell with words like diversity and waxing about the paramountcy of art in urban areas. She just needed a moment to organize her thoughts, which seemed to keep slipping through her fingers.

Isabelle took one last breath and traveled past the gates into the dense urban campus, navigating the small walkways of young students, so arrogant and hopeful they seemed to spray it in the air like a mist. She had signed in and shown her ID to an apathetic security guard and took a creaking elevator up to the art department.

As she shook hands with a secretary and sat in the tight, airless office, she was astounded at how big everything had seemed in her memory's eye. The office that had once epitomized artistic discernment was a small room with salt stains on an aged carpet. The meeting had been scheduled for ten, and it was ten fifteen when the university art director, a round old man whose narrow convictions about art seemed to line his face finally emerge into the office.

Isabelle stood from her chair, and they shook hands. He, like everything in college, remained nearly unaffected by time, only not as impassable as he had once been. He, too, had become smaller, perhaps more human than before.

He led her into an even smaller office, where they sat, and Isabelle extracted a copy of the business proposal she'd emailed to him earlier. He squinted at her business proposal on the desk until his eyes disappeared into the wrinkles of his face. His hand crossed on the desk before him, barely touching the proposal, as if it were an amateurish construct.

Isabelle's blood churned in her body. She straightened in her chair and began. "I've dedicated my entire professional life to this gallery. You, as a man in the field, know how important art is and how it can reach across cultures and remind each of the importance and fragility of our humanity. My gallery is presently in Logan Square, a neighborhood in the height of gentrification, and I believe this gallery will allow the neighborhood to keep its original voice and open up a much-needed dialogue in that neighborhood."

He nodded.

"If possible, I would love to have you stop by and see in what way we can open up a beneficial partnership for the students here."

She almost predicted his answer.

The wrinkles in his face softened, and he said with barely an inflection in his voice, "I will have to pass your proposal to the board. I'll have our secretary schedule another presentation for them."

She attempted a smile and left the office nearly choking to maintain composure.

The secretary, whom she hadn't paid more attention to when she had arrived, looked up from his desk. His face gave way to sympathy, informing Isabelle that her attempts to appear cool were failing.

"Didn't go so well?" he asked.

Isabelle stretched her lips into a pained half smile.

The secretary raised a finger to his chin to indicate his consideration. Isabelle didn't know why she was standing there in defeat, listening to him. By the looks of youthful appearances and piercings, he was most likely a student himself. He contained the spray of youthful arrogance, and maybe she was fixed before him on the grubby carpet because she wanted to rip that self-assuredness away from him. She wanted to whisper viciously, "Your dreams won't come true. It's all a lie."

The secretary, unaware of her ill-intent, continued, his voice saturated in affected sympathy, "If the director isn't interested in your proposal, maybe you should try minority funding."

It was spoken in such a deadpan voice.

How could she have thought that with her dark skin, afro, and breasts that they would take the business proposal as seriously as from a white man? No, they had special funding for her kind because her art gallery and the art it held would not be regarded as simply art. That was something not relegated to her. This was a reality she had reluctantly accepted a while ago and had exhausted the few minority grants and funding she could get for this year. Those organizations had been kinder and more helpful, but unfortunately, she had depleted all those contacts.

So here she was, a woman with her black art. Judged and regarded as one thing, lessened in the eyes of the beholder. Not a part of a legitimate art community, but something other, something lesser. Filtered through speculation and stereotypes and hobbled, unable to provoke in the way that art should.

She blinked at him and turned on her heel and headed back out through the campus to the subway, where she rode the Blue Line west to Logan Square. The snowfall numbed her aching parts. She listened to the soft drag of traffic, decelerated under the ceaseless snow, and the muffled, leery footsteps and huffing breaths stolen by the cold.

She lingered before the glass door of the gallery in this moment of peace before she charged in, taking a moment to ready herself for the war of egos that made the frigid temperatures hospitable.

Readied, she tugged open the glass door of the store front. A three-foot origami bird suspended in the window looked down at her. As she moved through the open space, she slowed at the silence falling over the gallery. From the phone call she'd received from the co-owner, Curtis Newman, she thought the gallery was the scene of a nuclear holocaust. Isabelle glanced around, looking for the source of panic, and instead, everything stood intact, the walls now carrying a new artist named Russell Cowell. His wide canvases were a juxtaposition between Chicago's gritty cityscape, human portraits, and negative space. To Isabelle's delight, his work had been selling, and his series of portraits dedicated to the delicate beauty of his girlfriend, a bartender at Stratosphere, garnered the most attention. Isabelle even recalled nights at Stratosphere having her drink order interrupted by a few admirers of the artist coming into the bar to gawk at his girlfriend and compare her to his work. When the poor woman shooed them off with a strained smile, she admitted to Isabelle that it wasn't the first time it had happened since his exhibition.

The artist's meticulous yet whimsical play on the human form was stunning, and the buzz had been wonderful for the gallery.

Hammering footsteps rushed toward her, and Isabelle now turned to the sight of ratty blond dreadlocks whipping at the air, attached to a face crimson in anger.

"It's about damn time you got here," Curtis said, crossing his arms.

Russell, a generally docile lumbering giant, walked at a slower pace behind Curtis. He rolled his eyes at Curtis's drama crackling the air. Isabelle struggled not to express her exasperation at Curtis, too.

"Did you get my message?" Curtis asked, his voice shrill.

"Honestly, I couldn't understand it," Isabelle said, recalling the screaming coming from her phone earlier.

"This asshole is leaving us for a residency at the Nichols-Griffin Art Institute," he said, continuing to scream.

His voice resonated off the walls and pierced Isabelle from all directions. She gritted her teeth to keep from yelling back at him. Instead, she turned to Russell, who shrugged.

"Are you still going to help out here?" she said.

"No, he's not," Curtis said, then threw his hands in the air and blew out a dismissive sigh. He spun toward Russell and, looking up at the tall man, jabbed a finger into his chest as if it were a weapon. "You wouldn't be here if it weren't for me."

"Are you mad I'm leaving or that you weren't offered the residency?" Russell said, looming over Curtis.

"Oh, fuck you!" Curtis said.

"Wait," Isabelle said with a shake of her head. "Russell is leaving and you're trying to leave, Curtis? You do know you're part owner, right?"

Curtis sneered at Isabelle. "No one wants to be here but you. Shit, we can barely keep the lights on."

He sped toward the back of the gallery toward the offices in a frenzy of pinwheeling dreadlocks and limbs.

Isabelle turned to Russell and gave him a weak smile. He began to deeply apologize for his withdrawal from the gallery, but Isabelle just shook her head, pulling on her distended, yet present, etiquette. She held out her hand with her shoulders back and her face steady.

"I'm glad you had a chance to show your art and work here," she said as he took her hand. "Please ignore Curtis—you and I both know he's childish."

Russell nodded and looked down at her from his towering height with a face full of remorse.

"Are you sure there is nothing I can do to get you to stay?" she asked him.

Russell stared back at her helplessly.

She sighed. "Fine, but when you get there, let me know what the gallery is offering so I can at least be aware of what the competitor's offering."

Russell nodded. A slow resolve settled on his face, almost as lovely as his painting, and in consolation more generous than she anticipated, he agreed to close the gallery for the rest of the week. Isabelle took him up on his offer and walked past the gallery space into a small network of storage space and into her small, cramped office. She stared out through a window, reinforced with metal bars, into the frozen night. She sat at her desk, and in the corridors of her mind, she tried to hold back the fear that her imminent doom had come, that if she didn't respond quickly, the doors of her gallery would close. And that smug, pale leathery face of the art director of her university rotated around as if swung on the end of a pendulum, back and forth. She could almost hear his words to the board, mostly likely pleased that he hadn't sunk any money into that black woman's gallery.

She breathed steady breaths, holding on to the sides of her chair, watching the snow and ice collected along the bars of the window before her. For a moment, she wondered what it would be like to be buried alive in the snow, here in the small, dim office, enclosed by old gray file cabinets, her refurbished computer, and a dusty phone.

She heard footsteps behind her and straightened herself, unscrambling her wits.

The night came and went, and she lay in bed listening to the hollow, cold breeze wailing against the building. The hissing snowy cry across the building seemed as though it were rising from within her. She turned over in her bed, closing her eyes, and focused on her breathing. She gently pulled in air and slowly exhaled in a vain attempt to steady her mind and body. Her stillness of mind and the rest she needed seemed just out of reach—only brushed by the very tips of her fingers. The more she tried to focus, the more ardent her breathing became and the further sleep drifted away. And now without even the reassurance of her clock, she felt the slow creep of weary morning greet her. At this tipping point, she surrendered to the rise of another day where she would drag the cumbersome sandbags of her exhaustion.

But now, she surfed the weary crescents of this night turned morning. The wail of wind grew to a blast, and for a moment, she saw this old building that creaked and bled out its warmth tumbling down upon her. She saw heaps of old bricks, plaster, and wood give way, burying her, with her solitary hand reaching out from the mound into the cold air. These mornings plagued by hot, watery red eyes and a restlessness that made her turn in her sheets till she was roped tightly in them were precursors to death, if nothing else. If that happened, if the wind or some unnatural force did overtake this building, who would grieve her death?

Surely, her parents would and her long-knotted string of extended family netted throughout Milwaukee, but here where she lived and toiled with the near megalomania of artists and struggled to keep the art gallery afloat, would anyone grieve? And despite herself, despite her successful efforts to drive him out of her mind, she saw Noah, staring at her with gaping eyes, struggling with words, calling her the wrong name, and trying to profess his affection for her.

Isabelle didn't want to find solace in the haunting memory of his touch, his sweet, invasive kiss, or how deep he'd been inside her, but there it was. In this cold black morning, shackled to thin sheets and heavy blankets that held no warmth, comfort was a rare commodity. And her defenses refused to fight it back as memories of his touch and the weight of his body settled down next to her body.

10

The next night, Noah stepped into Hank's apartment and shut the door behind him. He stood at the threshold and surveyed the emptiness of the apartment with limp indifference. He clucked his tongue and shook his head. He walked over to Hank, who sat on the couch, leaning over and holding his skull in his hand. At Hank's feet, a small fleet of empty beer bottles watched over a crumpled afghan at the end of the couch.

Noah's heart fluttered in his stomach. "Have you been sleeping out here?"

Hank grumbled what Noah took as an affirmation.

Noah walked a lap around the apartment, trying to assess the damage before he offered his diagnosis, with the contemplation he reserved for fried hard drives. He silently took in the opened empty closets, the half-full room. He joined Hank on the couch, which was solely accompanied by the flat screen perched on the floor. As Noah landed on the couch, he toppled a few beer bottles over with his feet. He produced a small joint from his cigarette box, lit the end, and sucked. He held in the smoke before exhaling the sharp smell of burning weed in the air.

"I was pissed you didn't show up for work today," Noah said, recalling the mounting work orders waiting for them back in the work room.

Noah hoped Hank would have come into work. But he had been alone most of the day, hunched over his workstation, staring at computer entrails under magnifying lamps, unable to work. Remorse sat in the center of his chest and festered as he replayed the events that had led him to Isabelle's apartment. The hot sting of embarrassment still made his ears burn. He wanted to pick at these emotions like he would a hangnail, but he certainly couldn't do that with the part-time guys who came in to help out with the work orders.

Now glancing at Hank and smelling the tang of his body odor drifting from his body, he knew he'd have to leave his hangnails unpicked and his dread firmly in place.

"She was moving out when I got home from work."

Hank plucked the joint from Noah's fingers and inhaled it before erupting in violent coughing. Noah slapped Hank on the back as the coughs finally subsided. Hank glanced down at the empty bottles at his feet and found one that had a swallow of old beer. He reached for it and tried to drink. Noah quickly seized it from his hand and stood up.

"What the hell, man?" he asked.

Hank shrugged and shame emerged on his face.

"Yeah, I'm going to need you to get your shit together," Noah said. "If I'm remembering right, you wanted to break up with Andrea."

Hank sighed, stuck the joint in his mouth, and dropped his head back into his hand.

Noah went into the nearby closet and gathered Hank's coat, causing the empty hangers to clang and ring out like cymbals in the echoing apartment. Noah flung the coat at Hank's head, causing him to fall back and drop the joint.

"You're a single man now," Noah said. "It's time we go out and enjoy it."

"It's cold out," Hank said. "I'm slightly drunk and a bit high."

"Even better."

Noah bent down and shoved Hank until he put his coat on. He collected the joint that had stopped burning on impact with the ground and stuffed it back into his cigarette box. He hauled Hank off the couch, pushing through the room. Their footfalls rolled in an echoing staccato as they left the apartment and entered the hall.

"We're going to get you laid tonight," Noah said as Hank's head lolled back and forth.

The two of them took to the stairway at the end of the hall, zipping up their jackets in a useless attempt to fortify themselves against the cold. Ahead, he heard someone traveling up the steps against their descent. A hard thrumming in Noah's chest made his feet slide on the edge of the stairs, and he gripped the railing as if the building had shifted. Isabelle shook loose snow from herself and paused in the stairwell.

Hank nodded, ambivalent in his intoxication, and Isabelle gave a flat smile. Hank pushed past her and stopped at the landing, waiting for Noah to follow him. Noah gaped back at her, his feet rooted to the stairs. His hand was fused to the railing.

"Hey, Isabelle."

"I see you have my name right."

Her face stared back at him, immobile, giving off no expression, and her arms were crossed before her chest. She blinked back at him as if he were a stranger. Noah's grip strained around the wood of the railing as his stomach careened within him. He opened his mouth to say something to her. Only dry air passed his lips.

"Are you going to let me pass?"

"Uh, yeah," Noah said, pressing himself against the wood.

Isabelle jostled past him, touching him for a moment. Noah nearly lost his footing at the contact. Thoughts of her body in the morning light haunted him.

"Hey, join us," Noah said as his words collided into each other, barely comprehensible.

She turned and glanced down at him. A short-lived resistance yielded to warmth on her face like a blush. She took a step downward, toward him. Noah's hand unwound itself from the railing and he opened it to her.

"Yeah, Noah's going to try and get me laid tonight," Hank called up from the landing.

Noah cringed, turning back to Hank and nearly growling at him. He turned to Isabelle, and she recoiled, slowly withdrawing up the stairs.

"Maybe next time." Her face was once again indecipherable.

"Yeah, maybe next time," Noah said, following Hank to the landing.

He glanced back up at the empty stairs. The remorse he had carried with him throughout the day began to pinch at his insides once he and Hank pushed against the hostile cold of the night.

11

Hank ordered the beer on special, some lager made locally that left a lingering sour bite in his mouth. Then, he ordered the shot on special, a suspicious sweet blast of liquor that tasted like pineapple. He leaned up against the bar, unhinged, scanning the faces of Stratosphere and wondering if anyone knew how high and drunk he was. Through the murky blue light of the bar, he glanced at Noah, roosted next to him on a stool. Noah was hunched over, wilting over the bar.

Hank leaned over to him, and in breathy, wet whisper said, "You need a drink?"

The weed he smoked earlier and the undetermined amount of beer he'd drunk had released Hank from the nauseating guilt. He was liberated from the heavy responsibility to determine what was next. With Andrea, he always knew what events would follow his day, like scenes from an old movie.

"Who should I talk to?"

He nudged Noah and asked his question again. Noah sighed and pursed his lips in retort.

"Hey, asshole," Hank said. "You were the one who said I should be out here."

"I know, I know."

"Wingman me."

"Okay, okay."

Hank took a gulp from his beer again and sucked back a wince at its taste. He eyed his friend, flipping through the events that led them here. The long pause, the tense exchange that took place between him and Isabelle.

"Do you like our neighbor?"

Noah's eyes wavered and settled on the bar.

"Whoa," Hank cried out. "Really?"

"Shut up. I just want to sleep with her again."

"That good, huh?"

Noah cleared his throat, and his eyes darted around, betraying him.

"Yeah, right, okay," Hank said, eager to take advantage of his newfound nerve before it deflated with thoughts of Andrea and his apartment. "Wingman me."

"Stop saying that."

"You don't get too unhappy—I was the one who was dumped."

"I thought you were the one who broke up with Andrea."

"Does it matter?"

Noah looked over Hank's shoulder and nodded. Hank turned and followed his glance and spotted the woman he'd shared a cigarette with several nights before at Stratosphere. His heart fluttered and heat swelled to his face. He swung back to Noah, knocking over his beer. Noah, much soberer than he was, caught it before it tumbled onto the bar.

"Is that really her?" Hank asked. "What should I say? How do I look?"

Hank began pulling at the collar of his sweater. He snatched the beer from Noah's hand. He upturned the bottle and downed the rest of the beer in one gulp. He slammed it on the bar, garnering a snarl from the bartender. He turned back to the woman. Her gait was so agile that she skimmed through the dim air as if it were water. A shudder jolted the length of Hank as their eyes met.

"I should go home," Hank said, reaching for the empty bottle.

"This is what you wanted," Noah said. "It's too late now."

Noah's words were passed like a confirming blessing, and Hank's clumsy feet inched forward, shuffling through the density of the crowd. Toes of nearby guys were crushed under his boots as he advanced on the woman who floated toward him.

"So, are you going to buy me another drink?" she said when they were inches from one another.

"Yeah," Hank said.

She sailed through the crowd, and bodies parted in a perfect path in front of her, leading back to the bar. She leaned back against the bar, and her night-colored hair swung around her face. She pulled Hank closer and circled him like he was her helpless prey. It could have been the potency of the weed Hank had consumed earlier, but the moment unfurled at a glacial crawl. Her hand dragged across his shoulders and her lips curled into a smile as the moon rose in the sky. She said something and Hank smiled at her. She said it again, and this time, one of her eyebrows traveled up her forehead.

Hank shook his head. "What?"

"My drink?"

"Oh, yeah," he said, leaning over the bar. "Vodka martini?"

"You remembered."

Shortly, the bartender came with a martini and the same bitter lager on special. He handed the woman her drink, and they sipped together, returning each other's smiles.

"What's your name?"

She sipped her drink in consideration and tilted her head.

"Is your girlfriend home?"

"I don't have a girlfriend now."

She returned a cool chuckle. "Is that my fault?"

"Would you like it if it were?"

"Let's have another drink and get out of here."

Hank's pulse quickened, and he blinked at her several times as if she'd vanish like an apparition. He cleared his throat and asked, "What is your name?"

She smiled, and there was a sharp calculation in her eyes, a visible juggling, a flexing of power for its own sake. Hank could see this but her face was too beautiful, too dangerous to deny it. She swallowed her drink and whipped her head, clucking her tongue at the strength of the vodka.

"You have two choices: you get my name or I go home with you."

Hank gaped at her, and his hands and feet grew numb. The fog from the weed began to lift, and the clarity of his vision upon her grew blade-sharp. She was nothing like the woman who left the emptiness back in his apartment.

"Now get me another drink," she said, "before I change my mind."

Urgency rushed over him. Without another thought, he ordered her another drink and didn't ask for her name again.

12

Snow, gold from the glow of streetlights, fell in spinning sheets through the frigid air. Noah bundled his coat and stepped out of Stratosphere. He shuffled past the line and the hardened faces of the smokers. Underneath his coat in an inside pocket, he grabbed the joint out of his cigarette box. He waded through the snowdrifts and stiffened against a chill. Alone, he stepped into a shadow against the cold brick and lit his joint. He pulled in the rough smoke. He held the burn in his lungs until pinpricks danced in his skull. A sweet stupor wove through his body. His gaze traveled up through the fragments of white falling around him. Tiny points of cold touched the surface of his face, and before he could give himself over to this ease, he felt the heaviness of someone's gaze on him. He quickly dropped the joint out of view and behind his back.

A woman emerged from within another shadow in the narrow alley, as if it were a portal between rooms. She was wrapped in an oversized fur coat, and her pink lips were wrapped around a cigarette.

"Marcie," Noah said, slipping into a familiar blend of arousal and disdain.

"Did you follow me out here?" she asked.

He had been unaware she'd been at the bar. Had she seen him in Stratosphere and hidden out here? Noah's brows knitted themselves over his narrowing eyes. He slid into disgust and hit his joint again. He blew smoke in her direction, and it diffused in the snow.

"I stopped following you a long time ago," he said.

"Only because I made you."

"So, why are you out in the alley?" he said. "Nothing good ever happens in alleys."

Her smooth face brought a flood of memories of autumn nights years ago, memories glazed over by too many lines of coke, excessive amounts of liquor, and lust so blinding that Noah had lost all semblance of himself. Toward the end of that autumn with her, in those black hours of night, woven tightly between her limbs, she'd dragged him into a deep, longing hatred of everything but her. Even now, with the blatant knowledge of this, he could still taste her. His tongue could never forget the tang of her spaces . . . her lips. Her eyes assessed him, and he stepped out of his shadow and next to her.

He cursed himself for it. He gritted his teeth, and his already tense muscles contracted until he was certain they would pop.

He passed her the joint. She chuckled and inhaled slowly.

"How's business?" she asked.

"Good," he said. "I've hired part-time guys to help with the workload."

There was an easiness to their words, like the way old enemies talked to each other. The brutality of their long-ago fights had left a lingering intimacy that their sex never had. Marcie had been with him when his father first started to have lapses in his memory. She had been lying next to him in September five years back when his mother had called, terrified, her gruff voice screaming that his father had crashed the car. Marcie hadn't been much of a comfort once he returned from the hospital early that morning, his head swimming from confessions his parents had been hiding from him for years. Noah stood there in the florescent glow of the hospital room, his father in a pale gown and held to the bed by a network of wires and tubes, and listened to his father admit he was diagnosed with early onset dementia. It was as if those words had precipitated his descent. His father's license was taken away, and his mother enlisted the help of a live-in nurse.

Noah needed Marcie. He needed her to be beyond the parties, beyond their pointless squabbles. But she couldn't give up the night for him, no matter how much he asked. Nights pleading for her touch, for her comfort, hardened him over. And one night, when the moon rose, he departed.

Now, Marcie smiled and drew closer to him. In all the years that had elapsed between them, through the icy air and twirling snow, the scent of her flesh remained saccharine.

"Are you still stripping?"

An apprehensive hush fell upon them. Noah acknowledged his misstep and cleared his throat apologetically. There was no need to tear into old wounds. Certainly, they didn't want to enter into the grisly battles that had ended them. Noah didn't want to express his disapproval, and Marcie had never had any interest in it whatsoever. She would take men's money but never their opinions. Despite himself, he respected that. Depending on his mood, he even admired it. Time had passed, and they had worked out a peaceful treaty, if not a stalemate that left room to navigate shared locations and bars they were too proud to give up.

Marcie accepted his apology by passing his joint, from which Noah took another puff. The silence between them was interrupted by a drag of metal as a plow truck passed along the street.

"You know, you're the most honest man I know," she said.

Noah snorted and choked on smoke from his joint.

"Seriously," she said.

There was a mourning in her voice that caused Noah to turn to her—a gentle shake in her words that caused his heart to flutter. He stared at her face, a bit older, not from time but from something else. Maybe too much life lived in the nights.

"You okay?"

"Yes," she said.

Her face was hidden from him, and before they left the alley, she said over her shoulder, "Hank shouldn't trust that girl he's talking to."

"What do you mean?" he asked.

She frowned, walking out of the shadows toward the street. "She hangs with a rough crowd."

"You're one to talk," he mumbled to himself.

Noah put out his joint against the cold brick and returned the stump to his cigarette tin. He walked back to the door and peeked into Stratosphere. Hank and the girl he was talking to were nowhere to be found among the glowing blue faces. He sighed, relieved, and took to the street, pressing his luck that a few devoted cabs prowled the street even against this cold. After a few minutes with numb limbs, after his hope had waned to a shivering desperation, a cab pulled along the road. Noah climbed over the mound of snow into the cab and traveled back to his apartment in silence.

There, he grumbled as he stomped through the ignored walkway. His frozen hands fumbled the keys, and as he stuck them into the doorknob, he halted. An authoritative notice posted from the city addressed to the landlord warned that soon, the gas would be shut off. Noah squinted to take in the words and pulled back from the threshold to take it in. He grimaced at it, already preparing the angry email in his head. What good was "all utilities included" if the landlord never paid them?

He shivered again with a combination of cold and nerves, pushing past the shut-off notice and into the hall.

He climbed the steps and slowed as he passed Isabelle's floor. His chest tightened, and again, images of her skin and her lips assaulted his mind. Everything about her felt different from any woman he had been with. He felt a painful longing. And the clarity of this, solid in his chest, made him stand there in the hall. He hadn't even felt that way about Marcie with all their common history.

This was new and unnerving. This was outside his normal bid for women. Outside his witty lines and ease with women. He considered walking up to her door and knocking on it. He even took a step in that direction, but he knew that, like before, he would battle for words.

Noah sighed and turned toward the stairs and his apartment. He buried his pining for Isabelle deep inside.

13

Jones sifted through the refrigerator, desperate to distance herself from Derek. She heard her phone buzz and rattle off the nightstand in her bedroom from the kitchen. She sighed as nausea fluttered in her stomach. Since her meeting with the finance director, she had been receiving panicked house calls from the editor of the magazine. At first, when her phone would ring, Derek would simply ignore it from the glowing screen of his computer, most likely looking at the nonexistent downloads of his app. Come to find out, no one would pay to send pictures of their apartments via mobile app to reimage in free-flow or feng shui or have their kitchen enlivened by color. The app used a preference profile set up by the user to link and suggest products. When the user purchased the product advertised in the app, Derek would get paid. Unfortunately, this didn't happen. Not even a week after the launch party, financial ruin ran the company dry as if someone had sucked money from a tap.

The downfall rocked Derek so absolutely, like waves crashing, one after another, on a shore, drawing back more and more fragments of him. All his valuable friendships and money had been squandered. He deleted contacts from his phone, and yesterday, swaying in a drunken rage, he swore to outlive his friends to piss on their graves. And Jones tried to distance herself from the wreckage in the way she would watch a natural disaster on the news, clucking her tongue and shaking her head in vacuous gestures of sympathy. But when the winds of his failure died down and the all-clear was given, what Jones found was a glassy-eyed naysayer who needed her to stroke the remnants of his ego. But now, as she crossed the living room toward the hall into the bathroom, he glared at her with suspicious contempt, brows melded together in a dark line over his eyes.

"Who's that?" Derek asked.

Since his launch party, he'd grown caustic, shifting between various states of unrest with his computer not too far behind him. The screen flickered on marketing articles or some TED Talk of some successful CEO—someone he equated his own unrecognized brilliance to.

As she passed through, the living room was saturated with the smell of his musk and burned coffee beans. She picked up her phone and saw Isabelle's number on the screen. The muscles in her back unwound with relief. No call from the office. No need to lie about her promotion anymore. Vindicated, she shook the phone in Derek's face as she entered the living room. As she got within view of his computer, he quickly closed the window, concealing whatever he was glaring at.

There was an edgy pause between them. In that moment, Jones was certain they both could feel those heavy secrets brewing between them like rot or dark mold. He was hiding something from her, too. A pang of guilt lingered on his face. There was pressure from all the unspoken words that needed to be said, but she certainly didn't have the strength to sort through them. And Derek, weary from being on his feet, still smelling like labor, slumped on the couch with his computer cradled in his lap like a lover, wasn't in fighting shape. The launch party hadn't instilled enough faith for him to quit his job at the coffee shop—one of his few decisions that Jones thought wise.

Jones tiptoed back as if landmines were underneath the floorboards. Once in the kitchen, she returned Isabelle's phone call.

"Come over," Isabelle said. "I'm watching art documentaries."

This was all pretense, of course, for them to fold themselves tightly onto Isabelle's couch and drink cheap wine and gossip until they stretched the bounds of proper decorum. She thought of her nagging exhaustion from work and Derek sitting there on the couch, under the dim glow of his computer, festering in his own stink.

She returned to the refrigerator and grabbed a month-old Sauvignon Blanc.

"Going over to Isabelle's," she said quickly, walking through the apartment.

Derek grimaced at her. "You're going to leave?"

She came to a halt, feet from the door, and pressed her palm against her forehead. He glared at her with almost a look of betrayal. How dare she abandon him in his time of need? Shouldn't she stay and smooth the battered edges of his pride? She staggered forward toward him, but then back-stepped to her previous position. His persistence strained her and tested her already labored patience. She had nothing to offer tonight.

"I'll just be downstairs."

He blinked at her as if she had said she was crossing the Atlantic to a remote country. He continued as if she'd said nothing and gestured to his computer screen. "Have you seen these numbers?"

She shook her head.

He clipped off bitter laughter. "Of course not. Why would you care?"

She crept backward toward the door. He clearly needed a target for his failure. "Isabelle's expecting me."

"What about me?" he said, too shrill.

Jones was now against the door. She slowly closed her hand around the door handle. "I'm not doing this."

His faced soured, and he sneered. "Go then."

Jones felt a rush of relief as she pushed out of the apartment and moved through the hall, chilly from the winter seeping in from cracks in the doorways, windows, and foundation. She was down the stairs and knocking at Isabelle's door. Isabelle opened it, already waiting for her. Isabelle led Jones through her creaky apartment, sighing against the blast of coldness outside. They gathered in the living room, snugly on the couch beneath old blankets, and empty wine glasses waited on the coffee table. Jones unscrewed the top of the inelegant bottle and filled each glass to the rim. She spilled a bit on the table, but Isabelle didn't acknowledge, only bringing the glass to her face as quickly as she could.

The opening of an American-produced French documentary filled the small screen of the tiny flat screen suspended from the wall. A rolling warm countryside played before them, bright blue sky, lush vineyards, and ancient vibrant architecture bathed in the bright yellow warmth of the sun. Jones's stomach tightened against it, thinking about the blackened city's snow and the gray coldness narrowing in on them within this building so close to degradation. It was as if the gray, merciless cold was tearing at everything. She turned to Isabelle, who had drunk nearly half of her glass of wine. Her friend's face was knotted in sadness as she glanced at the screen.

"You okay?"

"No."

"Not sleeping?"

"Yeah," Isabelle said.

"The pills aren't helping?"

Isabelle smiled and sipped from her glass. "The pills make me feel like a zombie. I'd rather be tired than feel nothing at all."

Isabelle gave her a warning look, a line drawn before them. Jones swiftly changed the subject.

"Are you ready to talk about work?"

Isabelle softened a bit at this, as if a tender wound had been exposed. She shrugged.

"One of our artists is leaving the gallery," she said.

"Curtis?"

"I'd be so lucky. No one else has the patience to deal with that narcissist. No, it's Russell Cowell," Isabelle said. "He's been getting a lot of attention."

"That's good for the gallery, right?"

"He's taking up a residency with the Nichols-Griffin Art Institute. He going to leave at the end of the month. He helps keep the place running. On top of that, his art is the only thing selling right now. It's how I've been able to keep the lights on."

Russell Cowell was a talented artist with a great story behind him. Jones was surprised it hadn't happened sooner. But she wouldn't share this with Isabelle. She felt a sudden kinship in Isabelle's anguish. She turned to the screen, and the credits yielded to the Eiffel Tower overlooking the city.

"I can do a story in the magazine," she found herself saying before she could think about what that would mean for the already struggling publication. "In fact, I'll make you the cover story."

Isabelle turned to her. Her face wavered in an uncertain hope.

"You don't have to."

Jones, unsure herself, rolled the idea carefully in her mind. She was the director of her magazine, and besides a new office and managing crises, she hadn't made any sort of executive decisions in her new role. She finally drank from her wine glass to help the impulse settle into a decision. Jones grinned at Isabelle and raised her shoulders. Derek wouldn't allow her to help him, but Isabelle would.

"I'm the director now," she told her friend. "There isn't much room in this issue, but I'll see what I can do. That's what friends do for one another."

Isabelle glowed, and something came unhitched between them. Gossip followed, laughter rang out, and wine glasses were filled again and again. The beautiful summer in Paris was ignored on the wall in the chilly apartment. After a few hours and a couple of woeful glances at the clock on her phone, Jones knew she should return to her apartment. She hugged her friend goodbye and left her the last swallow of wine.

Her steps faltered from the wine as she walked into her dark apartment. She tiptoed, groping through the still darkness, aware that she was the only one breathing. Derek had left to parts unknown, and a rush of relief stirred within

Jones as she began to settle and dress for bed. Solace met her alone in the bed and carried her down into sleep.

Jones wasn't sure how long she was asleep—it could have been hours or minutes—but hard, wet footsteps paraded into the darkness. There was a quick plop onto the mattress, jolting her fully awake, where Derek usually slept. Her jaw tightened to keep the heated rage within her. She slowly peeked over her shoulder, where Derek sat, swaying slightly in the bronze streetlight trickling in from the cracks in the blinds.

"Jones," he said, his speech taxed in drunkenness. "Joooonnneesss."

She screwed her eyes tight and held her breath, pretending to be asleep. The muscles in her tensed jaw started to ache. She felt him look over at her for what seemed like a long time. His rocking movements pitched the bed back and forth. The stench of the liquor from his heaving breath filled the air.

Jones had never so desperately wanted to be alone as she did now. It all rushed over her as quickly as Derek had entered the room.

"Are you awake?"

There was a feebleness in his voice, and she knew she had outlasted his efforts. The mattress shifted one last time as Derek lowered himself into the bed. He burrowed himself into the covers next to her. After a heavy, resigned sigh, Derek gave in to sleep. Jones felt a chilling dampness at the foot of the bed as Derek drew in closer to her, and she felt the wet soles of his boots touch her ankles. Snow dripped off them onto her feet, chilling her to the point of shivering. She gritted her teeth and dared not move, knowing she didn't want to wake him for the immense dread of their speaking.

14

Hank was acutely aware of his limbs at this moment. His legs shook as he plowed through feet of snow to his apartment. His arms hung at his side, languid, disconnected from the nerves and tendons that pulled at them. Quaking against the cold and his fears, he thought for a moment that he couldn't get the key to the door. It took several tries, and he was nervous the woman he'd met at the bar would leave him.

The night was still around them, and the cold seemed to silence all the noise the city normally carried. Most of the lights in the apartment buildings were off, and it was as if the walls of the surrounding buildings and the stretch of icy white road belonged to them alone.

He heard the soft breathing of the woman behind him, the warmth of her breath on the back of his neck, and the slow crawl of her hand on his shoulder. In a spell of dizziness, Hank was suddenly virginal. No woman besides Andrea had ever touched him the way this nameless woman was. Her fingers pressed through the fabric of his coat, and then the key, as if on cue with her touch, slid in the lock.

"Some landlord . . ." she said, eyeing the gas shut-off notice on the door.

Hank grimaced, more concerned with the woman at his heels than his remiss landlord.

Hank made his ascent up the stairs, trying to manage his disjointed, fickle limbs, as the woman trailed behind, so controlled. Her hips rolled along, and her shoulders were serpentine in her smooth advance. Again, Hank fumbled with the keys, but with quicker success, they were in his apartment.

Hank reached out to take her coat, and she walked around the empty space. A quizzical look lifted the features of her face. She laughed to herself, settled on a conclusion that she wouldn't share with him. Her eyes moved from the barren room to Hank, and he felt his knees weaken. She appeared so out of place in the emptiness that he expected the air around her to simmer and for her to fade like a mirage.

"You really don't have a girlfriend anymore."

He nodded, then said, "You want anything to drink?"

"What do you have?"

"Beer."

She sighed, now disappointed. "I guess it'll have to do."

Hank stepped into the kitchen and returned with two bottles as quickly as he could, fearful that if he idled too long, she would vanish. The woman was now sitting on the couch, digging in her purse. Once he entered the room, she leaned back with a sharp, almost jagged smile. Hank couldn't help but notice that her skirt rose, exposing more of the black stockings underneath it. He gulped, and the sound was so perceptible, crashing off empty walls and rooms.

She laughed and reached for her beer.

As she took a swig, she said, "I've never met a man as nervous as you are. Is this a joke? Do you do this all the time?"

"No," he said, standing frozen to the floor in front her.

"We should do something about that," she said, and held out her fist before them.

Her fingers uncurled and exposed the spoils of her purse, two pills on her upturned palm. She smiled at him expectedly as if she'd performed a magic trick. Hank eyed them carefully before he chose one. She popped the pill in her mouth and grabbed the beer from Hank. She took a heavy swig of the beer. The dangerous smile reappeared on her face. She glanced at him, her eyes growing wide with expectation.

"What is it?"

"Vicodin," she said flatly. "Take it."

She sat on the couch, causing her skirt to inch up a bit higher. Little fabric hid the length of her slender legs. Heat tickled the back of Hank's neck, and his cock stirred within his pants. He placed the pill on his tongue and drank from his bottle.

A silence passed over them, and the building creaked and groaned as if it labored around them to shut out the cold. The woman moved through the arched doorway of the kitchen, still in Hank's sight. She poked around a partially empty box that sat on the countertop. Her face held amusement, as if she were uncovering a lost artifact, witnessing a man of a bygone primitive culture. Hank realized then how exposed he was, and his face grew hot and florid. She openly regarded him with lighthearted mockery, yet he knew nothing about her.

"Are you really not going to at least tell me your name?"

She grabbed something within the box on the counter, and her expression changed almost imperceptibly. She looked at him and smiled.

"A guy like you," she said, "is going to have to earn it."

Hank groaned and met her in the kitchen. "What does that mean?"

She slipped something out of the box and slinked over toward him. She stopped short a few inches in front of him. Hank was disoriented from her closeness, no longer annoyed, and now studied her beautiful lips and the sly upturn moving from the corners of her mouth.

"That means you're going to have to earn my name, Hank."

"Why?"

Her hand reached up to his shoulder, and her finger brushed along the back of his neck. The stroking of his skin caused him to tremble, and it became the only thing he could feel. She grinned again with delight at this.

"That's why," she said, pulling back from him. "For me, there isn't anything new. I've done everything. I've slept with a bunch of people. Some of them, I don't know their names, don't remember their faces."

Hank pulled back with a gasp, and blood rushed to his cheeks. The woman tilted her head, coming to another silent conclusion. She smiled at him with narrowed, focused eyes.

"You don't like this?"

"No," Hank said in a thin whisper.

"You know, I have no regrets for the things or people I've done," she said. "But you . . . you remind me of a time when things were new. When things were unknown. Just look at yourself. It's actually quite beautiful."

"I've done things," Hank said, and snorted at her with hollow conviction.

The woman bent over, and deep laughter expelled from her. Her cackle boomed over him, so great and so infectious that Hank found himself chuckling alongside her, shaking and enjoying a sudden warmth that burst within him. He shut his eyes and gave in to it, rolling and clutching his sides. When he opened his eyes, the world sparkled in dazzling luster. He suddenly remembered the pill he took.

He looked at her, no longer afraid of her astonishing beauty exciting the atoms around her. All that mattered at this moment, in this chemically encouraged stillness, was that she was there before him. She stared at him with eyes as intrigued by his boyish naïveté as he was with her beauty. He eyed her up and down, taking her in boldly without fear now, and stopped at the small framed photograph that she must have taken from the box.

She noticed his attention on it and held it forward for their shared examination. She held a college picture of Andrea at the pinnacle of beauty—how Hank always wanted to imagine her. She was youthful, a smile eclipsing her soft face. He remembered getting that picture developed because he had never seen her look so true, so open, and so his. He remembered taking that picture, on some spring day in Ohio, before going out with their small-town friends to not do much of anything.

Andrea had been outside, laughing in his backyard as he chased her with the camera. She stepped back and looked at him, and he captured her there, with the sun inflamed behind her head. And there she was within his frame, warm, enduring, holding up all their shared thoughts and the heavy, hopeful, terrifying promise of love.

He spoke no words and absorbed the harsh blast of cold rattling the glass in the windows.

"Was this your girlfriend?"

"Yeah."

The woman placed the picture back into the box and sat in the living room as Hank followed her. He sat next to her. He filled his nostrils with her sweet scent. His eyes dropped to her legs, inches from his, and the gentle rise of her skirt.

"What happened between you two?"

Hank drew in a breath. He paused and examined it, now drunk and detached. He was floating above all of it, ready to dictate it as flippantly as he talked about the weather

"Are you sure you want to know?"

The woman rolled her eyes. "I wouldn't have asked if I didn't want to know."

"You want to hear about my ex? Isn't that what scared you off the first night we met?"

"No, it was your creepy friend looking at us and smiling," she said.

Hank chuckled and thought of that night with Noah. Then, he looked at the woman and his expression turned grave. "We grew up, that's what happened. It wasn't black-and-white anymore. It became gray."

The woman crossed her arms and one of her eyebrows rose. "That makes no sense."

Hank cried out and jumped up from the couch with his arms stretched out. "I couldn't do it anymore. And I don't know when it happened. But all of a sudden, I stopped answering her texts. I stopped picking up her almond milk at the grocery store. I mean, who the fuck drinks almond milk? And then there was this one night, when all I wanted to do was watch the game in peace, and here she comes walking in front of the TV, trying to cuddle in the middle of the game, and all I want is a few hours—just a few fucking hours. And I know if I don't cuddle with her, I'll hear about it for a week. So I give up, I cuddle with her, and I even let her change the channel."

Hank turned to face the girl, no longer detached, feeling himself seized by guilt. The emptiness around them took his voice and flung it back in anger. Knots formed in his abdomen and his face hardened as he continued his confession.

"There she was, holding on to me, trying to love me, and I was pissed. All I could think about was how big she'd gotten over the years and how hot and heavy she was lying next to me. I knew then that I couldn't love her anymore."

He stared at the woman on the couch, and her face was imperceptible. He deflated, and his shoulders sagged. He knew it was only a matter of time before this beautiful stranger left him.

Her face revealed none of her thoughts, and she slipped her sweater over her head. The orbs of her breasts gleamed in black lace. Hank's cock stiffened in his pants as he made out her pink nipples through the lace. His heart dropped to his stomach, and his limbs became independent from his body, flimsy at his sides.

The woman stood up and out of her boots, then released her hips from her skirt and peeled off her stockings. Her clothing lay in a pool at her feet. She walked over to him, once again in an unbroken, rolling stride. She began unbuttoning his flannel while he tried to swill in a breath. His chest heaved as she tugged the flannel off him.

"Why?" he asked.

She reached behind her back, undoing the clasp of her bra and shrugging it off.

"It's cold out, and I'm drunk," she said. "And you're just so damn sad."

He nodded, took a look at her breasts, and led her back through the vacant apartment into his bedroom.

15

Noah's day carried on like an unending tug of war. From the very start of his journey through the mounds of snow and the sidewalk, a valley of ice and puddles, his body was wrecked with cold that wouldn't leave him. Even at his workstation, with a space heater turned up, blasting him with dry heat, he continued to shiver. The potted tulip he'd bought to give his father had died from the cold. Ice crystals ravaged the blossom, and it slumped over in death. He took the pot out with him this morning and tossed it in the dumpster out back in a vain attempt to alleviate his guilt.

Noah had hoped that the workload today would be manageable, but due to Hank's idea of an online ad with a twenty-five percent off coupon code, a flood of people came banging through the door. Each person brought with them broken computers and smart phones, ushering in gusts of frigid air and dirty snow that would later turn into brown puddles. He assigned one of the part-time guys to mop duty, fearing some patron would slip on one of those puddles and sue his business into ruin.

Around noon, he looked up from the microscope of his workstation, amongst the smells of burning metal and Thai food, and realized that Hank hadn't arrived. He picked up his phone to call him, but the door opened again. Another customer came in with an iPad with a cracked screen, willing to pay double for an express order. Noah sighed and got back to work. It wasn't until after six o'clock that he thought of Hank again, when he went to set the alarm and lock up his store.

He stepped out into the street, walking toward the Damen train station against the breeze. He checked his phone for any missed calls or text messages. He had gotten two calls and a voicemail from his mother. No doubt, they were laced with maternal manipulation. But nothing from Hank. How could he have missed a whole day's work without at least sending a text message?

The train delay lasted a tortuous amount of time, but then he was off it, down the platform steps, and charging down his street to his apartment. He rushed up to Hank's door and knocked. He heard no movement from within the apartment, just the cold breeze on the front door causing the gas shut-off notice to flap against a glass pane.

The gas shut-off notice—another jab from this cold, ugly, gray day. He had to email the landlord before the building froze to death.

Noah bit his lips back in fury and hammered his fist on the door as if he were going to break through the wood. This time, he heard the scurry of uncertain footsteps, slow in their approach toward the door.

"I hear you," Noah said through the door.

The door cried out in a painful creak as it was opened. The woman from the night before stood there, wearing one of Hank's tank tops. She was a pubescent wet dream, with her breasts nearly exposed, freely roaming the confines of the shirt that was barely long enough to cover her crotch.

Noah started to speak and stammered. He cleared his throat and fought the cartoonish urge to pull at the collar of his jacket. A cavalier smile arched along her face as she stepped out of the way to let Noah pass. From the rear of the apartment, stumbling in a post-drunk, post-sex daze, Hank emerged shirtless in a pair of gym shorts. He raked his hand through his hair and made a half-hearted attempt to grin at Noah.

Heat rose to his face and his fists tightened again. He cut a narrow grimace at the woman, and said, "If you don't mind, can we have a moment alone?"

"I don't want to get in the middle of a lovers' quarrel," she said, impervious to Noah's anger.

The two of them stared at each other, prepared for a face-off. Noah sighed, suddenly aware of his pulse in his temple.

"Please," he said to the woman.

Her face was set, again, in the smug smile, and she regarded Noah and the panic in Hank's eyes. Without another word, she slinked into the bedroom. Hank's shirt skimmed her ass and exposed her rear to the men. This display was deliberate and manipulative, and despite themselves, both men watched her walk away. Once she had left the room, Noah's simmering anger returned.

"You couldn't call?"

"I didn't have time."

"You couldn't break away for five minutes?"

Hank grinned as if recalling the day and shrugged at Noah as if he should've understood. And Noah did, on some level. He knew the pull of escaping into a woman for a day, but it wouldn't be at the cost of their business. He thought of Isabelle and the morning he had spent with her, and how he'd longed to extend it, even for a moment.

"Do you even know her name?"

The dogged smirk on Hank's face stretched into pride as he shook his head. A groan rattled through Noah's chest and throat. As if beckoned, the woman came out fully dressed and preening, like she hadn't just spent the entire day fucking Hank into a state of stupidity.

"Where are you going?" Hank asked as his face shifted to panic.

He drew close to the woman and encircled her with his arms. She said nothing for a moment, pleased. She kissed Hank slowly. Noah choked at the wet sound of their lips smacking and tasting one another. He looked away, trying to keep his mind from what she must've done to him or what she must have let him do to her.

"You have my phone number?" Hank asked her as they parted.

"Yes," she said, "I do."

Hank glanced down at his feet like a bashful schoolboy, and said, "Have I earned your name yet?"

A nauseating blend of horror and disgust rose in Noah's stomach, and he felt himself back-stepping into the couch. His eyes widened, and he sat down, unable to tear himself away now.

The woman held Hank's gaze for a moment. Noah watched her as she clung to this moment of silence, almost like she was tasting it. Noah's fluttering horror hardened into anger, and he, an unwilling participant, fought to remain silent. Finally, she waved her hand in the air in nonchalance, and said, "Gwen."

She turned on her heel and zipped up her coat, and over her shoulder, she said, "I'll call you."

Gwen moved toward the door and shot Noah a hostile glare before she passed through it. Hank dawdled behind her and closed the door. Hank fell with his back against the door and let out an amorous sigh.

"Man, what the fuck is wrong with you?" Noah asked.

Hank balked as if he were injured. He sat on the couch next to Noah, and said, "Did you see her?"

Noah blinked back at him. Hank bit back a hissing sigh.

"You were the one who said I should go out and get laid."

"Yeah," Noah said, "but I didn't think you'd miss a day of work."

"Oh, come on. Don't be like that."

"Are you kidding me? I understand you're going through a hard time without Andrea, but I can't run the shop by myself, man. The workload is getting crazy. You and I both know we can't hire anyone else, so I'm going to need you to step it up."

Hank lurched back in defense. "I missed a few days. I'll be in tomorrow."

"I sure as hell hope so," Noah said.

Hank's mouth shortened into a thin, pursed line. "What is this about? Coming to my place, knocking on the door like the police."

Noah sneered at his friend. He knew the determined look on Hank's face, the squaring off of his shoulders, the ring of scorn in his voice. And even though he'd traveled down this path with his friend so many times and knew the outcome, it heaved at him like gravity. They slipped into their primitive nature, like bulldogs snapping at one another's flesh.

"Then please, tell me," Noah said, "what is this about?"

"You're jealous."

"Of you? Did you even know what hole to put your dick in?"

Hank gaped at him, stalled for a moment. A bolt of guilt forked along Noah's chest. Hank shook his head as if he were trying to steady himself against the sting of a blow.

"You talk to Isabelle yet?"

Hank's words lanced at him with surprising accuracy. Noah seethed at him, and for a moment, he felt blinded, knocked completely off-balance. He was muddled before he found his composure. He cleared his throat and made his way to the door, huffing through the apartment. He turned and looked at Hank, who was now deflated, maybe in his victory, maybe in the now emptiness of the apartment. Hank's eyes were wide, gaping down at his feet. But this time, he wasn't gleeful with anticipation. He was broken, under the fever of something septic.

Noah suddenly wanted to say something to him. The same base nature that had caused him to fight with Hank made him want to reach out and comfort him. But Hank was his peer, his business partner, not his little brother.

He had chosen to let Andrea go, and no words from Noah would change that.

Instead of comforting words, Noah said, "Be at work tomorrow."

Hank nodded, his face fixed and solemn, before Noah stepped out of the apartment.

16

Noah preheated his oven and absently glanced over the directions for a frozen pizza, a rigid disc in his hand that promised, in twenty minutes, it would be enough to satisfy him. He skeptically regarded it. He tried to think of anything that would keep him from the raw truth of Hank's words. He unwrapped the pizza from the plastic and placed it in the oven. He left his kitchen and walked into the living room toward the window.

Heavy white flakes rode wind currents. The snow simmered endlessly underneath the spotlights of streetlamps lining the dark street. A violent shiver passed through Noah, and although he had tried to avoid it, his mind was clinging to the memory of Isabelle's warmth. His thoughts stayed fixed on her like due north. The more he spun around, the more his thoughts returned to her.

As a distraction, he pulled his phone from his pocket and contemplated listening to his mother's voicemail. He knew the dementia had eroded his father away into something barely recognizable. Noah wanted to call his mother and tell her he wasn't prepared to face the mortality of a man who had always seemed indestructible. The man who encouraged Noah to start his own business. He helped him organized the paperwork. He provided the initial seed money it took to start it.

His father had owned a hardware store, and his hands grew callused from handling the metal parts. He, in part, was like Noah, learning the interworking of things, ready to repair any broken mechanism with his wide hands. The hands Noah watched protect his mother and guide him. To face the shell of that man of force who loved Noah and his mother and watch him so gently decline into a cruel elongated death was like falling into a chasm. The only certainty was his father's death, but everything else that made up the world around him had lost meaning. What was left to be trusted? How could he explain this to his mother? How could he travel down to their South Side home, square in the middle of the Irish neighborhood, and gape at the void his father had left? He wouldn't be able to bear the pictures hung on their walls of what once was. Noah couldn't accept all those memories of holiday and family meals coming to such a bitter end.

He shoved the phone back into his pocket, assured that his mother's voicemail would only take him to a darker place.

He retrieved his pizza from the oven. The melted cheese sizzled softly as he placed it on the counter. Now the frozen disc had been under heat, transforming into a limp promise that couldn't possibly feed him. His TV's dull noise accompanied this sad meal, and he forced himself to eat several pieces with a beer until the threat of heartburn stirred in his chest.

The rising sting at his sternum brought Hank's words back to his mind. Maybe he was jealous of Hank. Had he forgotten, along the perpetual crusade of libido, what it was like to actually like the woman he was sleeping with? He had spent so many nights traveling the spaces between women's thighs. He had heard a chorus of moans and impassioned screams. He'd spent years in relish, in a boastful recklessness, sampling the many varieties of women. He had stepped into bars, eyes zeroing in on them as if they were prey, weaving words and leaning upon lies to bed them. He'd done this without remorse, with an increased urgency, in the wake of Marcie.

She had been real. The feeling he'd had for her burned and hurt and tore at him, whereas all the others had been impulses. And he had resigned himself to this until he had felt Isabelle's warm skin and tasted her kisses. Until she had held his cock in her hand and he froze, transfixed, over her.

Isabelle could burn, hurt, and tear him. And that's exactly what he wanted.

He dropped the pizza, and with a splat, it landed on the plate. He rushed out of his apartment, through the hall, and down the stairs. He stood in front of Isabelle's apartment and held his fist before the door. He readied his words in his head, stacking them neatly, preparing them for her. He planted his feet and resisted the pull to go back upstairs.

Hank was right, even in his folly.

Noah knocked twice on the door and waited. He heard nothing for a moment. He feared he had knocked too softly and considered knocking again when the door opened.

Isabelle stumbled back a few steps and gaped at him. They stared at each other for a tense moment. Warmth poured past her threshold. Noah felt as if he could stand there all night, gorging on his closeness to her.

"Hello," Isabelle said, strained with her concealed emotions.

A dizziness started in Noah's head and drained to his stomach. He took a breath, and the air fought for space in his lungs past this feeling. In the moment, as he focused on her and everything began to grow fuzzy, he thought how wonderfully unsettling it was to actually care for a woman again.

"Isabelle," he began, and neatly laid out his gathered words before her in the hall.

17

Jones woke before her alarm. She sensed she was alone in bed. She lay there, staring through the window out at the gray cold, her eyes following the skeletal tops of barren trees reaching out to her window. She stretched her muscles individually, fortifying herself in the solitude. She fought to get up, to start her day, to face those eventual battles that waited for her just beyond her bed.

The hiss of a coffee grinder warned of Derek's presence. Jones stilled in bed to hear his footsteps moving along in the kitchen, following the clearing of his throat. She bristled at the sound of him. She wished for a secret panel somewhere, hidden within the bedroom wall, that would let her downstairs unnoticed. She even pictured herself opening the window and diving for those brittle old branches from trees along the rear of the building and scaling down to the sidewalk.

There was burning in her gut because she knew that Derek, with his insufferable morning cheeriness, was up making her coffee. She could smell the rich aroma carried from the kitchen. He'd been doing this lately, his insufficient peace offerings—coffee, remorseful looks, and a side serving of compliments. Some mornings, she would let them thaw her. She would attempt to see the man she had fallen in love with. His face would hold his clever-fox grin, and he would be shirtless, exposing his sinewy chest and his broad back. He seemed as if he was preparing to go out there and face the world alongside her. With his back to her at the counter, he would fuss with the coffeemaker and the cheap appliance would gasp and gurgle as if drowning. She gazed forward at his beautiful muscles pulling at his shoulder blades under the flesh she no longer kissed. She tried to remember when Derek and she first held each other's gaze so long ago, when she could get drunk off the mere sight of him. The hot, sticky summer night he had swaggered, impossibly arrogant, into the bar she had been in. Derek had brought with him a swell of blistering heat, as if he were the source of hot pavement, the humidity clinging to her skin, and the sweat gathering in her scalp. But those memories, his presence, now had the ineffectual blunt of a dull knife. All that was left, as she watched him on those mornings, was the sear of her guilt.

A muted guilt had hardened into something ugly, something she couldn't shake. There Derek was, once imposing, bending all those around him, the very source of heat, lauding his greatness . . . simpering in defeat. She missed who he had been deeply.

Every morning was like this. Derek skipping about their kitchen, masked in his false glee. Then after he had given her coffee, a bagel, or a scone, he would return to the couch, exhausted after his dynamic performance. He would place his computer in his lap, eyes watching Jones, ready for her to leave, so he could dump money into his business without a plan and most certainly without her advice.

The burden of her disgust wasn't easy. It set down seeds in her and bloomed into something grotesque. There were moments when she couldn't bear the sound of his breathing. She could give him all the time in the world to recover from his failed business. She had offered to help, but his pride wouldn't allow it. She understood his heart was broken, but wasn't that the nature of life? The blows, the scrapes, the injuries from those eventual battles turned into unavoidable losses.

And during his morning productions, between his smiles and his witty quips, she tried to steer the conversation. She tried to reassure him the world had not come to an end. He would only smile at her blankly, and she could see him shut down and shrink before her eyes.

So yes, she wondered if the branches of that tree, suspended in ice, touching at her window, could support her weight and aid her in an escape. If she fell, surely, the branches would break her fall on the way down, and of course, there was all the snow out there that could account for some sort of cushioning.

She heard him moving, then the hiss of steam from the coffeemaker. The knots of her anger railed against her. And now, instead of escaping, she wanted to charge into the kitchen and claw at him until she found the man she had known, the man who had dreams and arrogance. She wanted to pull off his flesh, to crack him like a hard shell, and hope the memory of him was inside there.

Maybe then, at last, she could unchain herself from the guilt.

She held her breath and stilled her body in bed. She heard the wind rush against the trees followed by a soft snap as frozen branches cracked off and met their end in the snow below.

Her alarm whistled, jolting her out of her thoughts. She heard Derek down the hall with her coffee mug in hand. There was a grin on his face that was supposed to be charming but read as imbecilic. She sat up, tired and in no way equipped to handle him.

"There's a bagel for you in the kitchen," he said, handing her the steaming mug.

Heat from the mug burned her palm. She yelped and sent the mug across the bed and shattering onto the floor in five pieces. Brown coffee streamed along the comforter, soaking through it onto Jones's legs. She kicked back the comforter, drawing her legs up to her body. Derek dropped to the floor, collecting the remains of the mug. His face was wide in shock.

"Derek," she said, her voice growling, "can I wake up before you start handing me hot coffee?"

There on his knees, he began to wilt.

"I'll take care of the mess," he said.

Jones sighed and wished she hadn't spoken. She stepped off the bed to meet him down at the mess.

"Let me help."

He glared at her coldly. "I got it."

"Please, just let me help."

"I've fucking got it, all right?"

Jones jumped back, standing up. The force of his voice nearly knocked the air out of her. Derek stood up, too, looking down at the broken pieces of the mug. The quick anger in his face was gone. Nothing was left but the familiar defeat.

"I'm trying, Jones," he said to her in a barely audible voice.

Jones startled, hearing the current of blood throb in her head, and said, "Okay."

She shoved past him, stepping over the mess and toward the bathroom.

The air within the office crackled with tension and hadn't been better than what she'd left at her apartment. Jones had spent the first part of the day questioning this— maybe a manifestation of her own anxiety had tinted her view. But as she peered through her window from her office, she sensed the hesitance in people's movements. There was an uneasy hush through the cubicles and an urgency with which people stared at their computers and regarded their projects. She wanted to attribute it to the vice president of the publishing company coming by, but this particular breed of apprehension was laced with an ominous feeling that rendered her inert.

Jones grappled at nothing for a moment before tiptoeing to the finance director's office. She closed his door behind her and sat down.

"What do you know?" she asked in a hushed voice as if speaking a profane blasphemy.

The finance director looked like a cornered animal behind his Wayfarer glasses. He pushed them further up the bridge of his nose and shrugged.

Jones screwed her face into a grimace. "What is the gossip? I know you know. You always know."

The finance director slumped in his chair. "The vice president is coming in today to talk about a buyout of the magazine."

Jones gripped the armrests of the chair. The panic hit her so hard she coughed up a few nervous giggles of disbelief. She shook her head at the finance director, now aware of how small and cold his office was.

"It's true," he said. "I think the guy who had the job before you knew this. It's why he left. He told me last night when I met him for drinks."

"Okay," Jones said. "Okay."

She smiled at him and hoped it was convincing. She stood on rubbery legs and made her way toward his door and headed back to her office. At her desk, she pulled out her purse and began rummaging through it. She dug past lip gloss, loose change, and tampons and stuck herself with the sharp edge of her keys. The jagged teeth of a key dug underneath her nail, and she yanked back her hand as if trying to save herself from a bear trap. She examined her hands and noticed them shaking. There was nothing she could do to save the magazine. This buyout was happening right underneath her.

In her purse, she found what she had been looking for. She plucked out her bottle of Xanax and took the pill with a mug full of cold coffee at her desk.

The rest of her day was a countdown until the board meeting with the vice president. She accomplished very little, merely half-heartedly responding to emails. Minutes stretched and twisted into choking cords, but thanks to Xanax, there was no sharpness to her anxiety. She returned to her emails and considered making some phone calls that she had been putting off when movement caught her eyes.

Through the window, she saw the vice president stroll through. She was an older woman who had grown handsome with age, wearing the lines on her face like one would wear expensive garments. Behind her intrepid stride, a four-man infantry of suited men followed. Against the artistic orthodoxy of the staff, they were well-bred nobility. The vice president stopped in the middle of the office and spoke and gestured as if she were showing off a used car.

Three of the men stopped and looked upon the man at the center of the group before reacting.

This man at the center was younger than the others, but judging by the impudence in his stance and the consideration within his face, it was evident he was in charge. He had handsome sharp features with high cheekbones. He had strong shoulders and a build that couldn't be contained within the straight lines of his suit. He said something to the vice president, and the men around him nodded. Jones could've attributed her Xanax to this, but she enjoyed the way he didn't have to move. With a few words, the men around him buzzed and pulled out an arsenal of iPhones and tablets, taking down whatever he had said.

The party continued, but the man in the center paused, lingering behind, staring ahead, suddenly tense. He turned to her office, locking eyes with her through the glass. A quiver skated along her legs. She understood why the men had moved when he spoke. His blue eyes shot back at her, and she wanted to dive underneath her desk, but she was arrested before him, waiting for his signal on how to react. He commanded attention, and one wanted to carry out his commands.

Yet slowly, his full mouth swung into a crescent smile and his face lit brilliantly, finding radiance from the skylights above. Jones floundered against this affront of kindness. Then the smile was gone, and he stepped back into the group and into the boardroom, out of Jones's view.

She sat back in her chair and waited for the quivering in her legs to pass.

18

Isabelle had a sleepless night yet again, watching the night dispense to another bleak winter day. She closed her eyes and summoned her strength before she stepped into the back entrance of the gallery. The lights were off, and she moved silently through the gray shadows of the late morning. In the shrouded gloom, the murals, canvases, and small sculptures roosted on pedestals and slumbered. Isabelle envied them as she headed toward the back offices and storage space.

Curtis announced his presence with the glitchy pop of electronic music. The music settled into Isabelle's skull in the form of a headache. She bit back her lips, trying to curb her annoyance as she followed the noise into one of the storage rooms. One half of storage was crowded with piles of paper, steel ropes, hooks for mounting pieces, brooms, and industrial light bulbs, and the other half had been cleared out for Curtis and his canvases, easels, and oil paints.

When Isabelle entered the room, he stood in front of a canvas, dreadlocks tied back. His hands were cocked on his hips, and paint was splattered on him as if he had butchered some animal with multicolored innards. He turned toward Isabelle and nodded. Isabelle tried to speak, but her voice was overthrown by the music's volume. Curtis grimaced and knelt to turn off the speaker at his feet.

"We need to talk," Isabelle said.

"Must we?" Curtis said with his back to her once again, searching his canvas. "I'm sort of busy."

Isabelle bit back her contempt. "Oh, and I'm just here so you can have a punching bag to work through your mother issues."

Curtis faced her and rolled his eyes in retort. Isabelle gave him an icy smile.

"What do you need?" Curtis asked.

"I have a way for us to make additional income."

"So do I."

"Well, my way is legal," Isabelle said.

"What is it?" The lines of Curtis's grimace deepened.

Isabelle turned around in a circle, taking in the room. "We rent out the rest of the storage for studio space."

Curtis drew his hand up to his face, absently smearing green and blue paint onto his skin. He shook his head, and his dreadlocks bucked around as if they were reaching out to her.

"I'm not sharing my studio space."

"This is a solution that works."

This idea had come to her in those grave hours of the early morning. It was a time when logic usually unfurled and she was left with nothing but manic fear whipping at her. But somehow, in the mad acceptance of her demise, the space within the storage room rose to her mind like an air bubble burping up through mud.

"How does this work?"

"No one is hardly attending anything showing in this weather. And the gallery has bills to pay, and so do I. This will give us a steady stream of revenue until I can manage to sell that," Isabelle said, jabbing her finger at his dripping canvas. "Plus, we're going to need more art than yours on the wall. We can get it in-house from the artists renting our space."

"Well, I told you I have an idea," Curtis said.

"I'm not going to prison," she said, walking toward her office.

"I don't like this."

"Look, we're in the red here, Curtis," she said. "If we don't do this, you won't have a studio space to worry about."

Curtis, now solemn, looked down at his green and blue hands. He exhaled a defeated puff of air and sulked back to his canvas. She would give him another hour or so before she rallied him to prepare their storage room. Isabelle could count on him to be obstinate, simpering, and childish, but he would comply. She was the reason the gallery shuffled along, and without her guidance, it would have been closed long ago. Isabelle began to believe that his fits were just a veiled effort to save face because he hadn't come up with the solution himself.

Hours piled upon themselves like the snow outside. The gallery was lit and the art pieces were alive and vivid for an audience of no one. Isabelle had seen some of the pieces for weeks, and what once titillated were now stale coagulations mounted on the walls. She stood behind the white desk in the lobby, looking past the pieces to the abysmal day and the people outside the glass who moved through with hurried paces, bundled with their scowls. She uttered hollow prayers, hoping one of them would step in.

In spite, Curtis had quickly removed Russell's artwork from the walls. The whole situation gnawed at her with a surprising sadness. Her sadness was swift to remind her that a virulent exhaustion had come to perch in her bones.

The door opened, and a mechanical bell chimed overhead. A surge of cold air billowed around Noah as he entered, stomping his boots on the mat as if he were trying to kill something underfoot.

Isabelle was now hopeful to see him, with his chipped-tooth smile fastened to his face. She felt embarrassed and a bit silly, not quite able to look at him as he approached slowly. Once at the desk at the far end, he scanned the gallery.

"Whoa," he said, his mouth slack-jawed.

Last night, he came to her door, eyes full of penance, uttering apology after apology. There at her doorway, she found herself dumbstruck, again failing to escape the undertow of his pleading face. As a token of remorse, he offered to come by and look at her computers at the end of his day. Isabelle accepted his invitation, merely to free herself to close her door again—to escape the want in his eyes. But now as he stood next to her, practically twirling to take in the gallery. She knew this was just an excuse to see her, a safe pretense for him to navigate and see if it had been more than just alcohol and an opportunity. Isabelle knew, as she ushered him to her office at the rear of the gallery, she would be back under the scope of his wanting eyes. And she would have to reconcile that now there were no doors, no wrong names to separate her from him.

As they reached her office, Curtis's head peeped out of the storage room. He regarded Noah suspiciously and looked as if he were readying himself to say something. Isabelle shot him an admonishing glare, and his head retreated into the storage room.

Noah sat down at her desk and restarted her computer. The old dusty machine whirled as its entrails went to work.

The screen flickered, going from black to blue and soon to the start page. Isabelle had worked on this computer, knowing its oddities and regarding them in a benign contempt, but now she was embarrassed. Noah was a series of meticulous movements over the stressed, clicking machine, opening up windows and background programs that Isabelle didn't know existed on her computer. He hummed, and his fingers grazed quickly along her keyboard.

He turned to Isabelle, flashed his smile, and said, "Your hardware is pretty old, and your OS could stand an upgrade."

Isabelle barked in laughter. "What?"

He stood up face-to-face with her in the forced intimacy of the small office. The closeness of him, just barely a foot away, propelled all the blood out of Isabelle's head. Her head, now an empty backdrop, played out the night of him on top of her. Inadvertently, they stepped closer to one another, and Isabelle wondered if he could see inside her head.

"Isabelle," he said, "I'll take care of your computer."

"Okay."

"Don't worry."

Her mind recounted the way Noah's weight felt pressing down on her in the same manner that his lovesick eyes bore down on her now.

19

Jones was completely outside herself as she stepped from her office toward the boardroom. She would have possibly felt frustrated if everything weren't so far removed from her, as if she were peering through the screen from some place laid-back, warm, and familiar. To her left was the financial director, walking the chain-bound shuffle of a man on death row. He appeared, looking over his ever-present Wayfarers, ready to be blindfolded and whisper dying confessions. The art director and a few editors were behind him, in the same manner of trepidation, following the same grave path to damnation.

They gathered together at the end of a long table as if their closeness would promise them safety. At the opposite end of the table, below the skylight, was the vice president and the straight-faced herd of suited men. For what appeared to be a long moment, the two groups were silent like that of parties readying for a duel.

That prolonged moment spiraled into a surreal paradox punctuated by adjusting in chairs, clearing throats, checking phones, and it nearly caused Jones to laugh—how one moment, she'd felt completely in control, guiding the oversight of the quarter three issue, and now here she sat, alongside her colleagues, as if beckoned to the principal's office.

"Thank you all for coming today," the vice president began. "We had you, our senior staff, attend this meeting to discuss some changes to Chicago Modern Art Magazine. I would like to introduce to you Todd Nicolas, from the Nichols-Griffin Art Institute. He and his team are here to negotiate the acquisition of our magazine."

Jones felt the distance between her and what was happening in the room dilate. She strained to hear the next words spoken, as if they had to travel a great distance to get to her. One of the more bookish of the suited men materialized a briefcase, and from the briefcase, a folder, and from that folder, he extracted a stack of papers. The suited man passed the papers to the rear of the table to Jones and her colleagues. The others sat nearly stock-still with fear as they shuffled through the sheets.

Jones looked down at the papers in front of her. She didn't want to touch them, suddenly worried she would become contaminated. She stared down at the papers which outlined Nichols-Griffin Art Institute's vision. The mission statement, written in bold script, read like supercilious rhetoric. And just when she thought she could float away further in her chair before these men in suits, she thought of Isabelle and the toil that men like this had brought down on her friend.

Another man from the group began to speak about projected dates for the acquisition and a promise of a smooth transition—a promise so hollow that it sounded as if he didn't even believe it himself. He continued to drone, and words rolled into nonsensical noise. Her colleagues around her nodded their heads in a coerced sanction, and Jones followed their lead, staring blankly ahead.

Then in the center of group, Todd Nicolas spoke, the startling man in charge, penetrating them all with blue eyes.

"Look, I know this seems intrusive, but I'm here because I like what this magazine does," he said. "All I want is for Nichols-Griffin to enhance what you've all been working on. Of course, it will require a bit of restructuring, like all change."

Heavy plains of clouds shifted like tectonic plates, and light from sun, no longer buried in winter's bleak squalor, spilled through the skylight onto Todd Nicolas. Around Jones, colleagues tensed, and the sighs were almost audible as they gave into an uneasy relief.

Jones wanted to hate him. She looked at Todd through the strain. His sharp features lit up as if he were a messiah, and she understood why his cadre of men in suits stared at him with devotion.

Once more, the droning man in the suit continued to speak his garble. Jones began to drift again, but Todd's gaze fell on her and, discreetly, he smiled. Jones startled and glanced down at the paper, now moored to the room by his presence. She crossed her legs to keep them from shaking.

Could this all be her imagination? Was it the Xanax? Why had she taken it at work?

She slightly veered her attention from the paper, toward Todd Nicolas. He remained transfixed on her, and as their eyes met yet again, his smile deepened. It traveled higher upon his face that somehow managed to steal the sun where none had existed. This confirmation thrilled her, and despite the Xanax and her legs being crossed, they began to shake under the table. Jones dropped her eyes to the papers. She stayed that way until the meeting was over. She was only aware of her heartbeat when she and the others went back to their respective offices.

Jones sat still at her desk for a moment in a fleeting attempt to still her heart from Todd Nicolas's smile swimming in her mind. In truth, there was much at risk with the change coming. How would her team deal with this, and what did Todd Nicolas mean by restructuring? Did that mean people could possibly lose their jobs? Stones of dread grounded her, and Jones's heart hushed. She now wondered how to tell Isabelle that she was in league with the dark empire that had acquired her gallery's most successful artist.

Knuckles rapped softly on Jones's door, and Todd Nicolas stepped in. He simply smiled at her for a moment, and again, his face found unseasonal sun. Jones, grappling for something, snagged a pen off her desk and began to frantically click the end of it to replace sound where conversation should be.

"Can I help you?" she asked, then silently cursed herself for the meekness curdling her voice.

"Are you Emily?"

"Jones," she said, now harsher, trying to compensate. "I go by Jones."

He winced in apology, pulling air between his teeth sharply. "Sorry, they barely tell me anything before a meeting."

"It's okay," Jones said, if only to say anything. She wanted him out of her office. She couldn't trust herself with him inside her office.

"I heard you are the new director of the magazine," he said.

"Yeah, started last week," she said, "and now this."

She wanted to palm her own face but resisted the urge.

Todd Nicolas chuckled, and said, "Look, I know this is . . ."

"Scary," Jones offered.

He smiled, and then nodded. "Yes, but I believe in this magazine, and I'm excited at what it brings to Chicago's art community."

"Me too."

"Jones," he said, hesitating on her name, "I would love to hear about your vision for the magazine sometime."

He stepped deeper into her office and pulled out a small card from inside his suit. He placed the business card on her desk. He then quickly stepped back as if he had crossed some forbidden boundary.

"Please call me anytime," he said.

"Sure." Jones was now in conflict with her quivering legs.

"Maybe we can have dinner and talk about it."

Jones nodded as he continued to retreat from her desk as if being chased out by that boundary line of decorum that was supposed to separate them. Todd Nicolas rejoined the men in suits in the main office space being led out by the vice president. Jones watch them move out of the office, and in her mind, she counted the steps it took for them to arrive at the elevators and out of the building. Once again, she wrangled control over her legs and her heart beating against her ribcage.

When calmness had settled upon her, she picked up his business card and examined it with a reverence she reserved for great works of art. She glanced through the office and up into the skylights, where the clouds had closed in and withdrawn the sun.

She sighed to relieve the heaviness in her chest and stuck his card into the safety of her purse

20

Isabelle wasn't naïve about men, but something happened to her as she watched Noah squat down to access the wires at the rear of her desktop computer. This was an obvious stalling tactic on his part, but she welcomed it. His company had been an amicable warmth on a cold day. She admired his odd brand of handsome and his fleeting goofy jokes that would elicit that chipped-toothed grin. She had already decided she would sleep with him again, provided he continued to call her by the right name. Sex with him again would be a simple transaction. What troubled her wasn't his company, not even the length he had gone through to be in her presence again. It was whether she could trust the ease that she felt around him.

Isabelle let him linger around the gallery after he had finished a sweep of her computer and networks. They strolled slowly from wall to wall, and Noah glanced at each piece and gave his opinion. He spoke sparsely, and although he tried to hide his ignorance about the art, it was obvious. Isabelle, in response, would offer a limited explanation for him. Some of the art on the white walls was beautiful, but most was provocative, making harsh verdicts on the degradation of modern society. Isabelle tried her best to appear modest about all of this and failed. Her fervor drenched her words, and as they spanned over the work to the last canvas, she now found herself ill with fear of how pretentious she must've sounded.

At the last wall, Noah was silent before a canvas of a man's black silhouette joined by a woman and a child. Behind them was a massive mushroom cloud, and destruction appeared to rush up behind them in volatile reds and oranges. Flames twisted out from the explosion and a harsh line hinted at the force barreling toward them. Noah turned toward the title card to the picture and stooped down to read, AMERICAN FAMILY. His face flashed in disgust, and he turned and looked at Isabelle for justification.

"You don't like it?" she asked.

"Maybe I'm not an art guy," he said, "but that's not what I think of when I see the American family."

Isabelle tilted her head, and asked, "You see something more what . . . picturesque?"

Her voice was sour with derision. Noah appeared injured, then his shoulders squared in defense.

"I just think that sometimes artists make fun of shit just to make fun of shit," Noah said. "Family is . . . family is . . ."

"Family is what?" Isabelle asked, this time with no insult in her voice, only true curiosity.

"I don't know—sacred."

Isabelle puckered her mouth as if considering the taste of this word. She rolled it around in her mind and felt like she had to rearrange things in order to find a place for it. Eventually, in their silence, watching Noah's skin transition from pale to red, the word found rest. Isabelle smiled slightly and gave him a quick kiss.

She left him in the gallery amongst the paintings to check in with Curtis in the back office. He was covered in even more paint than he had been when she had last seen him. Now, he stood barefoot in front of the canvas, flexing his long pink feet, inspecting his work for an answer. When Isabelle asked him to close the gallery, he nodded in reluctance.

As she left, he said after her, "I like that guy."

"But you hate everyone."

"No, just you."

Isabelle sucked her teeth and left the rear offices, carrying her heavy winter coat like a child. Noah was eager to help her into it, and Isabelle was awkward as he slipped the coat over her shoulders.

They walked to the front door and stood staring out into the dark night. Unconsciously, they linked hands, joined in the fear that the cold could overtake them separately. They leaped against the breeze, and Isabelle bit back a cry as together they ran through the snow. A rising glee bubbled up in Isabelle, and laughter pressed past her lips as they half ran and slid toward the train station. Noah added his own barking guffaw to her own and ran up to the platform and into a train that carried them home to their apartment building.

There were at the apartment door, and Noah pulled out his keys as Isabelle absently picked at the gas shut-off notice.

"You think he'll pay soon?" Isabelle asked.

"He'd better," Noah said darkly, his shoulders poised to attack. It was a show for Isabelle, and in spite of herself, she enjoyed it.

They shuffled upstairs, shaking themselves free from the snow, and made their way up toward Isabelle's apartment, but she was behind him and gave him a gentle push, urging him toward his apartment above hers. Laughter squeezed into the narrowing space between them. Noah's arms surrounded Isabelle, and she was flooded with the smell of saccharine aftershave and cigarettes. Together, they climbed the stairs side by side while Noah clutched her against his body.

Once in his apartment, he reached for her coat, pulling it off her. He was no longer awkward, now in the familiarity of his home. They stood close to each other, listening to their heavy breaths—the sounds of anticipation. He slowly raised his hand up to her face, and Isabelle closed her eyes and leaned into his palm. His fingers were warm on her skin. Shivers crawled along Isabelle in an attempt to thaw out for the man whose breath she had fallen in sync with.

Noah kissed her lips softly, a gentle preamble to the intensity that was there. It ignited them in a whirlwind of motion. Isabelle pulled at Noah's sweater, and he pawed at the buttons on her blouse. Kisses tasted and licked at one another, scouting one another. They stumbled backward, feet nearly succumbing to the castaway layers of winter clothes.

Isabelle was now in the bedroom, surprised that he had placed his bed in his room just as she had. She lay on her back, pulling herself onto the bed. He stood there, erect and swollen with lust, his wide chest heaving. Isabelle braced herself for an onslaught. There was steady force, a slight flexing of his flesh, restrained in his muscles. He crawled on the bed, kissing her neck. His lips gently lapped at her flesh. His mouth was delicious on her skin, and lust forced her to grasp Noah's head and push it down along her body.

He understood and even delighted in this compliance until his face, his lips, were between her legs. He nibbled and licked until she bucked in pleasure. Groans hissed between her clenched teeth, and Noah's finger traveled along her neck, toward her chin, and found her mouth. With his strong hand, he parted her lips and teeth, freeing her moans.

They fucked until they ached. Time waned away, and once again, it was just their breathing. Isabelle finally untangled herself from him. She tasted the mix of their sweat in her mouth. She still tingled from his touch, still felt the haunting where he had entered between her thighs. That suspicious calm fell on her again, and she found herself wanting to return to his arms.

Noah maybe sensed this, or maybe he just wanted to touch her, so he pulled her back into the embankment of his lanky compact body. He began to speak, but a scratchy noise came from his throat.

"Are you still nervous around me?" Isabelle asked.

Noah huffed, then said, "No."

Isabelle, with her head on his chest, raised her eyebrows in question.

"Yes."

"Why? You've been with tons of other girls."

Noah glanced around his room, then he reached for tissue paper from a Kleenex box on his nightstand. He tended to the used condom on his cock for something to do. Isabelle rolled away with her arms crossed. Noah looked back at her with a helplessness overtaking his face.

"You owe me this," Isabelle said. "Give me a reason to believe you're okay."

Noah sighed. "Yeah, I've slept with a bunch of girls, but I didn't feel anything with them. But you . . . I feel something, okay? I like you. I'm sure you want to run away now."

"Honestly," Isabelle said, "I don't know what I want to do."

"It's just that the last time I felt this way—well, I got really fucked over."

Isabelle thought for moment, and then said, "Where is your weed?"

"Huh?"

"I can smell it through the vents when you smoke."

"You smoke?"

"I'm a hipster who owns an art gallery in Logan Square, and I fight all day with a white guy with dreadlocks. Yes, I smoke weed."

Noah snorted, and then crossed his room toward his dresser. Isabelle admired his pale, firm ass as he pulled a bowl from the first drawer and brought it back to them. He handed it to her and grabbed a lighter from his nightstand. Isabelle lit the piece and took a deep pull from it. She passed it to Noah, who did the same.

Isabelle held it in until her eyes began to water and she convulsed with coughs. She shook the entire bed, gasping for air, and Noah laughed at her expense. She gave him a playful swat and settled into his arms. The comfort she was wary of around him deepened.

"You act as if I'm not human," she said.

"I don't mean to."

"I'm going to tell you something, and you can't run away."

"Okay."

"I have insomnia. Sometimes, I can't sleep. Sometimes, it's just me alone in the dark."

She shifted in the bed, putting her back to his chest. She couldn't look into his face. Isabelle focused on his breathing, her head rising with his inhalations. She wanted to stay here tonight. Even if she had another sleepless night, at least someone would be there.

"Sometimes, it gets really bad. I tried to do everything right. I kept a sleep journal, exercised, avoided the TV at night, no drinking past a certain point . . . but nothing helped. Medication seemed to make it worse."

"And now?"

Isabelle draped her arm over his narrow chest. "Being in your bed helps."

"Well, okay," Noah said, and kissed her forehead. "You're human, after all."

21

Jones failed to avoid Derek this morning. She emerged from the bathroom, and there he was, poised on the couch, staring at his laptop and those absent sales. She floundered, undecided between rushing into the bedroom to avoid him or moving slowly so as not to attract his unwanted attention. In her hesitation, he looked up and caught her in his glance. His disappointment lingered over his head like a poltergeist, malevolent and searching. And before she could fully dress, he was up and pacing, with her in his crosshairs. He voiced his theories on his business failure—some sensible, like his failure to beta test, and others bordering on paranoia, like the willful sabotage of his partners. Jones offered a few of her ideas, which he abruptly dismissed and began talking over her.

When Jones managed to extract herself from his mania, she arrived at the office late and frustrated. She had already missed a meeting and started the day playing catch-up. While drafting an email to the editorial staff, Derek had sent her several text messages, expounding on his presumptions as if she'd never left. She ignored him, of course, but ever persistent, he began to call her office. Jones ground her heels into the carpet underneath and inhaled a Xanax, and after his third attempt, decided to take his call.

"Jones, I'm sorry to bother you at work," he began.

"Not sorry enough," she said, mostly to herself.

He, of course, didn't hear this. "They want out."

"Who?"

"My business partners," he continued. "I knew they had it in for me."

Despite her mounting frustration, Jones considered this. If her conversations with Derek were any indication of how he spoke to his business partners, they had every reason to abandon ship before they were overtaken by the current.

She sighed and pinched the bridge of her nose. The tingly afterglow of her Xanax began to warm her limbs, and the small amount of concern she had gathered for Derek dissipated. "I'm at work."

There was movement at her door, and she glanced up. Todd Nicolas leaned one of his shoulders against the doorframe with his arms crossed over his chest. This gave the impression that he had been there a while, spying on Jones. He was dressed in his typical bespoke suit, without a tie, and the first few buttons were casually undone, exposing the top of his strong pale chest. He stared back her, stoic and beautiful. The arcs of his high cheeks, the slope of his nose, and curve of his lips echoed a marble bust crafted during the Italian Renaissance. A pang of fear bubbled through the Xanax's sedation, and for a moment, she feared she was in trouble and that maybe he had come here to let her go. But as soon as their eyes met, a slow smile illuminated his face that nearly overwhelmed her.

Derek's voice in her ear became distant, and she hung up the phone without another word. Todd laughed at this, and Jones was certain he was aware of the effect he had on people.

He raised an eyebrow and nodded at the phone. "Was that important?"

Jones straightened in her chair. "Not in the slightest."

He continued to stare at her, his expression not hostile, yet indecipherable. And if it had been anyone else, Jones would have scoffed at them. Yet even in the silence between them, there was something pleasurable about his presence, some quality of kindness or hopefulness she picked up around him . . . or that could have been the aftereffect of his attractiveness. Beauty that remarkable on a man could have become a canvas for whatever one needed it to be. And at the thought, she sobered and cleared her throat, breaking the spell between them.

"What can I do for you?"

"Take an early lunch with me."

His request, soft and amicable, parted his smile. Jones wasn't sure she heard him correctly, and her brows met in skepticism. His presence, aided by her own consumption of Xanax, altered her perception. Nothing seemed right—but in the most remarkable way.

Todd grew nervous from her silence, and Jones couldn't quite commit to pity while staring at him, because even in this, it brought another dimension to his beauty.

"I'd simply like to discuss the magazine with you," he said, breaking the trance between them with sudden formality.

Jones fought back a smirk, dropping her hands in her lap. She wasn't sure how to feel about any of this. The thought of Derek withered against the brilliance of Todd's smile.

He led Jones out of her office and through the editorial floor. She swallowed her nervousness as they strolled toward the elevator, worried someone would catch a hint of this nascent attraction between them and turn it into gossip. She surveyed the room, and most people averted their gaze from the new boss, reluctant to become the object of his scrutiny. This somehow assured her. She shouldn't even entertain any feeling of attraction to him. He was, in fact, her new boss, a completely unknown variable to the magazine. For all she knew, he could be taking her out of the office to fire her. She didn't know what his motives were, and even if he was attracted to her, would this be a case for sexual harassment?

Jones tried to hold on to her better sense as they stepped into the elevator, but the doors closed, leaving them alone. And in that small space, nothing existed but their proximity to each other that unfortunately extended to the Town Car that waited for them down on the street. The Town Car cautiously traveled the wintry streets. A steady downpour of snow cloaked and enclosed them within the car. His earthy smell filled her lungs, and he seemed to occupy every space within the cabin. She was aware of the strain his muscular thighs placed on the seams of his pants and the gentle drumming of his fingers on the leather seats.

Jones's agitation began to slice through the fading effects of her Xanax. And she didn't want to be sober next to this man. Because in her sober mind, she wouldn't be able to process this attraction. She would have turned over to reason—to the fact that he was her boss and she was in a relationship.

"Why am I here?" she asked.

"I'd like to get to know you."

She tilted her head in suspicion. "I work for you. What else is there to know?"

Todd Nicolas raised an eyebrow and pressed his index finger against his lips. "Fine. Fair enough. Keep your cards close—I can respect that. Well, let me tell you what I know about you." He sat back and crossed him arms. "You studied journalism and art history, and after you graduated, you came to this magazine, which barely could justify the cost of ink and the paper it was printed on. And I heard that you're extremely smug and arrogant and determined to do things your way. You gave your bosses a terrible time. You railed against the rules and set parameters. And you were nearly fired more than twice."

Jones swallowed hard. Had she misread this entire situation? The air within the car became thick.

Todd leaned in closer and smiled. "But because of those things, you saved the magazine time and time again. You doubled its circulation and created quite the influential publication for the city. You've created local artists with the stroke of a pen. You're amazing, Emily Jones, and the only reason I'm interested in this magazine."

Jones blinked at him incredulously.

He turned away from her, to her great relief, and squinted through the snow.

"When my father died, I'd inherited all his companies, holdings, and stocks. And I sold all of that to try to be a part of something." He glanced back at her intently. "Something real, something beautiful. A lot of people think I'm going to fail. But I believe you can help me succeed."

Jones nodded, utterly baffled.

The car slowed at a light, and then turned. Todd held his hand out, and she took it. He smiled and shook it. His was soft and warm on her skin, and they both held contact for longer than what was customary.

Another dazzling smile overtook his face, and the car pulled alongside a restaurant that Jones could barely make out through the snow.

He finally released her hand. "I hope you like sushi."

22

In the smallest room, in the office space offset from the workspace, wedged tightly in the corner was a mini-fridge. Overhead, dry, hot air blew in from the heating duct. Hank carried in Thai food from the restaurant below the shop. The cold had made venturing to any place further than downstairs a torture not worth enduring. In the room, two old ramshackle chairs crowded the wall for dominance. Across from the furniture, a tiny refurbished TV hung on the wall. On its flickering screen, a meteorologist, red-faced in a sadistic fervor, warned of the decreasing temperatures. The screen flashed to a reporter downtown on the street. The reporter was an unnecessary sacrifice to further this point. He huddled within a parka, his face also a shade of red but due to cold, and he spoke a few words of caution. And then back to the warm studio, where the meteorologist, the harbinger of the icy apocalypse, promised record-breaking cold and snow. The reporter, as if it were something mystical, gravely called the weather patterns the Polar Vortex.

Hank, an unbeliever, shook his head as if the weather could be ignored. And even if this record-breaking cold did hit Chicago, the people here were strong. This wasn't his first winter here. He had earned the right to balk at the meteorologist. Hank reached for the remote and turned through the channels. All that was on was women arguing about current events around tables. Reconciling his fate, he sat and amused himself with how much pad Thai he could get into his mouth with chopsticks.

Noah entered the room, and his gait slowed as the two eyed one another. He also carried a dish from downstairs, and before Hank could smell it, he knew it was ginger chicken. They stared at one another as the words from two days ago persisted like broken bones that hadn't been set. The hovering anger had begun to solidify around them. Throughout the last few days, they found themselves avoiding eye contact in the workroom and through the hallways of their apartment building. Their discord found a shaky balance where Hank would come in an hour early and Noah would leave an hour late. It ensured no shared commutes and no extraneous time together.

Yet, Hank wanted to talk to him. The space was too small not to speak, and he couldn't eat at his workstation. When they spoke, words were sparse and only related to work.

Noah settled down into the chair next to Hank, inches away, and pulled a fork from the bag of Thai food. If they had been talking, Noah would have teased Hank for his chopsticks and handed Hank the extra fork he always had for his friend. But there was no laughter. There was no extra fork.

Hank turned back to the weather and continued his unsuccessful campaign with his chopsticks. In the static of their silence, they listened to the oncoming, unrelenting calamity of the Polar Vortex.

Gwen sat on the end of Hank's bed naked, smoking a cigarette. She held it gently in her hand, carelessly flicking ash on the hardwood floor. Hank licked his dry lips and pulled his body out of bed and into the bathroom to wash off the sweat and aroma of sex. Over the hiss of the water, he heard the chirping of a phone. He turned to the noise and pulled back the shower curtain enough to see Gwen, passing the haze of steam rising from the bathroom with her phone to her ear, moving from the bedroom to the front of the apartment.

He heard her gentle murmuring and was seized by panic. Who was on the other line? Was it another man? The last few nights were one long stretch of relentless sex, the numbing plunder of flesh upon flesh, and left little room for conversation. Hank realized they hadn't discussed the length or the terms of this arrangement. She could very well put on her clothes and disappear into the snow and never see Hank again. Things like that happened more often than not, and he would be left in his still-barren apartment.

He quickly ended his shower before he even had the chance to clean himself. Shivering and wet, he lost his footing getting out of the tub. He gripped a nearby towel rack. He caught himself and heard the plaster crack behind the rack. He wrapped himself in a towel and leaned against the door, trying to make out her conversation.

There was a jet of Gwen's giggles, and Hank's stomach retracted into his chest. He was certain she was preparing to leave him. He thought about hiding out in his bathroom all night, but then he realized it was his apartment. He adjusted his towel, and then strolled in, pantomiming nonchalance, passing Gwen to his refrigerator. He pulled out a beer, next to the half-empty bottle of Vodka that had been bought for her.

In the same forced ramble, he made his way to the couch, now admiring her figure visible underneath one of his shirts.

She smiled at him, and said to the phone, "I'm with someone now. Yeah, yeah . . . okay, bye."

She hung up the phone, and Hank drank from his beer to keep from asking who she'd been talking to. She plopped next to him on the couch. A wicked smile crept along her face, and she played with the edge of his towel tied around his waist.

"Do you want to go out with me?"

There was a contrived innocence in her voice. Hank detected it immediately, but he knew that he couldn't stop her from going, which left him with the only option of going with her.

Once again, Hank was no longer the master of his extremities as he called an Uber on his phone. Gwen took his phone and added an address. And as if being driven by her, he was slipping into black jeans, black boots, and T-shirt, ready. Gwen had dressed with ease, combing her fingers through her wild bed-hair and running her index finger along her bottom eyelids to wipe away her smudged eyeliner. She looked feral in her anticipation, and Hank held his reservations as his faced tightened.

His phone buzzed in his hand when the Uber had arrived. Gwen pushed through his door, and Hank followed her, leaving no slack in the invisible tether between them. They charged through the cold and into the car. Gwen gave directions, and Hank couldn't hear her over the rise of mania rushing into his head. His thoughts had now beccme an indiscernible hum of white noise. Breaths fogged the car's windows, and streaks of light and ropes of white rushed past.

Hank had never been so unable to plot the course out in front him. For all he knew as they barreled through the darkness, Gwen could be taking him off the edge of a cliff. But maybe after this night, when the sun had risen and she was hampered with a hangover, they could talk. He could convince her to stay at his apartment on a trial basis and to fill the vacancy. She had been there every night of the week.

She now sat next to him with her phone in her hand, texting, the blue glow from the phone striping her skin. She turned to him in the bleached glow, smiling like the preamble to a horror movie. Hank reached for her thigh, desiring some material proof that she was the woman he had been in bed with earlier.

Gwen must've sensed this and placed her phone in her lap. She said, "You'll have fun."

Hank remained uncertain, and Gwen took his hand.

"I promise."

The car came to juddering halt along the ice. They were let out at a nondescript row of houses, hidden in shadows and snow. Hank glanced around, looking for some landmark, but there was only a long strip of repeating architecture and barren trees in the darkness, and snow masked everything, including the street signs. Hank could have been anywhere in the city.

An agitated dog barked in the window of a nearby house. Bass grumbled in succession, and figures flickered against the yellow glow from within the house they approached. Gwen stepped into the house, and Hank was so close behind her he nearly stepped on her heels.

Inside, the air was a thick soup of burning weed, spilled liquor, and sweat. People crushed upon people, churning about, and their collective voices strained to be heard over the hip-hop. Hank wrestled his anxiety as he wove through the crowd behind Gwen to her undetermined destination. He noticed the variety of the people enclosed around him. There was something adverse about them, something in their narrowed side glances. Hank couldn't feel his toes in fear. This underlining aggressiveness reflected his anemic suburban gentility. The men around him were clad in a hyper-urban armor. Their varied ethnicities blurred into handkerchiefs tied around heads, oversized clothing draped over muscular frames, and scowls tight over lit blunts. He had no dominion here in this no-man's land on this no-name block. None of these harsh faces were familiar, and if they regarded him, it was only for a moment. He thought about his grandparents and the housing project his parents were desperate to escape. Where had she taken him?

He felt invisible and was almost comforted by it.

Gwen waved at three men in a rear lounge room, occupying a couch with stains stretching across its surface. She and Hank settled into empty plastic chairs in front of them. Hank felt the plastic chair bow underneath him and feared that he might fall.

One of the men before him was a younger black guy whose face twisted in the coldest frown Hank had ever seen on a person. Fear swelled in Hank's chest each time he looked at the man's scowl, so he chose to focus on the next man who, despite the worn features of a crimson face and a gin-blossomed nose, remained affable with a joint pinched off in his fingers. This man's empty hand trembled slightly, and so did his feet, all moving to an internal metronome. And at the end of the couch, taking up most of the room, was a wide, plump, bald man. This man's skin was glazed in sweat. They took turns giving Hank suspicious glances.

"Who's he, Gwen?" said the frowning black man.

"Who's this dude?" said the fat one. "He cool?"

"Now, Kelvin," she said to black man, "I would never bring someone who ain't cool up in here. This is Hank, my friend. I'm showing him around."

She turned to Hank and introduced them. "This is Kelvin, that's Shakes, and that's Don."

Shakes exposed his jagged grin and pushed a quivering hand through his greasy hair. He handed Hank his blunt. Hank nodded in appreciation and took a pull from it. There was an odd chemical burn to the weed he inhaled, and his abdomen seized painfully as he battled not to choke in front of these men. He handed the blunt back to Shakes and smiled at him feebly.

Shakes took a puff from the blunt and adoringly held it before Hank. "A little extra in this. Good shit, huh?"

And as if those words were enough to signal the chemicals, the room altered around him. Colors grew saturated, and his clothing was rough on his body. Hank moved through layers of passing fear like walking through a series of rooms until he found something that felt like calm and rested there.

The men were distorting in front of him slowly. Their faces were made from hot wax, pooling around them, to reveal a truer face. Kelvin's scowl seemed to fold on itself until his head was made completely of downturn eyebrows and frown lines. His brown wrinkles shifted and deepened, one of them now a mouth, and Hank wondered how wrinkles could speak.

"Dammit, Shakes," the winking line said, "you just fucked this dude up."

Shakes's smile stretched and pulled far outside the confines of his head, and his yellowed, crooked teeth made a long cobblestone path. His hand was flittering hummingbirds, constantly moving.

"Ah, he's all right," said the yellow stretch of cobblestoned teeth, somehow encased in chapped lips. Then, a long, pink wet creature parted the stones and drug itself over the lips. "You okay, right, man?"

It was a question directed at Hank, and he found it impossible to answer, so he simply giggled an affirmation. A hand stretched out, arching so far up into the sky, and came down softly on his shoulder. He looked up, following the long path the hand had taken to get to him, and Gwen was the source.

He nearly gasped at her beautiful shining eyes. They were black and wide as if they belonged to a deer, and she seemed to blink with great effort. It was as if those eyelids had too far to travel just to close. She had all the stars in the sky in her eyes. Hank leaned over to her, and he saw a comet shoot past them. He made a wish, whispering it softly to no one.

"I have to speak to Kelvin for minute," she said. "Are you going to be all right?"

"I'm fyyyne," Hank said, waving at her dismissively, and the chair wobbled underneath him, no longer made of plastic but constructed entirely out of bungee cords.

Gwen got up from her chair and was ushered off through clouds with Kelvin. Hank noticed one of the clouds was a particular gray and descended on the two as they talked in a corner of the room. He didn't like the gray cloud, and Gwen smiled at the frown lines upon lines upon thick eyebrows, but she didn't seem happy either.

"You ain't right," said the shiny round mass that once was Don, shifting and bubbling on the brown couch.

Something underneath his skin moved as though it were trapped. A set of knuckles pressed against the surface of the skin. Underneath the trap of fabric and glossing pink skin, something was alive, pressing tight like the rubber of a balloon. What was it?

"What the fuck is with this dude?"

"He's fine, Don."

"Mother fucker, he's staring at me."

"Be happy somebody is."

Contours and bumps gathered to a point on the skin. They withdrew into the bulk, and then pressed forward into the outline of a face. They protruded through, blindly rolling along, and turned toward Hank through the fabric and skin. The face smiled at Hank, and he smiled back.

Hank peered back at Gwen in the gray cloud. He wanted to show her the smiling face in the skin. But she was preoccupied, and her face was now grim. Hank noticed tiny flashes of static around the cloud as Kelvin slipped something in her hand. Gwen placed this small object into her purse, and then withdrew money and handed it to Kelvin. Hank heard the rumbles of thunder from the cloud around them.

23

The days that followed in Jones's office were ones of stress. The beautiful Todd Nicolas and his men waged a full-scale invasion on the magazine. During the official announcement of the buyout, Jones wondered if a mutiny would break out. In her Xanax-induced reverie, her colleagues took to the office with lit Molotov cocktails and pitchforks. But no riots broke out among the cubicles, just fretful faces shooting Todd and his team leery glances. An icy distance and passive aggression took ahold of them.

None of which Todd seemed to catch on to. He spent his first week catering lunch for the office and going to each cubicle and introducing himself to each employee. He offered compliments and cracked jokes, and with each day, he wore down at the barrier between himself and his new employees.

His efforts were quite effective with Jones. He would pass her office and smile at her quickly, like small tokens traded in secret. The first few occasions, Jones had convinced herself it was mere coincidence that she should happen to feel the warmth of his smile. Over the course of the week, it continued to happen, and Jones smiled back. Once she acknowledged this clandestine exchange between them, it happened regularly. Posted behind her desk, she would count the times he would pass by, always with at least one member of his team trailing behind, to smile. She began to think this was his only motivation to move along the office at all.

And although she was afraid of how problematic it was to be attracted to her new boss, she couldn't help it. There was so little indulgence in her life, and the work was mushrooming with the new restructuring, managing not only her team but being introduced to a whole new network within the Nichols-Griffin Art Institute itself. She often felt as though she were cramming two entities together, and she was certain she would destroy them both. Her Xanax bottle grew emptier and lighter until only a few pills rattled within it.

The workdays stretched into nights, and the pressure for a polished edition of the magazine bore down on Jones. She knew that in light of the change Chicago Modern Art Magazine would have to prove a worthy investment.

Yet through all of this, Todd Nicolas's smile was the oscillation of a lighthouse on a black night. And this frightened Jones. Her heart fluttered and her legs bounced underneath her desk. There was rising desire for this man in her, and in each of her attempts to evade this, she buckled each time he peered in at her with his faithful smile. This small admission of his desire for her stirred so much in her. Then at the end of the work day, no matter how late, she would pass through the cold evening to her apartment and Derek.

Guilt would rip at her insides, and she would spit acid at Derek, who, none the wiser of her promotion or this festering attraction to another man, would awake early each morning to brew her hot coffee. In bed, slowly sipping from the mug, she would ache deeply from the weight of Derek's love until she saw Todd Nicolas smile.

The office emptied out, and the overhead lights were shutting off. Jones had taken too many Xanax and lost time. She knew she would be alone at this an hour later and would have to close the office. But here in this office, even laden down by due dates, at least she was in control and far away from her drafty apartment and Derek within, who was probably looking at the stats on his app.

There was a knock on her door, and Todd stepped through.

"Hey," he said.

"Hey."

She stared at him for a moment, aware of the emptiness of the office. Her throat began to tingle with the promise of this privacy and what they could do.

"Do you have plans tonight?" he asked.

"No."

"Come with me. I want to show you something."

There were so many reasons she should've said no, but in the commerce of those smiles between them, she couldn't possibly deny him. He was standing at her door, and his hand was outstretched. She pushed herself up and away from her desk, traveled over the chasm of reason, and took his hand. They walked through the office, back lit from the city outside. They rode the elevator side by side in a supernatural repose as if they'd been close like this for years. Downstairs and outside, they hugged the walls of the building while a taxi pulled up.

Todd opened the door and stepped back to let Jones in as the cold whipped at her. Once inside the moving car, Todd directed them deeper into River North. The night around them glimmered along in wisps of white carried along the shiny glass walls of skyscrapers and within the bends of golden streetlights. Contained in the warmth of the taxi, now aware of Todd's very physical presence, his breath adding fog to the window, snow melting in his hair, Jones forgot the cold. She allowed herself to immerse in the glow.

The taxi let them off in front a sleek modern building. Its glass and steel stretched up several stories, and its illumination poured onto the street corner. Nichols-Griffin Art Institute arched over the doors they pushed through

"Mr. Nicolas," said a cheery old woman in a gray security uniform behind a round desk in the lobby.

"Hey, Greta, did your daughter get the flowers?"

A handsome smile stretched over the woman's face. "Sure did! She loved them."

Jones and Todd moved forward into another elevator, taking it to the fifth floor.

"So, are you wooing your security guard's daughter?"

Todd grinned sheepishly. "No, nothing quite like that. She was in an accident. I told Greta to take off more time, but she insisted that her daughter is okay and she can work."

"That's nice of you."

"Yeah, but the board thinks I'm too nice to my employees."

"What do you think?"

They stepped out of the elevator and into a wide, dark, open space with floor-to-ceiling windows overlooking the city. Tips of skyscrapers within the skyline were cut by the thick cloud cover of a lingering storm. The snow and the wind itself surged, pressing up against the windows in blows as if they wanted to join them. Jones had almost forgotten the character of Chicago. She had been too cold to look around outside, only concerned with the few feet in front of her and how many steps she took until she was someplace warm.

They faced one another for a lingering moment.

"I think I'm the boss and I can do what I want," he said, and it was spoken with arrogance as if he were stating the most common fact.

His words stung at her and reminded her why she shouldn't have been here with him.

"Stay here," he said.

He walked to the far wall, and Jones turned from him and toward the windows. She began to think about Derek and his coffee in the morning, his wet shoes in her bed, and his failing app. The guilt she had been escaping had found her. She should put an end to this attraction she had with this man before it was too late.

Then with a loud snap, light flooded the room and she was aware of several flat rectangular shapes hanging suspended in the air as if floating. They were underneath the spotlight, and all trapped in the air on fine wires extending from the ceiling and anchored in the floor. It was a terrible way to display the art—strung up in the middle of the room, unprotected, contrived, and fervently trying to be innovative. She walked closer toward them and saw the art mounted within each rectangle.

It was Russell Cowell's portrait of his girlfriend, a simple bartender at Stratosphere. She had seen a few of his pieces, but here, surrounded by the series of portraits of this woman, she felt the warmth of the artist. His gentle brush strokes along her bare back, the softness in her face, the slope of her hip. He had managed to exalt a woman into something ethereal. Jones was embarrassed and wanted to look away at first from the naked form of the woman stretching out before her. But she couldn't pull away from this act of adoration by a man in love. So much a bitter reminder of how she used to be touched, of how she wanted to be touched. She could almost feel the artist's fingers along the woman's thighs. Jones saw the power of this artist's love for her—she felt his love for her. How could a man ever look at a woman like that? How could he feel like that about a woman? Surely, it couldn't have sustained itself, but something in those colors fleshed within the oil pigments hoped for it, a half-whispered vow and a murmured promise.

She suddenly saw why Isabelle grieved for Russell's departure and why Todd Nicolas, in all his power and influence, had taken him away from her. Jones turned to him, and the tingle returned in her throat and filled her mouth with an acrid taste. She shook her head. Even in Isabelle's small gallery, the manner in which she displayed the art was exponentially more tasteful than Todd Nicolas's exhibition. It was as if he didn't know how to harness so much beauty.

"Why am I here?" Jones asked.

Todd approached her, his eyes gleaming, as beautiful as the art that surrounded them.

"You feel it, too, don't you?"

He paced around the room, slowly circling Jones and the floating art. When he finally stopped, he was standing behind her. The back of Jones's neck tickled through her hair as he breathed her in. She began to tap her feet underneath his adoration and her back stiffened. Todd sensed this and stepped back.

"I'm sorry," he said. "I didn't mean to make you feel uncomfortable."

Jones spun around, and he was wonderfully clumsy— somehow powerful and fallible all at once. Uncertainty was kind to his face. He cleared his throat and smiled, and it passed so quickly as if it had never happened. He now shifted his gaze toward the hanging art and gave a sweeping gesture toward it.

"It's beautiful," he said. "Isn't it?"

"Yes."

"You know, I suffered from a really bad bout of depression."

"Really?"

Todd narrowed his gaze at her, and Jones's stomach twisted. "I tried to commit suicide and failed."

He held out his wrist to her and pulled back his sleeve. A vertical line of raised flesh sat an inch up from his palm. He then flashed her the corresponding one on the other wrist. Jones touched his scars with her fingers, and then blushed.

The muscles along Jones's back tensed and raised goosebumps along her skin. She stepped back, feeling as if she would slip and drown in all this tension and this terrible beauty locked in the man before her. She looked away, facing another portrait of the artist's lover. Desire was potent from everywhere in this room, and she was drowning in it. She turned back to Todd, who now glanced back at her, his face, his strong form so utterly, ghastly exquisite.

"I feel it," she said, and bit back a soft breath from the relief of finally admitting that attraction.

She felt all of it here, surrounded by the painted murmurs of love, the promises of what could be. Her shoulders grew slack for moment, muscles in her back unknotted themselves, and she was helpless before him. Jones was so unnerved by this that tears stung her eyes. Her breath quivered in her. And then the alleviation passed and malice replaced it. His smiles had brought her here to the room's garish allure, with nothing for him to lose. She had fought for her promotion, and he had undone her so swiftly.

He must've sensed this, and he pulled her so quickly to him that she had to lean on him completely to keep from falling. She let her weight drape over him, her hands on his broad shoulders, her face only inches from his, and his hands along her back with his fingers tangled in her hair.

"It's okay," he whispered to her.

The closeness made her insides turn to liquid and the pleasure of it was too much. Jones couldn't remember the last time Derek had held her this way, and with him now in her mind, she pushed Todd away. She took several shaky steps back. They both stood, chests rising and falling, trying to wrangle their breaths. Jones shook her hair back and straightened her coat.

"This was . . ." She swallowed. "Great, but I should be going."

"Don't you feel it?" he asked.

"I have a boyfriend."

"Are you happy with him?"

She didn't answer because she would tell the truth. She didn't think she would be able to resist him again.

"It's been a long day," she said. "I really need to go home."

"Let me take you."

"No," she said. "No, no, that's fine. I'll take the train."

Jones walked away from him toward the elevator. Her footsteps were impossibly heavy, each one its own act of rebellion against her weak legs.

"I want you to make Russell Cowell the cover story of the magazine," he said to her once she was at the elevator.

Jones spun toward him. A tremor rocked her completely as she thought of the promise she had made to Isabelle. Sweat began to needle at her scalp, and she shook her head at him.

"I have a cover story already," she said.

"Change it to Russell Cowell."

She swallowed, already wondering how she could piece together an explanation to Isabelle. He turned away from her, decided.

"Why?" she asked him as the elevator opened behind her.

"Because this will remind you of what you felt between us," he said, "and because I'm the boss."

She didn't say another word as the elevator took her down to the street, and a night never felt colder or blacker.

24

Over the last week and a half, Noah had fallen for Isabelle. She had quickly become his addiction and he hers. He had rejected a front of indifference that he usually reserved for these situations and was constantly by her side. Noah would arrive after work in front of her door, brandishing some sort of small gift—a flower, a bottle of wine. He would flash his smile, aware of how embarrassing all of this was because it was also new. He worried that she would deny him, tell him to go back to his apartment, declare her own space, but she would step aside and allow him to come through.

Along the days and the nights, they gathered their naked bodies and drank deeply from one another. They'd cling to each other against the sound of the cold raking against the apartment building. Sometimes, they would even argue in jest, just to hear their voices together and to give the heat between them an outlet while their bodies rested after sex. Between their collective puffs from Noah's blunts, Isabelle would speak poetically, almost in song about her love for art, and Noah would talk of the abstruse theories on technological singularity and computer advancement. They laughed at the strange configuration they made.

He listened sympathetically when she confessed the trials of her insomnia, and when he told her about his father, she took him to a flower shop tucked away in Logan Square on a block he'd never seen before. The shop was run by a genteel Muslim woman who welcomed them when they came in, shaking the cold and snow from themselves. In the humid nursery amongst groves of flowers behind glass, along tables and shelves, Isabelle took him far from winter and into another season. Noah was light-headed and giddy in the thick floral perfume of the small shop. There, he picked out another yellow potted tulip, this one stronger than the one before and nurtured under the love of the store owner. Isabelle bought the flower as a sign of compassion, and Noah brought it home and set in the middle of the living room on the coffee table.

At Isabelle's persistence, she suggested they journey out into the world only to make it as far as Stratosphere. Noah had the notion that this was some sort of test to see if their dynamic could withstand a public space. Arm in arm, they pushed through the swell of people and the murky blue lights to the bar. Outside the confines of the apartment building, Isabelle was hesitant bumping into Noah, who awkwardly smiled at her, scanning her for reassurance.

The tense figures lurched their way up to the bar and ordered drinks from the woman behind the bar. Isabelle knew the woman from Russell Cowell's portrait series. Noah didn't quite hear her over the low blast of music. The bartender handed them their drinks, grinned, and told them they made a cute couple. Noah clasped Isabelle's free hand, grasping at the statement as if the bartender had somehow bestowed a blessing on them. He led them to a round booth at the rear of the bar where the crowd was thin and out of full range of the speakers.

"She said we are a couple," Isabelle said, then laughed.

"Aren't we?"

Isabelle froze with her straw between her lips. She fumbled with her drink and opened her mouth to speak. Noah silenced her with a shake of his head.

"I'm only kidding," he said, diffusing the tension with a smile. "We're good, right?"

Isabelle nodded.

"Then we don't have to define this."

He placed his arm around her and she moved in closer. If this had been a test, he suspected that he'd just passed it.

Isabelle relaxed against him, and soon, the awkwardness slowly crumbled. Under the dim blue light, close to him with a drink in hand, Isabelle whispered softly to him about work. But this conversation, like the few they'd had in his or her bed, was different, heightened by being in this space where it had started. And although Noah wasn't in a rush to title their relationship, he wouldn't be opposed to it.

This felt good. This was good.

Isabelle had sipped the last of her drink, and Noah had finished his drink a while ago.

"One more?"

"Yeah," Isabelle said.

Noah proceeded back into the crowd at a slow shuffle, nodding at a few familiar faces, toward the bar. He ordered another round from the bartender, giving her a generous tip for the earlier compliment. An influx of people now pressed into Stratosphere, and the way back to the booth had grown hazardous with a drink in each hand. Through his drag forward, he spotted Marcie, his ex-girlfriend's scowl flaring underneath the blue lights. She returned his look and waved at him to join her.

There was a hope that he could pretend that he hadn't seen her. But in his peripheral vision, she moved toward him like an approaching storm. He plowed forward, and a stray elbow emerged from the darkness and slammed into his wrist. He saved Isabelle's drink, but half of his spilled down the front of his shirt. He surveyed the damage as whiskey soaked through to his skin.

"Hey," Marcie said, appearing supernaturally from the shadows of the crowd.

She reviewed him, shaking her head in dismay. Marcie pulled a wad of tissue from a small clutch underneath her arm and began to dab at his wet torso.

"Marcie," Noah said gravely, scowling at her.

She pursed her lips at him, and he felt himself sliding into the past. He was inert against it, dripping and caged against a compact wall of people. He lost sight of Isabelle. A swarm of guys laughing in their own amusement eclipsed her.

Marcie's gentle pats felt as if they became a full-on assault. This gesture of kindness was off-putting and historically meant she wanted something. His scowl redoubled, and he frantically shrugged her off, nearly spilling the drinks again.

"What?" he said.

"You're a mess," she said softly, still coming at him with a fist full of tissue.

"Stop it."

She placed her hand gently on his chest, and it slowly slid up his neck until her cold hand was on his cheek. He sidestepped, teeth clenched and eyes narrowed.

"What the fuck do you want?"

Marcie blinked at him, and then cackled. "The girl you're with—who is she?"

"No one."

"Bullshit. You like her."

Heat rose to Noah's face. His stomach skittered in his abdomen. He edged back into the group of guys still laughing. One of them nudged him roughly back into Marcie.

"She is none of your damn business," Noah said, and now the drinks were heavy in his hands and his fingers were numb from the cold glasses.

"Oh, don't be such a bitch. You're a good person," she said, then added darkly, "You deserve to be happy, and so do I."

"I have to get back," Noah said, looking for a break in the crowd.

"Is she a good person?"

The pack of guys behind them began to stir, and Noah and Marcie moved deeper into the bar to avoid the fray. They stood in a patch of inky blackness, wedged deeper into the strangers. The air was dank with sweat and breath. Marcie leered at him, appearing perhaps more comfortable in the darkness. She fell into a brief contemplative silence. Noah's rapid heart rose to his throat and nearly choked him. He could see her arranging ends and pieces, trying to get at something. And after all these years, Noah was still a pawn in her agenda. He could no longer be restrained by the drinks. On the wall, he found a ledge where forsaken empty glasses and bottles sat.

"You listen to me," he said, jabbing his index finger at her face, "whatever you're doing—I don't want any part of it."

Marcie pushed his finger out of her face. "She must be truly wonderful." Then, she smirked, and said, "But does she fuck better than me?"

"Noah?"

Isabelle worked her way through a few people to join them. There was a tense silence between them as Isabelle tried to work out what was happening.

"Noah, who is this?"

"No one," he said sharply, turning to Isabelle.

"I'm Marcie," she said over his shoulder.

"Let's go," Noah said.

He grabbed Isabelle's hand and plowed through the crowd despite the protests made by a few as he collided into them.

"What's going on?" Isabelle said, yanking her hand from his grasp.

"Nothing."

He continued forward, and Isabelle reluctantly followed him to coat check, where they collected their things and ventured out into the night. Noah's hands trembled against his nerves as he lit a cigarette. He marched ahead as Isabelle's frustration turned into a muted simmer. The train arrived as they ascended the platform, and they took it west in seething quiet. Noah shivered until they arrived at their apartment building. He walked solemnly up the stairs and to Isabelle's door.

She slowly unlocked her door and rested her hand on the door handle.

"She's the girl you told me about," Isabelle said. "She broke your heart."

Noah shuddered violently and nodded. Isabelle sighed, and then hugged him. What had been frustration in her face softened. She nuzzled her face into the crook of his neck and kissed it. Isabelle opened her door and led him inside.

Images of Marcie shifted through more shadows. Her face and the lines around her mouth held an inky blackness as she unrolled her smile. She opened her mouth and an awful hollow sound rattled Noah's head. He stepped back but felt restricted, as if moving through thick tar. She grew closer to him, and for a moment, he thought he was back at Stratosphere. Noah was worried for a moment that he'd been tricked. Had he made it back to Isabelle's apartment and into her arms? He began to protest with a violent strain, and then his eyes snapped open to the night around him.

He lay in Isabelle's bed, covered in a fine layer of sweat. He wiped away the plastered hair on his forehead. He didn't know how late or early it was. There was a period of respite as he climbed out of the pit of his nightmare and back into reality. His feelings were short-lived as the hollow sound from Marcie's mouth had followed him into the real world. He felt a sudden heavy panic under his ribs as he heard the noise once more. He listened until logic gave way and the howl was only the wind pushing against brick, using alleyways like chambers in an instrument. His breath was shaky, and he felt for Isabelle, who should have been next to him. His hands unfolded over the empty sheets next to him. He squinted in the darkness until shapes assembled themselves into the room around him.

Isabelle was perched up, sitting on the side of the bed. She appeared inanimate, carved from the material of night itself. Her naked form was outlined in the silver glow of streetlights. An intense worry coiled her face, and she blinked, staring at nothing. Her hand rested on her knees. And Noah knew she had been this way for a long time.

She startled when he sat up. He swung his legs over the edge of the bed to be next to her. He placed his arm around her, and she was cool and stiff to his touch.

"You okay?"

"Go back to sleep," she said.

He didn't move and joined her for a moment, looking out at the darkness. Jagged shadows from barren trees against the window migrated from one corner of the room to another and back again as car headlights from the street below slowly rolled past. He remembered his dream and nearly expected Marcie to be there with whatever plot she was working on.

He didn't want to think about her and grabbed Isabelle tighter. She grew uneasy from his company and began to fidget with the edge of her sheet. He had stumbled across Isabelle's intimate misery of insomnia and refused to let her suffer alone.

"Please go back to sleep."

"Only if you let me hold you."

There was an objection made by her in the form of a sigh and a yawn. They lay back in bed, and Isabelle was back in his arms against his chest. She was a plank in his arms, and Noah wondered what thoughts kept her awake.

"I can't go back to sleep unless you tell me what's wrong."

"Noah, what are we doing?"

"Well, if you want to spend all night worrying, please don't do so on my behalf. I don't know what we are doing, but I'm holding you. I'm looking for any reason to touch you. I'm looking for any reason to spend time with you.

I'm going to try to do this until you get sick of me. How is that?"

"This is just happening so quickly."

Noah inhaled deeply, and Isabelle's head rose on his chest. "So, what are you saying? You want to be my girlfriend?"

She angled her face on his chest until their eyes met. The heaviness in her expression was indecipherable. She turned away from him and placed her hand on his chest. Her body became soft and pliant against his.

"If that's what you want."

Noah bit back a chuckle. "Yes, that's what I want."

He wanted to reassure her. He resisted the urge to pull her tightly against him until there was no separation between them. He closed his eyes, dazed. It was doubtful if Isabelle would join him in sleep, but in his slumber, he wanted to hold her.

25

Hank had attempted to reach out to Gwen since the party, but all attempts had failed. The night of the party, they had traveled back to his apartment. In Hank's rapturous high, swinging from searing terror to elation, his thoughts crashed and stacked upon each other in a jumbled heap. He watched Gwen all night. He kissed her. She thrilled him, and she carried in her small hands and sharp smile the command of his mortality. And it was certainly the drug, whatever had laced the weed, still searing the lining in his throat and lungs, but that night, when he had her lips, they were the softest thing he could remember. That night he drifted high enough to expand into his own cumulus cloud, to scrape at the outer rings of the atmosphere. He devoured her. She graciously allowed him, and he was scantly aware that she was on something, too. Her head lolled back, and her mouth was slack as he pulled off her clothes. Her fingers jabbed into the muscles of his back as she pulled him into her. Gwen's skin was electric on his palms, and he came quickly, then bumbled into sleep.

When he awoke, she had vanished, and then a wall of agony toppled onto him in jagged blocks. The comedown on whatever he had smoked had left him drained as if someone had taken a rusty spoon and emptied him out. The next morning, he shut his blinds and turned off all the lights. Hank, up on his depleted legs, sought the darkest corner of his apartment like a dog sniffing soil for the perfect place to shit. In all his efforts, the sunlight had somehow found him, scattering from cracks in blinds, spaces under the doors, and even his eyelids didn't protect him. To escape the light, he fled into his closet with a blanket and holed up there as if it were a storm shelter.

In his melodrama, Hank, again, wished he could die because of a woman. He was the punchline at the end of a cruel joke that Gwen was playing on him.

He was racked with clammy sweats, a stomach rocking on choppy waves at sea, and a knifing headache. He ached for food and yet couldn't keep any of it down. Was his stomach ruined because of the laced weed or a smoldering anger for Gwen? Admittedly, before the donning of his outerwear, shirt, and shoes, he'd pulled out his phone. He called her three times. Each time, there was the strident drum of her dial tone and a woman's mechanical voice informing him that the mailbox was full. Crestfallen, he turned on his side and brought his knees to his chest.

The sky was a smoky dusk before Hank emerged from the closet. He went to bed early, trying half-heartedly to accept that she had left and may be gone permanently. The trap had snapped. The joke had run its course. His thoughts buckled, and he gave in to sleep.

Hours, or what felt like minutes later, Hank's door intercom buzzer lanced through the night. He shot straight up, grabbing his chest as if his heart had burst from his chest. He sat up in bed, collecting his bearings alone in the darkness. He reached for his phone on a fold-up chair that was acting as a nightstand. The screen read 2:44 AM and the missed attempts of Gwen to reach him. Hank scrambled out of bed. In haste, he collided into the doorframe as he made his way to the intercom to buzz her in.

He waited by the door, making a bitter vow that he wouldn't let her in. A deep need for reciprocity churned his insides. He heard through the door floorboards objecting under light footsteps. He pressed his face against his peephole. The lens he looked out warped Gwen into cartoonish portions, her skin chalky and the tip of her nose, a vivid red, pulled impossibly forward. Around her eyes, she was puffy, and black mascara tears trailed along her face in streaks.

Hank dismissed his frustration for her as if casually turning the channel on his TV. He stared back at the watery-eyed woman as she leaned against the door and quaked with sobs. She had been otherworldly when he had met her. A pure sexual being, exclusively carnal. Not quite a woman then, but more of this elevated concept, a lurid fantasy. Now, with the door as a barrier between them, she was more human to him than she had been when he'd first touched her. This discovery was a wondrous confusion. He was locked in place, and for a moment, he watched her crying. She was vulnerable tender flesh, and in her angst, she had come to him.

He opened the door. She rushed in, winding her arms around his neck. Her sobs choked in his ears. She was fallible, and she was here with him. He needed nothing else but this.

"I'm so scared."

"What is it?" he asked.

"I fucked up," she said.

She didn't offer more than that. She closed the door and wiped under her eyes. She walked over to his couch and rifled through her purse. She brought a cigarette to her lips and continued to search her purse. Gwen cried in frustration and slapped her knees with both hands.

"Can I get a light?"

Hank reached for her cigarette and went to his kitchen. He stuck it in his mouth, turned on his stove, and leaned forward to bring the cigarette to the flame. He exhaled slowly, aware at how the landscape of his empty apartment had changed now that Gwen had entered. The air vibrated slightly, and he was grateful she was here despite the shape she was in. He breathed the cigarette again.

He entered his living room and sat next to her. He stared back her, withholding her lit cigarette like it was a bargaining chip.

"Where have you been?"

"Dealing with things."

He hit the cigarette again, and smoke discharged from his nostrils. He glared at her, unsatisfied. She looked back at him as the unanswered questions hardened between them.

"What do you want from me?" she asked.

"The truth," he said, and handed her the cigarette.

"You make it sound as if I'm lying."

"The party we went to—what was that?"

She took a long drag from the cigarette. She regarded him mutinously, and Hank realized that all that jarring humanity that had led him to open the door had been packed away somewhere. It was just out of reach behind bars, to be observed but not attained. He knew he wouldn't be able to get to her, and his chest constricted. Gwen was now closed off to him again, as warm and safe as if this was her home and he was the brazen interloper.

"It was a party," she said coolly.

"What do mean, you've 'fucked up'?"

"I had a fight with my roommate."

"Roommate?"

"Yeah, roommate."

Hank now didn't know what to do with himself. He wanted to find his earlier anger. She had abandoned him in the middle of the night, dragged him out into some unknown part of the city, and he could even argue that she'd put him in harm's way. She had played him—to what means, for what purpose, he didn't know. He looked for his fury, maybe a smoldering cinder of conviction, but his disappointment was tremendous. He couldn't rouse the sense of righteousness it would take to be angry at her again. She sensed this in him and leaned forward and kissed him for his concession.

He thought of pushing her off him. But he wanted her here with him in his apartment. He wanted that more than his anger. In his incurable, nascent arousal, he kissed her back and she pulled off her shirt. And this signaled a rush of confused fingers, tugging off her jeans, pulling at the elastic band of his underwear. Her abrupt hand was cold on his cock, and he gasped. And without the interruption, she leaned back on his couch, liberated herself from her jeans, and straddled him there.

He let out a guttural moan, sliding inside her. She ground herself against him and grabbed fists full of his hair and pulled like she wanted to tear it from the roots. She was warm and wet crashing down on him, skin slapping against skin. She descended on him over and over again. Parts connected. Motion in a furious desperation. Maybe they were both trying to outrun a truth that had been too close. He was being led somewhere into peril. He closed his eyes and parted his mouth, unable to breathe, unable to feel anything but a horrible, fervid vertigo.

Hank thought about his upstairs neighbors and how many times he had been forced to hear them through the floor. He had heard them walking about his head earlier this evening. He knew the noise that he and Gwen were making was loud enough to travel through the walls. This was something that he never would have done with Andrea— her sense of modesty was too great. The thrill traveled up Hank's back, and he joined Gwen in her cries.

She grabbed the back of his neck and tugged back hard. Hank delighted in the pain shooting through his spine and whimpered and shuddered. His voice sailed over them, and he moaned for her, an offering to her. She put her mouth on his ear and whispered harshly. He couldn't make out her words.

Hank adjusted underneath her. She yanked back harder on his head.

"Don't move," she said again, pounding herself against him quicker.

She arched her back and drew in a ragged breath as her thighs clamped around him. In the vise of legs, he came and brayed out in desperation. He cried out for her humanity that she refused to give to him. And now, post-orgasm, he at least knew what he had been running from, what he had hoped to lose in fucking her. He shrank inside her as he could feel her blank stare on him. There was a lurch along his back and horror that she would abandon him. She would simply fall in the pit made from all her secrets.

She scared him deeply.

He opened his eyes, and she stared at him darkly, just as he'd imagined.

He was so scared. Words were snared up in him as she climbed off him and walked toward his bedroom. He sat cold, wet, and deflated from her, trying to work out what to do next.

"Are you coming?" she called from his bedroom.

He locked his front door, cut off the light, and complied.

26

Jones needed to refill her prescription. In her lap, out of the line of sight, she counted the last three little pills at her desk. She decided she would have to save them. She placed them carefully back in the bottle like they were raw gemstones. The day was approaching its end, and Jones had sustained without her Xanax and without the presence of Todd Nicolas.

In between scheduling appointments, dealing with the new cover story he had forced upon the magazine, and subduing the frustration of the staff, she caught herself looking up from her computer and down the aisle of cubicles for his straight shoulders, his flash of blond hair— those elements of his ghastly beauty. It happened once in the beginning of the day, a simple glance up from her computer at her door. At first, she didn't realize who she was looking for until her gaze pressed on for five minutes uninterrupted. Maybe her compulsion was driven by a need for resolution, but soon, on every hour, and now in the last hour of the day, she was peering up from her desk and out into the office.

She told herself, scrolling through her emails, that it was good he wasn't in the office. But then again, she did want to discuss the new cover story with him. Possibly in the clarity of a new day, out of the isolation of his gallery, his trying to touch Jones, and her desperately wanting to yield to it, she could tell him how horribly unprofessional their interaction had been. If there were feelings, it would serve as a hindrance to the magazine.

She would say this to him. But the truth, the reason she kept searching for him with the obsession she would a misplaced object, was that there were feelings. There was something troubled yet kinetic with him, and when he had his arms around her, she had wished to stay there. She thought about how the scar on his wrist felt on her fingertips. She wondered what could've driven him to suicide and how such a beautiful man could carry something so dark. Why had he told her this? She loathed Todd for that. Even though she would huff at him about this breach in conduct, she was injured that this workday had come and gone without the sight of him at her door.

She would have glowered at him, possibly chastised him, but she wanted his smile nonetheless.

She placed her pill bottle back in her purse and took out her phone. The screen glowed with three missed calls. One had been from Isabelle, and the other two had been from Derek.

She had slinked out of the apartment this morning without speaking to Derek. She couldn't stand to look at Derek, and the night with Todd Nicolas crushed the walls of her chest. She'd had to sidestep him completely—the grisly hit-and-run of Derek's affection and her rebuff. The coffee mug on her nightstand was left untouched. The artisan bagel in the toaster was cold. Tonight, if she came home, she would have to sift through that. But now, with only three Xanax as a safeguard, she couldn't formulate a plausible excuse.

She instead called Isabelle, who was inexplicably cheerful on the phone. Jones instantly didn't trust it. But her suspicion buckled into guilt. She knew she'd have to share with Isabelle that she wouldn't be the cover story in the magazine. At this point, with all the reworks needed to make the deadline, Jones possibly wouldn't even be able to get her in a small article. Maybe Isabelle would be open to other options. Jones could have facilitated a meeting with someone or offered some discounted advertising in her magazine. So, when Isabelle asked her to dinner, Jones had quickly said yes.

The weather had let up in a way only a Chicagoan could appreciate, moving from the subarctic teens to a cool thirty-eight degrees. The ill-fated Polar Vortex was set to miss them and pass southeast, leaving the city untouched. Jones had her reservations on how factual this claim was, but the temperature hadn't dropped and the sun withdrew hours ago. The snow hadn't fallen all day, and residual snow piles occupying corners, alleys, and parking lots deteriorated into mounds of black and brown slush. Outside was so tolerable that Jones agreed to travel to a restaurant called By Land and By Sea in Logan Square next to Isabelle's gallery. When she had stepped through the doors into the restaurant, she was flushed, nearly grateful. She found Isabelle at the booth, staring about her in the manner of giddiness that she'd spoken with earlier on the phone. The restaurant itself was starting to fill up, and the rumble of conversation, chairs against tiles, and silverware against plates surrounded Jones.

Isabelle was light, and her face was taut as if restraining a smile.

"Well?" Jones said, sitting across from her.

"The guy in the building."

"Yes?"

"Well," Isabelle said, then paused, clutching her hands on the table as if information was there. "I think it's getting serious."

Jones involuntarily teetered back away from the table and into her booth. She knew the last week had been busy for the both of them, but she hadn't expected this.

"What do you mean by serious?"

"We're dating."

A scowl whipped across Jones's face. "But he sleeps around."

Isabelle drew in a sharp breath to protest, but a waiter materialized between them, unaware of the crackling between them. Jones quickly ordered as sweat dropped from her armpits into her bra strap. She remembered what she would have to tell Isabelle and wheeled her skepticism back while her friend ordered. She knew her usual, at times harsh, candor wouldn't help her. She smiled at Isabelle in amnesty. When the waiter left them, any would-be anger dissipated and Isabelle sat in front of her in a foreign state of glee.

She talked about the week she'd had with Noah, and shortly, the food was set before them and Jones had hoped that would act as a deterrent. But Isabelle continued with her stories and analysis of the man upstairs. Under the table, Jones twisted her napkin in her fist.

How could Isabelle let herself lapse into this fleeting happiness? As Jones sipped from her wine and glanced down into her plate, there was a burn in her stomach that felt like betrayal. She was embarrassed by this, but it was there, despite the fact that she held on to news that would hurt her friend. How could she harbor such animus for Isabelle when she, herself, was pursued by two men? Isabelle was supposed to be her companion, her ally, and now, here she sat in front of Jones, a defector, a traitor.

The waiter came around again, refilling glasses. Isabelle continued as if reciting a jovial sermon. She practically hovered in the booth. She barely paused to take a breath and only picked at her plate with her fork. Her wide orb of hair was more coiffed and her makeup more thoughtfully applied. A soft plum enriched her mouth, and her skin shimmered. Jones squinted at her, recognizing something underneath the glimmer of her friend, shining like a coin underneath the surface of water.

"You're in love."

Jones hadn't intended on saying it aloud. The words had the ring of a damnation, and it surprised them both. Isabelle stopped and gaped at her. She reached for her glass and regarded her as she sipped. Jones ran her fingers along the hem of the napkin in her lap.

"I don't think I'm in love," Isabelle said, "but would it be a problem if I were?"

The napkin dropped from Jones's lap and was lost under the booth.

"No," Jones said, "absolutely not."

Isabelle was pleased by this answer and continued to talk about Noah's visit to her gallery. Jones's hand slipped into her purse next to her at the booth. She closed her fist around her Xanax bottle. She considered excusing herself to take the pill when Isabelle flagged down the waiter for another glass of wine. It was then that Jones decided she needed to switch to something stronger.

"Vodka on the rocks with a lime, please."

An hour later, the restaurant was nearly empty. The waiter's forbearance had turned callous, and Jones's fingertips tingled in intoxication. She had abdicated telling Isabelle about how the artist who had left her gallery would now replace her on the cover. Isabelle was so happy, and it was charitable to leave her that way—at least for this night. She couldn't face her friend's disappointment. The tab, larger than what any of them had intended on spending, was paid. The women, arm in arm, carried each other out onto the street in search of a cab. Their heeled boots splashed in snow slop, and a collective giggle was visible as misty breaths in the cold. It was too late to endure the train ride, and a cab came quickly up to the curb before either of them could rethink the decision.

The two had a small conference in the cabin of the car on which way would get them home quickest. Jones heard the protest of the cab driver—a familiar grumble emitting only from men who hated when a woman issued directions. Before he could interject, Jones quickly directed him down the street, and after a jerky cab ride, they were home. They uttered swears and tipped nothing, and Jones and Isabelle strolled up to the building.

Isabelle eyed the door to the lobby thoughtfully. She was less drunk than Jones, who stood behind her. Jones caught herself swaying slightly. Isabelle reached up and touched the gas shut-off noticed plastered on the door for a week now as if hoping it wasn't real. The notice was ripped and warped from the harsh winter, yet still stern.

"Is the landlord ever going to pay this?"

"I'm sure he has," Jones said, making a mental note to herself to email him as they made their way through the door and up the grinding stairs. The thought of the landlord made her think of the cab driver again and the inevitable disregard that would follow her email.

The landlord was a man who believed his undoubtedly tiny little gonads, fetid between his legs, required her silence and compliance. Jones was now reminded of the squalor that surrounded her in this building. Dank smells of soiled carpet filled her nose, and her gaze ran along the familiar jagged trail of the cracks in the wall. She looked back at her friend for solidarity, but Isabelle's back was turned and she was waving goodbye and journeying up to her floor.

Jones opened the door to her apartment, and a feeble, dim light pulsed from candles plunked over nearly every surface. An attempt at romance transformed the apartment into a ghastly tomb. Battered red roses coiled in cellophane lay on the coffee table, and a few stray petals had dropped from a battered blossom onto the floor. Melted candlewax overpowered the haunting stench of burned chicken and some herb. Wax rolled from a nub candle and cooled in a hard puddle. It all seemed so alien that, in a panicked second, she thought she'd walked into someone else's home. How long had it been this way?

Jones dropped her coat and purse in a nearby chair. She followed the melee into the kitchen, and Derek sat at the small table, slumped and conquered over a plate of chicken grown cold and viscid. Shadows flickered over the downturned features of his face, and his phone was glowing. He didn't immediately register that Jones had entered the room. He shook his head, and then looked up at her with rheumy eyes.

"I wanted to do something nice for you," he said in small voice, and each word came out choked.

Jones tried to speak but couldn't find any words. She backed out of the kitchen as if she'd walked in on a cornered predator. She wanted to escape all of this, and she felt her lungs flutter and her intestines sear. She was too drunk for all of this. She looked around at the candle nubs on the coffee table and on the windowsill in the living room. Nausea crashed into her, and she stumbled slightly, grabbing out to air, looking for something solid.

Derek came out of the kitchen armed with his phone, and the screen pointed to her. "I called you."

"I didn't get the call."

"I called you all day. I called you at work. I called your cell."

He thrust the phone at her, two inches from her nose. There had been several calls made while she was at dinner. She hadn't heard any of them.

"Why didn't you pick up?"

Jones backed away with her arms up. She was dizzy now, and she felt more drunk than she had been in a while.

"I was busy with work," she said.

"Did you screen my calls?" he said, marching toward her.

He was close enough that she felt the heat of his body. His breath was sour with whiskey, and his face was furrowed in so much rage that it appeared to be a mask. His wide chest heaved, and his arms were away from his body as if he were about to attack. His gait was uneven, and Jones knew he was as drunk as she.

"Work has been crazy," she offered, trying to hold her ground.

"And that's an excuse?" he asked. "What if I'd been in a hospital? What if something had happened to me?"

"Nothing has happened to you, Derek."

"You wouldn't care if it had."

"That's not true."

His face softened slightly. He seemed hopeful that second. His arms rested at his body, and Jones took a breath.

"Kiss me," he said, moving even closer until there was no space between them.

Jones turned her head in reflex.

"Please, kiss me."

Derek leaned down toward her face. His lips were parted in a gentle pucker. Jones swatted him away, and Derek expelled a strained roar. He seized her shoulders and forced his mouth on her. His mouth was rough on her face. The assault pinched her lips between his face and her teeth. Jones jerked away from him and felt the coppery taste of her blood in her mouth.

"Why won't you let me touch you?" he screamed.

Jones's chin quivered in defiance. He huffed back at her as if he would hurt her. He glared back at her as if she had no other alternative but to submit to him and his touch. She snorted dismissively and moved away and began to blow out one candle after another.

"What happened to us?" he asked, deflated, backing into a chair.

She spun to him. "Us?"

A tear fell from one of Derek's eyes, tracing a path along his cheek and hanging on his chin.

"I'm here! I'm here in this fucked-up apartment with you. I'm here in your misery. I know you lost your friends and your money. I know—"

"Shut up!" he screamed with an incredible force. He'd seemed to rattle the apartment, maybe even deepen the cracks along the walls. He lunged off the couch and to the closet. He plucked out his coat and rushed out the door.

Jones continued to blow out the remaining candles, aided by her shaky breath. She sat on the couch, and her head swam in the stench of burned wicks. She found her purse underneath her coat and fished for her pills. She sighed, relieved when they were in her hand, and swallowed two of them without water.

27

Noah was immobile in Isabelle's bed. His face was relaxed, and gentle movement fluttered behind his eyes. Isabelle suspected he was dreaming. She had managed a few hours of sleep before some force hauled her awake. She now sat up in her room, wide-eyed and utterly conscious. She drifted in the steely silence from thought to thought, following one after another in circles. Each thought somehow led her back to the statement that Jones had posed earlier during dinner, like passing a landmark along the tracks.

Had she fallen in love with Noah? Had it happened this fast, and to what extent?

She watched the deep blue shadows along her skin. They consorted along the valleys and divots made from the bodies underneath her comforter. The glow from streetlamps cut the deep blackness of her room into geometrics. Outside through the blinds, icicles dulled and dripped into a slow stream. The drops of melting dirty city ice created a soft pulse on her windowsill. There was a soft scuttling of something within the walls of the apartment, at best, plaster falling from within the walls and at worst, some undetected vermin fleeing the cold. In the night, the apartment was at its most menacing. There were no sounds of the residents to camouflage its cry of decrepitude. There was only the quake of old pipes and the whistle of wind in the hall as air rushed in from the broken panel in the front door.

This was the night when Isabelle was confronted with the familiar passage of her fears. She would normally explore her morose fears, but this night was different.

Instead of plotting the way doom would come to her, she instead watched Noah's face and thought of his chipped-toothed smile. She felt heady with this thought, and her foot brushed his hairy shin. There was still the lush agitation of where his mouth had been between her legs and, like muscle memory, his weight had been upon her body. The very memory of their sex sustained her wonderfully, and afterward, sweating in his arms, his laughter rang melodically, which she now replayed like the thrill of a new song. All that took up new residence within her, and now the space for anxiety became limited.

Noah groaned and kicked. He kicked again, expelling the comforter and sheet from his body. His naked form lay sprawled out before her. His wide chest undulated with his breathing. He groaned again, and his brow creased in distress. Isabelle smirked as she thought of those internet videos of puppies whimpering from nightmares. She reached for the cover and pulled it over him. She knelt and kissed his forehead, and his face relaxed once more.

She circled back to Jones.

"You're in love."

Isabelle couldn't be certain. That would have to wait for the morning. Isabelle sighed, her eyes falling on the shadows in the room. She told herself she didn't want to analyze this. It all felt so utterly fragile to her and could crumble under the slightest question. She lay down on the bed next to Noah. She listened to him breathe and stared up at the ceiling. Light filtered gray through the clouds, and the room turned into shades of black and white like an old film. The first sounds of the morning stirred outside on the street. Isabelle sailed between sleep and consciousness with deep, long blinks.

When she came to, Noah was over her, kissing her like she had kissed him hours earlier. His face lingered over her, and his chipped smile pulled across his face.

"Hey," he said.

"Hi," Isabelle said in a muffled voice.

It was a moment of perfection. His face made up the entire field of her vision and there was nothing else in the world but him. His smile, so peculiar, became the onset of a chill along Isabelle's arms—a chill that raised bumps along her forearms and thighs. This smile of his became hers. And there in the brevity of gestures, she had a completion when a cherished object was found.

He pulled back from her and strolled away. He was still naked, his back a strong knitting of muscles and his ass pale, round, and utterly vulnerable. His footsteps were soft as he exited the bedroom, and then the hiss of running water could be heard.

Isabelle swam from the sudden discovery of this fondness for him. She nearly reached out from her bed, wanting to protect him from everything.

The moment had passed, and Isabelle was rewinding it over and over again. New details bled into her consciousness, and as she lay in bed, she bit her lip to keep from calling him back into the room. She wanted to stare at him naked, all his inharmonious loveliness before her eyes. She wanted more details nestled into her memory.

The water was turned off and was replaced by the gruff clearing of his throat. He reentered the room, and he was heavy and alert. He found his clothing and tugged on his pants and put his arm through his shirt. He looked back at Isabelle with longing, but the world was calling to him. He smiled at her sadly, as if it were continents that separated them instead of a work day.

"Do you have the day off?" he asked her.

"Yes," she replied, then she stretched back on the bed in a humorous display of enjoyment.

Noah chuckled. "Lucky."

He went back out of the bedroom, and Isabelle followed him. They both moved slowly through her apartment. There was a relish in the dull pain of this parting because it meant the pleasure was real. He stood at the door, and Isabelle leaned against him and pressed her face against the cross-stitch of his back muscles. He turned around and kissed her quickly. He opened the door and stepped out swiftly, and they both knew if he'd hesitated, even a bit, he would be back in the bed with her. She waved as if he had climbed aboard a boat and there was a handkerchief in her hand. He set sail down the hall and down the stairs.

Isabelle idled at the door until the cold from the hall stung her toes. She closed the door and made her way through her apartment and back to her bed. She hauled the covers over her head and sank into a silliness. Her stomach fluttered, and between her fingers, her lips, and her legs, she knew with a defined clarity the truth of Jones's statement.

ii

Marcie placed a silk robe over her naked body. She strolled gracefully over the plush rug, and with each step, she paused to dig her feet into the lux fibers. She was on the twenty-second floor of a high-rise off Michigan Avenue in South Loop. She was on display, high in the rooms and walls made of glass and concrete, like jewelry in a case. She had spent the last few days here tucked away from her life, only removing her clothes for one man, who lay, lightly snoring, in the morass of sheets in the California king mattress. In those few days, she had ridden, flexed, and devastated him raw. She had bent her body across him with such fervor, with such calculation, that he belonged only to her. And she had him as he cradled her breasts while she sat on top of him like she was the very giver of life itself.

He was the man she had spent years dancing for. He was the man who had whimpered for her, who had spilled open to her. He was confined by his job, his responsibilities. Labored and beaten, driven by capital, by profit as CFO of a finance company. But there in the small room of their private dances, between the lines of coke, he would unfold before her. They traveled his fears, the futility of a career-focused life, and the loneliness, the irreverent predictability of it all, and he followed her into the night. And there, she had promised life—or maybe death, depending on how he chose to look at it.

There, between her lips and cupped in the palm of her hand, was the gift of vibrancy, the seeking of power. of audacious recklessness.

"Let's travel down this alley. Don't be frightened."

"Let's snort this until our noses bleed."

"Let's dance until our feet ache."

"Watch while I fuck her."

"Watch while I fuck him."

"Watch while I fuck them."

"Fuck me."

She was his unbridled carnality. She was his savior from his fluorescent-lit, air-conditioned world, carpal-tunneled wrists, and boredom by boardroom. Marcie was his American dream. His destiny. His elegant, coke-snorting, pill-popping destruction. He could feel with her. He could feel his power and his despair. He could feel it all with her.

She had left him in the bedroom and walked around his apartment. The furniture was clean and sleek, no doubt the handiwork of some overpriced interior designer. The couches were made from white leather, and the end tables and coffee table were a pristine black wood. On an exposed brick wall was generic art, impressionist shapes that revealed no passion. The living room was sterile, devoid of any real color. The stainless steel modesty of the kitchen was the same. The entire living space was a showroom and no genuine life was experienced there.

That's why she was here. As she walked along the couch, she let her hand extend along its length and dug her nails into it, creating creases along the supple leather. She took the cigarettes on the end table.

Marcie opened the glass door to the patio and stepped out on it. From the height she stood, she saw the entire skyline of Chicago dulled by the gloom of winter. Thick clouds were pulled through skyscrapers like the even teeth of a rake. The temperature outside had reached the high thirties and would likely stay that way. There was a winter storm miles out of the city, and according to the news, there was a high probability that it would miss the city.

It was the perfect day to fly to Miami.

Marcie lit one of the cigarettes and breathed in the smoke. She was tingling with anticipation, and she wouldn't be able to sleep until she was on the plane leaving this city. She had coaxed her dear CFO into buying her a new phone with a new number to cut ties with her old life. She didn't expect to receive any collect calls from her ex, but she wanted to ensure her liberation.

The CFO had a vacation home in Miami, so she was certain he would return to this city, but she would not. She was sure she could squeeze a few months of staying there after his departure. It was a simple exchange in commerce. She would make her life there. She would liberate herself from all the stifling weaknesses threatening to usurp her.

She could live and thrive in her dark nights, by her own rules, without regard to anyone else. It had to be that way— how else could one live? This was who she had always been, working jobs at night, baring herself before men. She loved the drunken rush of being on stage under the harsh glare of lights and lustful eyes. She would slither along the cold metal pole, and her nerves would sharpen. She had been a classical dancer before she became an exotic dancer, part of a company, but it was nothing like the clubs she worked.

When Marcie traveled those sordid spaces, those black nights, there was no need for her to display courtesy. She existed exclusively for herself.

Marcie puffed her cigarette and tried not to think of her son. She failed and saw him sucking from his inhaler and heard the haunting howl of his cries. She leaned over the edge of the balcony and looked at the swarming dots of people moving on the street and the current of traffic glowing along the streets. Her head began to spin with vertigo.

She remembered the all-out invasion of her body. When she had pissed on the strip of the pregnancy test, the revulsion had been immediate. But a small part of herself, an inaudible flutter, kept her from aborting the baby. It seemed as though it could have been her chance to change, to join the world—the world that everyone spoke of. Maybe she could emerge from the night, and she rounded her thoughts around this as she battled mercilessly against fatigue and swelling ankles. She prayed her clipped hopes that she would change to no god in particular as heartburn cauterized her esophagus. Movement whirled around in her inflating womb, and she tried to be excited, but it wasn't there. Around her, the fellow natives of her life continued to snort up and party as if on a crusade, and in her certain state, she was no longer welcomed—an outcast among outcasts.

She would still smoke cigarettes, like she did now, coaxing a guy she used to fuck to buy them for her in order to avoid the scathing stares of salesclerks. With the cigarette between her lips and her hand on her belly, she seethed, waiting for the day the child would be out of her.

And when the day had arrived, the guy she used to fuck took her to the hospital. He had hailed a cab and held her hand through the mind-numbing pain. She had spent a total of eighteen hours dazed in pain that wracked her to her core. The room was full of doctors and nurses and interns. They were all speaking to her, but she was in too much agony to respond. She cried and wept and swore until hoarse. There was so much fluid coming from her and she was frightened by it. She felt herself rip, and then shat on herself. A nurse whose face she couldn't remember told her this was normal. It was the first time in her life that she had felt shame in being naked in front of people.

This embarrassment was as traumatizing as the birth itself.

The baby came, adding his cries to her own. She didn't want to hold him. She simply wanted to be through. She wanted it to all be over, to have those doctors, the very witnesses to her humiliation, take him away.

A week later, the guy she used to fuck moved in to help and became the guy she was fucking again. He played house with her and also began to provide her with good weed and pills. He dragged her back into the world she had left. Days passed, and she still felt as though she didn't want to hold her baby. Then weeks passed, and those became months and soon years. She did enough to keep the child alive, but she couldn't give up residency in her world.

But now the guy she was fucking went to prison, and he once again became the guy she used to fuck and now called her collect. She couldn't be alone with the boy. Her child represented a failure of hers, an ugly mortality.

She looked out over the balcony, grateful to be above it and out of reach. She flicked her cigarette high into the air and watched as the breeze took the ashes over and below. There was no room for her child in Miami. She accepted this and, in the cool solitude, found a solace in this. Maybe, away from him and all the history compressed in his tiny body, she would find the fragment of freedom, of power that she'd lost.

Marcie headed back into the apartment before the cold became too much. Inside, she sat down next to the couch where there were several store bags from a shopping excursion the CFO had taken her on. It was done completely at his invitation. They had taken a private car north from his apartment on Michigan Avenue, and he took her to the mall, spending copious sums of money on her. He strutted around the submissive salespeople with her on his arm as a prized showpiece. Marcie saw that it had turned him on more than her, and she now dug into the bags to retrieve a shoebox containing a pair of Manolo Blahnik high heels that cost double what her rent had been.

The CFO stepped from his bedroom without any clothing. Marcie resisted the urge to look away. It was still awkward seeing him naked in front of her. She was still used to being the naked one, and their altered dynamic would take some adjustment on her end. He was ignorant of this and smiled at her. He wiped the sleep out of his eyes and walked to her side.

"Are you ready to leave?"

She opened the shoebox and admired the five-inch red heels. The shoes' shells were made from fine suede. Marcie smiled back at him. "Yes, but I have a few things I have to take care of back home. Don't worry, I'll make the flight."

"Good," he said. "I'll call a car for you when you're ready. But I want you to do something for me."

"Sure."

There was lust gleaming his eyes. Marcie knew this expression. She had seen it many times during the many dances she had performed for him. It was comforting that with or without his clothes, this was a constant.

"Put those shoes on for me."

Marcie took them out of the box and slowly guided her feet into them. She rose off the couch gracefully, pitching her balance as she stood. She let her robe open and fall to the floor.

28

Isabelle didn't have to be strong alone in her apartment on her day off. She had been alone for hours, and the most she'd managed was to shower and put on clothes. Her body was lead, and exhaustion rolled over like condensed fog. Her muscles were liquefied, and her spine was rigid. She, in much pain, folded her feet underneath herself on the couch and lolled to the sounds of daytime television. At sporadic intervals, the fog would lift and Isabelle's eyes would open to TV judges casting insults on those foolish enough to exploit themselves and commercials for seedy-looking lawyers offering to mitigate lawsuits for the wrongfully injured. Isabelle reached for the remote, confident that silence was a better alternative. She turned off the TV and extended herself along the couch.

The last few hours of the morning gave way to afternoon. She lay there rolling in futility, hoping her mind would yield to sleep. Each time she closed her eyes, an unsettled prodding forked through her and she felt those old anxieties of doom reaching up through the darkness of closed lids. She considered pacing or turning on the TV once more. But she knew that fear would still be there, and all she could do was relent to it. Her only solace was that they lacked the sharpness they had at night. The sense of dread was a toothless gnawing. In the cold gray of afternoon, however fragile, she could follow the narrow path of logic.

Yes, her art gallery was on the brink, but her Craigslist ad for studio space had already had eight responses, and tomorrow, she would meet with two of the artists. Yes, Jones hadn't talked to her about the story for the magazine, but she was busy with the new owner. And yes, she had fallen in love with Noah, but she was almost certain he was in love with her as well.

She could nearly make her way through these thoughts. She felt limp. Her incongruent parts started to realign, snapping with a practically audible click. She was close to at rest, at the mouth of deep sleep, when footfalls so explosive and irregular ascended the stairs in the outside hall. She jumped, awakened. It was as if someone was trying to break into one of the apartments. Isabelle's earlier ease instantly evaporated.

There was a series of violent knocks on an apartment door and a muffled voice crying in the hall. Isabelle sat up now, scanning the living room for her phone. She held her breath and looked at the brass door handle and locks on her front door. Would they be enough to keep whoever was trudging about from entering here? It was as if her anxiety had brought those ghastly thoughts into the corporeal world. She lived in a city where the threat of violence was a reality. Isabelle swallowed and eased her feet to the ground, with the blind hope that the floorboards wouldn't betray her. She would head to her room, putting distance between whoever that was and herself and search her bedroom for her phone.

She heard the muffled intonation of speech. The voice was soft, belonging to a woman. This stopped Isabelle in midstride as the muffled speech called out for Noah. She made her way toward her door, hopping quietly on the balls of her feet, and peered through the peephole. Whoever it was stood out of her range of vison. A manic gait stormed up to another floor of the building. The voice was now screeching for Noah at full volume over her head.

Isabelle cracked the door and glanced out. She saw nothing, then tepidly edged into the hall. Grimy wet carpet soaked her bare feet. The cold air was vaporous with cheap cleaner and ancient dust. The voice above flooded her with adrenaline. She should've called the police, but this woman was screaming for Noah.

"Noah! I know you live here!"

Isabelle was halfway up the stairs when she realized she had forgotten her phone. She heard shuffling from the hall down the stairs. And there, on the stairway, was Marcie, Noah's ex, staring down at her with a face tight with distress. The woman was draped in a fur coat, perched on hazardously high heels. She was more beautiful now in the gray light than she had been in the darkness of Stratosphere, but her eyes, now transfixed on Isabelle, were wild and unsettling. Had she heeded the call of Isabelle's anxiety?

They both stood there, sizing one another up. The cold now heated in tension. Isabelle, empowered by this morning and the still palpable memory of Noah's kiss, confronted her.

"Noah isn't here," she said. "He's at work."

"When will he get back?" Marcie asked. Her voice was distended, and she spoke between clenched teeth.

Isabelle realized that Marcie was half-turned and something moved behind her. There was a shift in the shadows behind her as if they belonged to her and someone else. Isabelle arched her neck to see, and Marcie adjusted to reveal nothing.

"Why do you need to know?" Isabelle asked.

A small hand, nearly two times smaller than Marcie's, reached from behind the shadow and clutched at the end of her fur coat.

"It is better that I talk to him."

"Well, he won't be back until later," Isabelle said.

Marcie had a phone and a gaudy metallic clutch in her hand. Her phone rang, and her face grew flushed. She took a shallow breath, her face softened, and she answered it.

"What?" Marcie said, her voice velvet. "I know the flight leaves in an hour. I know. I'm dealing with the kid right now, but his father isn't home."

Isabelle recoiled and reached for the banister to prevent herself from falling. The burden of her exhaustion had doubled back onto her, and she considered collapsing onto the drafty, filthy stairs and closing her eyes. Did she hear correctly?

It couldn't have possibly been true.

"A kid?" she said in breathy whisper.

Noah never mentioned having a child with this woman. Isabelle was caving in on herself.

Marcie turned from the phone, and both women were beginning to drown in panic. From behind the bulk emerged a small child with a backpack. His entire presence was gray, with dirt from his old jacket to his greasy hair peeking through his knit hat. His lips were stained pink with Kool-Aid, and a line of dried snot crusted the tip of his nose. His dark eyes were wide in his tiny face, darting from Isabelle to the hall and back again. The child appeared to be plucked out of one of the dirty mounds of snow littered with trash. He couldn't have been spawned from Marcie, who stood before Isabelle in her nimble, nearly a comically prototypical beauty. This boy appeared to be forgotten. This child was a ploy to extort money on 1-800 commercials for children in an impoverished country after a major natural disaster.

Isabelle felt the stairs rock beneath her feet as if she were on a boat at sea.

"Yes," Marcie said, "this is Noah's child."

Marcie opened her clutch and extracted several folded papers. She quickly shoved them into Isabelle's chest. She turned on the stairs and crouched down to face the child.

"You're going to stay with this nice lady until your daddy comes home from work. Then, you'll live with him from now on. Mommy's moving to Miami," she said, and pushed past Isabelle.

Isabelle shook her head, gasping at the air. She stumbled down the stairs after Marcie, lit with horror. At the bottom of the steps, before the woman could push her way toward the sidewalk, Isabelle grabbed her arm.

"What the hell are you doing?" Isabelle cried.

Tears burned her eyes and elongated the image of Marcie in front of her. The pace of the world was moving too fast around Isabelle. She couldn't keep up with it. She needed Marcie to stay and answer questions. But Marcie had hardened like marble in her resolve. She opened her clutch again and pulled out an inhaler and placed it in Isabelle's palm.

"I almost forgot to give you this," she said, and wrenched her arm free.

Her phone rang again, and Marcie answered, her voice rolling into purrs. She shoved through the door and out of sight. Isabelle was readying to follow the woman out into the street when she remembered she didn't have on any shoes and began to feel the cold in her feet.

She closed one palm around the inhaler and the other around the papers. She'd left the child alone in the hall. She rushed up the stairs, tripping up the last few as the child came back into view.

The child had sat down patiently on the stairs with his arm neatly placed over his dirty jeans. He stared back at Isabelle with a solemn face—a face of someone accustomed to being left behind.

29

A slate-colored mass of clouds eclipsed the sky, and around midafternoon, a darkness descended like night. The first manic flurries streaked across the window of Noah's shop. He wondered if the slight warm-up in the temperature was only winter drawing back to issue a forceful blow. Over the crackling radio, between music, the DJ issued a furtive warning about the impending snow levels that could break historical records.

He sighed and returned to the scattered parts of a hard drive on his desk. Outside his workspace, he heard Hank speaking to the part-time employees. One was gathering his coat in preparation to leave in an effort to avoid the storm. The other one was pleading his case to do the same. Noah shifted on his stool and stifled his wheeling irritation. He and the staff knew that Hank wouldn't take much coaxing and would let them off early despite the avalanche of work orders. The hostility between Hank and him still continued to crackle, and their staff had caught wind of it. Lately, they had been angling the two of them against each other like kids in a divided household.

Noah turned from Hank's muted conversation with the employees. He walked through the workspace into the rear break room. He opened the refrigerator habitually, looking for nothing in particular, when he heard the chirp of a missed call from his phone tucked deep in his jacket pocket hanging on the coat rack along the wall.

He retrieved it and on the screen were eight missed calls from Isabelle and several texts demanding that he call her. He scrolled through the texts, and as they progressed, they deteriorated into monosyllabic cries. He felt her urgency, and by the time he called her, fear was shifting into him.

"Where have you been?" Isabelle said, breathless and sharp.

"At work. Are you okay?"

"No. Jesus, no."

"What is it?"

"Marcie came over and dropped off your kid."

Noah strained to hear her voice. The words weren't lining up in any order he could understand.

"You never told me you had a kid."

"What? I don't have a kid. I don't know what you're talking about."

"He's here in my apartment. I'm looking at him now."

The walls within the break room had moved in several feet and were about to close in on Noah. He started to pant. The air in the room had grown thin.

"I have a kid?"

"Yes, Marcie tossed him to me like he was fuck—" She lowered her voice as if she wasn't alone. "Like he was a piece of luggage."

"He? A son?"

"Why would you not tell me this?"

"I don't know anything about this!"

Noah was screaming now, and Hank walked into the break room and their two employees stopped moving. One had one arm in his coat, and they were both at the threshold of the door. Their collective glances made it difficult to breathe. The ceiling and the floor conspired against Noah and threatened to crush him. He hurtled back into the muddled past, back to those foggy drunken days with

Marcie, back into the perpetual sex. Their many trysts without condoms. The fucking at whim. The arguing and brutal fights. Her fists on his face, her nails clawing at his neck. Her vengeance, and then utter withdrawal from him when he fell into grief. And his departure, followed by her withdrawal from everything, everyone—all the parties— and then her sudden reemergence about nine months later. In her wake, rumors were spoken in clandestine exchanges, as if passing treasonous information, about a child.

Noah had worried whether it was his. Surely, if it had been, she would have approached him about it. And at first, there was fear that the child had been his, rooting itself deep down, but it had been placed among the topics they didn't talk about, buried down inside him next to his father's dementia and his mother's assignment of guilt. Years had passed, and he'd assumed he was cleared.

He was now hyperventilating. A stupor was rising over him, and he could hear Isabelle's screeching whispers and couldn't comprehend any of it. Color drained from his face, and he looked over at Hank as if he was reaching out for a lifeline while sinking.

Hank immediately reacted. He turned to their employees and pushed them toward the door. He waved them off and even said shoo as if they were vermin he was sweeping away with a broom. He rushed back into the break room and shoved Noah into a seat.

"Put your head between your legs, man."

Hank took the phone from Noah and began speaking to Isabelle. He fell silent and gaped back at Noah. He nodded and drew his lips into a tight line. He hung up the phone and gathered both of their jackets.

"We're closing down early today," Hank said, forcing Noah's arms into the jacket. "Besides, a storm is coming."

Hank walked Noah toward the door and began to close down each of the workstations and turn off each of the lights. Noah was swaying a bit, trying to piece together the information. Could it be possible? Could he have a son? And it occurred to him that if this were true, he knew nothing about this child—not his face, not even his name. How would he tell his parents? Could his father even understand what was happening? Hot anger licked at his insides, and his knees could barely support him.

Hank took Noah by his shoulders and walked him down the stairs onto the street, past the glow of the Thai restaurant beneath their shop. The temperature had plummeted, and Noah's jacket did little against the chill. He embraced the cold breaching his body. It was a reprieve from the venom that was infiltrating him. Hank walked him like he was an infirmed senile. Noah was grateful he didn't have to think, grateful to give himself over to his friend.

He glanced up at the sky, which was nearly black. Snow flooded his vision. It whipped at his face and threatened to part his skin. Snow whited out everything, even obscuring the black sky it fell from. From this angle, Noah felt as though his feet were leaving the ground and he was rushing up toward the sky.

Hank called a cab off the street, and after a long, treacherous ride through the escalating storm and the blinding white, Noah and he had made it to the apartment building. They plodded through the snow, which now quickly reached their ankles. The gas shut-off notice fluttered like the wings of a small bird. They forced through the door and up toward Isabelle's apartment.

Noah stood frozen at Isabelle's door a moment, like he had before he'd confessed his feelings for her. He was quivering from the cold and terror. Marcie had never lost any fight, never bowed down before any quarrel, and in the brittle peace that they had forged, she had never truly forgiven him for leaving her. She had never forgiven him for loving her and wanting her to step out of the night to be with him. She had kept this from him as a final blow, her A-bomb, her endgame. That night at Stratosphere, she knew he was happy, that he was in love. And through this door was a child who would threaten all of that.

"It's okay," Hank said.

Noah knocked on the door, and Isabelle opened it. Her face was blank, completely unreadable. She was reeling from this, too, and guilt swirled about Noah's stomach. She refused to meet his eyes. She stepped to the side to let him pass.

Noah walked carefully into her apartment as if the floor would give way under him, and Hank came in behind him the same way. On the couch, sitting stiffly, was a small fearful boy whose gaze was planted on the floor. The child's small dirty hands clutched a backpack to his chest, no doubt filled with his belongings. Noah, a mere six feet away, could smell the sharp stench of urine and sweat wafting from the child and overpowering the living room. The child became aware of Noah's gaze and looked up at him with wide eyes. The child's breathing was slightly rattled, and Noah could hear the gentle wheeze of each breath as if it had to press through layers of mucus.

The child seemed feral, like a cornered animal. Noah was afraid to blink. Everything that had happened in the last few minutes had altered his world so severely that if he closed his eyes for that half second, more would become unrecognizable. And yet here this boy was, more real, more substantial than anything else in the room.

Noah choked on air, and the anger in him became too much to contain. Hot tears lanced his face, and his core quaked savagely with sobs. He muffled his mouth with his hand and moaned. Hank rushed up behind him, and Isabelle was at his side, her tears mirroring his own.

Noah's thoughts cluttered within him. The numbing shock had dwindled and so had the tears. Hank had absconded to his apartment as if someone's dropping a child on Noah was a contagious condition. He looked at the child's sooty face and started picking apart his features, questioning whether any had been inherited from him. Noah wondered if this boy was indeed his, or had this been a poor manipulation on Marcie's part? This detonated a nagging in him that threatened to upset his stomach.

Isabelle stood along the wall in her living room with her arms wrapped around herself. Noah picked up his phone and began his sixth attempt to call Marcie, and each time, the phone went to voicemail. He considered leaving her a scathing message but it seemed useless. Marcie knew exactly what he wanted and wouldn't answer.

Isabelle gestured to Noah and he came to her and they stepped into the kitchen.

"What are you going to do about this?" she asked, her voice a whisper.

"I've tried to call Marcie."

"She's halfway to Miami by now, if she got out early enough to miss the storm."

Isabelle faced him, finally meeting his eyes. She placed her hands on his shoulders.

"Is it true? Is that boy your son?"

"I don't know," Noah said. He considered the timeline and filled in the blanks with likely conclusions. "It's likely."

Isabelle sucked in a bitter breath and squared her shoulders before him. She appeared to be readying herself for some battle that Noah wasn't aware of.

"Well, then, if he's your son, you should know his name. It's Eli, and he's almost five."

She went over to the table and handed him a collection of crumpled papers.

"Here's what Marcie gave me on him," she said. "A birth certificate with the father listed as 'Unknown,' his social security card, and a medical card that lists him as an asthmatic. And if he's going to be here in this apartment and in our—I mean, your—life, then we'd better give him a bath."

Noah nodded in agreement and peeked out into the living room.

"I think . . . I think Marcie did something to him. Like neglected him or something. He doesn't speak or move much. I don't know what's wrong with him, Noah, and I'm half tempted to call the police and file charges on that bitch." Isabelle's voice pealed and she wiped her eyes. "How can she dump her child on a stranger?"

Noah shook his head as the child readjusted on the couch. Was this his little boy? It was possible.

"We have to help him," Isabelle said, succumbing to tears in spite of her best efforts.

The boy drew the backpack into his lap. His movements were slow, and he glanced around at his surroundings once more. Noah became unsure with the way the child moved. He may not be his son. He may not belong to him. Noah shivered at this.

Isabelle grabbed his hand. "We have to help him." Her eyes were red and slightly swollen from crying, and Noah agreed once more.

With her hand in his, they stepped into the living room and approached the child. No one spoke for a moment. All parties involved were wary of one another. This day had completely traveled down a course that neither man, woman, nor child had expected. Even Isabelle and Noah were in the heavy stretch of silent minutes, strangers. Outside, the wind bellowed and growled. An impenetrable curtain of snow closed in around the apartment, and the tree branches just outside the window were invisible. They were all confined to one another.

Noah wanted to speak but he had no words. They were sinking, capsized in his stomach. But Isabelle was brave, and she lowered herself on one knee. She gave the child a small smile that didn't fit the face that had spent the last few hours grieving.

"Hi, Eli," she said. "I'm sorry I didn't introduce myself to you."

Eli lightened a bit. He appeared to contemplate Isabelle. That expression made him look like he could be a part of Noah. That he could be his son.

"I'm Isabelle," she said, "but you can call me Izzy. This is your dad, Noah."

Isabelle turned back and scowled at Noah until he spoke.

"Uh, hi," Noah said in a whisper.

"Like your mom said, you're going to be staying with us," she continued.

"Yeah," Noah offered weakly.

"Does that sound okay?"

Eli nodded, still uncertain. Isabelle smiled back at him. She stood up and appeared relieved, if only momentarily.

"Are you hungry?" she asked.

Eli nodded again, and Isabelle went off toward the kitchen. Terror started to claw at Noah as he and the boy were left with each other. He bit his tongue to keep from calling Isabelle back into the room with them. He was hapless now, trapped in the gaze of the child. He stood there petrified, glancing into the child's eyes. How was this going to change his life? And how much room did he have to give up in his apartment? Would Marcie ever come back?

Isabelle came back into the living room, distressed once more.

"The stove isn't working," she said.

"What do you mean?"

"Come look."

Isabelle led him into the kitchen, and Noah was practically stepping on her heels to get away from the child. He stepped up to the old gas stove and turned the knob. He kneeled close to the unresponsive eye and listened.

"What is it?"

He took a deep sniff, and his heart dropped into his stomach. "I don't hear or smell anything."

They looked at one another, arriving at a state of horror at the same time. Isabelle brought her hand up to her face.

"The gas is shut off," she said, and they returned to the child in the living room.

Noah moved past them on the couch and stared at the wall of falling snow that appeared to be static on a TV screen. It was then that he noticed small ice crystals crawling up the glass, spinning an ornamentation of silver. The cold had begun its siege upon the apartment.

30

Jones tucked her arms around her body as she walked into the apartment. She stopped at the window, and the world outside was entirely buried in snow. The weather had altered into a malevolent fury so quickly. The landscape of buildings and streets had become alien, and she felt displaced and illegitimate trudging among them. Cars were engulfed in white, and the wind currents forged snow mounds higher than the average height of a person and nearly dwarfed a few buildings. By now, most of the city had to have been buried. Jones edged into a dizzy panic. She hadn't seen the orbit of plow trucks, and she could barely make it on foot out there, let alone in any vehicle.

She began to take off her coat when Derek entered the room, huffing in his thickest down coat and wrapped in a blanket.

"Don't take off your coat," he said. "The gas is off."

Jones blinked at him incredulously, then frowned, unconvinced. She went over to the thermostat and turned the dial. There was a hollow silence where there should have been a shudder from the furnace. A shiver quaked across her shoulders, and she started to pace.

"Did you call the landlord?"

"Yes, of course I called the landlord. He didn't answer."

"Call him again."

"I've called him, like, twenty times."

"Call him again."

Derek vented a sound of exasperation and took his phone from his pocket under the blanket caped around him.

He dialed the number and placed his phone on speaker, and together, they listened to the dial tone rattle for three minutes.

"Let's get out of here," Derek said. "We can get a hotel."

Jones dropped her face in her hands as the chill set deeper in her body. "Have you been outside? We can't go anywhere. We can't walk or get a cab."

"What?"

Jones drew back with a sneer. "We're fucking trapped, and we're probably going to die here."

She marched into the kitchen. In the kitchen sink, there was a crusty plate and a coffee mug that was always used and never clean. Inside the mug, tipped a bit on its side, was a small amount of coffee that had formed a top layer of ice. Jones swallowed a scream.

She took her Xanax from her purse and placed a pill in her mouth. She went to the cabinet next to the refrigerator. Derek gingerly pushed into the kitchen with an extra blanket in his hands. Jones grabbed a fifth of Derek's cheap whiskey by the neck and opened it. She took a gulp and winced at the burn.

She and Derek exchanged the bottle and the blanket. He upturned the bottle, clearing his throat against the whiskey's bite.

"Do you think we're going to die?" he asked with a joking smile.

"Well, now I don't care if we do," she said, shaking her pill bottle and placing it back into her purse.

Derek scowled at her. "Why are you always taking those?"

Jones grunted and moved to the living room and sat next to his open laptop. She reached for it, and Derek leaped over the room toward his computer. Jones drew back her fingers just in time as he snapped it closed and tucked it under his arm beneath the blanket.

"Why are you always on porn sites?"

"Why don't we have sex?"

Jones rolled her eyes. "I'm not going to freeze to death having this argument."

She saw the whiskey bottle still in Derek's other hand and pointed at it. Derek handed it over as he sat across the room on a lounge chair. She took another drink of the bottle. She didn't really believe she would die today in the cold, but she kept her face stern. Someone should have to pay for this heavy misstep, and the landlord, with his lecherous stares and thick undetermined accent and origins, was not in the apartment with her.

"You shouldn't drink with Xanax."

"And you shouldn't have asked me to live here with you."

Derek's hands formed fists, and he slinked out and into the bedroom. Jones sighed, relieved to be alone. But her relief was clipped short when she saw her breath in small vapors before her. She leaned forward, contemplating joining Derek in the bedroom, when her phone purred in her pocket.

"Hello?"

"Are you home?" It was Isabelle.

"Yes—are you?"

"No, I'm in Hank's apartment—you know, the guy from the bar."

"What in God's name is happening? The gas is off?"

"Yeah, it's been a hell of a day," Isabelle said

A chill quaked through Jones's shoulders. "We're going to fucking freeze here."

"Hank has a space heater. Come up here."

Jones heard shuffling in the bedroom. "Is it cool if I bring Derek?"

She jumped up from the couch and headed to the bedroom.

Isabelle dropped down to a whisper. "It's a full house, though."

The cryptic nature of her voice halted Jones. "What is it?"

"Just come up here."

Derek had built a tomb with all the blankets from the closets. And in a desperate effort to warm himself, he had plugged in her hairdryer and set it on himself, his face flushed under it. Jones smirked despite her anger, allowing this only because there was the promise of heat in the other apartment. She explained this to him, and they left their apartment and took the stairs to Hank's apartment. The temperature in the hallways was glacial, and the wind blustered along the building. Jones doubted the apartment, the structure that was supposed to shelter her, would stand through the night.

At the door, Hank ushered them in. His living room was sparse and the couch was pushed out of the way on the far wall. In the center of the room, gathered around the small glowing space heater, was a woman Hank introduced as Gwen sitting on a quilt, and on another set of blankets was Isabelle and Noah. A small, grubby child sat next to them, cross-legged and clinging to a backpack.

Derek joined the semi-circle, and Jones stood back. She was wheeling as she wondered what had happened to the day and how she'd ended up in a refugee camp that had once been an apartment. She still had the whiskey in her hand and decided to take another sip. She walked up to Isabelle and winced at the sharp scent of urine. She gagged slightly, stumbling back.

Isabelle hopped up, her expression strained. She gripped Jones's arm and took her into the kitchen.

"Who's the kid?"

"Noah's son."

"I don't understand. Did he kidnap a child off the street?"

Isabelle glowered at her friend and quickly reported Marcie's abandonment. Jones nodded slowly and rolled over the facts. The day had been so ordinary a few hours ago. It hadn't been cold or snowing. An arguably productive day without Todd Nicolas at the office. But so quickly, with the passing of storm clouds, her apartment had become the start of an apocalypse. Outside the kitchen, they squatted on blankets around the heater like they were the last humans on earth.

"Isabelle, I know you love him," Jones said, "but this isn't your problem."

"I know," Isabelle said as her brows wrinkled across her forehead, and she pulled at the down coat around her wrist.

"I'm serious," Jones said. "Tell Noah to call the police and leave it at that."

Isabelle's eyes moved from Jones to a fixed point behind her. Jones turned around, and Gwen stood there with an unreadable smile on her face. Gwen's arms were crossed behind her back, and she tilted her head to the side in a poor display of innocence. Jones's stomach lurched as if she'd eaten something vile.

"She won't do that," Gwen said. "Just look at her."

Jones grimaced at the woman and sized her up. Gwen's audacity was offensive, and her tone was sweet, yet laced with insult. Jones readied herself as one woman fought for dominance over another. She knew this place well, where they could issue a slight kindly, where they would tear on another with aggression so nuanced, one wouldn't realize the damage was done until it was too late. Jones hadn't seen Gwen much around the building, but she was dating Hank and living in this apartment, and the two of them were in her home. Jones would have to tread carefully.

"I'm okay, really," Isabelle said.

"I just don't want to see you get caught up in anything out of obligation," Jones said, keeping Gwen in her vision.

Gwen walked up to Isabelle and grabbed her hand and smiled. "I know this must be tough."

"I mean, she practically left him on my doorstep," Isabelle said.

"How could she have done that?" Gwen asked.

"That doesn't mean he's your child," Jones said.

Isabelle and Gwen shot her disapproving glances. Gwen let her judgment idle and sneered at Jones.

"I know he's not my child," Isabelle said. "But look at him and look at Noah. I haven't decided what I'm going to do one way or the other."

"You need to break up with him or stop doing whatever it is you guys are doing," Jones said. "If you let him, he will drag you down into his mess and you will never get out of it."

Gwen smiled again, putting up a thin veil of concern. "Are you speaking from experience?"

Jones's lips twitched. "Do you mind? I'm trying to talk to my friend here."

"I'm sorry. I just wanted to help," Gwen said as she placed a hand on her chest. "We are all here snowed in for who knows how long—"

"And we are not your in-flight entertainment, and I've never even seen you before."

"I'm new to the building," Gwen said.

"Oh, I know. Has Hank told you about his last girlfriend, Andrea?"

"Jones, please," Isabelle said.

"She was really sweet, and she knew how to mind her own business."

Gwen snorted. "Hmm. I heard she was fat."

Jones stammered and said nothing. Gwen had tipped her hand, and Jones saw a crazy she wasn't prepared to deal with.

Jones held a hand up in surrender and with the other tipped a bit more whiskey into her mouth. She left the two women in the kitchen and crouched down next to Derek around the portable heater. The heater, enough to warm up a small office, blew burned, dust-laced heat. The temperature increased but not by much. The child sat closer to the heat in an unspoken agreement to allow him access to more warmth. This would have been noble if the child hadn't smelled so foul and the air wasn't rank with dried urine.

Jones buried her face in Derek's shoulder, attempting to mask the stench. She handed Derek the whiskey, and he took a swallow.

"I'm calling a fucking lawyer when this shit is over," Derek said.

Jones slowly came to with her head in Derek's lap and his arm around her. She was shrouded in a blanket taken from their apartment. The Xanax and the whiskey had pulled her under at some unknown point. For a few seconds, she didn't know where she was. But then she looked up to see Hank up, pacing with the phone in his hand. Noah's son was wound into a ball, and behind him, Noah was supine, snoring slightly. Isabelle was next to them, sitting up, her eyes glassy and her face worn.

"The landlord must've been skipping out on the gas bill for months. I'm sure the gas company has called him several times to notify him that they were shutting the gas down," Hank said.

"Isn't this illegal?" Derek asked.

Jones glanced at her phone. "No, the gas company can cut off the gas if the temperature is above thirty-two degrees."

"Well, it's not," Gwen said, narrowing her eyes at Jones.

Jones strained a smile. "Well, if you look at the forecast from earlier, this storm was supposed to miss us."

"Shitty luck," Gwen said from the couch on the far wall, sucking on the cigarette and flicking the ash on the floor.

Jones ached from lying on the floor, and she wanted to escape this house party from hell. She sensed it was early in the morning, but she couldn't tell the exact time. In the corner, the TV had been turned on and infomercials flashed on a local station while alerts and snow warnings scrolled on the screen below, followed by the school closings. She hoped it would be over, but outside the window, snow continued to fall.

She had the incoherent notion that the snow would never stop, that this would be her life. She shivered, and Derek looked down at her. He kneaded her shoulders with his hands and stooped down to kiss her. He was as lovely as he'd been every morning, making coffee for her. And in this cold space, amidst all the frustration, he was enough. Jones gazed up at him and caught a glimmer of the man she remembered when they first dated in the flicker of his eyes, in the manner in which he drew her close.

His tenderness was too much and she had no place to escape the downpour of guilt. He was there in this awfulness, beside her, keeping her warm and offering her blankets. She wondered why she had wanted anyone else and why she had been so harsh to him when all he'd wanted was for his business to be successful. Jones turned to Isabelle, who watched in her exhaustion the sleeping father and son, and in the dim glow of early morning, she looked like a shepherd keeping watch.

Jones sat up, and a sob folded in her throat.

"I need to talk to you," she said slowly in Derek's ear.

They excused themselves and journeyed back to their frozen apartment.

The sob stayed in Jones's throat as she confessed everything—the promotion and her attraction to Todd Nicolas.

"He doesn't mean anything to me. Just a guy I work with," she told him.

The words crawled up out of her, bubbling over, and by the end of her admission, she was shaking. But Derek was lowering his gaze and holding back his words. His face was dark as if he wanted to tell her something, but this passed and he opened his arms to her. She wanted to question him, to see if there were any transgression on his part, but his touch disarmed her.

He kissed her long and deeply, and she felt an erection jutting from his pants. Her old passion had life again and she couldn't breathe. She couldn't question it. She hopped up and wrapped her legs around his waist. He lumbered toward the bedroom. But he didn't make it in time. He stopped in the hall. They were determined and only removed each other's pants feverishly. Both were afraid this courage would dissolve. It was a matter of time before old lovers become familiar antagonists again.

Their bare bottoms prickled with the cold. He laid her on the floor and dropped on top of her. He plunged into her, and she keened at his girth. She squirmed underneath, trying to take as much of him in as possible, and he was maddened, growling and colliding into her. Jones was broiling in her coat, and she was not alone. Derek was damp and sweat dropped from his nose onto her. He was no longer tender but brutal and grunting. He pressed his face into the crook of her neck. He grabbed a fistful of her hair, and his other hand anchored beneath her ass. He thrust harder and deeper into her as if he was trying to reclaim her, as if he was trying to save them.

Jones rolled her head back and forth on the floor and didn't think about the secrets she had kept or Todd Nicolas. She was severed from it, and if only for now, pressing her hands against the hallway's walls, she was back in the past, before his pride or his app or either of their ambitions had disjoined them. She allowed herself to be the woman he had once met, and Derek was who she'd known him to be.

31

Hank would've never admitted the happiness of having his apartment full of people. The gas shut-off was horrible, and the snowstorm, one of historic magnitude, had threatened to freeze over the city. The blizzard had led to numerous cases of hypothermia and a few deaths among the elderly. The street they lived on wouldn't see a plow truck for at least a day or two. There were even stories circulating the news of cars with people being stuck in middle of Lake Shore Drive. Emergency responders were overloaded. Schools were closed. Retail shops were shut down. An entire city of millions was completely frozen in its tracks.

But the emptiness left by his ex-girlfriend, Andrea, had unearthed the rusty little portable heater he had used during his college years. To his relief, the heater had still functioned, even though the air it gave off smelled like burnt dust.

He was a hero for his sad group of friends and even looked out for Noah, who had been stunned since Marcie had dropped off his son. He watched his friend, now asleep on the blankets in front of him. Hank still couldn't believe she had kept that from him for five years. And he would hold his reservation on the matter until they'd dealt with the gas and it was back on.

Elsewhere, on a blanket and cushion taken from the couch were his neighbors, Jones and Derek, asleep in one another's arms.

Gwen pensively smoked cigarettes and checked her phone every so often. She had been doing this the entire night until morning. Hank contemplated yanking the phone out of her hand. He wanted her here with him. He wanted her to admire his resourcefulness in this time of disaster.

Isabelle stepped out of the bathroom. Her face was threadbare with sleeplessness. Hank hadn't slept much that night on the floor, but he had managed a few hours, and each time he awoke, she was up, staring over Noah and his son. Hank wondered if it had shocked her as badly as Noah.

"Thanks for letting us stay here," she said to him in a low voice.

"Oh, it's fine," he said. "Like playing third-world summer camp."

Isabelle laughed, and then stretched into a yawn. They both turned to Noah.

"He's going to need help, isn't he?" she said.

Hank nodded slowly. "You know, you don't have to be the one to do it."

"That's what Jones said—but I think I want to."

They fell into silence, and she settled down next to them on the blankets. She reminded him of Andrea and a sharpness twisted in his chest. Hank's attention was back on Gwen. She stared out the window and flicked ashes from her cigarette onto his floor.

Hank crossed his arms and settled into a light slumber. His apartment was a life raft, and they were all floating with no land in sight until Hank's phone rang in his pocket. It was the landlord, who spoke to him in a thick indecipherable accent.

"Hey," Hank said, "this shit is wholly unacceptable. I should fucking sue you."

His voice stirred everyone. Hank was the hero again, defending all of them. He was enlivened by a hot rage and barely recalled what he'd said to the man. He yelled and stomped his feet and argued while spittle formed at the corners of his mouth. But soon, his rent was discounted for the month and he found out that, by the end of the day, the gas would be turned on. Everyone cheered as if they had just been rescued, and soon, the landlord called Isabelle, then Derek, and each of them sought vengeance.

Hank turned to Gwen to celebrate. He wanted to hug her or kiss her, but she was preoccupied by her phone. She got up to leave the room, murmuring something into it that Hank wished he could hear.

After the blizzard, the city attempted to put itself back together. Snowplows cleared the streets. Walkways were shoveled, and salt was laid down. Ice was chipped away on windows, doorways, and stairs. People, no longer eremitic strangers, left their homes in eagerness to add their tales of survival to one another. They were all temporarily friendly in passing. Buses scuttled back to their routes, and retail stores reopened.

Hank and only one of the employees opened the store and played catch-up to the back orders. Hank had stressed to Noah that he would handle the store while he straightened out the situation with his son. And by the end of his work day, the world had returned to itself. Hank had walked into his apartment and noticed at his couch a small, sleek suitcase on wheels and next to it a large, dingy gym bag. The suitcase was easy to place as Gwen's, but the gym bag had him thrown. The fabric of the bag was caked with dirt and a fine layer of dust. The bottom of the bag was damp, and there was a trail of wet mud drying to its exact spot on his floor. Hank stepped over to the bag and nudged it gently with his foot. It didn't budge, and its contents were solid and heavy. He tried to image Gwen, such a slim woman, laboring with the bag up the stairs into his apartment while he was at work, but maybe she had help carrying it. Maybe while he was gone, she had strangers from her enigmatic life entering his home and going through the few belongings he had in his near-empty apartment.

A tightness formed at the base of Hank's skull.

He heard her movements pass from the bathroom to the bedroom, and his stomach fluttered. He had let some unknown agent into his home. He had offered her his bed, his room, and access to his things. He had seen her tears, and the urge to be her savior, to mean something to someone again, had driven him to this. He glanced at the set of keys he'd given her on the top of her suitcase.

He heard her phone ring and her voice. He quickly pulled off his boots and tiptoed high on his feet toward the bedroom's closed door. He held his breath and listened over the sound of his throbbing heart.

"I'm fine. I'm told you I'm fine."

Her voice was taxed.

"I'm staying with someone. No, you don't know him."

Her footsteps fell on the floor, and he jumped back to avoid being caught. He snuck back into the hall, ready to dive into the bathroom if the bedroom door opened. He felt ridiculous to behave this way in his own apartment, but he doubted direct confrontation would give him the information. Oddly enough, she had grown taciturn since she'd decided to stay with him. She would physically give herself to him. She would gladly, almost wildly, climb on top of Hank, and by the end of the night, it had grown late and he was too spent to ask her any questions.

"I don't have it," he heard Gwen say. "I swear I don't have it."

She struggled to keep her voice restrained, but shrill emotions undid her efforts.

"I don't have it. I don't have anything. I won't tell you where I am."

He couldn't endure the trepidation in her voice. It was like hot coals in his throat, and he knocked on the door. He cracked it and stuck his head into the room. She sat panicked on the bed, with her phone pressed against her chest.

"Are you okay?" he asked.

"Yeah," she said in a low whisper, then put her phone to her ear.

There was a metered voice shouting that could be heard from the speaker, and then Gwen said, "It's no one."

Hank narrowed his eyes at her even though her face pleaded with him to leave. He stayed planted to the floor.

"I have to go," she said, and hung up the phone, then powered it down.

The air was tense between them, and the features of Hank's face rose into a question. Gwen's gaze settled on Hank's empty closet. He had hoped she would fill that space left by Andrea, and he realized in a way, she had. But instead of those numbingly familiar memories of love that had grown stale with passing years, she had immersed his house in the mystery of her.

Hank was floating outside of himself, watching the distance grow between Gwen and him. Some very quiet part of him knew he should've told her and whatever or whomever she was escaping from to leave his apartment. But much as he had the other day, there was a pleasure in people seeking haven in him from the cold.

He crossed the room and sat on the bed next to her. He had witnessed enough to be given some explanation for her behavior. She would have to give him something. Some morsel of truth or the humanity that he so desperately wanted.

"You have to let me know what's going on," he said.

She lit a cigarette—a transparent stalling tactic. Hank swallowed back his chagrin. He wished she wouldn't smoke cigarettes in his apartment.

"I really like you, Gwen," he said. "I just want to help."

Her shoulders sagged. "I've done bad shit, and I know bad people."

She exhaled smoke into the room and said nothing else.

"The person on the phone wasn't your roommate," Hank said. "Did you date him?"

She shot him a helpless glance. "What do you want from me?"

Hank resisted a twist of pain in his neck.

He wanted everything. He wanted her to be as open and as vulnerable as he was. He wanted her to cling to regret and uncertainty like he had been in the aftermath of Andrea and all this damnable emptiness that was overtaking him. But he looked at her and her eyes were watery and the cigarette between her fingers trembled. She was there with him in a similar sort of desperation.

"I don't know anything about you," Hank said. "Nothing real."

She handed him her cigarette, and the end of it was smudged with her lipstick. "It's better that way."

Hank pressed his lips on the cigarette like he had the night they'd met. She was trying to seduce him into silence. "Why?"

"Because I can't disappoint you," she said.

"Let me be disappointed."

She bared her teeth at him in a sad grin. "The truth is I came to this city not long ago looking for more. I'm in between jobs. The guy I ended up with was a coworker and the complete opposite of you. And I'm trying to get away from him."

Hank gulped, and his face darkened. "Are you in danger?"

Gwen smirked and took back her cigarette. "You are naïve. No, I'm not in danger, and in answer to the question you really want to ask—neither are you."

There was something conclusive in the way she spoke. He stood up and left the bedroom.

"I'm going to order takeout," he called back to the bedroom. "Think about what you want to eat."

Although he hated that it was all it took, her answers satisfied him and he was light. He exalted that she needed him and found that he was now very much himself. Inspired, he looked at her bags. He stooped down and heaved the dirty gym bag, carrying it down the hall into the room. The trappings within the bag shifted, and Hank nearly toppled. One of his feet went up in the air as he swayed. He cried out, and Gwen flew into the hall.

She was twisted in horror, mouth open and her hands out. He kept his foot up as he wavered against gravity until his balance returned.

"Oh, God," she said.

"It's okay," he said, catching himself at the cost of his lower back.

He trailed into the bedroom and set it next to the closet. He dusted himself off and placed his hands firmly on his hips. He smiled, pleased, and knelt to unzip the bag.

"Let's get you unpacked."

"No," Gwen said, yanking his arm away from the bag. "Another time."

She was pallid, her cigarette still quivering in her hand. Hank bit his lips. The only time he had seen her crack like this was when she had asked him to stay. Her shoulders were drawn into her body, and her panic shifted into something malignant. He was nonplussed and wouldn't risk the rapport he'd had to struggle for. He nodded, and they returned to the living room and ordered Mediterranean from a nearby restaurant. Gwen smiled and continued with some small talk, returning to her cool smile.

When the food came, they settled the chicken on his plates and sat before the TV. She didn't argue with him on what he wanted to watch like Andrea would have. She didn't insist that they eat at the table. She simply sat next to him on the couch and ate.

Hank should have been contented, but in his mind, he replayed her reaction to her bag and her face of terror as he entered the room while she was on the phone. They played like a couple at the beginning of their relationship, but the vacancy he had intended her to fill was occupied by unanswered questions.

32

When gas had returned to Noah's apartment, the thermostat was turned up all the way. Eli dropped in front of a vent in the living room, staring blankly at Noah. Noah gave him an uneasy smile to which there was no response. Noah sighed and went to the spare room in his apartment, where he had spent the better part of the day organizing the plastic crates of used computer parts and old business files. He hadn't realized how dusty the room had become over the last few months.

Across the hall, inside the bathroom, running water filled the bathtub. He glanced to see Isabelle kneeling at the mouth of the tub, like it was a cauldron, sticking her arm in and stirring the water. They locked eyes, and a drained, half-hearted smile pulled at her face. Noah's insides dropped within him, and he turned back to the room at hand. He went to the closet in the room that had been serving as extra storage and found an old box containing a deflated air mattress. He blew off the dust, sending it into the air, and plugged the mattress into a wall. It roared as it inflated, unfolding and flopping and spreading along the floor.

He couldn't understand why Isabelle had been with him the entire day, as he called the police to file a report, and then left a voicemail for his lawyer regarding the situation.

She stayed at his apartment, on the computer, searching the internet for similar situations, and scoured his apartment for some food to prepare for Noah and Eli. After finding none, she went down to her apartment to find something for them. While Noah was on the phone, she sat next to Eli, talking softly and asking questions to which the child didn't respond.

Noah missed the numbness of the cold because, now thawed, there was no barrier between him and the newfound helplessness. It was a thorny vine piercing him, digging into places no one could see. He wished there were some way to expel it—some way to feel like himself again. He wanted to fight someone or drink—anything that would provide a moment of distraction, but then there was Eli, this strange child who was alarmingly quiet, floating soundlessly like a ghost along the walls of his apartment. His child, who had continued to shiver hours after vents had suffused his apartment with the heat of a mid-July afternoon. Noah realized that the child—his child—was quaking from animalistic fear.

Isabelle saw this, too, and when Noah stared at Eli, like a guiding compass, she gripped his hand or nudged his shoulder and led him out. He wanted to tell her she could go, but something in her touch told him she wouldn't.

Noah considered pressing charges for child abuse regarding the condition he'd found Eli in. She had been

277

gone for two days now. The number he had for her was only answered by a mechanical voice informing him that the number was no longer in service. According to Isabelle, Marcie was in Miami, but he had no real way to prove that it was where she actually went.

In the meantime, there was a child who had gone from abandonment to nearly freezing to death in his apartment. And Noah had to find a place for him to sleep. He decided to take the air mattress tonight and Eli would take his bed until he could come up with something more permanent.

The air mattress swelled completely and he unplugged it. When he looked up, Eli was standing in the hallway, gawking at him. Confusion and fear mingled in his small gray face.

"Eli, sweetie," Isabelle said across the hall, "your dad is just getting his bed ready. It's okay."

Eli nodded slowly and walked to her in the bathroom. His tiny legs and arms were quiet as if he were afraid to make any sound. And Noah's stomach lurched as his mind spun the type of conditions that would drive a child to such wordlessness. Most children he'd seen Eli's age were torrents of noises, words, and driven by a relentless curiosity. But here this child was, stepping next to Isabelle like a cornered animal at the bathtub, at the moment looking very much like a carbon copy of Noah, and in the next moment, a stranger with no connection to him.

"So, we're going to take a bath tonight," she said to Eli. "Is that okay?"

Eli consented and took off his jacket.

"Thank you," Isabelle said under a labored cheeriness.

Isabelle hands gently undressed the child and pulled back layers as if he were fractured glass and a wrong touch would shatter him completely. Noah watched, and a heaviness forced the air out of his chest. Eli stood gaunt without his clothes. His bones jutted from his pale skin, and his knees appeared like grapefruits in comparison to his narrow legs. The too-small pull-up brief he wore was swollen with piss. Noah could smell it from across the hall.

Isabelle's face was taut as she held herself from wincing. Noah crossed the hall, and the floor under him swayed and his hands shook. He dropped to a knee in front of Eli.

"We're going to get you clean, okay?"

The pull-up had to be ripped off Eli, and then peeled way. Eli stood shivering, with his face pale in fear. He glanced from Noah to Isabelle, and then back to Noah.

"Can you get in the tub?" Noah asked.

Eli peered over at the tub as if he were standing at the edge of a cliff being asked to jump. He shook his head.

"We'll be right here," Isabelle said.

"It's fine," Noah said, placing his hand in the water and smiling.

Eli stared back, unconvinced.

Isabelle shrugged at Noah in defeat.

Noah gripped the edge of the tub and dismay burrowed deep into him. He could barely breathe, and if not for Isabelle's and Eli's eyes, he would have yielded to the feeling completely.

If he couldn't at the very least give Eli a bath, then how was he going to care for him? He didn't see many children living the type of life that he'd lived. Occasionally, he would pass a small family in a grocery store or see a mother with her child on the train. And those children were jovial, incessantly squirming around, erupting with noise. He'd rolled his eyes at their noise filling the otherwise quiet train of docile adults, or he'd stifle his anger, maneuvering past the family in the narrow aisle of the grocery store. But now more than ever, he wanted this child, his child, to smile or speak or do anything that resembled those children.

Noah stood up and kicked off his shoes and tugged his shirt over his head. Eli and Isabelle both jumped back as he, in his socks and jeans, stepped into the tub and lowered himself into the warm water. He let out an emphatic groan.

"What are you doing?" Isabelle asked.

"It's so nice in here," Noah said, splashing around, and water crested over the rim of the tub onto Eli's feet.

Eli's face lightened, and he half-smiled.

"Come on," Noah said. "Join me."

Eli turned to Isabelle for assurance, and she nodded. Eli stepped up to the tub and with Isabelle's help climbed into the water. Once inside the water, he sat on Noah's lap and splashed the water in the manner Noah had. Noah's heart rose into his throat, threatening to choke him as he laughed through tears, but soon, his emotions subsided. He didn't know what to do next and looked at Isabelle for her help.

Her face softened as she acknowledged him. Next to her was a bag she had packed. She gathered some strange hypoallergenic organic soap bar from the bag. She dipped the soap into the water along with one of Noah's old face towels. She lathered the towel, slowly alternating her glances between both Eli and Noah. Her hands were slow and deliberate in the water, like she was preparing a religious rite. Eli watched Isabelle, and the tension dissipated from both father and son. Noah began to mirror the boy's joy as he sat on his lap in the water. Isabelle had the soap and the towel in one hand, dripping with suds, and with her other hand, she made a cup below the water. She brought this hand above the little boy's head and held it there.

She grinned at him, and in a whisper said, "Close your eyes."

He did as he was told, and water ran from her hand along the boy's crown, flattening his greasy hair, streaming down his temples and his face. A vast adoration gripped

Noah, as if he had witnessed a baptism. A crude, yet holy act completed by Isabelle had transformed her into someone so tender, into someone with a profound absolution, and he felt that she had poured the water over him.

Isabelle took the washcloth and held Eli's arms and gently scrubbed his skin. She stroked his body and soon excavated the blush-colored skin underneath. Eli squirmed only slightly, but soon, he languished in her touch, leaning back onto Noah. Isabelle continued to scrub the child until his eyes closed and he was lying folded up in Noah's lap in the water.

Noah stood and gathered him up in a towel. His jeans clung to him and dripped, trailing water throughout his apartment as he took Eli to his bedroom. Together, he and Isabelle dried the child and put him in one of Noah's old shirts. Despite himself, and with no other alternative, Noah slipped a pull-up on the boy. Eli was limp in slumber while they worked over him. Finally sharing sighs of relief, they placed the child in Noah's bed under blankets, turned off the light, and left the door slightly ajar.

Once in the hallway, Noah remembered that he was shirtless and still soaked. He pulled at his jeans, and Isabelle chuckled.

"That's a nice look for you," she said.

"Holy shit, I'm a dad now," he said back.

"Yeah, I know. Either that, or this is the most elaborate prank anyone has ever pulled on me."

Noah and Isabelle moved toward the living room. They tiptoed and spoke in whispers. Noah found a pair a gym shorts on his floor near the couch.

"On you? Are you sure you're not pulling a prank on me?"

"Yes, you're right. I was thinking in order for this relationship to work, you needed more baggage from your ex-girlfriend."

Noah smiled and sniffed his shorts and paused to consider their odor. He peeled off his pants and hauled on the gym shorts. Isabelle turned away to conceal her blush.

"That's disgusting," Isabelle said. "Are those things even clean?"

"Well, we've bonded now—I was hoping I could be a bit more open."

Isabelle's gaze dropped to her feet. "Yeah, we have."

Noah stepped closer to Isabelle and circled his arms around her waist. "Thank you—but you know you don't have to do this."

Isabelle chuckled. "Everyone keeps telling me that. But you clearly need help."

Noah winced.

"What I mean is that I care about you," she said. "And if you have a kid, then I have to care about him, too, right?"

She said these words so simply, so matter-of-factly, that Noah wondered if he had misheard them. Had the water in the bathtub changed all of them? The child was now clean, deep in a contented sleep, and Noah was a father, and what did that make Isabelle—the consolatory mother? Did she want that? He evidently needed that. He needed her comfort, her gentle guidance, but did he want it?

She arched on her tiptoes and kissed him. She had read the doubt scrolling across his face. And she gave him her answer, as she had the night Eli had come to them. He kissed her back deeper, and together, they shut off the lights, locked the doors, and settled on the air mattress. Battle worn, Isabelle dropped into a quick sleep that surprised him. She lay across his chest, and he listened to her breathing. He inhaled her scent, and soon, he was half off into a dreamless state when the hushed swing of the bedroom door awoke him.

He opened his eyes, and Eli's silhouette floated into the room. Eli's steps were so hesitant Noah was afraid if he moved, the child would scurry out of the room and out of sight. Eli stopped at the foot of the air mattress and assessed Noah and Isabelle, unaware that Noah was watching him through the darkness. Eli crawled onto the mattress, redistributing the weight, causing Isabelle to stir and turn away from Noah. Eli froze on all fours on the foot of the mattress, and then after a moment, he pulled up the blanket from the end of the bed and slipped inside. He lay down and curled into a ball. Noah tingled with the thrill of having him in the room. He wanted to bring Eli closer but he didn't want to upset him.

As Noah closed his eyes, he thought about his father, who seemed indestructible when he was Eli's age. What would his father have said about all of this? What guidance would he have given Noah in this strange territory? Somehow, overnight, as one thoughtlessly flipped a switch, he had gone from bachelor to a man with his own family. He closed his eyes and thought of the potted yellow tulip that he had bought with Isabelle. The plant had somehow survived the night without heat. Somehow, with a supernatural fortitude, it had endured. Its blossom was still bright gold and its stalk still erect, slightly bowed by the flower's weight.

That night, he dreamed in yellow and of his father

33

Jones's voice was strained and her words clipped when she called Isabelle and requested that they meet for lunch. Isabelle had been floating around Noah's apartment. Somehow, Eli and Noah had clung to her, and she had spent the morning as a conduit between the two as they orbited one another. At her friend's cryptic insistence, she left them. Before she exited the apartment, she stopped at the door and the man and boy glared back at her with round, pleading eyes.

She trailed through snowdrifts toward the train and fought the urge to return to Noah's apartment. When she had talked to Jones and her strange voice, they debated other restaurants. But the conversation quickly gave way to routine, and after a train ride haunted by Noah's and Eli's faces, she arrived at By Land and By Sea feeling outside herself.

She sat across from Jones at a table overlooking the white street. Jones's face was taut and her expression illegible. On the table in front of her was an empty glass with melting ice and a slice of lime that looked as though it had once held vodka. Isabelle gaped at her, and a sickness collided into her. She was unsure whether she would be able to eat.

"It's a bit early for vodka." Isabelle tried to smile.

"Blasphemy," Jones said in the spirit of forced humor.

The women plunged into silence. Jones grabbed her empty glass and tipped it, verifying she had drained all the vodka from it.

"I don't think Eli is adjusting well," Isabelle said suddenly.

"Well, is that your problem?" Jones said curtly.

Hostility flickered between them. Isabelle's mouth soured, and she sucked on her teeth.

"Why did you call me to lunch?" she asked.

"I told Derek about my promotion."

"Okay," Isabelle said uncertainly. "Shouldn't that be good news?"

"I've decided to be honest," she said, "with everyone."

Isabelle glanced around, hoping for the attention of a waiter that was at another table across the dining room. She turned to Jones's empty drink in envy.

Jones's face darkened and hardened, and Isabelle's muscles tightened along her sides.

"I know your gallery is struggling," Jones began, her words following one another in slow precision, "and I believed that I would have been able to help you with that. But in light of the merger and the new direction of the magazine, I'm unable to assist you. I regret this deeply."

Isabelle pulled back in the seat to get a better view of Jones, looking for something that resembled her friend. She chuckled humorlessly at the coldness, her unsympathetic delivery she would have given to a stranger. The person at the other end of the table surely wasn't the woman she had spent the better part of her twenties with, in bars, in shops, in each other's home, in the very art gallery Isabelle was fighting to keep open. Isabelle had seen Jones treat Derek this way and had assumed that he maybe deserved it. She questioned whether he had now, facing the blunt force of her friend's callousness. She couldn't find any remorse in Jones's face.

"How long have you known this?" Isabelle asked, recalling the length of time Jones had kept her promotion from Derek. Reason would have it that Jones, like most information she possessed, would mull over it before disclosing it while the injured party went along obliviously.

"A few weeks," Jones said in the same distant tone. "It's mostly due to the new ownership—"

Her words were suspended in the air, and she looked away toward the waitress. She had succeeded in bringing her to the table where they swiftly ordered drinks, skipping the meal outright. Once a few sips of alcohol were ingested, they resumed, and from Jones's tentative nature, Isabelle knew there was more prowling underneath Jones's hardened features. Isabelle then wondered how many pills she had taken with her drink to deaden herself enough to confess this to her friend. Isabelle wanted to lunge across the table and slap her to force the feelings she ran from.

"The new owner of the Chicago Modern Art Magazine is Nichols-Griffin Art Institute, and they've requested that we put Russell Cowell—your Russell Cowell—on the cover," Jones said.

Isabelle kissed her teeth and grimaced. Her mouth tasted of bile. A stinging rose up between her ribs and she blinked, gaping around to see if anyone had witnessed her cascade into devastation. She struggled to maintain composure but it was sand in her open palm. She stood up, and her chair screeched behind her, drawing a few stares from the nearby tables.

"I have to go," she said, and snatched up her purse and coat.

Jones wavered, and a short-lived panic burst on her face. "This is all my fault."

Isabelle tugged her coat and attempted not to meet her eyes.

"I have feelings for him," she whispered. "He did this for me."

Confusion stopped Isabelle with one arm in her coat.

"We bonded over Russell's work."

Isabelle rubbed her face as if she was waking up from sleep. She knelt, lowering her voice. "But what about Derek?"

Jones shrugged helplessly.

"You're a fucking shit show," Isabelle said. "You sit here doped up on damn Xanax and judge everyone else because you think you're not messy like the rest of us."

Jones pulled back her lips and sneered. "I'm not like you, Isabelle. You're about to take care of someone else's kid when you really need to be focusing on your gallery."

"When did you decide to push people away? When did you decide to push me away?"

Isabelle slipped her other arm into her coat and left Jones before she could reply. She forged ahead, against a blast of arctic wind and through the small canyons and valleys of snow toward her art gallery.

As she predicted, it was empty except for a small rustling in the back, followed by a hard snort. Her blood pulsed in her temples and along her neck. Her nerves were raw, and something akin to fear spurred in her sides. She crept quickly toward the back, keeping close to the wall.

In his back studio, Curtis threw back his dreadlocks and hunched over a stool. He brought a rolled up five-dollar bill to his nostril and inhaled from a small white line of coke on top of the stool. Dried paint was spattered over his front and into the tendrils of his hair. Behind him on the easel was a shredded canvas that he had been working on for months. As quiet as Isabelle's approach had been, he had sensed her in the back hall and looked up at her.

He gave a grunt, clearing his nasal passage of the coke. His face was marred by a rising mania. His pupils overtook his irises. His eyes were so wide his face could barely hold them.

"It's all over," he said.

"Curtis, you shouldn't do that here," she said, keeping close to the wall. "Anyone could come in."

Curtis upturned his head and guffawed. His laughter was harrowing in her ears, a wild subhuman howl crowning in the emptiness of the gallery. He clawed the canvas off the easel.

"Can you believe it?"

"Believe what?" Isabelle said, tasting her coppery fear in her mouth.

"Russell Cowell would be nothing without this gallery!" he continued, stomping in circles, as petulant as a child.

When his gaze moved off her, Isabelle stepped back. The more distance between them, the safer she would be.

"I gave him this opportunity! I'm the better artist! I was always the better artist!"

Isabelle nodded, moving back even more. Curtis stopped and recognized her fear and moved toward her with his hands out as if he were trying to coax her closer to him.

"You believe I'm a better artist, right?" he asked as his face contorted into something Isabelle couldn't identify. "I was the one who deserved the residency at Nichols-Griffin, right?"

"Yes, yes," Isabelle said, pressed up against the wall so tightly the back of her skull ached. She drew in a breath to scream.

"He's a hack. He's a goddam hack. He's a sellout. Painting portraits about love!"

Curtis roared in more crazed laughter and spittle hit Isabelle in the face. She knew he was the temperamental embodiment of an artist. She had seen his moods reach peaks and plummet to lows, but nothing as horrifying as this, nothing as base as this. It occurred to her, as his laughter railed against her eardrum and his spit dried on her cheek, that her entire world had shifted into something awful, and yet she had known it was coming all along. This was the moment she had been waiting for on those sleepless nights. The disruption that had stalked her disembodied was here at her apartment, in her relationships, in her business. It had taken Russell Cowell and with him the lifeblood of her gallery. It materialized Eli at her steps and had dragged Jones into a blind betrayal.

As sadistic as it felt, she was almost vindicated. She was no longer afraid.

The worst had already happened.

"He paints about love. I know love. I can paint love," Curtis said, then crouched down before the ruins of his canvas, then held his hands out to Isabelle. "I know love."

His eyes were glimmering and watery as he knelt in front of her. His rage subsided and he was paltry without it. He aimlessly picked at the wreckage at his feet. Something had caused this. This outburst wasn't solely about Russell. That was Curtis's go-to, his trusted punching bag.

"This is our gallery," Isabelle said. "And you can paint whatever you want. You don't have to paint about love. I have enough love for both of us."

"There may not be a gallery anymore," he said in a quiet voice. "They're raising the rent on the gallery at the end of the winter. Can you believe gentrification is working against an art gallery?"

Isabelle's breath stopped short. "We can move."

"How?" Curtis asked. "We're still in the red, and the two artists who were supposed to be renting the space backed out and the other one's check bounced. We are out of money."

Isabelle had no more words, no more ideas, and no more inspiration. Everything seemed to be dragging her underwater.

"I'm going to do something," Curtis said in a mumble. "I'm going to fix this somehow."

She turned away from him and headed into her small, dark office. She heard Curtis sniffing more coke and starting another destructive campaign against the ruins of the canvas. She got up and shut the door and submitted to doom. She slid down the door and brought her knees to her chest. She wanted to be angry at Jones but couldn't muster the strength it would take. Instead, her thoughts took her back to Noah and Eli imploring her to stay.

34

Jones forged through the last few days in a haze. Derek had nearly disappeared. Whole days passed without seeing his face, the only reminders he had been in the apartment a closet door opened with his coat missing, his computer moved from the couch to the kitchen table, or dishes left in the sink. She was relieved that he existed on the fringes of her days. Since they'd had sex, she couldn't settle her emotions for him. She had hoped for a resolution between them and maybe he would start behaving like the person he used to be. When they did see each other at the end of the day, words were few. They remained cordial and customary. But something changed in Derek, too, a slight increase in distance. She hadn't recognized it immediately until she was at her desk midday at work, trying to remember whether he had made her coffee that morning. He hadn't made any since the day she'd told him about the promotion. In fact, each morning when he rose, there were no sounds in the kitchen, merely a quick goodbye from the other room and the closing of the front door.

Jones considered this and in response gave herself nearly exclusively to work. She scheduled an appointment with Russell Cowell, who insisted on having his own photographer for the cover. Jones looked over the work of his appointed photographer for competency. She agreed to it, not realizing it was his girlfriend who moonlighted as a bartender in Stratosphere. She thought of those two— Russell Cowell, coasting on a wave of success for painting his girlfriend, and in return, she would photograph him.

Russell sat across from her in the small boardroom. He was an oafishly large man, and his very size made him look sheepish and composed, as if he were accustomed to being an imposition. He was more pleased about working with the woman he loved than being invited on the magazine cover.

"Why do you want her to take your picture so badly?" Jones asked.

"Because she sees the best in me." He beamed.

Jones didn't argue and set a time for his interview. He lumbered out of her office, and she sighed to herself. The man was completely oblivious to the havoc his beautiful portraits and their declaration of love were piling on her and the people around her.

Jones had tried to call Isabelle for days, but the phone went straight to voicemail. She even drafted several remorseful emails. But when she read over them, the words were trite. On her commutes to and from work, she even lingered a bit in the cold hallways, hoping to bump into her.

She even considered knocking on Isabelle's door and even Noah's door. But the thought of seeing Isabelle contented, playing substitute mom for Noah and his child, was too much. It posed too many questions and exposed the failing within Jones herself.

All the people around her were constructing relationships, weaving into the reckless passion.

She sat in the conference room, and her leg began to shake under the table. Outside the window, Todd Nicolas was back in the office and met Russell Cowell in the hallway. He looked up at the mammoth artist and grinned and talked empathically. He appeared even a bit star struck as Russell walked away. Then, his attention shifted to Jones in the conference room. He stepped in and glanced around before he closed the door behind him.

Jones's face grew hot, and she looked down at the samples of Russell's girlfriend's photographs. She pushed them across the table toward Todd.

"His girlfriend is going to take his pictures."

"His muse?" Todd Nicolas said, grinning in delight.

Jones smiled and tried not to laugh. "He's a romantic."

Todd grabbed a few of the photographs and examined them. "She's pretty good."

"Annoying, isn't it?"

Todd shook his head, then stared at Jones. She swallowed and pulled at the crease in her pants underneath the table. The air thickened around them, and she was swimming in him once again.

"I missed you," he said.

Jones opened her mouth, nearly daring to share his sentiment. Instead, she stood up and made her way to the door.

"Wait, please," he said, rushing up behind her.

He was so close she felt the warmth of his body. She strained not to lean against him, not to yield to his pull. She was too smart for this. She wasn't optimistic like Isabelle or maudlin like Russell Cowell. He was her boss and she had a job to do. Love was a force that grew stagnant between people, and when that end came, people were left broken with hollow reminders of who they were to each other. Left with sad tokens and cold coffee in mugs.

"I understand this is complicated," Todd said, "but please don't keep walking away."

She turned to him, ignited, her head pounding. "Do you know who Isabelle Boldwyn is?"

Todd shrugged.

"She has a small art gallery, and I was doing a cover story on her. Well, when you made Russell that offer, it took away her best-selling artist and you also co-opted her story. I get that it's business, I really do, but chasing your 'feelings' for me is affecting our business and my friendship. She was my best friend, and now her gallery is a breath away from closing. It's beyond complicated. We will never work."

"Please let me fix it, then," he said, bringing his hands to her shoulders.

"Why are you doing this?" she asked.

Todd Nicolas was all she could see. Despondency rose on his face, and Jones was transfixed in an urge to kiss him.

"Three years ago, I almost killed myself, and if Greta, my security guard, hadn't found me, I'd be dead now. I lived my life in so much fear that I wanted to end it. But I have a second chance. And art brought me back, art like Russell Cowell's. It reminds me of what I could have lost and why I'm glad I'm here. And for some reason, you do the same thing."

The haze Jones had dwelled in all week parted. Everything was crisp in an alarming detail. She was aware of the dust particles in the air between them, the few strands of blond hair the fell away from Todd's hair, the lucid construct of his eyes. He drew in close and kissed her, and the suddenness, the pleasure of him, left her clutching onto his arms to remain standing.

She would have given in completely if she hadn't heard the daily rumbling of the office. Jones ripped herself away from him and roughly used the back of her hand to wipe his taste from her mouth. She staggered for a moment as tears of alarm glistened in her eyes.

"I can't do this," she said breathlessly. "I'm in a relationship."

Todd stumbled back into the table. His face darkened in rejection. They stayed this way for a moment, both grasping for equilibrium. Todd brushed back his hair and straightened his suit coat.

"Please, let me help your friend. Let me at the very least do that for you, if you don't want to be with me," he said. "I'm so sorry for the discomfort I've caused you. It won't happen again."

Jones stepped aside, and Todd passed through the door. She silently watched him walk through the office, and the haze and heaviness of the day surrounded her once more.

Todd Nicolas's kiss haunted Jones. It prowled the edges of her mind like movement in her peripheral vision that disappeared when she turned to it. She told herself she did the right thing— the only responsible thing in her opinion. She wanted to believe she and Derek were in the beginning stage of some sort of reconciliation. The snowfall picked up again, not at the rate of before, but enough to ensure she traveled the city in a gray day and black night from the office to her apartment. At each place, there was a nagging ache left by either Todd or Derek. Both of them had become evasive.

Todd Nicolas's visits to the office had become nonexistent. During the first day of his absence, Jones had been able to keep her head focused on her work. But the next day, the ache, the familiar longing, kept her looking up in a wild hope that he'd buzz through the office with an announcement or some novel idea that would upend productivity. But he didn't come, and as the week reached an end, Jones went to the office of her finance director. She pretended to request the last quarter's profit report, but in truth, if anyone in the office had information on where Todd was, it would be the finance director.

"I've noticed that Todd Nicolas hasn't been here," she said as he handed her a report she didn't need.

He squinted through his Wayfarer glasses as he scanned through all the gossip he was a receptacle for. His lips curled into a keen smile. Jones's heart throbbed, and she knew he was somehow aware of her attraction to Todd. But the smile quickly vanished, and upon confrontation, she understood he would deny any accusation.

"I heard he went to New York for a week or so to check out the art of some anti-Trump collective," he said nonchalantly.

As she left his office, the duration of the day was plagued with wondering whether he did know something.

Back home, Derek had left a vacuum where he used to reside. He continued to pile on hours at the coffee shop, and when Jones asked about it, he casually said that some girl was let go and more time became available.

This, however, didn't explain the late-night creeping into bed that night. She attempted to go back to sleep but merely listened to the sounds of him slipping off his jeans and putting on pajama bottoms. She felt him go around the bed and hover over her to ensure she was asleep. He then made a clandestine departure into the living room, grabbing his computer on the way. What was he hiding from her? Why was there a sudden shift between them?

Jones lay in bed, awakened by a gnawing curiosity that quickly turned into the urge to urinate.

She gently pulled herself out of bed, making great effort to move silently. Was Derek punishing her for not telling him sooner? Was this the cost of her success? She lurked out of the room, pausing in the shadows. Should she have not tried for the promotion? Should she have let herself become damned from his business failings? Could that have been the bottom denominator of love, bearing the woes of the other's circumstances? She let herself move into the shabby apartment. She woke next to his cumbersome disappointment every day, but she had always been apart from it.

She would never carry his mantle.

In the darkness with his laptop on his knees, Derek hammered down on the keys. The screen illuminated him in blue, and there was a peculiarity in his face that she was unable to work out, a look that gave way to something like desire.

"Are you coming to bed?"

He jumped and shut his computer, masking himself in darkness. He stammered before saying, "Did I wake you?"

"No, I had to go the bathroom. How long are you going to be out here?"

"Not long."

Jones wished she could see Derek. The glow from the outside left most of the room in various degrees of darkness. They had been divided by so many secrets, so many barriers, but even if she could see him, it wouldn't have made it easier to speak to him.

"We haven't really talked since the night the gas was out."

She heard his loaded sigh from where he sat on the couch and tried to picture the exasperation on his face. It was odd, now, finding herself beseeching him instead of the other way around.

"I'm sorry," he said flatly, "but it's late. You want to talk now?"

Jones bristled and held herself. She strained through the night to see him and saw nothing.

"I guess not," she said, deciding she should listen to her bladder rather than travel down the void that stretched between them.

She stepped into the bathroom and submitted to the cold seat.

Jones had tried to be in step with Derek. The night they had slept together had been over a week ago, and the likelihood that it had been just a one-night occurrence, and any hope she had for them was misplaced. Her unresolved feelings were suddenly interrupted by a searing pain. She winced, muffling her cry from the burning her urination had caused her.

Winded and pale, she wiped and touched herself to see if she would draw back blood. She saw nothing on her fingertips and was relieved. The extended sensation of pain brought questions she couldn't answer tonight. She gently wiped herself, testing her pubic area for pain, and went back to her bed, where Derek lay on the other side on the far edge.

35

Hank sat on Noah's couch and rubbed his palms against his jeans legs. Initially, he had been supportive of Noah and his new family, but now, he felt uneasy in his friend's apartment. Noah's and Isabelle's voices talked to the child in the other room. Their voices both held a cheery lilt, and everything spoken adhered to affirmation and assurance. The people he'd known a month and a half ago had been possessed. He was unable to cope with the suddenness of this transformation.

At work, while navigating the small workspace, Noah's conversations revolved around Eli and Isabelle. Hank strained to recognize him. Noah was enchanted by the boy, detailing the grisly details of potty training, discussions with a lawyer for sole custody, and Isabelle's unwavering advocacy. It was as if Noah had been waiting to be this man all along. Hank saw no resistance in Noah—no suspicion. The guy who cried out for him to be a wingman, who had slept with more women than Noah thought possible, spent his break online shopping for kids' clothes and wailing about the waitlist for the good schools in the neighborhood.

Collective laughter burst in the other room. Hank considered leaving Noah's apartment. He wasn't quite sure why Noah had been so insistent on him stopping over after work. Was it to boast? To have a witness to this instant-made family?

Hank's encouragement eroded into a strange sort of contempt. It wasn't solely directed at his friend, but he did feel left behind. He was free from Andrea, lost in his newfound singleness, clinging to Gwen, and Noah was reading blogs about parenting. It had all happened too fast.

Noah, at last, stepped into the living room, flashing his chipped smile.

"Hey, sorry about that, man," Noah said. In his hand, he carried a paper bag and handed it to Hank. "This is for you."

Hank opened the bag and saw two dime bags of weed, a piece, grinder, and two half-smoked blunts. He quickly closed the bag and looked up at Noah in stark horror as if someone else was blinking behind Noah's face.

"This is your lucky bowl," Hank said. "Man, I can't take this."

Noah laughed. "It's yours now. Use it wisely. You must take up the mantel and toke, my friend."

"Are you sure? You have a kid—you're not dead."

"I'm sure," Noah said. "We all know Marcie had Eli living in some shitty-ass conditions. I can't do that. I gotta do what's right."

Isabelle came out to join them, holding Eli propped up on her hip. Noah turned back at them and smiled, his face fixed in pride. Hank's contempt crumbled at the sight of the three of them. It appeared as though the three of them had all been looking for each other for so long. And now that they'd all found one another, Hank knew he couldn't argue or question something so true. A connection like that between people had to be respected.

Hank lowered his head and smiled, closing the bag, and held it close. "Thanks for, uh, packing me lunch."

Isabelle glanced at Hank, then Noah, and rolled her eyes before laughing at the two of them.

Hank stood up, bent over, and kissed her on the cheek amicably, and then looked at the toddler draped on her hip.

"Have a good night, Mr. Eli," he said, mimicking the same tone he heard Noah and Isabelle using with him in the other room.

This action seemed to please all three of them, and Hank descended the stairs and entered his apartment. He entered slowly, in the hope to overhear Gwen or catch her in the act of something. She continued to elude any questions he had with sex or by disappearing for nights at a time in the past weeks. He'd given up on her volunteering any information and resorted to spying.

He had convinced himself it was innocent enough, merely picking up her phone when she left the room when a text message came on the screen early this week. On the screen, he'd read, "WES ASKED ABOUT YOU. WHAT DO YOU WANT ME TO SAY?"

Hank had set the phone back on his dresser in his bedroom, and while Noah waxed on and on about throes and triumphs with Eli, Hank's innocent curiosity was quickly altered into paranoia. Wes became a faceless figure looming in his mind. When Gwen kissed him, questions arose. And later, when he was heaving and grappling at his oscillating thoughts, sweat on his brow, post-sex, he clenched his teeth to keep from asking them. Gwen would rise out of bed, dress herself, and leave him subdued and alone for the night. The next morning, he stepped out for work as she would enter, giving him a tired kiss, swatting away all of his concern.

"I'll meet you at Peppermint," he now heard her say in the other room.

He took one of the joints from the paper bag and lit it. He inhaled slowly and swallowed back a cough. This alerted Gwen in the next room, and she came out. Her face was startled until she saw Hank.

"Hey," she said, reaching out for the joint.

"Are you going out?" he asked, and as he posed the question, he wished he hadn't.

She pulled back on the joint with a sharp drag before passing it back and narrowed her eyes at him. Gwen went to the closet and gathered her coat.

"I won't be long," she said as she moved to the door.

"I was hoping we could make dinner," he said, sounding more desperate than he intended to.

Gwen tilted her head at him, and the tension tightened between them. He wilted under her gaze and took to the comfort of the joint burning between his fingers.

"I'll play house with you later," she said, then left quickly before Hank could respond.

Hank found the ashtray on the coffee table. An ashtray he'd asked Gwen to use, but she insisted on disposing of cigarettes in mugs and cups and flicking ash anywhere she pleased. Whoever Wes was, Gwen probably wouldn't disregard him the way she did Hank.

As Gwen closed the door behind her and stepped out into the night, the current of his thoughts drifted back to Andrea. The months away from her had elevated her into a sort of sainthood. She didn't smoke and hated it when Hank would drunkenly puff on cigarettes or hit joints every now and then.

The weed had failed to calm his nerves. In fact, it made the idea of Wes more corporeal. He paced back and forth, at odds, yet again, with the vacancy Andrea, and now Gwen, had left in his apartment. He walked to the kitchen, opened the refrigerator, and surveyed its contents. There wasn't much there looking back at him but the empty shelves. Andrea, aspiring to be a chef, had always packed it with exotic cheeses, strange meats, and open jars that held parsley and cilantro. Containers upon containers were stacked on each other carrying a French dish she had seen online or chicken soaking overnight in some marinade. The refrigerator had not only carried evidence of her, but the best of her.

All that was left now was half-eaten takeout in Styrofoam and a plastic milk jug so old that it swelled, bloated with rot.

It could have been the weed, but he craved one of Andrea's dishes. He longed for the joy in her face as she spun recipes from foreign lands into beautiful dishes.

He stepped out of the kitchen while Gwen trekked through the snow to Peppermint, a loud dance club in Wicker Park. Above him, Hank could hear the muffled voices of his upstairs neighbors. Overhead, footsteps followed one another to the living room. Everyone around him was living life while he was stuck and utterly alone. Hank grunted from this pang of sadness.

He ran through his apartment toward his closet. He flung open the door and glared at the heavy old gym bag he had carried in for Gwen. And there it was, the evidence that he wasn't alone. That this woman was in this apartment with him and occupying space. He sighed as this comfort warmed him, but then he realized he still knew nothing about Gwen. She gave him nothing real to hold on to.

He kicked at the bag, and whatever it held was solid and in stacks. It didn't feel like clothing. He dragged the bag out of the closet and into the center of his bedroom. He recalled Gwen's panic when he grabbed it to bring it into the closet. Since she had been here, she never once moved or looked inside while he was here. His pulse quickened, and he slowly unzipped the bag.

Inside the bag were wads of twenty-dollar bills made into tight cylinders by rubber bands. The entire bag was stuffed with money. It was more money than Hank had seen in one place in his entire life.

A bitter breeze lanced at him, and he hunched over in an attempt to shield himself as he approached Peppermint. The loud thump of bass came from the small club, and he fell into step with it. At the door, a massive muscled man puffed on a cigarette. He clung to a woman who hopped up and down in his arms to keep warm. They laughed and talked in a slurred drunken dialect. Hank slowed when he saw them, as if they were obstacles in his way. The couple ignored him, staggering, crunching snow underneath them. They pushed their way back inside, opening the door, and red strobe lights and the roar of music spilled out onto the street.

Hank didn't have a set plan when he came here. He had tried several times to call Gwen and demand some explanation for all of that money sitting in his apartment. He knew it couldn't be legal and was possibly dangerous. He considered calling the police, but he was too afraid of being implicated in whatever she was doing. He was a black man in America, and guilt was easier attributed to him than innocence.

He had heard Gwen say she was here, and it only left him with one option.

But beneath that, he was relieved to be out of his apartment. He'd much rather chase Gwen for an explanation and bring her back home.

He pulled in a sigh to still his nerves and stepped into a small line of shivering people. He avoided eye contact with anyone, afraid they would detect why he was there. The line moved quickly and the doors opened, and he was met with a blast of hot air. Inside, the club surged with people. Bodies shoved in upon each other. Voices, loud and hoarse, became an underlying note to the peal of music. Above, revolving red lights imbued the room in a throbbing crimson. Lights and the images of figures reverberated off the mirror-lined walls, and people pressed Hank, elbows and hands nearly propelling him to the corner of the club along the wall.

He was a few feet away from the speakers where the painful assault of music washed out complex thought. Thrown back from the tide of people, he'd been reduced to the singular urge to search for Gwen. He scanned the crowd, finding that in the glow of the strobe light, all faces were familiar and yet strange. He stood back, searching the faces that tossed and flickered like flames, and the calming effect of weed he had smoked regressed into mild paranoia. For a moment, he thought he had done more than enter a club in Wicker Park—a club he'd passed and shuddered at because it seemed way too unbridled for him. No, he'd followed Gwen into someplace outside this realm. He looked at scarlet faces twisted in expressions of laughter and drunkenness and imagined he had caught a glimpse of Hell.

Sweat dripped from his forehead and stung his right eye. He quickly checked in his coat and fought along the flux to the bar. He grabbed a beer and continued forward when he found the bulk of Don, one of Gwen's friends he'd met at the party. A few feet away, Don's mass parted the tide of people, and next to him, as if riding a vessel at sea, was Shakes, quivering and moving in excess. Shakes was the first one to see Hank, his face sharking in recognition.

"Hey, I remember you," he said, and Hank suspected that for him, this was quite the undertaking.

"What's up, man?" Don said, and offered his hand. Hank took it and shook it, a misstep by the pinched displeasure in Don's wide face.

Shakes fished deep in his pocket. His movements were sluggish and his eyes half closed. He furnished a few pills and handed them to Hank. Hank was jarred and took them to keep them out of sight. He placed his hand behind his back and let them drop on the floor. He swallowed down a wave of nausea recalling what had happened the last time he'd accepted something from these two. He had no intention of hallucinating in the throes of this club.

"It's good to see you guys," Hank said over the music, trying to produce an aura of nonchalance. "Have you seen Gwen?"

"Yeah," Shakes said. "She off somewhere with Kelvin."

Don plowed a trench through the people, and Hank became a passenger following Don's mass while he bulldozed a path to the bar. There, Hank, as a gesture of good intent, bought them both a shot of tequila. The two men quickly sucked down the liquor. Instead of gratitude, they asked for another shot. Hank supplied them again.

"I have a question about Gwen," Hank said. "What is she hiding from?"

Don and Shakes exchanged uncertain looks at one other. Hank was motivated to buy another round of shots for them. Shakes inhaled his quickly, and Don was a bit warier. His pudgy face set in a grimace on Hank before he took the shot.

"It's not what," Shakes said. "It's who?"

Don gave Shakes an admonishing smack on his chest. Shakes wavered a bit on his feet, and Hank was frightened he might capsize into the crowd.

"Is it Wes?"

Don stiffened and Shakes twitched, all pointing to an affirmative. Don rolled over, perched on the bar, and ordered a whiskey. He looked like a nervous bull sipping on his drink.

"I'm only telling you this because you've been keeping Gwen safe," he said in a lulled tone barely audible over the crash of music. "Wes ain't nobody to us. Just some crazy mother fucker that Kelvin did business with and Gwen got caught up in. But be easy. He's here tonight, and they're trying to work shit out."

A prickling skittered across Hank's back as he attempted to process what Don had said. He looked around for Gwen, determined more than ever to rescue her from this club and these people. He recalled her in tears at his front door and her layers of secrets. Tonight, he could take her from this.

Gwen waded through the pressed bodies toward them, and alongside her was Kelvin who bore the same scowl he had when Hank had met him. Gwen seethed at Hank, and she narrowed her eyes at him. Hank's entrails sloshed inside him, and he was certain his stomach would betray him in the face of all this.

Behind them, a man slinked, his face dead set on the group. He wore a black T-shirt, baring solid arms and a battered fist. His snarl revealed sharp teeth, and his pallid skin radiated the red from the strobe lights. A wide silver septum ring dangled underneath his Roman nose. His dark eyes simmered on each of them like they were targets. The man before them appeared to have experience in coercing by force, and in his measured movements, it seemed as though he was ready to do that. Even amongst the multitude of people pushing through the club, he was isolated and processed personal space distance that others did not. His wordlessness was threatening, and the entire group bristled at him.

Hank felt something in him clipped, and he knew as he looked at this man, the apex predator of the small grouping, that maybe his first suspicion about this club was right. Maybe he was in hell. Maybe this was his punishment.

The moment of tension passed, and Kelvin ordered a round of drinks for everyone. He began talking to the man in a hushed tone, both of their faces stern as they began their negotiations. When the man's eyes were off him, Hank pulled Gwen close to him.

"What the hell is going on?" he whispered in her ear

"You shouldn't be here," she said back to him, alternating between fear and rage.

"I need to know what is going on," he said, turning her slightly away from the group. "Is that Wes?"

"How do you know that?"

"Is he dangerous?"

"You need to go, now."

She made a half-hearted attempt to shove him into the crowd, but Hank didn't budge. He was light-headed from the distress and vodka. He grabbed Gwen's shoulders, tears nearly rising to his eyes. He wanted her with him more than he ever had before. He was swimming in it, and she was more beautiful and wild than she had been when he first met her.

"Please just come with me," he begged. "You don't have to do this."

"You don't know what the fuck you're talking about. I'm not your ex-girlfriend. I don't need you or love you."

Shadows and red light passed over Hank's face. "I found the money."

Her face twisted, and her mouth closed and opened as if she were a fish out of water. Hank was preparing to plead to her when a cry over the music stopped him. Wes threw himself into Kelvin, who stumbled backward into Shakes. The two of them bounced off Don. The three men collected themselves. Their daze quickly evaporated, and the three circled Wes, their faces all entwined with the same vengeance and emboldened by their numbers. They stormed down on him with swears and fists.

Hank grabbed Gwen's arm and tried to pull her back. She wrenched from his grasp and joined her friends, adding her voice to the chaos. A swell of heat passed over Hank, and he was dizzy. He shuffled back into the churning crowd. The noise around him and the strobe lights recast everything in a brutal red. No one would notice a fight. Hank gasped for air and steadied himself on a nearby person who shook him off. The ground seemed made of sand, and he was sinking into their altercation. The crowd was forcing him closer into it.

Shakes, not aware who was behind him, drew back for a blow and his elbow caught Hank in the eye. In the collision, there was a flash of light, and then his vision blackened. He cradled him face, swaying from the ache.

Gwen's shrill scream brought the world back into focus. When he opened his eyes, Kelvin and Shakes jumped back, but Don wasn't quick enough. Wes darted at him, and Don bellowed out, finally drawing the attention of those around. Wes had now become the predator that Hank had feared.

Wes pulled back, and in his hand flashed the sharp point of a switchblade. Don clenched his stomach, and blood streamed from between his fingers. The world didn't make sense. There was so much blood. It continued to pour from the wound. Don sputtered, and his mass dropped. He almost took down a nearby woman in his descent. His eyes fluttered, and he caved in on himself. More screams cried out, and the music came to a halt. For a moment, the silence rang in Hank's ears, and confusion broke into panic as more people caught sight of Don bleeding on the floor.

Shakes kneeled to the floor over Don and began yelling, descending into panic.

Kelvin stood helpless between Hank, Gwen, and Wes. Hank stared at the dripping blade and knew his turn would be next. Wes glanced over at Kelvin and at Gwen. He sneered at her, then chaos ignited. People erupted into movement, surging toward the exits. Hank tugged Gwen into the crowd, steering them past fearful faces and toward the exit.

"Oh, God! Oh, shit!" Gwen said, her pale face too stunned to resist Hank as they stepped outside into the cold.

The crowd dispersed into the street, still carrying with them their alarm. Most of them continued to run, and Hank with Gwen in hand joined them, panting and storming through without a coat, too drunk on his adrenaline to care. He was reduced to the singular desire to flee. In the distance, maybe a few blocks out, a siren howled. The crowd itself grew less frantic outside the club. A few of them, now at a perceived safe distance, stopped to recount what had happened. Hank continued to push through them, through the numbness, through the suspicion that Wes was pursuing them. Hank swallowed at every alley they passed, at every corner draped in blackness.

They clamored up toward the train station and platform. Hank scanned behind them to make sure they hadn't been followed. A few train patrons sensed their panic and distanced themselves.

"Are you okay?" Hank asked.

"He's going to find out I was the one who took the money," Gwen said.

Gwen's skin had grown sallow, and she wrapped her arms around herself. A breeze fluttered the ends of her hair, and she was spectral as though she would be carried away by the wind. Hank took her toward the heating lamps in an effort to keep her from freezing. Under their warm glow, he saw the spatters of Don's blood on her cheek.

36

In the past few weeks, Noah was swept up in the new form his life was taking. Most days, he would struggle to stay afloat in the fear. Any free time at work was spent Googling parenting techniques and tactics on childproofing his home. Everywhere he looked, there was peril in his apartment from the electrical sockets to an amassment of empty beer bottles by his trash can. And the spare room he used for storage of computer parts made him nauseated every time he passed it. Every day, he dealt with the imminent threat of not being near a bathroom while spanning the chasm of potty-training.

Most parents had months to prepare, and then years before the baby became a child. When his anxiety would stack up on itself, as when Eli would stare at Hank in unending need, Noah reminded himself that the child was here now. Those years may have been stolen, but now here Eli was, and with him a force so primal rose up out of Noah. He took days off work and refashioned that spare room into a bedroom, flooding into home department stores and toy stores. While Isabelle looked after Eli, he painted the room in sky blue, and by the end of the day, his body was a network of aches and burning muscles. He accessed all his resources, pooling them together to fashion some life, some semblance of security.

His feelings for Isabelle reworked themselves around Eli, and his child became a vehicle in which they showed affection for one another. Washing him, reading to him, comforting his cries while stealing glances at one another. Noah stretched himself to care for each of them. And what had started off as an experimental fantasy had cemented into a reality for them. The brief interludes in which he did find himself alone, out amongst the cold, in a train car, his thoughts returned to his father and mother. How would he explain Eli to her? Would his father even respond to Eli? How could he look to them to aid him in the construction of this life and these new demands when dementia had taken so much from them? Those questions added bitterness to his days and weight to Isabelle's touch and to Eli. Smiles and laughter from Eli came forth like a soft stream, which startled both Isabelle and him. But soon, they rushed forth from Eli, and he began to run around the apartment, calling out for them both. Noah and Isabelle were reduced to "Noey" and "Izzy." His voice was playful harmony. Noah deduced he wasn't as advanced as a child his age, but in time, Noah hoped to change that.

One night at the end of a workday, Noah had baked cheap oven pizza, and after a scornful lecture, Isabelle was determined to make sure at least Eli ate properly. Isabelle came into his apartment using the keys Noah had given her shortly after Eli had arrived. She had a shopping bag of food.

She unloaded one of the bags in the kitchen and met Noah and Eli in the living room carrying the other one. Eli sat blithely in front of the television where cartoon animals danced. Noah glanced up from the screen of his laptop from the work orders at his shop. She leaned down and kissed Noah quickly, and then ruffled Eli's hair.

"Izzy!" Eli said in his cheerful tune.

Isabelle pulled out a box of crayons and a notebook. Eli smiled in appreciation, turning his attention, even if momentarily, to them. His small fingers worked a crayon out of the box, and in wide slopes, he scrawled on the paper.

"Help me in the kitchen," she said. "At some point, you're going to have to figure out a way to feed Eli without microwaved or precooked food in cardboard boxes."

They opened the door to the kitchen to keep an eye on Eli, and Isabelle unsheathed raw chicken from plastic. She instructed Noah to cut vegetables. And for a moment, there was the sound of them working and Eli humming from the living room. Noah smiled to himself in secret pleasure, but when he glanced at Isabelle as she turned the knob on the stove, she was fraught and tension rippled through her.

"You okay?"

"It's the art gallery," she said. "It's coming apart."

Noah placed the knife down and caught her by her waist. "I don't know what to say."

"There's nothing to say," she said, then peered into the living room at Eli. "He's so beautiful. I mean, all of this is so beautiful. And none of its mine. All I have is a crumbling gallery."

A spasm shot through Noah's face. "What? I couldn't do any of this without you. This is as much yours as it is mine. Look, there's something I need to tell you."

A dryness tightened Noah's throat. Words and phrases crackled in his head, and he readjusted his feet. His voice had evaporated, and he was unable to talk to her. Anxiety brought him back to the first night they'd shared together and how the wrong thing had caused her to push him away.

This new life seemed unimaginable without her, and the possibility of not sharing it with her muted him. Her concern, her uncertainty frightened him deeply when she suggested that all of this could fall apart.

He wanted to give her comfort, but the words were tangled, lost in the pathway from his mind to his mouth. Instead, he kissed her. They returned to their task and the intensity passed, leaving the sting of Noah's failure. He cut the remaining vegetables and went to check on Eli.

Eli was busy dragging the crayon rapidly over the paper, propped on his knees on the coffee table. He stopped when he sensed he was being watched. He turned to Noah, and a bashful smile pulled over his face. He held up the paper and offered it to Noah. Noah took the paper from the notebook and studied it carefully. Hard strokes and the jagged lines of crayons converged to create the green stem of a plant leading up to a yellow burst. Noah smiled at Eli and followed his son's gaze to the yellow tulips that sat in bloom on the coffee table.

Eli pointed and grinned. "Look, Noey!"

Noah nodded, and they both shared a moment of pride. Isabelle came out to join them as he handed her Eli's picture.

"Well, it appears we have an artist here," she said, examining the paper.

Noah focused on the tulips, and their brilliance took on a new form in his apartment. It was almost as if they heralded something greater, something that Noah was on the verge of with Isabelle and Eli. Even if he was unable to find the words, he would have to get them out of this apartment with the horrible landlord, the creaking boards, and walls with spider-web like splinters in the plaster. He could no longer accept the squalor in the building. He couldn't protect them here.

"I love you," he said.

"What?"

He turned to her. "I love you."

He opened his arms to her, and Eli smiled, jumping up to encircle their legs in his tiny arms.

Later that night, Noah awoke to Isabelle shaking his shoulder, standing over him. Her face, partially masked in darkness, was wide with fear. She was speaking rapidly, and emerging from sleep, he couldn't quite gather her meaning. Her brows creased, and she yanked at his arm, pulling him from the warmth of the bed up into the cold night. Noah shivered and stared at her, trying to follow her words, as if she was speaking into a radio at the wrong frequency. And then, one of her words ripped him from the last tendrils of sleep.

"Eli!" she screamed, taking ahold of his arm and dragging him through the apartment toward Eli's room.

Noah's heart plummeted in his chest as Eli labored in a rattling breath. Noah dropped to his knees at the side of his bed and pushed Eli's hair back from his face. Eli stared back at him with large eyes, lips parted, pulling one wheezing breath after another, his small chest extending and falling too rapidly.

"When did this start?" Noah asked, pulling the blanket off him.

"I-I don't know," Isabelle said, clasping her hands together. "Should I call an ambulance?"

Noah looked at Eli and sat on the bed, gathering his tiny frame into his arms and on his lap. Eli's eyes were mad with panic, and he reached out his tiny hand on the side of Noah's face. An ethereal calm passed over Noah with his son in his lap. He turned to Isabelle.

"Did you say that Marcie gave you an inhaler?"

Without another word, Isabelle raced across the hall and threw open the medicine cabinet. She tossed out bottles of aspirin and toothpaste. In her rapid movements, she dumped mouthwash and it splattered over the toilet and floor. She found the inhaler, holding it in her hand, and nearly lost her balance on the slick tiles below her. She tripped back into the room with her arms spinning like fulcrums.

She handed Noah the inhaler. Noah stared into Eli eyes and placed the inhaler between his lips. Eli's hand didn't move from the side of Noah's face.

"You have to breathe," he said.

He depressed the inhaler, and Eli's gasping breath sucked in the medication. Noah pulled him close and up to his chest, wrapping his arms around him. Eli's chest fluttered like beating wings against Noah, and Eli encircled his arm around Noah's neck. Noah breathed in calm, rhythmic breaths. Soon, Eli's huffing subsided and fell in sync with Noah's breathing. Noah stood, bringing Eli into his bedroom and into his bed.

Isabelle placed her hand on his shoulder, and they settled under the covers. Their watchful gazes locked on Eli.

"Thank you," Noah said.

Isabelle slid closer to him and closed her eyes. She made an effort to rest, and Eli was in deep sleep in his arms. Noah watched both of them and felt a twinge deep in his stomach. They were his family now, and there in the darkness and half shadows of night, he knew he had to try to see his father once more.

Noah sat in his car parked along the street of St. Rose Community Living Nursing Home. The four-story building was draped in ice and snow, and several streams of smoke were carried from its roof as if it were breathing. Dusk closed off the sky earlier tonight. The first streetlamp turned on, and the building was lit from within. Shadows and movement oscillated behind windows. And Noah was content for a while, sitting there with the car running, alone with only the potted tulips to keep him company. He hoped if he pictured his father behind one of those many windows long enough that he would be prepared for the reality. He had researched online multiple horror stories of dementia and Alzheimer's diseases and what they did to those inflicted. With each tale, he tried to recast his family as parts in the tragedies, but recalling the scenarios kept him in his car.

Isabelle had inspired him to do this. How could they have a family, how could they make what they had real between them if he had unresolved issues with his parents? She was at her apartment faithfully watching Eli. He couldn't return to her without some story, some resolution.

Noah held out his phone and listened to this mother's voicemail again. The old burn of her guilt came back and seared him, and before he could rethink it, he dialed her number. There was a brief dial tone, and then his mother picked up.

"Noah?"

Her voice was hoarse and rattled in relief.

"Yeah, Mom."

There was a pause, then the voice on the other line rumbled into a whizzing sob. Noah clenched his jaw, and tears blurred his vision of the tulip into undulations of amber in the glow of the streetlights.

"Noah, where in God's name have you been?"

"It's complicated."

"I was preparing to show up at your job—you know that?"

"I'm sorry."

"God, Noah," she said, and buckled into more sobs laden with thick sniffling. "We raised you better than this."

"I know, Mom, but something has happened to me."

Noah swallowed, and the heat coming from the vents in the dashboard became overwhelming. His mouth was dry, and words became knotted within him. He tried to speak and cleared his throat several times.

"Where are you?"

"In front of the nursing home."

"You're there?"

Silence hushed the line between them. On the other line, he heard a muffled tapping and a sharp metallic flick. He pictured his mother wherever she was lighting a cigarette. And as if to confirm this, she blew into the phone, expelling smoke.

"At some point, you're going to have to see him," she said. "You're going to have to deal with this before there is no more time."

"I know."

"You don't want the regret, Noah," she said. "I don't want you to leave this way. If you can't see your father, then come see me. I'm staying home tonight. The house is practically falling apart with me gone all the time. I mean, can you believe the snow we've been having this year?"

Noah agreed, grateful to have any reason to pull him away from the nursing home. He traveled south along Lake Shore Drive, taking him far from the luminous walls of high-rises south into the suburb of Beverly. Squat, post-war, bungalow homes sat along narrow streets, entombed in snow, locked in ice. Noah turned onto the road, and muscle memory took him along the path home, as if he were part of a migrating flock driven by instinct and design. He grew up in this neighborhood, blossomed from these narrow yards, and conceived ideas about the world beyond within the small span of those blocks. And although he now lived not too far from that place, years of being away had stretched into oceans.

His car stopped at the light on the block where his father's hardware shop still stood. He had sold it over six years ago, and now, Noah knew it was due to this diagnosis. Although it was no longer his father's, it still belonged to

Noah in memory. He glanced over at the old, rusty, accordion gate stretched over the windows. The store itself was dark in slumber, closed off to the world. But the sight of its brick façade dragged him back into the past. He could almost walk up to the store, unlock the gate, and pull it back and enter. The shelves would hold columns of tools and in the back would have been a wholesale key cutting machine, which his father had won in a bet on a horse race. Below the counter in which the key machine was posted, fine silver shavings gathered from the keys that had been produced. The air would have a rich bite of mechanical lube. Within those walls, gilded as any temple, Noah had discerned what it meant to be a man.

The light turned green, and a car behind him gave a punitive honk.

He was a few blocks from home. The houses were as certain to him as the pattern of lines on his palm. Now miles outside of the Chicago's center, the night was deeper. The light from a crescent moon made the snow lucent. He parked in the driveway of his childhood home, and for a moment, it was easy to believe he wasn't a father and he wasn't in love. He was sixteen years old. Inside, his mother would smoke a cigarette near an open window, and his father, strong hands covered in the dirt and wear from the day, would feign annoyance. He would pull her close and peck her on the neck, and she would playfully swat at him.

Over the laughter, the sound of meat could be heard sizzling in the pan and the Bears playing a home game on the television. There would be rightness to the world, a resonance Noah hadn't noticed until it was now threatened.

He climbed out of the car and brought the tulips with him. The door opened, and his mother stood waiting. Her body seemed compromised by the weariness of her husband's illness. Noah knew he was also a culprit in her state. He had left her the sole inheritor of it. He walked forward and held out the plant in its clay pot. She hugged him, and they stepped into his home. The barrier between the present and the past broke, and memories rose alongside him. Pictures were hung all over the walls, a testament to their lives at various stages. All ringing notes of the previous years, but as his mother led him into the dining room, he noticed there was nothing of the present.

There was nothing to celebrate, no more dinners shared, no more stories, no more kisses on his mother's neck.

The inertia he had during their phone call had dissipated. He smiled at his mother, now realizing what had been given to him, what he could give to her. He recounted the story of how Eli and Isabelle came into his life. His mother gaped back, nonplussed, fumbling for a cigarette. As she lit her cigarette, Noah sensed she reached for anger. She had been dealing with so much alone, and now here he was, unveiling another surprise. Her wrinkles furrowed and expanded. Before she could protest, Noah pulled out his phone, showing her a video of Eli, running along the apartment. His small form was shockingly fast, and he was scooped up by Isabelle in the small screen of the phone.

His mother gasped, and her hand was at her mouth.

"I'm a grandmother?"

"Yes," Noah said, and the haunting past around them was drawn back like a curtain.

37

Isabelle had to keep treading water. She had to stay above the fray. She had to claw her way past her exhaustion. She opened herself and allowed Noah and Eli to fill in the cracks. They gave so much to her, the boundless joy of measuring Eli's development, and Noah's finding new ways to express his love for her. She shouldn't have been so willing, but she anchored down in what they had created. It appeared to be the only place she could take shelter.

Curtis's temperament had deteriorated greatly in the last week, and when no one was in the gallery, he destroyed more canvases than he painted. Isabelle held herself in her office. Snow filled in the spaces between the bars of the small window on the rear wall, and by noon, the room was nearly black. The entirety of her day devolved into an obstacle course of trying to contact established artists to show at the gallery. And most of the artists were notoriously difficult to get ahold of. Then when she grew tired, she stayed on the phone circumventing the secretaries of the holding company of the gallery's building. She paced in her dark hovel of an office with the phone attached to her head. Hours were wasted on hold as whimsical pop music blasted in her ear. By the time she'd had an opportunity to speak to someone who could make a decision, she was so feverish with anger that her words came out garbled. The property manager pounced on this sign of weakness, and by the end of the brisk phone call, Isabelle felt as though her situation had worsened.

She sank into her chair at her desk and clicked through her emails from the new computers that Noah had installed. There were several emails, mostly spam, but one stopped her in her tracks. It was from the president of Nichols-Griffin Art Institute. She glanced over it, and it had been a lunch invitation sent out a few days back for today. She looked at the clock on the screen, and she had missed the time by an hour.

Isabelle picked up her phone, aware of the conventions she'd broken, but if it hadn't been for the Institute, she might have had a night's sleep. She dialed the number on the signature.

"Office of Todd Nicolas."

"Yes, this is Isabelle Boldwyn. I'd like to reschedule with Mr. Nicolas, if possible."

"May I place you on hold?"

Isabelle stiffened at the idea of spending another minute on hold. "Yes."

Thankfully, there was a brief silence and the secretary returned to the phone. "Mr. Todd would like to know if you are interested in joining him for dinner tonight. If you aren't, he could work in something at your earliest convenience."

Isabelle held her breath at the thought of joining someone who, in her quietest thoughts, she regarded as an enemy.

"I can join him for dinner," she said.

"He'll have a car pick you up at your gallery around seven."

Isabelle hung up her phone and tension bit at her stomach. She didn't quite know what his motives were. A small part of her wondered if he had somehow been made aware of the state of her gallery and this was just a ploy to gloat. She hadn't paid much attention to Todd Nicolas. She'd seen a few small pictures of him in the art sections of papers, but that was the extent of it. They orbited different venues, populated with different types of people. Mr. Nicolas's halls were populated with the well-to-do, the educated elite, and the students indoctrinated with his passing notions of art. And Isabelle's gallery was forged with gritty street artists, some living hand over fist. The walls of her gallery were a myriad of colorful angry critiques on societal woes, sculptors of manic passion, and exhibitions of conceptions so vague she could barely understand them at times. She wanted to be smug and believe that her art was of a purer intention that had little to do Mr. Nicolas's success.

She had been in her office for hours and finally stepped out to stretch her legs. She had expected to see Curtis out in the main gallery, but he wasn't there. An uneasiness gripped her as she called out for him. She walked through the back halls and stopped at his studio's closed door. Behind the door, she heard subdued moaning. She froze in midstride, and her mind flashed to Curtis lying on the floor injured.

She flung open the door and on a desk was a slender woman in a T-shirt pulled up over her head, her breasts exposed. Curtis was stooped down on his knees, lapping between her bare legs. Isabelle yelped and shut the door, heat rising to her face. Behind the door, she heard frantic movement and voices. The woman, now dressed, pushed through the door with an apologetic expression staining her face. The woman scurried out of the gallery, and Isabelle's gut shifted as she opened the door again.

Curtis pulled up his underwear, and she winced at the sight of his pale concaved ass.

"What the hell are you doing?" Isabelle said.

"She was looking to rent the gallery space, and one thing led to another."

Isabelle dropped her face in her hands and resisted the urge to throttle him. "We need that money a lot more than you need a good lay."

"Do you know how badly I need a good fuck?" he said, pointing at his still erect penis through his underwear.

"Dammit!" Isabelle said, rushing at him with a raised fist but stopping herself as he flinched.

"Look, I'm sorry, okay?" Curtis said, finding his jeans on the floor and slipping them on. "Besides, I thought you were with your boyfriend again."

"And that makes fucking someone here okay?"

"Don't worry about the gallery," he said. "I have a plan that will fix all of this."

"What plan is that? I've been calling the landlords and artists. You have no plan."

"Fuck you."

Isabelle considered hitting him this time. "Why don't you paint something to sell on the walls?"

She turned to walk out of his studio, and he came running up behind her.

"You know I've been trying."

"No, you've been snorting coke and breaking things," she said. "And I have something to tell you. I'm having dinner tonight with Mr. Nicolas."

Curtis stopped behind her and she turned to face him. His face grew pallid, and his thin bare frame appeared as if it couldn't hold the weight of his dreadlocks. Under his eyes were gray pockets of flesh, and for the first time, she saw the toll this had all taken on him. There was no witty retort on his lips and his shoulders sagged.

He barked out a humorless chuckle. "Mr. Nicolas from the Institute? Everyone invited to the party but me."

Isabelle was preparing to defend herself, but this left her grappling for words. Curtis turned around and shuffed back to his studio.

"I'm going to fix this," he said to her before closing the door.

At seven o'clock, a black Town Car pulled in the front of the gallery. Isabelle swallowed, zipped up her coat, ard stared at the car from the shadows of her gallery. Curtis had left a while ago without saying goodbye, and a swell cf guilt tightened Isabelle's chest. She still didn't know why she had agreed to this meeting with Mr. Nicolas or what she hoped to solve. His art institute had brought so much tumult to her gallery, and maybe it was inadvertent, but what could a dinner solve?

She stepped out of the gallery, through the cold night, and into the vehicle. She only spoke to confirm her identity to the driver and quietly rode through the city toward River North. Her anxiety had her fixed to the seat when the car stopped in front of the sleek glass building. The driver cleared his throat, peering back at her through the rearview mirror, and Isabelle smiled sheepishly. She stepped out of the car and surveyed the building, and a part of her shrank at the magnitude of all it. She didn't want to feel timid in the face of this, and she gathered the pieces of her indignation and moved through the doors.

Inside, she signed in with an older woman at the security station and took the elevator to the floor she was instructed. The elevator opened to a massive gallery where Russell's works were hanging from wire, backed by metal, and lit from above. Large windows faced the city and in the center, waiting with his gaze on the artwork, was a slender man in an oxford shirt.

Isabelle bristled at him, and it was as if she was back in the offices of her university, begging for funding and grants. Anger bubbled up in her as she looked at the artwork that once covered her gallery walls, strung up by cables. The display had the effect of a crucifixion.

As she approached him, she wondered what else was going be taken from her. How many blows could her gallery endure, and was this another one of the many indignities she would have to suffer to keep her dream alive? Was this spectacle just a display of Mr. Nicolas's arrogance? An opportunity to show the grandeur of the Institute and remind Isabelle that she was small? That her gallery was the other, a bastardization of art, and if she did possess something of value, then clearly it would be better served with men like him?

He heard her footsteps and turned to her and smiled.

Isabelle stopped, and for a moment, the warmth of his smile disarmed her. She hadn't expected him to be so young and so handsome. She remembered what Jones had said, and despite herself, there was a pang of sympathy.

"Hello, Ms. Boldwyn," he said. "Thank you for meeting me. I apologize for the strangeness of all this."

"Being lured out into the middle of the night by a man I've never met?" she said. "No, not strange at all."

He laughed, and then regarded her with gentle eyes. She couldn't quite read his expression, but she sensed thoughts behind it.

"I've been to your gallery before," he said. "It's where I first saw Russell's work. It's quite a beautiful setup you have."

"Thank you," she said flatly, then walked around his gallery.

"What do think?"

She paused and crossed her arms. "I think your display is a great disservice to Russell's work."

He flinched, and emboldened by this, she continued, "It is ostentatious, and I understand it's all in admiration, but his pieces are hanging from the ceiling like fish on a hook. But maybe I'm a traditionalist. Maybe that's why I have a small gallery and you have all of this."

Isabelle knew she should have kept her opinion to herself. He had the upper hand. She was on his turf, in his space, but she wouldn't yield completely. He considered her words and again, his face was indecipherable.

"I'm sure you didn't bring me here for my opinion," Isabelle said. "Why am I here?"

Mr. Nicolas turned back to the artwork. "We have mutual acquaintances."

"Yes, Jones."

"I'm sure she has made you aware of the complicated nature of our relationship."

"I was more focused on no longer being in the magazine—your magazine—but yes, she did mention something."

"For that, I'd like to apologize."

Isabelle turned on her heel and began to walk toward the elevator.

"Wait, where are you going?"

Isabelle stopped and glared at him. "Did you send for me just to talk about Jones? Because I'm sure she made you aware of her boyfriend."

"Please don't leave. I know about the trouble you've been having with your gallery."

"So? Are you proposing I pimp out my friend in exchange for your help?"

"No, that's not what I'm saying."

He was flushed and fumbled with his hands, at odds with himself. "Look, I understand that she is involved with someone. And I know it's stupid, but I care about her. She wants me to help you. I can't be with her, but I can help you."

"Well, honestly, I'm not sure if Jones and I are even friends anymore. Thank you, Mr. Nicolas, but I'm going to have to respectfully decline your offer."

Isabelle called the elevator and stepped in.

"And thank you for your time, Ms. Boldwyn," he said. "I'll take your consideration about the art display under advisement."

They held each other's gaze as the elevator door closed. The afterimage of his face burned out before her, and as it disappeared, she finally decrypted that behind his enigmatic presence was a deep sadness.

38

Jones ignored the abdominal pain for about a day. The muscles in her lower stomach gathered in sharp knots as she sat behind her desk and in meetings in conference rooms. She would have minutes at a time when she wouldn't feel anything, and in relief, she assured herself that it was her imagination. Maybe this was all a product of stress or her cycle was changing. But over the course of the day, as she adjusted in her chair, the rub of fabric over her skin would ignite an ache so searing it would restrain her. But worse yet, each visit to the bathroom was met with varying degrees of sharp pain. By the end of the day, she had forgotten her work entirely. She closed her office door and furtively googled her symptoms. Jones picked up the phone and with a quivering voice scheduled an emergency appointment with an OB/GYN the next day.

At her apartment, she didn't sleep much, and although Derek was in the living room, under the glow of his computer, he was out of reach. She lay in bed and held herself to keep from unwinding. The next morning, she rose from bed earlier since she had her doctor's appointment at seven. She called a cab to take her to the doctor's practice at Northwest Hospital. Greeted by the hospital staff, she filled out paperwork and was led into the small patient room. She changed into a hospital gown and small currents of air traveled up her back and chilled her. She sat on the exam table and tried not to stare at the stirrups on either side. Jones wished she had someone with her. Someone either to confirm or deny her suspicion about the pain. The doctor was amiable, asking questions, taking blood, and nodding as she described her symptoms. She fought a grimace during her pap smear, and then she was promised that she would be called in a day or two with the results.

The pain came in varying degrees of intensity, and she decided to take the next few days off until she received the results. Inside her apartment alone during the day, there was no respite, like she had hoped, only the sounds of the old apartment. She heard the building creaking and bowing against the breeze, the occasional crash of ice falling from the gutter, and the dreadful skittering of something between the walls. She tried to read, but she merely looked through the book and at the uneven floorboards underneath her. There in the silence, there was nothing but her hatred for this awful building, and in the wake of the gas being cut off, she certainly had grounds to move. Jones wondered how Derek would respond to her asking them to relocate. She had the capital since her promotion, and since Isabelle had been avoiding her calls and email, she had no obligation to stay in this building. And the realization of that left her with an ache echoing her cramps.

The next afternoon, Jones sat on the couch, wrapped in a blanket, making another valiant effort to read when her phone rang. It was her doctor with the test results.

"Hello, Emily," the doctor said.

"Hey."

"I'm sorry to inform you that you have tested positive for chlamydia."

Jones's insides turned to liquid and a ringing started in her ears, nearly making it impossible for her to hear the doctor.

"We're going to start you on azithromycin, and it will clear up in the next week. I advise you to avoid any sexual contact for two weeks once you start the treatment. And you might want to talk to any sexual partners you've had."

Jones struggled to listen to the doctor over the numb ringing in her ears. She gave him the address of a pharmacy nearby where she could pick up the antibiotics and hung up. She stumbled up to her feet, clutching at the wall for support, and staggered to the bathroom. In the bathroom, she dropped to her knees in front of the toilet and heaved up vomit until there was nothing but thick bile coming from her.

When Jones returned from the pharmacy, that crazed panic took ahold of her. It was impossible for her sit, so she began to orbit her apartment with her phone in her hands.

She tried to call Isabelle, but as she expected, the call went to voicemail. She walked along the apartment, listening the floorboards groan underneath the blow of her footfalls. Jones stopped and glared at the place on the floor where she had fucked Derek, and the panic grew dark. Tears and sobs came from her until she was shrieking howls of anger.

He had been the only man she had been with. Even when given another chance to be with someone else, she had stayed true to him, in the awful apartment and in his awful unmovable business failure. Ropes of disgust wound around her stomach, and she ripped the sheets off their bed and tossed them into her tub. From under the sink, she pulled out a bottle of bleach and upended it over the bedding. She wanted to kick in the skittering walls, to bash out the sputtering pipes, break the drafty windows. She wanted out of this apartment and away from Derek.

A notion in her core told her that whoever Derek had slept with, he had done it here. She could see him while she was out, taking some strange woman into their apartment, sitting on their couch, maybe even drinking from one of the cups in her cupboard, and leaving this woman's lips and fingerprints on them. Everything around Jones was contaminated by this, even her body.

She thought about taking the bleach and pouring it over every surface in the apartment, but instead, she went to Derek's computer in the living room. She opened it up and stared at the login screen. She typed in the password he used since his he was an undergraduate at school. The screen blinked at her and denied her access. Even this appeared to be an admission of his guilt. Her hands hung over the keyboard as she searched herself for the password. She knew it would be something simple. Derek was linear minded and not much for complex thought, which in fact was why his business had failed.

Jones, by impulse, typed in the business name and opened his internet browser, and the homepage was a seedy hookup site, a website filled with foul profile pictures of half-naked women staring back lustfully at the camera. The website was set up for dates, but Jones knew the true nature of the website was sex. Her leg began to quiver, and she held her head as she scrolled through his message history on the website. Most of them were failed attempts to reach out to heavily made-up women. But he was persistent, and there was one response from a woman and a long thread of correspondence between the two. Jones looked at the date it started, and it was the night after he had made dinner for her and she didn't show up. Her stomach lurched within her, and she shut the computer. She didn't want to know any more. She couldn't bear it.

There on his computer was evidence of a whole other relationship with some woman, whom he had written to regularly. Jones knew this was where the chlamydia had come from, and whatever obligations, whatever threads that had kept Derek and her together, were broken.

Her body, her thoughts, even the apartment around her took new shape. And for a moment, she fumbled around the apartment, adjusting to the form of things. Her hands brushed along the walls and her feet dragged on the floor. She couldn't trust any of it.

She drifted out of her apartment without her coat and down through the cold, musty hall and leaned up against Isabelle's door. She knocked lightly on the door.

Isabelle opened the door, her face marred by contempt. She stepped aside as Jones squeezed through.

"Who the hell said you could come in?" she said. "Oh, and I talked to your boyfriend Todd Nicolas. That guy is a piece of—"

Isabelle stopped and looked Jones over. "What is it?"

Jones drew in a shallow breath, and her chin trembled. She tasted bile in her throat. Through vision obstructed by tears, she saw Noah's child rising from where he sat on the living room floor in a pile of crayons and notebook paper. The child moved to Isabelle's leg, sensing Jones's distress as well.

"Please don't turn me away," Jones said as hot tears fell from her eyes.

Isabelle pulled her into a hug, and Jones shuddered in tears.

Jones was folded on the end of her couch. Her face was puffy, and her scowl was set. The television was on at low volume, and her thoughts flickered rapidly. She had been grateful for Isabelle's comfort and her support. Jones had told her everything from Todd Nicolas to Derek's cheating on her. She allowed herself to feel all her emotions. She wouldn't take any Xanax tonight. She sharpened the heat of all her rage, and Derek deserved nothing less.

The lock clicked and spun as he placed his key in the door. It was late into the night, so he was slow and measured as he stepped into the apartment. He staggered back at the sight of her on the couch and quickly hid his surprise behind a smile.

Jones grimaced at him, and they glared at one another. Derek looked away as he took off his coat. Jones opened his laptop and entered his password. Derek's face grew flushed, and she turned the computer to him.

"Have you noticed a burning sensation when you piss?" she asked.

Derek blinked at her, and his face drained of color.

"You gave me chlamydia," she said flatly. "The gift that keeps on giving."

Derek's mouth fell agape.

"So, I suggest you get tested and end it with whomever you're talking to."

Derek stepped back and swayed slightly. "Are you sure? Chlamydia?"

"No, you're right—cramps and burning urine are absolutely normal. Maybe it was something I ate? That new Cajun place on Fullerton."

Jones hopped off the couch and rushed toward the bedroom. The shock in Derek's eyes was making her ill all over again. Derek followed her and stopped at the opened door of the bathroom and pointed to the bedding losing its color to the bleach.

"What happened?"

Jones whipped around and jabbed his chest with her finger. "Did you fuck her in our bed?"

Derek opened and closed his mouth. Jones brayed in hard laughter, and Derek froze from the force of it. It was all so undeniably terrible. And Jones reveled in the magnitude of everything crumbling between them. There was no place to stand and nothing to hold on to. She could only tumble onto the daggers of her rage.

"I'm sorry," he said, "but I was so—"

Jones bit at her lower lip, and she wanted to laugh again and cry all at once. She was still lost, still misplaced in the face of his candor. But in the new arrangement, within her and outside of her, she saw new things. Jones appeared different from this angle, and so was Derek.

"You left me when I was broken," he said. "How is that love?"

"No, your pride was injured. That was it," she said. "If you were afraid to fail, you never should've started your own business. You don't give up—you learn. You do better next time."

Derek stomped away from her toward the living room, and Jones was quick on his heels.

"You fucked up, Derek. It wasn't the end of the world. But let's get one thing straight—I didn't leave you. I stayed here in this horrible apartment and waited and waited and waited for you to get your life together. And every time I tried to help or talk about it, you walked away. I stayed here. And you cheated on me."

"Oh, don't make it my fault."

"I stayed here and hid my promotion for the sake of your ego. I made myself smaller for you."

"No one asked you to."

Jones snarled. "You're right, and now I have chlamydia."

Derek tightened in a glower. He was barely recognizable, and Jones pulled back.

"She was better than you. She was really good."

Jones cringed, and her stomach tilted. "I'm sleeping in the bed, and I think it'd be best if you sleep on the couch."

Derek shriveled, registering the sound of his own cruelty. He went to touch Jones. She shrugged away from him, and his shoulders dropped.

"What are we going to do?" Derek asked in a small voice that sounded as if it were a part of the creaking floorboards, the skittering walls, and the cold breeze against the apartment.

She headed to the bedroom, and at the door, she turned to Derek. He was more than a resident in the apartment. The walls were more than walls around him with their cracked plaster surfaces. They were borders to his native country where he was a citizen. He would do more than live here. He would die here, small and beaten. She was aware of the stench of coffee and his sweat. It pained her with a sour taste in her mouth. She closed the door behind her, tried to block the current of sounds around her, and wished she felt like herself again.

39

Gwen didn't leave Hank's apartment in the days after the stabbing at Peppermint. Hank tried to comfort her and even suggested they go to the hospital where Don was recovering. But Gwen refused and only sat on his couch, staring blankly out the window. She curled up on the couch, her nerves set on edge, smoking cigarette after cigarette until the air was stagnant with the smell of burned tobacco. She still refused to use an ashtray, only a wineglass that held a sludge of pinot noir and crushed cigarette butts.

In the mornings, as Hank layered himself in his scarf and down coat, she'd stare back at him with pleading eyes, and when he returned, she would arch up on the couch, ready to run or scream. It was clear that Gwen was awaiting the same fate as Don, waiting for Wes to find her and get his money. But the gym bag remained untouched in the closet.

Hank was grateful to have her around in his space, speaking, however infrequently, to her. What had happened in Peppermint left him unnerved and brought the two of them closer together. But it had also divided him from those around him. He didn't speak to anyone about it. How would anyone understand? He couldn't go to Noah, who had been comparing the merits of different daycare centers. During the day, Hank slipped into a stream of thought at his workstation. He worked out scenarios where he reported what he knew to the police. He wondered if he was an accomplice in the sordid matter with Gwen staying at his place. And if Wes did find Gwen with him, he was certain his life would be in danger. Hank recalled Wes's size and the dangerous glare in his eyes and the glint of his septum ring. Wes possessed enough agility to take on Kelvin, Shakes, and Don.

Hank couldn't free his mind from the endless tide of blood coming from Don. In the night that had followed, one without sleep, one of double-checking the locks on the door, he had been surprised when Gwen ended a phone call reporting that Don had survived the knife wounds and was out of surgery. Hank slid into the fear that immobilized Gwen on his couch.

He imaged Wes stepping through the crowc at Peppermint and hunting him down. Hank would stand no chance against him. He had never been in an actual fight in his entire life. He would probably fold under one punch.

He assured Gwen that everything would be okay, but he couldn't be sure himself. In the quiet icy mornings when he opened the shop and walked along the street, every shadow and dark pocket in the alley could've been Wes. At any moment, he expected the man to lunge out of some dark corner between buildings or behind a parked car with the same switchblade pointed at him. At first, he attributed this fear to his imagination, but his office was in Wicker Park, a few blocks away from Peppermint, not even a full mile away. Wes could've easily tracked him down, and this knowledge dug around his shoulders and neck like a yoke.

The fear had become a palpable entity dressed as Wes, poking at him throughout the day. During his lunch, Hank picked at his frozen dinner and waved off Noah's concern. But the workday had ended and night felt even worse. He tried to find a viable excuse to avoid being left alone to close the shop. But there was none. He was alone with empty workstations and opened computers, dreading each shadow and each sound coming up from the streets below. His stomach curdled as the sun plunged behind the rooftops. He walked down the stairway leading out to the pavement. He paused at the door and gripped the door handle. He flattened his face against the cold glass of the door and scanned the street. The block before him was cast in the neon glow from the neighboring Thai restaurant. Outside along the sidewalks and in cars along the streets were the last campaign of unflappable commuters, pushing their way home. Hank joined them and ambled against the biting cold to the train. As he moved, a crawling tingle, like someone's glare on his back, stopped him. He pressed against a closed storefront, his back on a brick wall adorned with graffiti. He looked out into the crowd. He squinted to see over the heads of people across the street in black alleys and in tinted windows of cars as they drove by. He waited for the feeling to pass, but it didn't. The longer he stood along the sidewalk jostled by the lashing cold and people strolling along the sidewalk, the more convinced he was that someone out there was watching him.

He rushed to the train, and when he departed at his stop, he walked purposefully in circles around the blocks of his neighborhood. Once in the shady overhang of barren trees, he turned around and repeated his course. His mouth ran dry, and he stepped to the rapid pulse in his throat. When the cold grew too much to endure, he crossed onto his street and into his apartment.

He stepped inside his apartment and looked through the peephole, half expecting Wes to be staring back at him, but instead he saw the empty hallway.

"Is everything okay?" Gwen asked.

Hank responded with a wan smile and joined her on the couch, where he presumed she had spent the day.

"We're going to have to figure this out," he said, taking her hand.

"You're right," she said. "Wes won't give up until he has the money."

"It's a lot of fucking money," Hank said, then in afterthought, he left her to slide the chain lock across the door.

"You're scared?" she asked.

Hank's cheeks became hot, and his lips tightened over his teeth. "Were you ever going to tell me you're hiding drug money in my apartment?"

Gwen crossed her arms over her chest. "I was trying to protect you."

"How? By lying to me?"

"You shouldn't have followed me."

Hank pressed his face with his hands. "I can't believe this. Your life is a gangster rap album."

Gwen crossed the room and pulled his hands away from his face. She kissed him gently. "I've been thinking. We have a bunch of money. We can leave Chicago—you and me."

Hank stared at her and shook his head. "I have a life here. I have a business here. I love my life here."

"You didn't seem to love your life when I met you."

"Let's just go to the police," he said, holding her. "I can get a lawyer, and we can get that Wes guy thrown in jail."

Gwen jumped back. "No cops. And if Wes goes to jail because of us, life gets a lot worse for everyone."

Hank went into the kitchen and searched his refrigerator for beer. There was only Gwen's vodka in the freezer. He poured two glasses and returned to living room and handed her a glass. He sipped it and eyed her coolly.

"What was your plan here, with me?"

She tipped back the cup as if it were water. "I liked you. You see the men that I'm around. You are sweet and honest."

Gwen placed her arms around his shoulder and kissed his neck. The brush of her lips against his skin smothered his anger, and an erection tented his jeans.

"Because I'm safe here with you," she said in a breathy whisper in his neck, and her warm hands slithered underneath his shirt and up his chest.

Her hands dragged gently along his torso and stopped at his waistband. One hand dropped past the fabric and into his underwear and around his rigid cock. She squeezed him and he quaked. The other hand deftly unbuckled his belt and pants. They dropped to the floor with a thud. He clenched her ass, pulling her lithe body against him, and she moaned. He knew the whole endeavor with Gwen was foolish and now dangerous. But he was delirious with fear and lust. And he pulled at her clothes and undergarments until she was naked and heaving before him.

They fumbled to his bedroom, and Hank hoisted her up and flung her to the bed. She landed upside down with her feet in the pillows. He climbed on top of her, and she opened her legs. She brought her hand down onto his back and guided him into her. He growled as they locked into each other. Her damp warmth became a focal point to his untamed thoughts. Her nails dug into the flesh of his neck until the meter of him matched her panting. Her mouth opened and he breathed her in. She clenched around him and cried out, and he swelled deeper in her.

They weren't gentle. They were savage, clawing and pillaging one another. It was an act of survival and catharsis. Their bodies slammed into one another. Hank lost sight of the whole of her. In the darkness, under his weight, she was fragmented into lips and breasts and an expanse of skin. Hank dropped sweat down on Gwen, and her nails drew blood on his neck. Hank glanced up to the open door of his closet and saw her gym bag stuffed with the stolen money. A shock slid along his spine. And with his eyes on the money, thrilled by fear, by the new terrain that Gwen had brought him into, he came deep inside her.

Gwen's phone buzzed on the nightstand. Hank pinched his eyes closed, hoping the noise would end. The warmth of Gwen's body left his arms as she answered the phone. Her voice lifted the dim fog of sleep as she spoke into her phone.

"Kelvin? What is it?"

She sat up, and Hank opened his eyes. Silver light illuminated her wide eyes, and she began to shake her head to the intonations of Kelvin's muffled voice. She brought her hand up to her mouth and turned to Hank as if he, too, was hearing what was said on the other line.

"What happened?" Hank said, rising as his chest constricted around his lungs.

"When?" she said. "Oh, no. I didn't."

Kelvin's voice on the other end rose into screams, and she winced.

"I didn't," she said. "You can't blame this on me. It was your idea to go up against Wes. I only listened to you. This has to be him."

Her eyes shimmered over with tears. She sniffed back hard, shook her head again, and hung up the phone.

"Are you okay?" Hank asked, wiping the grime from his face.

Gwen placed the phone back on the nightstand where his clock read 3:58. She whimpered in a small cry, and her gaze moved unfocused along the room.

"Shakes has been arrested," she said. "Kelvin thinks I tipped them off."

"It's clearly not you."

"Kelvin wants to come by and get the money."

Hank hesitated and peered out the window and over the windowsill collecting the falling snow. A small dome of streetlight lit a few parked cars, capped with snow, down along the street. Beyond the circle of light was a nebulous darkness where Wes could've been stalking. He drew Gwen closer, more for his sake than hers.

"If you don't have the money, then you're safe," he said, then kissed her forehead.

They settled back into the covers. Gwen rested her head on his chest, and her tears dropped and traveled along the curve of his muscles.

"You're still naïve," she said softly.

"Give Kelvin the money and make him the target," he said. "You'll be safe with me."

She didn't say anything more, but Hank knew it would be a long while before she slept. He closed his eyes and looped his arm around her.

His sleep was desultory. The blackness behind his eyelids was a subterranean well of disaster. There, Wes surfed on currents of blood rushing from Don's stomach. He snarled with his sharp teeth and shiny nose piercing. In the ocean of Don's blood, Kelvin rested on the floating gym bag of money as if it were a log and Shakes floated outstretched, smiling up into nothing. And in the discord, Gwen was nowhere in sight in the long red horizon that drained from Don. A violent surge ripped Hank out of his sleep and into the world.

He reached out for Gwen, and his hand stroked nothing but empty sheets. He hurdled out of bed naked. His limp penis flopped around as he lunged through the bedroom and out into the hall. He called her name, peering into the bathroom, through the living room, and into the kitchen. He fumbled back through the apartment, looking for some sign that she would return—something that anchored her to his apartment. In the refrigerator, her vodka was gone. The wine glasses that held her cigarette butts had been cleaned and laid to rest upside down in the sink. The smell of cigarettes was less pungent in the air. He went to the bathroom and found not a single product that she used. There wasn't even a strand of hair in the sink.

His stomach shifted inside him and he shuffled into his bedroom. His closet door was closed, and he slowly reached for the knob and pushed it open. The closet was cleared, and empty wire hangers rattled and chimed on the bar above.

Chills bit at his bare skin. He searched the apartment, this time without urgency, and collapsed on his couch. Gwen had left and had taken the gym bag of money, and the void she had filled when she had been here, in his arms, had been ripped open. The emptiness gaped back at Hank and he tumbled into it. He rested his head in curled fists, and then noticed a picture frame propped up on his coffee table. Inside the picture frame was Andrea's smiling face, years ago. Her face exemplified who he had been and who he was now, naked and alone. Gwen had found it on the first night she had come to his apartment. He found it odd that she would put it here for him to find.

He picked the picture up, and the familiarity and the kindness Andrea reflected so pointedly tore at him. He had feared stabbing criminals, had housed stolen money, and consorted with people he would've otherwise run from. The world had been safe with Andrea by his side, had been consumed with her home-cooked meals.

His biggest problem had been knowing the ending. With Andrea, the world moved with clockwork regularity—inevitable marriage, house, kid, and dogs. Why had he hated that? Why did he reject that? He knew he had once had strong convictions on this, but now in this moment, they were misplaced. And if he could find them, they couldn't have held the weight of what he'd endured with Gwen.

He had gotten what he wanted. He had escaped Andrea altogether and flung himself into a place so strange, so devoid of order, that he couldn't find the direction back even if he had tried. He pulled the picture frame of Andrea up to his face as if he could reach into the photograph, into the time in which she was that person. He wanted the mercy of her kisses, the warmth of her breasts in his hand, and all she had brought out of him. But now he was alone, without Gwen as a barrier between him and the vacuum that Andrea had left.

A gnarled sob burst from him, and his tears dropped on the glass of the picture frame.

40

Isabelle lay in bed, still and sleepless. She stared up as tepid dawn light washed the ceiling of Noah's apartment. Through the thin walls, she heard the soft rumbling of Eli and Noah breathing in her ear. She could endure the strain of another day without rest because of this. Those tiny noises, sighs, soft snoring, and readjusting brought them close to her. Their proximity lulled her trapped state of weary consciousness. She was soothed by the act of watching them. She was a vigil against all the dread she felt.

The morning began with the well-rehearsed choreography Isabelle and Noah had fallen into since Eli had begun to live with them. Noah stretched and grumbled, tired but grateful to have company and purpose. Isabelle would rise with him, and they tag-teamed getting Eli ready, passing him off at points like a baton. Eli, half-asleep, handed from Isabelle and then back to Noah, was washed and dressed. And by the end of it, he was awake and whirred in between them. His small feet and laughter added song to their conversation.

Noah still hadn't solved the issue of childcare during the day, and he decided to stay with Eli during the morning as Isabelle dressed and caffeinated, readying herself for the world. Exhaustion tied around her ankles like lead weights, and she hauled herself up through the trains and bus toward the Nichols-Griffin Art Institute. The building was more impressive in the bleak light of day than it had been during the night, and people oscillated in and out of the glass doors. Isabelle followed the flow inside, signing in and taking the elevator back to the gallery floor. There, she envisioned Todd Nicolas standing before the art, but he wasn't in the gallery. Instead, the gallery was invaded by several workmen, clamoring and constructing walls within the space. Russell Cowell's portraits were gone.

Isabelle glared and backed into a staff member headed to the elevator, causing him to spill a file of prints. She knelt and helped him collect the papers with a sheepish apology.

"Do you know if Mr. Nicolas is in today?" she said.

Slightly perturbed, the staff member straightened at the mention of his name and pointed her in the direction of the office. She meandered through the halls, and her gaze drifted from the walls that surrounded her. The stretch of walls contained a rich parade of color, methodized composition, and deft workmanship within frames. The collection of work within the hall usurped that on her gallery's wall. She lingered, nearly forgetting why she had come on this mission to begin with. At the end of hall, she came to a secretary posted before Mr. Nicolas's door like a warden.

Isabelle introduced herself, and the indifferent young man said, "He's not taking any visitors today."

"Just tell him Isabelle Boldwyn is here," she said, and narrowed her eyes at him.

The secretary expressed a sigh of reluctance and made a huge show of picking up the phone and announcing her. His face widened in shock, and he stepped up and opened the door for her. She sneered at him and pushed through.

The door closed behind her, and Todd Nicolas had his back to her, leaning on his fist up against the glass of the window. The flux of snow and the cityscape outlined his form. His shoulders sagged, and his hair was rumbled and unkempt. He turned to Isabelle and looked as tired as she felt.

"I want to apologize for what I said to you," she said.

He grinned half-heartedly. "You were right about Russell Cowell's work. I took down the cables, and we'll get it mounted like it deserves to be."

"Well, I know art," she said, "and I know Jones."

Todd stepped closer to her, and she saw his sadness settle again on his delicate features.

"She has feelings for you. And in light of recent events, I think you have a chance with her," she said. "But you're going to have to be patient. She's been hurt, so it's going to take time."

He brightened at this, and Isabelle was startled at his radiant beauty.

She cleared her throat. "You're clearly an intense guy, so take it easy, man. Be her friend first. Can you do that?"

"Of course, I can," he said. "Does she know you're here?"

"No," Isabelle said. "But I did a lot of thinking last night. You seem to be the most emotional man I've ever met, and she tries to feel nothing."

"Why are you doing this?"

"Because, like you, I care about her and want her happy." Isabelle examined him from head to toe and kissed her teeth. "You might want to take a shower before you try to talk to her."

She turned on her heel, and at the door, Todd Nicolas said, "No one talks to me the way you do."

"Maybe they should more often," she said.

"I would still like to help you and your gallery," he said.

"Look, this doesn't have to be quid pro quo."

"Fine. How about a consulting position?" Todd said. "Just part-time, and we'll work around your schedule with your gallery. Maybe you can save me from making an ass out of myself on other exhibits like you did with Russell Cowell. Everyone seems to say yes around me."

"Let me think about it," she said.

Isabelle stepped back out into the day. She felt so venerated, so light she could have been carried away by the chilly breeze. She traveled back to Logan Square and toward her gallery with a new zeal. Isabelle tucked herself into her coat, and as she approached, she heard a violent crunch under her feet. She glanced down, and the sidewalk was shimmering with shards of glass along the snow. The glass led a trail to her gallery.

Isabelle sucked back a scream, and she could barely force air into her body. She flailed and drove forward through the snow until she was at the front of her gallery. She wept, and her strangled voice stepped through the broken edifice of jagged windows into the dark gallery. At her feet, the floor was littered in ruptured canvases, shattered frames, and remnants of installations. Her cry curled off walls defaced with black graffiti, scrawled upon like primitive hieroglyphics. The destruction was complete, as if some vicious storm had shredded all it could get its hands on.

The shock produced a dull pain in Isabelle's skull, and she grabbed her head. She forced herself to take in breaths, and when she was breathing normally, she called the police. She readied herself as she looked back at the wreckage, unable to hold on to anything but herself.

Hours passed before the police had left the shambles of the gallery. The reports had been filed. Pictures had been taken. Statements had been given. The officers were so efficient that none of them stopped for remorse. They were Chicago police officers who'd undoubtedly seen worse. This was petty vandalism. No one had been injured. No one had been murdered. A report could be processed. An insurance check would cover the damages.

Isabelle's muscles could barely move. She was made of stone with a broom in her hands, pushing heaps of glass in no particular direction. A numbness invaded her like a drop of dye smoking through water to change the liquid completely. All she had worked for and toiled for had been brushed aside and lay in ruin before her. There was so much glass, and she couldn't step without it cracking underneath her feet. It came from the windows, framed art, and even from the light bulbs above. She decided she wouldn't move for a while.

Curtis said nothing as he boarded up the front window with plywood. The slamming of his hammer was all that could be heard. When he finished, he glanced at Isabelle.

"It's going to be okay," he said.

His voice startled her and brought her out of numbness. She glanced down at the small pile at her feet and shrugged her shoulders with a bitter snort.

"Why? Why would anyone do this?" she asked.

She edged forward and winced at the sound of glass. Along the wall, she kneeled down to a split canvas and held it close to her. She showed it to Curtis and bit her lip. He remained stoic, and she continued her survey, flinching with every step. Nothing felt real. Isabelle released the broom, and it slammed on the ground. A place she had built and fought for was no longer discernible. How can she trust the world now? Had she fallen asleep somewhere and this was the design of some nightmare?

"How are we going to tell the artists that their work is destroyed?" Isabelle pushed glass off a ripped painting.

"I'll tell them," Curtis said in a calm voice, and rested a hand on her shoulder.

Isabelle walked away from him and paused at the crumbled ruins of a sculpture. Her breath was shallow as she recalled the dazzling provocation of the piece, now rubble before her. She bent down to touch it to see if it was real. The clay was hard and jagged on her fingertips. The violation rocked her, and she stumbled on her feet and into the wall.

"They got every piece," she said. "Nothing was spared. Not a damn thing."

Curtis was behind her again, putting his hand on her shoulder in consolation. She turned and studied him. He was serene in the face of all this destruction. Isabelle lurched, and his hand seemed heavy on her, as if it would crush her.

"This is a chance to start over," he said. "I have a few pieces at my apartment."

Isabelle narrowed her eyes at him.

"I know it looks bad, but this could all work out," he said.

"What do you mean?"

"We can rebuild and relaunch."

Isabelle bit her lips, and her focus drifted to Curtis's hand. "Are you worried that whoever did this would come back?"

Curtis's hand slipped from her shoulder, and Isabelle concealed her relief. She stepped back, and glass snapped as she backed away from him. Curtis noticed, and his face darkened. Isabelle's stomach pitched as fear tickled the back of her neck.

"You did this," she said.

Curtis blinked at her, unshaken. He slung his dreadlocks over his shoulder. He went back to the plywood on the window and inspected his job.

Isabelle looked around her as a new level of horror settled on the gallery. She could see him moving through here at night, ripping everything apart. Probably using the same hammer he used to nail up the plywood. Her knees buckled underneath her, and searing rage lapped at her insides. She stormed up to him, kicking up glass and debris.

"What the fuck is wrong with you? What does this solve?"

"Everything. The insurance money will cover all the debts. The artists will get paid in the settlement. And how can the landlord raise the rent after this?"

"How can you be sure it won't get pinned on you or me?"

"Of course, I didn't do it. I just had a few motivated people take care of it. We have foolproof alibis."

Isabelle could barely see anymore. A ribbon of fog glazed over her vison. A tiredness pulled at her.

"I'm taking a consulting job at Nichols-Griffin Art Institute. I was going to put the money into the gallery. We were going to be fine, Curtis," she said. "We were going to be fine."

"But I took care of it," he said.

Isabelle turned from him and to the gallery behind them. "No, you didn't. Look around—can't you see it? You destroyed everything. Everything that we were fighting for."

A tear trailed down her face. Curtis reached out to touch her in comfort, and she shrugged him away.

"We can make it new again," he said. "Better this time."

"No, we can't," she said. "But I can."

Curtis recoiled, and he clenched his fist and tightened his jaw.

"This," Isabelle said as she gestured around the gallery, "is why Russell Cowell is a better artist than you."

Curtis slammed his foot into the ground. "That's not true."

"Look at what you did to us," she said. "To me."

Curtis glanced around, and his eyes widened as if he saw it for the first time. His chin trembled. He shuffled forward and touched the battered walls. He turned to Isabelle, and sorrow was trapped within his face.

"When I get the money and pay off the damage and the artists who trusted us with their work, you take whatever is left," Isabelle said. "And stay away from here and stay away from me."

Curtis was wounded and grabbed the fabric of his jeans for a moment. He hunched his shoulders, and a grimace passed over his face. His chest raised in a large breath to speak. Isabelle stood her ground. She didn't blink, and he wavered and nodded slowly. Curtis glanced around and sighed in resignation. He dropped the hammer. He strolled out of the gallery, out through the back, and into the frigid darkness. Isabelle wiped her face. A hard breeze whistled between the wall and the plywood. She pulled gloves out of her pocket and onto her hands. She bent down for the broom and with one last look began to sweep the glass into organized piles.

Marcie clutched her fur coat as she sauntered through the massive terminal of O'Hare Airport. In the last month out in Miami, she had grown used to the tropical weather.

Her skin was bronzed from the sun. Her gait was smooth as she wheeled her suitcase behind her. She held her head high and swallowed down the burn of her recent failure. An entire time zone and several states couldn't hide her from all she hoped to escape. The CFO she had run away with, who had seemed beyond mortality with fervent pledges of affection, had revealed himself to be nothing more than a man. He was not only a man, but one in the worst sense.

In the wide beach villa, perched next to the water, windows opened to catch the rich salty air of the ocean, she'd peeled back his layers. Among beautiful art deco architecture and the fiery kiss of seaside sunsets, he emerged flawed. His charm folded beneath a whiny petulance, and while she sat adorned in her bikini, out on the stone patio, so free, his voice would call her back. He issued demands as if decrees, and any denial of such would be met with withholding of money and the reminder that she could be replaced like the Indian carpets on the floor or the beautiful trimming along the walls.

One morning, as she lay, eyes closed to the glow of the sun, he approached her. His shadow crossed the warmth of the sun, and when she stared up at him from the reclining lawn chair, he was a black silhouette against the blue of the sky.

"I have a business meeting, and I'll be gone all day," he said. "Please have dinner ready when I get back this evening."

Marcie blinked back at him and shielded her eyes against the bright morning. She waited before responding, hoping that laughter would follow this statement. That this was an awful joke and surely he knew who she was.

"I don't do dinner," she finally said.

"Please tell me, what do you do then?"

He left her alone, blinded from the sun. It was the first ploy of manipulation. Despite herself, she ordered dinner and set the table for two. He returned to the house as expected, and they ate in silence. And in the silence, she began to study the fractures in his façade. The CFO must've felt her scrutiny, the disapproval behind her icy glare, but his behavior didn't waver. Soon, each day began with a list of demands and questions.

"We're having dinner with my new business partners."

"Don't wear that. You look cheap."

"Don't you think it's too late to be going out?"

"Where have you been all day?"

"Take off your clothes."

"I need you here."

Marcie always did her best thinking at night. There was something to be trusted about the night, and in the hidden darkness, she was the true manifestation of herself. She turned over in the white sheets, and in the pearly glow of moonlight, she saw his age. Lines branched over his face, and the brutality of too much business seemed to weaken him. His bare chest was thin, and the curve of his ribs caught shadows. Skin puckered under his neck. His knuckles were swollen as he gripped at the sheets. All the kindred strength, the shared language that she had seen in him, had gone.

She climbed out of bed and put on a cream silk robe. A breeze from the open window filled her silk robe like a sail, and she drifted out of the bedroom to his office. At his desk, she opened the drawer and withdrew a small baggy of coke next to a modest stack of hundred-dollar bills. She made out tiny lines with one hand and counted the modest stack of money. She took one of the bills from the stack and used it to take in the lines. Marcie continued to tiptoe through the house. All the windows were open to the breeze, and she heard the soft rustle of palm trees outside on the property. The moonlight lit her steps and the beach further out behind the house. She opened the deck doors and traveled down the slow incline into alabaster sand as white as the snow she had left behind in Chicago.

All the neighboring houses were dark, and in the distance, over the bank of palm trees, glistened the festive skyline of Miami clashing against the night sky with its yellow glow. It was beautiful, and Marcie saw that she couldn't grab hold of the life she had planned there. And instead of the freedom she had hoped to gain, she had fallen into the chains of a man weaker than the one she had left in prison.

Black water lapped at her feet, and her toes dug into the wet sand. The silver light shattered along the ripples on the water and swept out as far as she could see. She walked into the dark ocean, and it was warmer than the air around her. She went slack and let her body rise to the surface of the water. The splashing in her ear took away the buzz of a nearby coastal street. Her hair reached out around her head, and her robe came undone and opened out like wings behind her. She was naked and free without remorse.

In the morning, it would be time go back to Chicago. The man she had come here with was weak, and she now saw his only strength had been in possessions. She refused to be one of them. She couldn't pretend to be just part of the beautiful ornamentation within his house. He barely condoned her walking out of the house, let alone trying to get a gig dancing at one of the local bars. Because she was unfamiliar with the terrain and the people, who were so tan and excessively preened, it left the sting of distrust in Marcie's mouth. She didn't recognize any of the people who milled out before her. Against the backdrop of the most startling sunsets and sunrises, a longing for her old life, her known riven sidewalks and streets, grew. She even missed her ex-boyfriend, and if he somehow called her, she decided she would answer. She thought of Eli and how sickly, how broken he had been, and she knew Noah would take care of him. In the fabric of his nobility, the child would be safe.

In the morning, when the CFO headed out, predictably with a list of commands, Marcie gathered the cash from his desk and various hiding spots. With the money, she had enough to fly first class and hold down for a few months until she pieced back her life and made a sizeable deposit into her ex-boyfriend's commissary.

Now, it was late afternoon when she returned to her side of the city. The cold was harsher than she had remembered, but the sweetness of nostalgia still held strong. Overhead was the dome of gray clouds, and even this early in the day, the sky began to darken. She dropped her luggage off at her former colleague's place, where they smoked a celebratory blunt and Marcie lined up a gig for next week. She took the train further west into Logan Square, invigorated by the blast of wind and snow. She had almost gotten her life back. Only one last thing to do—one last ache to attend to digging inside her.

Marcie stopped in front of Isabelle's gallery to see it boarded up and battered. She had hoped to find her there, but not yet defeated, she walked the street to the train and took it east back to Isabelle's neighborhood. The snow came down harder, and the tips of her hair hardened with ice. She picked up her pace along the street. She stepped into Isabelle's building as one of her neighbors was leaving. She wavered over the door before committing to a knock.

She heard Isabelle's voice and footsteps carry her toward the door. In a rush, she opened the door and halted her conversation immediately as she saw Marcie. She quickly hung up the phone, and a scowl tainted her face.

"Marcie," she said as if spitting venom.

"Hello, Isabelle," she said. "May I come in?"

Isabelle clenched her teeth and sneered. She stepped aside, and Marcie wiped her feet on the mat in front of the door. She curtseyed at Isabelle and crossed the room to a couch.

"Any more children you'd like to drop off?" Isabelle asked, sitting across from her as she crossed her legs and arms.

"About that . . ."

"Yes, about that," Isabelle said. "We have been taking care of Eli."

"We?"

"Yes, him and me."

"Charming. Well, I'm here to take back my brat. I'm sure he's probably driving you crazy."

Marcie heard rustling in the back room and the quick staccato of a child's footsteps.

"He's fine. He's really not a problem, Marcie."

A child rushed out of the room and into the living room. He froze as if a spotlight had been placed on him as Marcie's and Isabelle's gazes fell on him. He was healthy and pink-faced. His skin was clean and glowing, and he wore a small set of overalls over a bright red sweater. His hair was cut and styled, and his round face held all the features of Eli, but the child certainly wasn't hers. Her child had never moved so fast. Her child had never been that clean.

A mild shock gripped at her, and she clutched at her fur coat. She choked, and tears pricked her eyes. She held out her hand for Eli to come to her, and he hesitated, then scurried past her to Isabelle's side. Both of the women exchanged helpless glances, and Isabelle put her hand slowly on Eli's shoulder. It was protective and instinctual, as if she was his mother.

A deep burn twisted in Marcie. She had expected Noah would have just kept the child alive, but she never could've foreseen this. It made what she was about to say more difficult. But she truly wanted to be free, and here it was, the freedom she had always wanted, bittersweet but complete. She edged off the couch. She almost walked out.

She had lost Eli, but her child was safe and thriving, and that was all she could've hoped for.

But guilt anchored her in that spot, and if she truly wanted to be free, Isabelle and Noah deserved the truth.

"I didn't know he would be here with you," Marcie said. "I was coming to apologize."

Isabelle's face was stark, and she pulled Eli closer. Her eyes shimmered, and one tear dropped from her face and ran down her cheek. Isabelle's breath was shaky as she whispered, "Are you coming to take him back?"

Marcie wrung her hands and smiled sadly, and her own tears rolled down her face. She sniffled and pushed back her wet hair. "No, no. I'm not, Isabelle. I couldn't, not now. But when I tell you the truth, you and Noah might not want him."

41

Noah was once again parked in his idle car outside the St. Rose Community Living Nursing Home. Snow dusted over the hood of his car, and the afternoon light escaped from breaks in the clouds overhead. The rare sunlight found the inside of his car and heated the small cabin. It illuminated the potted tulip Isabelle bought for him. Eli was kicking and humming, locked within a booster seat. The chemical smell of plastic was heavy in the air from the new booster seat. Noah had bought it special to take Eli with him on this trip.

Noah rested his hand on the door handle and had tried to open it twice. He couldn't work up the nerve it took to get Eli to cross the street and enter the building. His throat was dry, and his tongue was a sheet of sandpaper in his mouth. Eli began to kick harder against the passenger seat, which bounced from the blows. The seat was supposed to hold Isabelle. Last night, when he had tried to talk to her, she was in a quiet mood. He assumed it had to do with the vandalism of the gallery. He attempted to comfort her, but she was locked in watery-eyed silence, and he feared his efforts would only further upset her.

This morning when he woke, she had been asleep. Noah had been so surprised to find her that way that he couldn't be moved to wake her. Instead, he wrote her a note and left it gently on his pillow beside her head.

"Noey?" said Eli.

"Okay," Noah said, and unbuckled this seat, then turned to Eli. "We're going to go inside that building."

Noah pointed, and Eli followed his finger and nodded.

"Can you be good for me?"

Eli nodded again and smiled. Noah's heart swelled, and he opened the door. His foot lingered, and then he lowered himself onto the frozen crunch of snow. Noah unbuckled Eli from the booster seat, and Eli hopped into the snow. He stamped down the snow around his tiny feet, finding pleasure in his footprints. Eli raised this arms and hands up to Noah as if they were branches from a tree. Noah scooped him up and perched him on his hip, and with the other hand, he took the potted tulip. He marched forward before his conviction could abandon him. He stopped at the greeting desk at the front of the building. As the receptionist doted over Eli, who relished in the attention, Noah scanned the lobby decorated in printed couches, antique rugs, and heavy, healthy plants perched on many surfaces.

The receptionist directed Noah to the elevator. He grew light-headed as blood coursed through his skull. Inside the slow-moving elevator, Eli touched his chin, and his hand was cold and sticky on his face. Noah smiled at him, and Eli beamed back. Noah's uneasiness was drained from him in that moment.

"Can you hold this for me?"

He gave Eli the tulip, and Eli wrapped his arms around the plant. Noah raked his free hand across his son's head. The elevator chimed, and the doors opened at the second floor. He was centered and used his other arm to support his son's weight. Noah checked at another station in which a nurse, a slender dark man, buzzed him in. The nurse was kind and lit up when Noah told him his name.

"I'm Leslie," the nurse said as he took him through the sterile white halls. "Your dad is quite the charmer—you should see what he can get the nurses to do."

Noah gave the nurse a weak smile. He was more concerned with the squeaking of his wet rubber soles on the linoleum. As they pressed forward, turning into another white hallway as completely indistinct as the one they left, Noah slipped into vertigo. The florescent glow, audible like soft breathing, buzzed overhead. Along the hallway were doors in various states of open and closed, leading into rooms, and as he passed one, he saw a figure moving listlessly. He paused as the old man, bent over in age like a twig, slopped against a harsh breeze, moving about the room as a pinball bounced off surfaces. His sparse gray hair was matted in multiple directions, exposing dry, pale flesh, and his face was as expressionless as a corpse's. Noah moved quickly in a surge of fear and collided into the nurse. Eli dropped the tulip and the nurse's hand shot into the air before them to catch it.

He handed it back to Eli and saw the panic drifting over Noah's face.

"I know this is a lot," the nurse said. "But you've made it this far. It's only down the hall."

The walk continued, and the nurse stopped in front of a room. He gave Noah a reassuring smile and returned through the network of white hallways. Noah was frozen, a few feet before the door, and the image of the man he had seen moments ago was replaced with his father.

What if he was too late? What if dementia had ruined his father before Noah had a chance to say anything? What if there was nothing there to recognize?

The dread became defeating, and he raised his foot to step back. And Eli, with one arm encircled tightly around the tulip, reached out the other and placed his hand on his cheek. Noah sighed, and the foot in the air landed before him, and then another, and he turned in front of the open door.

Inside, a band of sunlight spindled through the window and passed open blinds into the room. In the meridian of light, his mother, who had been half asleep, straightened at their arrival. Emotion betrayed her composure, and she placed her hand to her mouth as she sputtered a soft cry. Resting next her in another chair across from her, in a nest of pillows and blankets, was a man. He followed the gaze of his wife to Noah. Noah was rooted as he searched the face for his father.

The man in the chair was gaunt with disease. His skin dipped in around his cheeks, and his scalp was covered with thick silver hair. For a moment, he was a stranger. But like a blurred picture realigning on a screen, he became crisp. The hand that lay dormant bore a familiar wedding band and had the worn look of a hardware owner. The shoulders that reclined into the chair were still the broad shoulders Noah had clung to in the same way Eli held his. And the smile that arced over the face was crooked, following the same path as Noah's but without the chipped tooth.

"Hi, Mom. Hi, Dad."

Noah walked fully into the room. A heaviness in him loosened in his chest and was swept away in the gaze of his parents. Noah lowered his child to his feet.

"This is Eli, your grandson."

Noah's father tilted his head as the information was processed. Noah held his breath, and Eli crossed the room, his two hands holding out the tulip to Noah's father. The man looked at the gift and took it from the child with his familiar hands. He held the flower out in front of him and grinned at it, and then gave it to his wife. Noah's father then reached out for Eli. Eli hesitated and glanced back at Noah for reassurance. Noah nodded at his son, then Eli moved into his grandfather's grasp.

Noah's mother stepped out of the chair and placed her arm around her son as tears flowed freely from her eyes. And they joined his father and his son in the circle of light around them.

Noah strolled into his apartment around late afternoon with Eli still in his arms. Eli's dripping feet kicked idly, dropping snow and mud smear on Noah's thigh. Once on the floor, Eli padded through the apartment calling out for Isabelle, leaving footprints in his wake. Noah soared on his new joy. His parents' voices still ran through his head. His father had been more cognitive, albeit measured and slower than Noah remembered. His mother, every so often, leaned into Noah's ear whispering, "This is a good day." And it had been, as Eli, a spinning top dancing along the room, brought in a hope, a new beginning for all of them.

Isabelle emerged from the rear room, and Jones trailed behind her. Isabelle was creased with concern, and Jones knelt to speak to Eli.

"Is everything okay?"

She shook her head. "I wanted to talk to you this morning, before you saw your parents."

"You were asleep," Noah said with a smile.

She smiled briefly, then the same worry lined her face. "We need to talk." She glanced down at Jones and Eli. "Can you take Eli to my apartment for a while?"

Jones nodded and took Eli by the hand. As they left the apartment, Eli skipped behind Jones, his feet slopping and squealing on the wood floor in glee. Isabelle clasped Noah's hand and she glanced down at them. She pulled back a grave breath, met Noah's eyes, and turned up to the ceiling as if in silent prayer.

"I don't know how to tell you this," she said, "but I love you."

Noah's heart wanted to burst in his chest. He brought Isabelle closer to him and kissed her forehead, breathing in her scent. There was still dread in her face but Noah didn't care. He kissed her lips, and it still felt like it wasn't enough. He pecked at her right cheek, and as he kissed her, his lips tasted the wetness of a tear. He pulled back, and her expression was knit in distress.

"My gallery is in utter ruins, and although I can build it back, I've lost my business partner," she said, and sighed, wiping at her face. "And I don't think I would've gotten through any of that if it hadn't been for you and Eli. I don't know how it happened, but you two are my world."

"I love you, too," Noah said.

"Marcie came by," she said, and the floor seemed to shift underneath Noah.

"Is she trying to take Eli away?" Noah could no longer stand. He moved to the couch and pressed his hand down on the couch as if it couldn't be trusted before he sat down.

"No, she wants to sign over her rights. She doesn't want to take care of him," Isabelle said, but then her chin trembled. "But she lied to us." Isabelle whimpered, and then said, "Eli isn't your son."

The room seemed to narrow as if it was going to crush Noah. He gripped the couch cushion underneath him, and his throat nearly closed. Each breath he pulled in was labored. He couldn't have possibly heard Isabelle right. He tried to pose a question but could only stare back at her. Once again, he was without words to give to her.

"But she doesn't want him, Noah," Isabelle said as her voice rose in desperation. "She'll give us Eli."

"He's not mine?"

"She said she doesn't know who the father is," Isabelle said. "She gave him to you because she knew that out of all the men she's been with, you would take care of him."

Blood rushed to Noah's face, and his vision turned crimson. He stood and paced a few steps and whipped forward toward Isabelle.

"How long have you known?"

"Since yesterday," she said in a whisper.

Noah almost growled at her. Tears slipped down his hot face, and he slammed his fist into the wall. A crack in the plaster fissured at the place of impact. Isabelle gasped and held a hand to her mouth. Noah staggered away and made his way back to the couch. He rasped in air through his flared nostrils, desperate to keep his air in his lungs.

"Why didn't you tell me last night?"

"What happened with the gallery, and what she said— it was just too much," Isabelle said, strangled with her weeping. "It was all too much."

"He's not mine," Noah said, and then horror reached him. "My parents . . . my fucking parents. How am I going to tell them this?"

"We can keep him," Isabelle said, sitting down next him, grasping his hand. "We can keep him. It can be the same."

"You think I want to take care of Marcie's kid?" Noah said. "He's not even mine. Hell, he's not even yours."

Isabelle drew back to the edge of couch. "So what? We give him to a woman who won't even take care of him?"

"He's not my son."

"You saw how badly she took care of him," Isabelle said. "You're just going to abandon him like she did?"

"I don't want this," he said.

He was so happy just a moment ago. And the visit with his parents had given him so much joy, and now he could see their eventual disappointment mingling with his and choking them all. He glanced around the room, and Eli was everywhere. In the corner of the room was a toy truck, overturned and forgotten. The television played the nauseating cheer of a kid program. Even the hardwood underneath him carried a cyclone of Eli's tiny footprints. Noah looked to Isabelle for help, but her devastation left nothing for him.

She was expressionless and resolved. She'd had a night with this information and a night's sleep, all leaving her clearheaded. Noah was almost resentful, but she stooped down at the couch and kissed Noah deeply. Her fingers ran patterns on the back of his neck.

"Marcie admitted to me that she doesn't want her child. She wants us to have Eli," Isabelle said. "And I intend to make sure he never suffers."

"I can't."

"She left him with you because you're the best man she knows."

Noah had another surge of anger and hauled back from Isabelle. "I can't. He's not mine."

Isabelle crossed her arms along her chest. Her eyes were glazed with tears. "Well, I guess he's mine, then."

As she opened his front door, she looked at him. "I'm not some mammy for Marcie and you. I guess you're not the man Marcie thought you were."

Everything was shattered and falling into pieces around him. So quickly, there was nothing to hold on to. He couldn't reach for her. She walked swiftly through the door and slammed it behind her, leaving Noah with the sounds of his breathing.

42

Posters were plastered along the insides of windows for DJ Heavyrox with their promise of a good time, and Jones regarded them with a sneer as she headed into Stratosphere. She hadn't had a good time in so long, and it certainly wouldn't be found behind a deejay under the glow of a MacBook computer. Behind her was Isabelle, whose sour face etched the same resentment. Once more, Jones had forced her to come out, but not before a harrowing quest to find a babysitter, which required her to pull every bit of clout and authority in her position. The result was the pimple-riddled fifteen-year-old daughter of a production manager at the magazine. The production manager settled into thinly veiled relief and a few hours without her snarky daughter. The teenager grunted in monosyllable and hid her bumpy face in the screen of an iPhone. Jones restrained Isabelle from yelling at the girl long enough to get her into the cab and to Wicker Park.

They pushed through the crowd and up to the bartender, Russell Cowell's girlfriend from his portraits. Her affable face and lithe form spun from behind the bar. The bartender conjured up the art hanging in the Nichols-Griffin Art Institute and Todd Nicolas standing before them in his grand admiration with the radiance of a city night upon him. Jones recoiled momentarily at the thought of him. She had come here to forget about the murkiness she'd slipped into around him.

The bartender pulled back empty glasses to replace them. She was art in motion, rich oil paints made real in smooth flesh underneath the blue luminosity of the dim bar lights. The bartender's hair slipped from behind her ear like a long, dark, arching paint stroke. A pang dug at Jones's center. And soon, Jones was no longer seeing the bartender move. She glanced through her and saw the smile lines along Todd Nicolas's cheeks, his uncanny aptitude to catch the winter sun on his face, and the urgent necessity of his kiss.

The bartender leaned over the bar at the two of them and spoke. Jones was a bit off-balance as the trance was broken, but Isabelle had been very much present.

"She'll have your strongest vodka on the rocks, and I'll have tonic water with lime," Isabelle said.

The bartender gave Isabelle a passing glance and went to receive their drinks.

"Tonic water?" Jones said, shaking off her embarrassment and turning her attention to Isabelle.

"I don't want to get drunk," Isabelle said. "Hell, I don't even want to be out, but you pulled the my-boyfriend-gave-me-chlamydia card. I can't exactly say no to that." Jones frowned, and Isabelle quickly said, "Sorry."

"Well, I never thought I'd have to be finding a babysitter for you," Jones said.

"Is she a babysitter?" Isabelle asked. "Did you find that teenager in a pack of feral dogs?"

Jones chuckled. "As long as your Wi-Fi holds up, Eli will be fine."

A noticeable silence stitched between them, and they both sipped on their drinks. A comforting warmth spread from Jones's stomach to her limbs as the vodka took hold. Jones's probing glance raked over Isabelle. Jones decided to address the concern she was reading on Isabelle's face.

"Are you really going to keep Eli?"

Jones couldn't quite believe the child belonged to anyone.

"Yes," Isabelle said solidly, and shifted back into the crowd away from the bar.

Jones scuffled behind her, wishing she hadn't spoken at all. She ushered her friend to the far wall and put her vodka at Isabelle's mouth. Isabelle cut her a disapproving look but sipped from Jones's glass anyway.

"If this is what you want to do, I'll support you," she said. "But he's not your kid or even Noah's."

"His mother doesn't even want him," Isabelle said. "So please don't question it, okay?"

Jones raised her hand in armistice and spilled a swallow of vodka in the process. Isabelle rolled her eyes. She grabbed Jones's drink and took another sip.

"And what are you going to do about Derek?"

The question came at Jones like a sharp attack. The answer had been something she had been trying to avoid.

What could she do about Derek? The air was stifling between them, and what goodwill they'd retained had devolved into a seething war. He would storm into the apartment with heavy punitive feet and Jones, by all accounts, would descend into wild anger at his audacity. She had become so unlike herself, traveling a new and unknown path of rage, that she was often left adrift. At some point, one of them was going to have to leave, and despite Jones's contempt for the ail-ridden apartment, she refused to give him a concession. And she had given him enough undeserved victories.

Jones looked at Isabelle, tossed back her drink, and shrugged.

Isabelle pursed her lips. She assessed the crowd around them and discreetly pointed to her crotch. "How are you feeling now?"

"The symptoms are gone," Jones said, emptying her glass. She was experiencing regular visits to the bathroom, and only the pains she had in her abdomen were phantom reminders of what Derek had done to her. "Look, let's not talk about our problems."

"What are we going to do—listen to the deejay?"

"He's a great deejay."

"What time is it?"

"It's not even eight o'clock yet. Have another drink."

"Well, unlike you, I can't get drunk."

"I know, you have a kid now."

"And an art gallery to rebuild," Isabelle said, then she grew somber. "Todd Nicolas offered me a job."

Jones tilted her head as her eyebrows arched on her forehead. "What? When did you start talking to him?"

Isabelle smirked. "When you stopped. He's actually a nice guy, and I think you should—"

Isabelle went blank, and her gaze shifted over Jones's shoulder and into the crowd. When Jones turned around, she saw Hank and Noah wading through the crowd looking just as despondent as the two of them were.

43

Hank was charitable when Noah knocked on his door, coat on, and suggested a drink at Stratosphere. Earlier that day, he had called Hank and told him Eli wasn't his son and he wouldn't be at work. When Noah arrived at his door, the toil was evident all over him. Noah's skin was pallid, and dark circles were embedded under his eyes. Stubble darkened his face, and the devastation seemed to come over him from a lifetime of misery instead of one night's confession. Noah had a beer as they waited for the Uber to retrieve them, and Hank had peeked out the window down into the swirling snow and shadows below.

Even though Gwen had left his apartment, the inkling that he was watched and pursued still raised goosebumps on his forearms and tiny hairs on the back of his neck. This worsened when he was alone, and he hoped as he now elbowed through the crowd that it would vanish. After his first drink, it did fade into the soft whir of Stratosphere. This bar was completely benign to Peppermint's predatory nature, and he was calm when he and Noah settled into a booth.

Noah's face curdled, and he said, "This was the booth where I met Isabelle."

"We could move."

Noah didn't hear him, but he glanced down at the booth and rested his hand on the vinyl seat as if he were in the presence of a holy relic.

"It's going to work out," Hank said helplessly, and drank from his beer.

Noah's head snapped up at him. His jaw was tight, and he shook his head.

"How?" Noah asked. "I've lost them both."

"No, you haven't," Hank said. "So, he's not your son by blood—that's not stopping Isabelle."

Noah raked his hand through his hair. "I can't do this."

Hank spotted irregular movement through the bodies of the crowd. Movement that was too fast, and his stomach lurched, expecting to see Wes or Kelvin charging at him.

But it was Isabelle dragging Jones through the people in the opposite direction.

"You may have to," Hank said, and then pointed with his bottle at them.

Noah jumped up in a surge of panic and glared at Hank. Hank sighed deeply and put his bottle on the table. He joined Noah as he headed in the direction of the women. For a brief moment, it was as though nothing had happened at all, that it was the first night Noah had pursued Isabelle and Hank was merely the wingman. Vertigo pulled at Hank, and instead of anticipating Wes or Kelvin, he expected Gwen to be on one of the stools by the bar. Maybe she was a part of this rewriting of time and she would be waiting here with a martini in her hand and a cigarette demanding to be smoked. If Hank could have had that night over again, he would have pushed past Gwen, maybe even looked for Andrea. But the stool where he had found her was occupied by a portly guy sweating in a tight leather jacket. And Isabelle was almost running away from Noah and had lost her friend somewhere along the way. Noah's face wasn't one of overconfidence but a wrench in consternation. Everything was wrong, and Hank wondered what he was even doing.

He wished he could have that night back at Stratosphere. But he couldn't, so he stopped and let Noah go off alone after Isabelle. He hauled through the crowd toward the bar. The first rumblings could be heard from the deejay's smooth music pouring from concealed speakers.

Jones was at the bar, and Hank decided to wait next to her. She saw him and smiled.

"You decided to get out of the way of them, too?" he said.

"It's seemed like the best way to survive."

When they both had fresh drinks in their hands, they clinked their glasses together and drank. Hank had the feeling they were toasting to mutual melancholy. She turned to him and smiled sadly.

"Where's what's-her-face?"

Hank snorted and scratched his head. "She's not around."

"Can I be honest with you?" she asked, and sipped from her drink.

"Sure."

"That woman was terrible."

Hank vented bitter laughter until his sides were sore. "I guess you're right."

"Oh, I'm right."

Hank and Jones stared over the heads of the crowds, through gaps in posters on the window, out into the street. There, just outside the bar, were Isabelle and Noah, both of their faces knotted in battle. The spoke heatedly, leaving clouds of breath between them. Hands and arms gestured at sharp, quick angles. Then, Isabelle shook her head, and her shoulders went slack. She pivoted away and ran in the other direction. Noah called out for her, but he, too, was defeated and trailed off in the opposite direction.

Hank and Jones now looked at each other. The earlier humor they shared was gone, replaced by the guilt of being spectators. Jones put her drink up to her mouth, and Hank swallowed from his beer.

"Have you heard from Andrea?" she asked.

He turned to her, and she was partly adrift in some reverie, or maybe the alcohol was taking ahold of her.

"No," he said. "I thought she moved out west."

"She's working at By Land and By Sea," Jones said. "She's a sous chef or something."

Hank's grip on his beer tightened. "Yeah."

"You should see her," Jones said, "and not worry about Gwen."

She turned and hugged Hank. Her grasp was a bit too tight, and it was clear that she was sliding into drunkenness. Hank nodded to the bartender and threw down a twenty. When her arm curled around him, more for companionship than balance, they made their way through the bar. The music soared into a breaking crescendo as they stepped out into the night over salt and ice. They stepped out on the edge of the sidewalk before a blackened mound of snow, and Hank held his arm for a cab.

"You know," Jones said softly, as if sharing a precious secret, "people are always telling you who they are by what they do and won't do to you. I don't know why I never listened."

"Maybe we both should've listened," Hank said as a cab pulled up to take them home.

Hank walked Jones up to her door and saw her safely in, and then took the stairs down to his apartment. His cold hands were stiff, and he fumbled with his keys for a moment. He paused for a moment, smelling the smoke of someone's failed attempt at cooking in the lower part of the apartment. His hands finally grabbed ahold of the right key, and as he steadied it, he realized his door was slightly ajar. The doorframe was splintered and cracked from a tremendous force.

Hank's head spun, and he stumbled against the wall to stay upright. He fought to suck in air and pressed the door open. From outside in the hallway, he examined the dim shadows of his apartment. The shadows were all familiar folds of darkness. He stepped in quietly and reached along the wall for the light. He held back a gasp as his entire apartment had been overturned. Cushions from the couch were strewn across the room, kitchen cupboards and cabinets were open, their contents scattered on the floor. The refrigerator had been emptied as well, and various foods were spilled and thawing, forming a viscous liquid.

As he stepped through his apartment, he noticed that nothing was taken.

He pulled out his phone to call the police, and his hand quaked so badly he could barely dial. Then a loud, shrill chirping from downstairs sliced though the silence. Hank rushed to his broken front door. At the mouth of the stairs, an onslaught of heat blasted him back, and black smoke slithered up along the hall toward him.

44

Jones awoke in bed from a piercing shrill that felt as though it was coming from inside her head. From the bed, she reached out with her arms to swat at her alarm clock, tossing it across the room. The noise continued, and she realized its pitch was too high to be her alarm. She sat up in the bed, still partly dressed in her jeans, too drunk to fully undress herself. She was alone in bed, and Derek had been lying on the couch, sleeping under the light from the television.

A gray smog hung in the air, and Jones blinked a few times, wondering if she was still suffering from drunkenness. Burning, noxious vapors and the wail of the smoke detectors slammed her into full consciousness. She grabbed one of Derek's discarded T-shirts and threw herself out of bed.

She careened on her feet. Her eyes stung, and she gagged on the air, retching to her knees. She tried to compose herself, and the air down near the floor was easier to breathe, but not by much. She hiked the collar of the T-shirt over her mouth and nose in an effort to breathe.

The cry of the smoke detector was beating down on her, and she could barely think. She shuffled, still low to the ground, through the hall into the living room.

"Derek!" she cried out.

She hoped that he was up so they could get out of the apartment together. The couch was empty, and all the windows were opened, venting the first flames crawling up along the walls. An eerie golden glow fell over Jones as the flames began to devour an entire portion of the room. The heat and the surge of smoke made her dizzy, and she clutched the wall.

Before her, the front door was opened. At the door, Derek was stooped down with a blanket over his shoulders. He turned and looked at her as if he saw nothing, as if he was looking through her. She reached out to him.

He took a step toward her, then his face hardened. Jones stretched her hand out to him in the searing air. The flame hadn't yet taken the floor that separated them. He could still cross the room to get her.

His face was florid under the blaze of fire and callous in anger. He looked at her hand, and then at her. He shook his head and dove through the door into an abyss of smoke and heat.

For a moment, Jones was blinded in anger. The shock left her coughing up spit. Flames flickered and inched from the wall on the floor toward her. She heard yelling above her and sharp creaking around her as if the whole of the apartment shuddered. The heat was unbearable in the living room and whipped her skin. She whimpered in pain as she scrambled back to the bedroom, closing the door behind her.

She pressed her weight into the window, and the glass felt cool against her skin. It refused to move and panic swelled in her. Outside the window, the she saw the framework of the fire escape. She saw a figure from another floor shoot by, leaving footprints in the snow, causing the structure and metal to vibrate in their wake. She banged on the window for her help. Once more, she tried to tug open the window.

She examined her room for something heavy and saw the flames nipping at the door, sliding underneath the crack. Flames bit through the walls and darkened the plaster. She wouldn't make it too much longer in the room.

Jones saw Derek's computer plugged up on the nightstand. She reached across the bed and pitched it through the window. It speared through the window, leaving a small breach in the glass, and tumbled over the edge into the night. Jones pushed on the glass, forcing a wider hole for her to escape. Heat licked at her back as glass cracked and gave way. She tugged herself through the jagged space in the glass, and the sharp edges sliced her sides. She screamed in the pain, but the cold air on her face was such a relief. She stabilized herself on the railing and attempted to take a few steps down the stairs.

The ice and snow combined with her weight was too much of a burden for her legs, and she fell through the air. She closed her eyes and didn't scream, as snowy metal crashed into her. There was sharp pain all along her body when she finally stopped tumbling one floor down from her apartment. She glanced up, and flames and a stream of black smoke shot out from her apartment.

Her hands were wet and dripping. She thought it was snow for a moment, but the liquid was warm. She placed them in front her, and they were drenched in blood. From the gash in her side, blood trickled out in a steady flow. She tried to pull herself up but was crushed under the pain. Jones looked down and saw that there were too many flights of stairs to the ground. So she stayed in the cool snow, watching the flames dance above her, until darkness fell on her.

45

Isabelle arrived at her apartment building with her thoughts on Noah. He had tried to text her, but she couldn't read any of them. She placed her phone in her pocket and stood in the hallway, wiping away the last of her tears on her cold face. Once composed, she stepped inside and paid and relieved the babysitter, who had put Eli to sleep in the last hour. She walked the sullen teenager down through the hall and out the front door. She watched the girl walk toward the direction of the train.

A chill forced her inside and up toward the creaking steps when an acrid smell of melted plastic stung her throat. She had made it up one floor when she saw smoke rise like a gentle fog from the ground floor.

Maybe someone's cooking had gotten out of hand. She couldn't be sure. She turned in the other direction toward the thin smoke. Isabelle heard scrambling movement. Fast footsteps slapped on the pavement. She stopped, and then pulled back up the stairs, out of sight, peeking slightly around the banister.

A man stood at the base of stairs facing the hall. He faced the flames, and bright light danced over his sharp snarl and his septum ring. In the flickering glow, he seemed subhuman—more predator than person. He was dressed completely in black, and in his hand, he held a red two-gallon gas canister. He emptied out the gas, splashing it along the hall and walls. The flash roared and slid along the liquid at rapid speed that he didn't anticipate.

He yelped and tossed the gas tank into the flames further down the hall. The flames flashed, and he guarded his face as he back-stepped. Isabelle pulled back a scream, afraid she would draw his attention. The man stared at the flames overtaking the ground hall as if the movement had put him in a trance.

Isabelle nearly lost her ability to breathe when she noticed in his hand that he had unearthed a switchblade from his pocket. He absentmindedly flicked the blade out, and then used his thumb to press it back into the hilt.

He did this with such a proficient ease, a numbness tickled at Isabelle's legs. She gripped the railing to steady herself, and the stairs groaned and popped under her feet. The man stopped the blade, and his gaze shot toward the stairs, locking eyes with her.

Isabelle couldn't scream and thundered up the steps toward her apartment. She heard his heavy footsteps in pursuit, and a sickly flush of adrenaline propelled her up the stairs. She flung herself around the corner, expecting his blade to come at her at any moment. Behind her was a draft of heat and the wallop of each of his steps, taking the stairs two at a time.

The man's hands scraped at the back of her coat. She screamed out and now, on her floor, barreled toward her door. She was a few inches away, and he was nearly on top of her. He clasped her arm. Without missing a step, she wrenched forward into the door of her apartment, slipping out of her coat and leaving it trapped in his fists.

Isabelle slammed the door and bolted the lock. Shaking, she leaned against the door. Her limbs were disjointed and she could barely take in air.

Eli, who must've heard the ruckus, stepped from her bedroom, rubbing his eyes. The sight caused tears to rise to Isabelle's eyes. Behind her, a booming force collided into the door, and Isabelle felt it snap through her body. Eli's hands dropped to his sides, and his eyes became two large discs.

"Get back in the room! Now!"

He scurried into her bedroom, and Isabelle backed away from the door. The man slammed into the door again. The room seemed to shake, and the doorframe protested and splintered. She held her hand to her mouth to keep from screaming. The man threw himself in the door once more, then over and over again, each bang harder and harder, and from the other room, she heard Eli's cries.

Isabelle turned to her bedroom, where he stood in the doorway. He was flushed with tears. Staring into his face, Isabelle's fear subsided and she checked her jean pockets for her phone, realizing it was in her coat outside with the man. She screamed out in frustration, and then hurled her body into her couch, pushing it across the door.

A miasma of smoke seeped in through the vents and underneath the door. The man continued to kick at the door and slam against the door handle.

Isabelle couldn't let anything else happen to Eli. He was hers now, and she didn't understand what this man was doing to her apartment, but it was clear they were in harm's way. If he got in here, she could only image what he would do to them.

Over the drumming of her heart, there was a chorus of smoke detectors ringing out from the closed doors of apartments. Soon, a warm, thick cloud quickly began to displace the air in the room.

The man howled behind the door and gave one last kick, then his footsteps receded down the stairs. Isabelle sighed in relief, only to choke on smoke. The temperature of her apartment had risen quickly, and now, instead of the man, flames were pushing through the door. The noxious smoke watered her eyes, and the floor snapped and slanted before her. She jumped back as a section of the floor gave way, rattling the walls and shaking the world around her. Red embers and sparks showered the air, and the room was lit below by a fire chasm where the floor used to be.

She rushed in the bedroom and Eli was crumpled on the floor. Isabelle kneeled down over him. His skin was blue. His breathing was rattled and wheezing. Isabelle cried out and dove over flames into the bathroom. She found his inhaler at the sink where she'd left it for the babysitter. She heaved a bit on the smoke, and faintness buckled her knees. The room was so black with smoke, and she couldn't get enough air in her lungs.

Every muscle within her was strained and wanted to yield. But she heard Eli wheezing and willed herself forward. She plunged over flames and scooped Eli into her lap. She depressed the inhaler in this mouth.

"Breathe," she said, cradling him closer as the floor lurched under them.

46

Noah was lost in every sense of the word. His efforts to collect himself were futile. He was cast off by Isabelle. He had betrayed her and abandoned Eli. And as much as he wanted to go to them, he couldn't. He was adrift in the night, led almost by instinct to a basement bar in South Loop. He entered an empty, tight, nondescript alley. Snow, blackened from filth and urban rubble frozen within it, crushed underneath him. Above him, erupting from gutters, icicles dripped down on him like bitter tears. He stopped at a rusty door he had been to many times and wrenched it open, dragging it across ice and snow.

Heat and thumping of bass met him as he took a pair of rusty stairs to another corridor. At this corridor, a Goth woman, cloaked in black leather, kept watch. Her venomous glare stared out at the dim door.

"Long time no see," she said.

"Is she here?" Noah asked.

The girl smirked at the rising tension in his muscles. A deep ache closed around his heart. He cleared his throat and tried to remain unshaken.

"Is she here?" he asked again.

The door girl's lips, smattered in black, pulled into a full sneer, and she held out her hand for him to enter. He strolled past her into the dark unfinished basement. Mostly male bodies were pressed upon each other in great numbers, requiring a false sense of camaraderie. The space was dank and dark and smelled of salty sweat. Men drank, grunted, and smoked, pulling absently at their erections. All eyes gazed forward and all were united, a part of one bestial entity, in the throes of lust, bowing before Marcie on the stage.

Scattered lights of blue and red splattered over her skin, burnished in sweat. Her body was bare before the crowd and her back to the pole on the stage. Bass detonated and her arm reached up, and as if by no effort at all, she pulled herself up along the pole, bare, arching into the air, through the fractured darkness, legs, breasts, and soft flesh. She hung upside down and exposed the full length of her body. She opened her legs and exposed herself to them brazenly. The crowd bellied and growled at her triumph, and she lowered herself to her feet to the cadence of a melody swallowed in the pulse of bass. She then scaled the pole once more as high up as it would take her, only a mere eight feet.

In the air, she closed her eyes and swayed her head. Her hair spun around and she held her body up with her thighs clasped around the pole. Marcie then extended her arms out as if she would take flight at any moment.

She was enraptured. She was utterly free.

Noah had the urge to spit. But instead, he waited patiently for the song to end and her to sweep up the crumpled bills tossed on the stage. She descended the stage as another woman stepped up. This poor woman looked too soft and too unskilled to follow Marcie. Marcie sneered at her as she left the woman to feed the hungry glare of the crowd. She pulled on a silk robe handed to her by a thick man in a security vest. Noah locked eyes with her, and she nodded to him. He fell in step with her through the main room into a better lit hallway in the rear.

Marcie's back was to him. "I know why you're here."

Noah's shaking hands closed in fists, and his heart thundered against his ribs. "How could you do this to me?"

She turned slightly, and her hair covered her face. "I'm not like you, Noah."

"What the fuck is that supposed to mean?"

"I need to be free."

Noah grabbed her and wrenched her around. He was seething, and air hissed between his teeth. Marcie looked up at him through her hair. Tears dropped from her chin.

"Hey, what's going on?" said the security guard, stepping into the hall. He quickly snatched Noah away from Marcie, pinning him against the wall. His two fists twisted up Noah's jacket, causing the collar to choke off his air.

"It's fine," Marcie said.

The security guard stepped away from Noah. An admonishing glare marred his face.

"If you touch her again, I break your fucking face," the guard said, leaving them alone in the hall.

A tense silence swung between them, and they couldn't face one another.

"Isabelle's going to keep him. I can't," she said.

Sobs were trapped in Noah's chest and he could barely inhale. "Why did you do this to me?"

"Because you're a good man," she said. "And I want him to have a chance."

Noah buckled in defeat, no closer to getting whatever he came here looking for. He turned and shuffled down the hall.

"Wait," Marcie said, and Noah halted. "Do you love him?"

She rushed to his side, and her brow was twisted and her lips were pulled into a line. "Please, tell me you love him."

Noah didn't feel much of anything as he bobbed in the back of the cab toward his apartment. The cab slid to a stop on the frozen street as fire trucks and ambulances barreled along the road. The cab driver swore, grasping the wheel tightly to keep the car from smashing into the curb. The car began to roll forward a few yards when another fire truck forced them to yield again.

"Chicago," the cab driver said, and his head lolled in grief as cars continued down the street.

Noah wanted to be polite and respond, but his mouth refused to compose words. He reclined back into the seat in the rear of the cab, and it felt as if he was sinking. As if instead of driving toward his apartment, the cab was penetrating the concrete, tumbling deep into the earth. He propped his head against the window and watched his breath rising along the glass and snow gathering on the street. The snow had begun to the fall, and when he had glimpsed up at the night sky, he could see low churning clouds of muddy gray and black.

The cab braked abruptly and flung Noah into the partition. His head bounced sharply off the plastic, and he bit down on the tip on his tongue. He clenched his head and tasted the metallic flavor of his own blood in his mouth.

"Are you sure this is where you want to go?" the cab driver said.

Noah's vision flickered, and it took a minute to realize it wasn't from the pain in his head, but a glow throbbing from outside the cab. A brightness akin to a noon day. Noah blinked and gaped out at ordinary buildings and trees that made up the neighborhood bathed in unearthly pulsing orange radiance. It seemed as though nothing belonged to him any longer, not even the street he lived on. His chest was tightened again and his thoughts evaporated quickly as he eyed the source of the light.

His apartment building stood aglow. The gashing teething of fire cannibalized the building from within and roiled in brilliance from every window. A river of smoke, blacker than night, teemed from the building and up into high stretches of the sky. An armada of fire trucks were positioned outside the building. Ribbons of water from their hoses bowed down on the building and were ineffective against the rage of the flames.

Noah dove out of the cab, his boots betrayed by ice as he slipped forward. He collided hard on his wrist, but he could only feel panic. He shot up and pushed forward. He heard the cab driver call after him and joined the crowd of people from the nearby buildings watching in horror under the glow of the fire. The temperature was warmer outside the cab, and a dank smell of smoke clung to the air. It was as if he was moving through a block party or a bonfire.

"Isabelle," he said in a weak voice over the murmurs of the crowd. He scanned the faces maniacally. "Eli."

A small cadre of ambulances were parked nearby, rear doors opened, administering oxygen to a few people wrapped in blankets. He ran up to them, again nearly slipping on ice. The people breathing in the oxygen were the couple in the building he'd never met.

"Isabelle, Eli," he said, turning toward the building.

His panic was absolute. It was all he was. He charged toward the building, toward the scorching heat, and a nearby fireman plowed into him. The force of the man's arms was stronger than he had anticipated. Noah plummeted into the snow and tried to squirm free when another fireman dropped onto him.

"My son is in there!" Noah said, his voice howling into the night. "My son!"

"Stop it!" one of the firemen screamed in his ear.

"Let us do our job," the other one said as they hauled Noah up and away from the heat of the apartment. "You'll die if you go in there."

This close to the flames, the air was so hot it was painful in his lungs. He heard glass shatter and the rumbling shift and collapse from within the building. He bucked against the men in vain, and their combined strength was too much for him. He shrieked, and his feet dragged helplessly in front of him as they pulled him toward the ambulances. Noah turned toward the building, and a deafening boom ignited the air. The ground underneath him rocked, and the crowd cried out. A police officer pushed the crowd back deeper into the street.

Noah held his face and was entirely supported by the firemen. They handed him off to an EMT. He heaved in air, and the world around him began to darken.

Were they dead? If they were dead, how could he live?

Noah collapsed to his knees. He could no longer stand. Snow puddled around him, and shivers invaded his body. He could no longer breathe. He squeezed his eyes closed. He let out a hoarse wail.

And then he heard tiny steps, and tiny hands fell gently on his cheek. And he knew.

Staring back at him covered in ash, skin as gray as it had been when he'd first seen him, was Eli. Noah coughed back a cry and ensnared him in his arms. He whimpered in the child's shoulder.

"My son," he whispered, and then looked up.

Isabelle limped toward him with the aid of an EMT, as if she had emerged from the flames when he had called her. She knelt to join them, and Eli and Noah opened up to receive her. No one spoke for a moment, and they only felt the warmth and certainty of each other.

47

When Jones opened her eyes, steely morning light greeted her from a window. She was alarmed by her surroundings and tried to get up but felt the pull of an IV in her arm. Her mouth was grainy, and she tried to speak. Her skin was itchy from the washed hospital sheets. Next to her on a table sat three dozen roses and a potted tulip, bright, cheery, and yellow. She craned her neck to see across the room. A hunched-over figure was curled up in the chair.

Her heart stopped in her chest. She felt the heat of the fire still and the way Derek had left her there. And now here he was? And how did she not die out there?

The figure stirred and glanced up at her. Jones drew back on the pillow, unable to make out the face in the shadows of the room. But the figure hopped out of the chair and into a shaft of light, and Todd Nicolas stared back at her. He burst into a dazzling smile, and he reached for her hand. He was beautiful and hopeful, and Jones's heart fluttered.

"Jones," he said, bringing her hand up to his mouth, and he turned toward the hallway and cried out, "Nurse!"

Within seconds, two nurses rushed into the room. One quickly began to examine Jones and fired off a series of questions while the other one left the room to page the doctor. Soon, Jones's hospital room was a flurry of activity as the doctor now surveyed her. The doctor, a stern-faced woman, turned her to her side to check her bandages. She then explained that along with the cut, Jones had suffered from extreme smoke inhalation, and after a day of monitoring, she would be released.

"How did I survive?" Jones asked in a raspy voice, and a nurse offered her water.

"One of your neighbors, Hank Parks, found you on the fire escape," Todd said.

"How did the fire start?" Jones asked, convinced that it was from an oversight of the landlord.

"The police are saying it was arson," he continued. "The guy who did it suffered third-degree burns over twenty percent of his body and barely made it out of the fire. Everybody else made it out of the building okay."

Jones shook herself, knowing that Derek was a part of that everybody.

A strange relief took hold of her. The apartment building was no longer. The collection of cracked plaster, groaning pipes, and warped floorboards that encased them all had burned to the ground, and in that was a startling liberation. There was no reason for her to hold or to anything or anyone but herself. To apologize to no one for her ambitions or conceal her successes. Derek had done more than leave her in the building to burn. He had let her go entirely.

Slivers tingled at her feet. A heaviness lay on her chest. Her mouth was thick, her cut still ached, and the stitches pulled at her side. A throbbing detonated in her head like a slow beat. But she didn't complain. She simply allowed herself to open up and feel all of it—all the pain, all the fear ebbing back and forth in her like a tide. She felt this without interruption for the first time in a long time. A brilliance dazzled in her eyes. She breathed in deeply, and a clarity sharpened the world to a pinpoint precision.

48

Soft snowfall rode the breeze into the new windows of Isabelle's gallery. She stared out the windows, watching the last of winter fall from the skies above. The weatherman said that within a week or so a warm front should roll over Chicago, but she couldn't trust his prediction. She crossed her arms, staring out onto the streets as a few people braved the cold, tucked into their wool and down to run whatever errands beckoned them out into the cold. There was a lightness on their faces, possibly a willingness—they, too, knew winter's end was near and something out of sight called. Even traffic flowed without its usual dire semblance.

Isabelle turned back to her art gallery, and contractors moved in flocks along the wall with white paint. They held paintbrushes and hammers and other tools she couldn't account for like soldiers in battle. They hung from ladders, as if on a trapeze, arms moving up into the reaches of the ceiling, installing new LED lights. Plastic tarp covered the expanse of the floor out in front of them, and over it, they moved with a jarring efficiency. Isabelle often regarded her own presence there as an obstacle to work around.

Mr. Nicolas, or "Todd" at his and Jones's instance, recommended them, and he had lauded over their quick work. But they would be done before Isabelle had booked any art to fill the place.

She tiptoed past the men and ducked under scaffolding into the back of the gallery. In her office, afternoon light broke through the barred window. She poured hot coffee from a coffeemaker on the file cabinet across from her desk. She warmed herself with the mug and considered having the workmen remove the bars. There was enough in the budget with the money she was making as a consultant at Nichols-Griffin Art Institute and the insurance settlement from Curtis's unnecessary ploy. She heard rumors that he had skipped out of the country, possibly to Europe. But she was sure he'd be back in Chicago one of these days.

It had been weeks since the fire, and Noah, Eli, and herself were growing restless from the cramped, sterile hotel room they were staying in. Yesterday, Noah had tried to take them up to see his father only to be stopped at the second floor and told by a nurse that it wasn't a good day. More and more bad days took hold of his father, and they all silently feared that his deterioration was only going to accelerate.

In the car, Isabelle had wondered why that was, and Noah, peering over at her, read the question in her face.

"Maybe he was holding on," Noah said, "waiting for me."

He then drove the car through the city to the nearby suburb, Beverly, that he grew up in. Eli kicked the seat after being told not to do for the fifth time. He grew restless bound up in the booster seat for so long. Isabelle craned around and flashed an admonishing look at her son. She then thought of how wonderfully strange it was to call him that, now that the guardianship had been finalized.

Noah was drunk in his nostalgia as the car circled the neighborhood of small homes. He recalled his tales of youthful follies for her. Isabelle tried to smile despite the fact that her and Eli's interest had waned. And Isabelle was certain as they made another loop around the same block that she, too, would start kicking at the dashboard in the manner that Eli was attacking the back of the seat when Noah pulled into a driveway of a small home dressed in snow. The house was of similar architecture as his childhood home, like a hopeful portrait of the past, and in its small yard, a snow-cloaked For Sale sign had danced desperately in the breeze.

Isabelle and Noah had fallen in love with it instantly. Hopefully, the sellers would accept their offer.

A chill shuddered through Isabelle in her office, and she sipped from the hot coffee. She lowered herself into the seat at her desk and listened to the sounds of construction and the men barking out in the gallery.

She knew that, soon, her makeshift family would have to leave the confines of the hotel. She just simply enjoyed their closeness and the sounds of their collective breathing in the small room at night. And since the fire, every night, the whispers of their breaths put her to sleep and she finally rested.

49

Hank was a series of tangled, pained muscles. He didn't know how much longer he would be able to live in his shop. The sympathetic looks of the part-time employees grew into burdens that he didn't want to carry any longer. Even Noah, who was a victim of the fire himself, changed his tone to one of pity. Hank would have challenged him on this, but he held back his feeling of betrayal. It was, by proxy, his fault that the building had burned down. He had set Gwen and her chaos onto all of them, and they were lucky to have survived it.

The days since the fire, he mostly worked, stooped over his workstation, when lights were turned off and long after the late-night Thai restaurant cooked its last Pad See Ew. He worked until his ass began to hurt on the stool, and then deposited his body on the tiny couch. The empty spaces of his apartment, the vacancy that Andrea had left, were long gone in the corporeal world. The apartment was now a blackened shell of crisp brick, heaping up snow in its punctured windows. Yet the memories of those empty spaces, the lack of Andrea, hung over him like bending before the gallows, and at night, even in his sleep, he waited for the blade to fall.

Tonight, he took a cab into the city. He tugged at the collar of his dress shirt and rolled his shoulders in the cheap tight suit he bought at a resale shop in Wicker Park. Sweat dampened his brow as the cab rolled deeper in the lambent glow of Logan Square. Fresh snow was falling, covering its blackened gray ancestry gathering in potholes and on the edges of curbs. He reassured himself that tonight would be beautiful and nothing could touch him after fleeing from a fire and dragging his bleeding neighbor down the rusty fire escape.

But the crumbs of bravado he clung to were tossed in the wind like the new cheerful snow as he stepped out of the cab before By Land and By Sea. In the glass façade of the restaurant, he appeared withered, and he wondered if parts of him were left to burn up in the apartment building. And if there were parts that faced the flames, which ones would those have been?

He pushed through the door and was greeted by a host who turned from kind to dissenting before Hank could tell him party of one.

"Can I request to be by the kitchen?" Hank asked, and the host nodded, probably happy to place the crumpled-suited man in the back away from the other patronage.

Hank sat in a corner table overlooking the swinging oak door to the kitchen. A plant was wedged next to his table and hung over the table so closely that it brushed the top of his head. When the waiter came, he ordered a glass of the cheapest white wine he could find on the menu and an appetizer. The cost of his modest spread would surely set him back more money than he was comfortable spending, but he tried not to focus on that.

Each time the door opened, he stole glimpses of the chaos warring behind the scenes and the clattering of dishware ringing out as if they were weapons. Bodies in white blurred over steel countertops, and flames burst from the stove. He attempted to discern Andrea among the bedlam, and the door would snap closed, and the night went on like this for hours as he nursed his wine and the small plate of food grew cold and inedible on the table.

The years he'd shared with Andrea unfolded in his mind, and he realized it was more than a lack of her that caused him to suffer, but it was what they could have been. When she walked away, he thought he had opened up to possibility, but he had closed himself off to it.

A series of waiters slammed through the door. Their outspread arms balanced entrées, and Hank glanced back into the kitchen. Just when he thought he wouldn't find her, a figure turned. It was her with a small skillet in her hand and steam rising from it, curling around her face. In that moment, she was the girl he'd met out underneath a tree in his yard, the body he had probed, the tears he had cried, but so much more. She was the woman she had promised him she would be. She was talking to another cook, and a small tress of hair fell from her white hat. She placed the pot quickly on the counter, and as she did this, she looked up and out.

It was as if this was the truest thing Hank had ever seen in his life.

They caught one another's gaze. Hank now remembered the beauty that he had lost in the years they had spent together. Of the hopes of their future and the certainty of them. How could he have ever seen her as anything other than this? His muscles contracted around his chest. How could he have ever seen anything other than this in her face and in her touch?

Tonight, again, he felt as though he would surely die.

She didn't move and neither did he.

The door flapped closed, and the connection was severed. Bile rose in Hank's throat and he forced it down with the overpriced wine. He threw down several bills and rushed to the door. He trailed onto the sidewalks and shoved his hand against the last of the cold breeze. Soon, very soon, it would be spring. The night glistened before him, streetlights blazed, buildings were luminous, and even the final snowflakes reflected brilliance. His heart was in shambles, and he hoped that one day, like the winter was regressing, this, too, would subside.

ABOUT THE AUTHOR

SB Gamble is an author, playwright, and a semi-retired party boy. He has written over several plays and short stories. His plays have been performed on the stage and over local radio in Kalamazoo Michigan. Over his career he won awards as a playwright with NAACP's ACT-SO competition and Kalamazoo's Black Arts and Cultural Center.

He currently lives and works in Chicago. He is driven to write works that underline his wild belief that people are all equal and have more commonalities than differences.

To stay in the know on his next projects please visit his website www.sbgamble.com and join the mailing list

www.ingramcontent.com/pod-product-compliance
Lightning Source LLC
Chambersburg PA
CBHW020503260626
47156CB00006B/1839